BLOOD ON THE SAND

Also by Michael Jecks

The Last Templar
The Merchant's Partner
A Moorland Hanging
The Crediton Killings
The Abbot's Gibbet
The Leper's Return
Squire Throwleigh's Heir
Belladonna at Belstone
The Traitor of St Giles
The Boy Bishop's Glovemaker
The Tournament of Blood
The Sticklepath Strangler
The Devil's Acolyte
The Mad Monk of Gidleigh
The Templar's Penance
The Outlaws of Ennor
The Tolls of Death
The Chapel of Bones
The Butcher of St Peter's
A Friar's Bloodfeud
The Death Ship of Dartmouth
The Malice of Unnatural Death
Dispensation of Death
The Templar, the Queen and Her Lover
The Prophecy of Death
The King of Thieves
The Bishop Must Die
The Oath
King's Gold
City of Fiends
Templar's Acre
Fields of Glory

MICHAEL JECKS

BLOOD ON THE SAND

SIMON & SCHUSTER

London · New York · Sydney · Toronto · New Delhi

A CBS COMPANY

First published in Great Britain by Simon & Schuster UK Ltd, 2015
A CBS COMPANY

1 3 5 7 9 10 8 6 4 2

Simon & Schuster UK Ltd
1st Floor
222 Gray's Inn Road
London WC1X 8HB

Simon & Schuster Australia, Sydney
Simon & Schuster India, New Delhi

A CIP catalogue record for this book
is available from the British Library

TPB ISBN: 978-1-47111-111-2
EBOOK ISBN: 978-1-47111-113-6

Typeset by M Rules
Printed and bound by CPI Group (UK) Ltd, Croydon, CR0 4YY

www.simonandschuster.co.uk
www.simonandschuster.com.au

Simon & Schuster UK Ltd are committed to sourcing paper
that is made from wood grown in sustainable forests and supports the Forest
Stewardship Council, the leading international forest certification organisation.
Our books displaying the FSC logo are printed on FSC certified paper.

This book is for Paul Moreton, an agent in a million,
for his undying enthusiasm, faith, and support.
Thanks, Paul.

And in fond memory of Shelagh Palmer and Roger Paul.
Two friends who will always be remembered
whenever Tinners dance Morris.

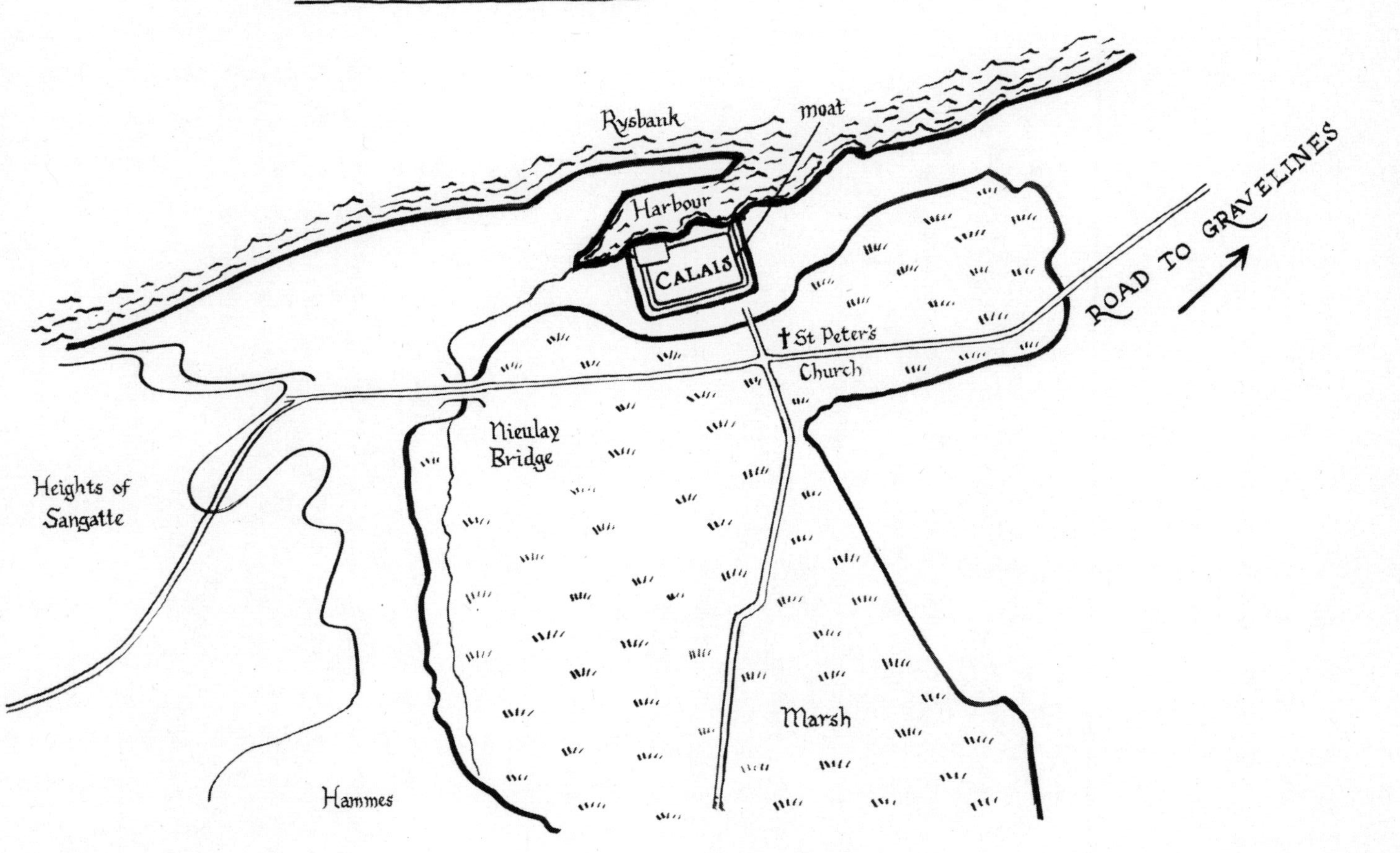
ENGLISH CHANNEL
Rysbank
moat
Harbour
CALAIS
St Peter's Church
ROAD TO GRAVELINES
Nieulay Bridge
Heights of Sangatte
Marsh
Hammes

CAST OF CHARACTERS

Sir John de Sully	Knight Banneret from Devon
Grandarse	leader of 100 men in the King's host
Berenger Fripper	leader of one vintaine of twenty men

Members of Berenger's vintaine:

- **Aletaster**
- **Clip**
- **Dogbreath**
- **The Earl**
- **Horn**
- **Jack Fletcher**
- **John of Essex**
- **Oliver**
- **Pardoner**
- **Saint Lawrence**
- **Turf**
- **Mark Tyler**
- **Wren**

Archibald Tanner	expert cannon-master or 'gynour'
Ed 'The Donkey'	apprentice to Archibald

Béatrice Pouillet	Frenchwoman who has joined Archibald
Marguerite	widowed Frenchwoman seeking her family
Georges	son of Marguerite
Sir Peter of Bromley	once Pierre d'Agen, he has renounced the French King and joined the English King's forces
Jean de Vervins	previously a devoted supporter of the French King, Jean has changed sides after an affront
Chrestien de Grimault	Genoese admiral of the French naval forces near Calais
The Vidame	an official and spy in the French camp
Bertucat	the Vidame's guard and 'heavy'

Author's Note

This book is the second in my Hundred Years' War trilogy, and covers almost a year of great courage and valour, as well as shocking brutality, while the English laid siege to Calais.

Calais: it was a name that resonated with English kings and queens for centuries, a proud foothold on the mainland of France, captured in late 1347 and held for two hundred years by the English Crown; a cause of shame and humiliation to the French until 1558, when the Duke of Guise retook it for France.

But what was Calais like for those who were besieging it in 1346? Thousands were encamped outside Calais in Villeneuve-la-Hardie, the bustling town of wooden sheds built by Edward III to house his army. Preparations for the town had been going on for some time, because he had a definite plan to take Calais, I believe. His Crécy campaign was well thought through, and while his first objective was to destroy the French army, his second was to take the port. That way he had a crucial jumping-off point whenever he wanted to re-enter France.

However, fascinating though the siege was, when I set out to write this book, I did not want it to be about the siege alone. There was too much else going on at this time. The 'Auld Alliance' with Scotland led to the sudden invasion of King David, with his rampage as far as the terrible battle of Neville's Cross, while at the same time the French were suffering from treachery at home as barons and knights tried to gauge which way the winds of power were blowing. There were many, like Sir Peter of Bromley and Sir Jean de Vervins, who sought new alliances.

Of course, there was no vintener called Berenger Fripper, and it is unlikely that one man was unfortunate enough to find himself in each of the battles depicted in this book. However, I have tried to give a feel for what it would have been like to be an English archer fighting in these battles.

It's been enormously enjoyable writing down the adventures of Fripper and his vintaine. I hope you get as much pleasure from reading their stories.

Michael Jecks
North Dartmoor
February 2015

PROLOGUE

Villeneuve-la-Hardie, outside Calais

There was a chill breeze coming off the sea as Berenger Fripper squatted on his haunches near the fire. It was dusk, and although the weather was dry enough now, it had been spitting all day from clouds the colour of old steel. The sort of weather to make a man want to be home again, in a tavern with a roaring fire and a quart of good ale in his fist.

Yet the weather suited his grim mood.

His vintaine had changed much since they had set off from England. The long march to Crécy had taken its toll. Many of his original sixteen men had died. Jon, Gil, Luke, Will, even Geoff, who had always seemed impervious to weapons. By the time they reached Crécy itself, most of his and another vintaine had been so badly mauled that there was scarcely enough to make one under-strength vintaine from the remnants of the two. Jack was still with him, and the boy Ed, nicknamed 'the Donkey'.

Sadly, Clip had succeeded in whining his way here, although

the day Clip died, Berenger would forswear ale and women and instead take up Holy Orders. The scrawny runt's constant complaining seemed to give him strength and vigour. When he stopped, the world would end.

Now he had new recruits, though Berenger eyed them without enthusiasm as they stood or knelt around the fire. He caught Jack's eye and the two men grimaced. They were both professional soldiers, and they knew how much work they had ahead of them to turn these into a fighting vintaine. At six-and-thirty, Berenger was feeling too old to start again. His thinning hair was already showing more grey than brown. This lot would turn it all white.

They were a mixed bunch, it was certain.

Over to the left there was the bulk of Aletaster. He was almost as fat as Grandarse, their centener, with a belt that could have encompassed Berenger, Jack and the Donkey simultaneously with ease. Red hair and small, dangerous blue eyes that never quite seemed to relax. Beside him sprawled the whey-faced, skinny little fellow the men had finally called Dogbreath, for the plainest of reasons. He had a whining voice and the appearance of a cur that's been kicked into abject submission; rather like Clip, but with more viciousness. There was the man they had named the Earl, for his fair hair and affable demeanour, listening politely with an expression of amused bafflement as Jack Fletcher tried to explain a fighting manoeuvre.

And finally, there were the others. The scum that always floated below the top of Berenger's pot of humanity when there was a little heat turned onto them: the fellows who wouldn't fit in, no matter what. Turf, so named for the colour of his face during the Channel crossing; Horn, the man who was almost as wide as he was tall, rather like a drinking horn; Pardoner, named not for his untrustworthiness, but for his habit of apologising every few moments; Wren, who was so small and dainty, he could have been a maid; Saint Lawrence, who seemed too good and kind to be here. Men wanted to stay near him. He carried himself like a priest, tall and elegant as an abbot, but with a certain anxiety, as though he constantly feared being exposed as an imposter.

What of it? Berenger thought to himself. They were all impostors here. That was why they were all content to be given a new nickname when they joined the vintaine. Whether they had arrived to win money and renown, or to escape a demanding wife, debts, or a length of rope, they were all welcomed. Their King had need of them all.

And Berenger felt a surge of affection for them. He would live in their company, teaching them, helping them, and in the end, no doubt, burying many of them, if God didn't call him first.

These were *his* men. His archers.

CHAPTER ONE

English Channel, Seinte Gryfys, Late September 1346

On the day of their capture, Berenger Fripper wiped the salt spray from a face burned brown and leathery, and kicked the writhing figure at his feet.

'Get up, Clip, you whining excuse for a man! I've seen better-looking turds in the midden. Get back on your damned feet.'

'We'll all be killed, ye mad bastard, Frip! Let me die in peace. Ach, you don't understand. My head is a' full of pain, man.'

'You shouldn't have gone thieving, then,' Jack Fletcher said unsympathetically, aiming a kick of his own at the man's scrawny backside.

'I was trying to get hold of some food for you!'

'You were seeing what you could thieve for your own benefit, more like,' Berenger said.

'You never complained when I brought you a squab or a barrel of ale, did you.'

'We never had to go and search for you before,' Jack said.

'If you were real comrades, you'd have helped find the man and avenge this,' Clip said bitterly.

Berenger was about to kick Clip again for the fun of it, when a sudden roll made him lose his balance. As he grabbed a rope, his belly clenched with the sudden need to puke.

Cog, he thought with disgust. A rotten, stinking, leaking bucket, rather. The air about the deck was fetid with the stench from the bilges, and the only reason it was safe from fire was that the whole vessel was so old that the timbers were themselves sodden. As the waves caught at her, she wallowed like a sow in mud. This wasn't a fighting ship: she was about as much use as a pastry bascinet. If the galley behind them caught up and accidentally rammed her, the hull would crumble like a dropped egg.

They were here on this godforsaken tub to help bring supplies. The last few ships heading for Villeneuve-la-Hardie, the vast English encampment outside Calais, had been attacked by the French or their Genoese mercenaries, and someone had decided that it would be sensible to install archers on the fleets coming to supply the English.

Today Berenger's men were on duty. Again. It made him wonder whether someone in his vintaine had offended a lord or some vindictive petty official. It was unreasonable that they kept being given the shit duties.

He felt a man slam into him, hard, and almost let go of the rope.

'Watch it!' he snarled.

'I'm sorry,' Pardoner gulped, his own face blenched and greasy with incipient sea sickness. 'I didn't mean to . . .'

'Shut up. Just keep hold of something. Hit me like that again, and I'll be pushed over the rails.'

He shoved the raw recruit back towards the rails, where Pardoner soon joined two others, Turf and the Saint, in emptying his belly. Berenger knew that if he were to go too close to them, he would soon be throwing up alongside them. The odour of vomit could do that to you.

A shipman hurried past, and three others were hauling on a rope as the shipmaster bellowed, his voice carrying clearly even over the howling and hissing of the wind. A fresh bout of nausea burned deep in Berenger's guts as another man barged into him.

'Look where you're going, Tyler,' Berenger grunted. He clung to the wale as the cog bucked, rearing over a high wall of water. She hesitated at the summit, and then plunged sickeningly, lurching to one side as she fell. Berenger was convinced the ship would continue to plummet, down and down, until she landed on the sea bed, but somehow she stopped at the trough and flung him to the other side of the deck, as though, like a small dog, the cog wanted to shake herself dry.

There were twenty-five ships all told in this fleet. The first convoy were bearing fresh soldiers, food, clothing and boots for the men besieging Calais. Standing here, Berenger could see them streaming away to the north and the south, a line of old cogs and fishing boats, all rolling and pitching in the grey seas. He wondered how many men were chucking their guts up on each of them. Probably as many as on this ship, he thought.

The stench of vomit came to him and he had to turn and stare at the horizon to distract himself, cursing his luck once more. Sitting out here on this lump of floating crap, waiting for the wave that would overwhelm them all, or for the first of the attacks that must surely come, he felt way out of his depth. God's truth, it was enough to make you throw up.

He looked ahead. John of Essex was up there at the prow, holding on to a rope and moving with the ship like a shipmaster born at the base of a mast. Gritting his teeth, Berenger made his way in stages to his side.

'Hello, Frip. Isn't this great?' the man said enthusiastically.

Berenger disagreed. He saw ships yawing and pitching and felt his own stomach lurch in response. 'Yes,' he lied.

'You know, I've always wanted excitement. Where I was born, my father never travelled further than five leagues from home. Did I tell you about him? He was a tanner, and a good one. I could have followed him in that trade, but . . . well, have you ever smelled the tanneries?' He made a face.

'Once smelled, never forgotten,' Berenger said.

'That's right. When you've got piss and dogshit all mixed up, and worked with it a while, spreading it over the skins . . . well, some men don't mind it, but for me, soon as I could, I ran away. I wanted *adventure*. I would never have got that back at home. I knew it would be different here.'

Berenger's mind was fixed on the image of dogs turds and urine. He swallowed down his latest bout of nausea and said hollowly, 'Adventure?'

His latest recruit gave a smile that made him look like a fox: cunning, but wary. 'I want to be able to make some decent money, not to end up a mere cobbler or tranter about my old home, without two farthings to rub together. One day, I'll be important. You watch me. I could be a centener, a man-at-arms . . . even a knight.'

'A knight?' Berenger scoffed. 'Are you serious?'

'Why not? I've as much brain as most of them.'

'You're the son of a tanner, and you think you can get your hands on a knighthood?'

'Others have. All I need do is show myself bold enough. I'll do it.'

Berenger wondered about that. The man had ambition, but ambition was never enough. This fellow had a lot to live down already. Berenger knew that until recently, he too had been the vintener of a small party – before his sudden fall from grace. If others could have had their way, this adventure-seeking tanner's son would even now be gracing the King's three-legged hangman's tree outside Villeneuve-la-Hardie.

'I reckon you should keep yourself quiet and unnoticed,' he said.

'Why?' The fellow bridled.

Berenger looked at him. 'You were found guilty of riding out for personal profit when the orders were to remain with the army. You've already lost your rank and position – you'd be well advised to keep yourself inconspicuous.'

'I wasn't riding for my own purse,' John of Essex said, and his face took on the obstinate expression Berenger was coming to recognise. 'I thought I saw men in the farmstead, and I was right. They waylaid us.'

'And so you were put in my charge and then we were all pushed up the gangplank to this old tub.'

'That's hardly my fault.'

Berenger looked at him. 'Is it not? Perhaps someone in a position of power took a dislike to you and your actions.'

'We rode into a small hamlet, got attacked and rode back. What is there in that to make someone want to punish me?'

Berenger frowned as he considered the boat now on their starboard side. It was a swift-moving galley, and it overhauled the rest of the convoy. At the prow was a man with long, mousy hair blowing in the breeze. 'Who is that?'

'Sir Peter of Bromley. Haven't you heard of him? He used to be named Sir Pierre d'Agen, but he fell out with the French King. Something to do with the King's latest favourite wanting some lands, and Sir Peter's being the best available. So, to satisfy his friend, King Philip gave away Sir Peter's lands and lost a loyal subject. Stupid prick!'

A shorter man clad in a cleric's gown with a fringe of almost-black hair went to Sir Peter's side and whispered in his ear.

Berenger watched as Sir Peter's vessel overtook them at speed. The galley was soon far beyond them, racing on towards France as though flying over the waves.

It was after midday, and Berenger was breaking his fast with a chicken leg and quart of ale, when he heard Dogbreath calling to him.

'Fripper, are they with us?'

Grumbling to himself about his poor eyesight, Berenger strained his eyes, peering in the direction Dogbreath was pointing. There were some hulls there, he felt sure, but a long way off. 'What do you see?' he said to Saint Lawrence, but the tall, fair recruit shook his head. His eyes were no better than Berenger's.

'Can't you see?'

'Yes, you fool' Berenger snapped, 'but I want to know what you—'

His words were suddenly drowned by the shipman at the masthead, who bawled down at the deck, 'GENOESE! Galleys to port!'

All at once, the ship came alive. Shipmen ran up the ratlines to the yard and began to let out more sail, while the ship's company rushed to their stations. Berenger and John of Essex made their way to the rail as the ship began to wallow, then with a creaking and cracking of ropes and timbers, she lurched to the larboard and began to hurtle through the waves. Their passage became more urgent, with a thrumming of ropes as the wind howled through them. Men temporarily forgot the slow agonies of their sickness as the ship strained like a greyhound at the leash. But she was an old, arthritic greyhound.

'Oh, God's ballocks!' Clip groaned.

Berenger followed the direction of his gaze and saw a galley ram the side of a great cog. Arrows were flying, and there was a loud crash and burst of flame as the galley fired a small gonne. Amidst the thick, roiling smoke, Berenger saw a number of shipmen thrown aside. One man was flung over the wale into the sea. Then the galley reversed, and the cog immediately began to sink down in the water.

Another galley crushed the whole of a fishing boat. The vessel collapsed like a felt hat struck by a hammer. It was there one moment, and then the prow rose up to the sky, while the rear was smashed aside, and in an instant both parts were sunk. The galley did not falter, but continued on towards their own ship.

'They'll take us next,' John of Essex said grimly.

CHAPTER TWO

At Villeneuve-la-Hardie, Archibald the gynour was up early that morning. He had been unable to sleep. Mares had troubled him as he tossed and turned under his blanket. In the end, he had got up and spent the remainder of the night sorting through his stores of powder and shot, testing the barrels for damage or leaks, and sifting powder to ensure all was still dry.

'You look tired,' Béatrice said when he returned to the camp late in the morning. There was, he thought, a slight edge of concern to her voice – almost as though she cared for him. He smiled at that thought. She had suffered so much in recent weeks, it would be a miracle if she ever felt able to trust a man again.

'I couldn't sleep,' he admitted. 'It was Fripper's fault, though. He spoke to me about the ships that keep making their way to the harbour to supply the town, and it gave me pause to wonder: will you be safe here, if I go away for a few hours?'

'I will see to my safety.'

'See to the boy as well, eh? I wouldn't wish for the Donkey to be harmed while I am away.'

'I will guard him too.'

'Good.'

He left soon after, walking up the north-bearing roadway, turning right, and continuing on to the city walls.

The town of Calais was itself held within a long rectangle of walls. To the north the city looked to the sea but on three other sides, the walls gave onto scrubby land with a miserable grey soil that looked insufficient to support any plants, and yet it brought forth a variety of trees and shrubs, while the fields further east looked productive. However here, near the walls, the land was wretchedly boggy. There was hardly any need to dig a moat. Even the trenches dug by the English were soon filling with water. Yet there was a wide, double moat, too, that curved from the east side along the south, and part-way up the western side.

Along the northern stretch of wall, and then curving slightly before continuing west, was the river that fed the estuary where the harbour lay. There was another moat here, as well as a long dyke. More defences protected the castle at the north-western corner of the town.

Archibald sighed as he took in the sight of the castle. It was tempting to think that he could pound it into dust, but alas, even the most massive gonne he possessed would do no more than scratch that rock. It was impregnable – as were most of the town's walls. For him to reach the town with his powder and shot was possible, but it would be at the last gasp. In truth, old technology would serve better. Large wooden catapults and stone-throwers would do more damage.

However, there was still work for his machines. This was what his dreams had told him.

To the north, for example, was the Rysbank. There, if he could position his gonnes safely, he would be able to command the entrance to the harbour. True, right now the Rysbank was protected by French defenders, but they could be driven off or into the sea.

It was a thought. Aye, it was a good thought.

'They're going to take us. We'll all be killed,' Clip whined.

'Shut up, Clip,' Jack said.

Dogbreath was eyeing the ship with a glower. 'There's no way I'll be captured by a poxed Genoese son of a whore!'

'They won't take us,' Berenger said. 'Not while we remain here fighting.'

'Frip? They're getting closer,' Mark Tyler said.

Berenger cast a look over his shoulder. The sea obscured the other vessel for a moment, but then it reappeared, the prow pointing to the heavens as it breasted the wave, and then started the long, gut-churning, swooping dive. It was definitely pursuing them.

'It's a fucking galley, Tyler. What do you expect?' he rasped.

Tyler flicked his lank, straw-coloured hair back from his brow. He was a tall fellow, with dark eyes that looked out of place in his pale face. Berenger had known him only a matter of weeks, but didn't trust the man at all. He had been involved in plundering a religious house, and Berenger preferred to keep to secular enemies. He saw little need to provoke God Himself.

Berenger glanced about him at the ship, his eyes narrowed against the stinging spray. He was weary after the last hours of rocking to and fro with the planks shifting under his feet, and felt like a man ten years his senior. Every muscle and joint ached, and his bowels felt weak, as though he was suffering from a fever, as well as the vomit that constantly threatened to gush like the spume from the wave-tops.

'I've had enough of this shit,' he swore, and began to make his way over the treacherous deck to the shipmaster.

A loose coil of rope, slippery planks, the sudden thunder of a fresh wave striking the hull . . . and Berenger was thrown from his feet. On his backside, he slid over the tilting deck and almost slammed into the wall of timbers on the farther side, but before he could do so, a hand grasped his jerkin, and he was drawn to a halt. He shivered as he looked at the sea in front of him. He had been *that* close to drowning, he knew. Wanting to thank his rescuer, he stared around at his saviour.

'Glad I'm here now, are you?' Tyler enquired.

Berenger jerked himself free of Tyler's hand and clasped a rope, hauling himself upright. 'Keep off me!'

'No gratitude?' Tyler said sarcastically and returned to watching their pursuer.

No, Berenger said to himself, *no gratitude, no friendship*. Only suspicion and disgust.

Back at Calais, Ed the Donkey stood huddled in a cloak near Archibald's wagon, grumpily surveying the grey seas.

Ed felt lonely. Twelve years old, he had been orphaned years before. He had come here to France to take his revenge, but the life of a soldier had proved more dangerous than he could have anticipated, and now he stood here staring out towards England and home.

Not that he had a home any more. The only home he knew was the one here, with Béatrice and Archibald the gynour.

At first he had thought the big man was terrifying: he reeked of the Devil. That was the smell Ed associated with Archibald – *brimstone*, the odour of Hell.

All the other soldiers tried to avoid Archibald: none of them liked the smell that followed him. Men made signs against the Evil One when he had passed, and even after a battle, Archibald found it difficult to acquire food. At Crécy, Ed had seen how

Archibald's great gonnes had ripped into the ranks of French men-at-arms – and had also seen how a mis-prepared gonne could detonate and slaughter all the gynours about it. Archibald had fought with all the zeal of a Christian that day. And recently Ed had grown fond of the old man.

It was not Archibald himself who made him feel more comfortable with his place at the gynour's side, though. It was the constant presence of Béatrice.

Ed had no sister. His parents died when French pirates appeared and destroyed his town. The young lad saw his father die, and his mother was raped and murdered. Béatrice felt like a mix of the older sister he'd never had and his mother. She was beautiful, and kind, and very understanding. He simply adored her.

He suddenly heard a little sound and his head snapped around. It came from over by a wagon. He stared hard. In the semi-darkness, it was hard to see much, but he was sure he could see a sack moving. It was the bag in which they kept their stores of oats. Not many people liked oats, but Archibald and Berenger had it in their heads that oats were a useful food for the men.

Ed reckoned a dog must have got into their stores. The movement was too large for a rat, surely? A rat that size would be bigger than a cat. He had no wish to confront a giant rat, he told himself. At first he shouted and threw a stick, then a small rock. A yelp came, but it sounded human rather than canine.

Ed hurried to the stores, and found a small boy rubbing his head. He turned wide, terrified eyes to Ed, but then saw how small Ed was. Standing, he was almost Ed's height.

'Keep away from our food!' Ed spat.

'I'll take what I need,' the boy responded truculently.

'You'll have to fight me first!'

'Reckon you can stop me?'

Ed had no desire to fight anyone, but he would rather fight than see Archibald's food pinched, and some thieving scrote of a vintener's boy was not going to walk away scot free. 'Yes!'

The boy was painfully thin. He looked as though he hadn't eaten in days.

'You're French?' Ed demanded. Ed had lost his family to the French, but in the last two weeks of fighting, he had come to appreciate that not all French were evil, in the same way that not all English soldiers were saints. And this was only a young lad. With the condescension of an older boy for one at least a full year younger, Ed dismissed him as a threat.

'Yes! This is my land!' the boy declared.

Ed shrugged. 'But it's my food, and you won't take it without permission. Still, if you're hungry I have bread. Do you want some?'

The boy eyed the hunk of bread Ed produced with all the ravenous desperation of a cur, then stared up at Ed's face as though suspecting there to be a trick in this act of generosity.

'I've been hungry, too,' Ed said gruffly by way of explanation. 'Come. Eat! What is your name?'

'Georges,' his visitor said, edging nearer to the bread.

'Where are you from?'

'My family lived in a town. You have destroyed it. We have nothing left, and I have lost my family.'

'I lost my family years ago,' Ed said. He held the loaf lower, ducking his head. 'Come, eat.'

The boy darted forward, snatched the bread and darted away a few yards, stuffing the food into his mouth as quickly as he could. He looked like a squirrel desperately filling its mouth before a predator could arrive.

'You want some drink?' Ed asked.

Georges nodded, and Ed fetched him a mazer of wine. The boy

drained it in one, coughing at the strength of it. Ed refilled the mazer and the boy took it back, sipping more carefully now.

'You'll be safe here,' Ed said. 'The men here are kind. They looked after me, too.'

Georges watched him doubtfully, but then nodded. As if by that one action he had passed responsibility for his well-being to Ed, he immediately wrapped himself up in Ed's blanket, lay down and was soon fast asleep.

Tyler. Bleeding Tyler, Berenger thought to himself.

There were always men like Tyler in any army. The stranger who stood at the outer edge of the men; the man who held the secrets of his past close to his chest; the odd one who wouldn't join in wholeheartedly. The one whom none of the others trusted entirely. John of Essex was bad enough, but he was predictable and, while dangerous, could be understood. Tyler was another sort of man entirely.

All the men in Berenger's vintaine had their own secrets. Any group of twenty men would have one or two whose secrets were close-guarded for good reason. In King Edward III's army, more than a few had been career outlaws and thieves. There were draw-latches, robbers and murderers in every centaine mingling freely with the honest fighters who had been brought by their lords or tempted by the promise of booty.

Many of them were pardoned felons. The King had need of more men to swell the ranks of his archers and infantry, which had been depleted in the short, vicious campaign that had taken the army down to the walls of Paris and back to Calais; therefore any man who could wield a sword or bow was welcome. For every man who could be counted on, who was reliable, there was another who was viewed askance by those who knew him, suspecting that his shifty manner meant he had something to hide.

And Berenger was convinced that Tyler was such a man.

'You all right, Vintener?' John of Essex called.

Berenger grunted, his attention returning to the galley behind them. It was gaining far too quickly. 'Shipman! How long till we reach the port?' he bellowed.

The ship's master, a dour old fisherman with a round face framed by grey whiskers and the expression of a man who had bitten by accident into a sloe, curled his lip as he peered over Berenger's shoulder at their pursuer. 'If he keeps on like that, us'll never reach the port, boy.'

Chapter Three

'They're preparing!'

The shipman's cries from the crow's nest came down to the decks during a brief lull in the storm, and for a moment, Fripper was startled to hear the voice coming from so high up. Then the deck pitched once more and he was forced to clutch at a rope. Staring back at their pursuers, he saw the enemy gathering at the forecastle. They were only a matter of yards away now.

'*Vintaine!*' he yelled. 'String your bows!'

Usually, before he went into battle, Fripper would find a strange peace washing over him, his breath coming more calmly. As a young man, he had known only terror, his heart beating faster, his armpits and hands growing clammy with sweat at the realisation that he was about to risk his life once more, but with age, that had deadened. Now there was only the sense of a task to be undertaken. Nothing more. It was just a job.

Not this time, however. Today, his fear was smothering him. Fighting on ships felt unnatural at the best of times. He had done so before, but on ships bound together, so that it was like fighting on land. To the vintener, the risk of drowning was more alarming than the thought of a stab to the heart or being hit by a crossbow bolt.

He was terrified, and the realisation sucked at his will. Clinging to his rope as the galley crawled ever closer, he could not muster the energy to draw his sword.

Berenger had come here to France with the intention of making money. Many years ago, his parents had died, and afterwards he had been taken in by the old King, Edward II, the present King's father. Growing up in the court, shown how to behave as a chivalric man should, he had loved the King like a father. But then the nation rose against Edward II, and suddenly his life was turned topsy-turvy. His King, his lord, was captured and held in prison; he himself was taken and gaoled. Only later, when the disastrous reign of terror of the arch-traitor, Roger Mortimer, had ended was Berenger fully free at last. He travelled widely, and when he returned to England, he was held as a traitor himself. Only the intervention of King Edward III had saved him. The King's son had shown him every courtesy, and perhaps then Berenger could have made something of his life. Maybe he could have settled and raised a family. But instead the lure of loot and pillage took hold of him. With no roots, no family, no land to hold him, he became a freebooter, fighting wherever there was a battle.

Having learned about chivalry when he lived in the King's court, he could have worked harder to become a knight himself, perhaps. But nothing had come of that. His life had progressed from one war to another – fighting those against whom he had no quarrel, purely to win the largesse of his master. At least in recent months he had been fighting with Sir John de Sully, but now Sir John was far away. Only Berenger and his men were here, and that felt awfully lonely. And he, Berenger, had absolutely no idea why he stood on this rolling deck facing a force of Genoese and French and about to join the slaughter once again.

If he survived this, if he came out after the Siege of Calais whole, he vowed that he would find a different life. He would forswear war and battle, and with God's help he would find a woman and settle down. He had said this many times before, but this time he would keep his word. That he swore.

'Should we loose, Frip?' Clip's whining voice cut through his thoughts. 'They'll kill us all if we don't fight.'

Berenger felt a shudder pass through his frame – a surge of anger at these Genoese, at France and, yes, at his King, for sending him here, to this poxy boat, to die. The spell of terror was broken.

'Archers, *draw*! Archers, *loose*!' he bawled, and set his hand to his sword-hilt. 'I don't give a fuck who these arrogant bastards are, but they won't take me without a fight!'

He could see them clearly enough. Burly fighting men, all of them burned by the sea's wind and sun, with dark hair set about swarthy features, wearing a mixture of plain clothing and mail, some with helmets or bascinets. Several were equipped with axes and polearms, while more stood at the rail brandishing swords or long knives.

Aloft, he saw the bowmen, their crossbows spanned and ready. Before the English could loose their first arrows, three bolts slammed into his men. The sound, like gravel flung against wet cabbage, made Berenger's belly roil. He hated that sound above all others. 'GET THOSE CUNTS ON THE CROW'S NEST,' he bellowed as he gripped his sword more firmly in his fist. It was a poor way to fight, this, with your hands cold and clammy, and damp from spray. No man could hold a weapon firmly in that kind of state.

A sudden lurch and he heard a splintering noise from beneath his feet. The ship gave a great shuddering roll, and then her rolling was stopped, but the deck remained at an impossible angle. Berenger stayed attached to his rope, the loose end wrapped about his wrist, while his men began to slide along the deck. Clip grabbed at a stanchion as he passed, and gave his hand to John of Essex; Jack Fletcher was halted by the mast, and he managed to hang on to a sailor who passed by him on his back. All about the deck, sailors and warriors were clinging to each other and any spare ropes or stays, rather than fighting the enemy.

Arrows flew over Berenger's head; he saw one pass through a sailor's body, to pierce the decking behind him while he shivered and cursed in pain. Another nicked Jack Fletcher's skull and stabbed into the mast itself, and he looked up at the fletchings over his brow with an expression of shock mixed with fury. Dogbreath swung on a rope, cursing volubly when a bolt flew by and almost struck his hip. Turf was curled into a ball at the wale, his hands pressed together as he prayed.

A man with a grapnel stood at the front of the galley, and Berenger lifted his sword to try to rally his men, but before he could do so, a calm, accented voice cut through the din.

'English, do you think to die today, or would you prefer to live?'

The speaker was a dark-skinned man with a well-trimmed beard and white teeth that stood out in stark contrast to his oily black hair. His voice was serious, but his eyes were alive with humour.

'Come, English, there is no need for us to kill you all. Surrender and you will be saved. Your ship is sinking already. Her hull is cracked like a dropped bowl. We could leave you to drown, but I don't think you would like that.'

Berenger gazed back at the tilted deck. There were three men dead – two men from his vintaine and a sailor – but as matters stood, the Genoese could pick them off one by one without effort if they wanted, and there was nothing he or the archers could do. Only four men looked as though they still had their bows: their arrows were lost. With the deck angled the way it was, there was no choice. They could not fight up the slippery slope of the deck and hope to achieve anything. They would be slaughtered before they had reached the wale.

'Frip, if we live we can fight another day!' Jack roared up at him. 'In Christ's name, we can't fight!'

'You have us,' Berenger said to the smiling face. At that moment, he hated his captor.

CHAPTER FOUR

Berenger stood on the galley's forecastle and watched as the oars dipped into the water and hauled the vessel away from the cog. The master of the galley had not been lying. The galley had a projecting spike that had punctured the English vessel as easily as a knife slipping into an inflated bladder. As they withdrew, the cog seemed to settle in the water, like a hound sprawling before a fire. Soon the entire deck was level with the waves, and then the seawater was crashing over and through her, and the masts leaned further and further from the vertical until, as the galley pulled away and took the wind in her sails, the old cog rolled over and all Berenger could see was her rounded belly as she sank.

A young, fair-haired shipman was standing not far away, and Berenger saw John of Essex put an arm about his shoulders as the lad began to sob. Strange how men could become so affectionate towards what was a mere assemblage of cords, pegs and wood, he thought. But then he realised that he too had a sense of loss. Perhaps it was just that the ship represented home. With her sinking, Berenger was as bereft as any of her sailors.

'You are the master of the ship?' the Genoese asked.

'No, I am a fighting man. You killed the master – a bolt from a crossbow.'

'The fortune of war, eh? Is a shame. I will say prayers for him.' The man looked suitably solemn for a moment, but then a smile flashed and he looked more like a pirate than a priest. 'But first we must bring you to solid ground again, yes? You would like that?'

Berenger nodded. He had never enjoyed working on ships. They were essential, of course, for travel from England to the King of France's lands or beyond, but that didn't mean he had to like the experience. The sooner he had his feet on dry land, the happier he would be. He would feel safer.

Not that it would necessarily be true, he knew as he looked about him. The Genoese were in the employ of the French. The King of France had paid them handsomely to come and sail for him. They were simple mercenaries, he thought with disgust, available to the man with the largest purse. They had no sense of honour or duty.

'Your men, they are thirsty?' the Genoese asked. He was watching a shipman who had been pierced by a pair of bolts, and who sat, panting, at a companionway. 'That man is in great pain.'

'A little drink would be received with gratitude,' Berenger said. He could not help a grimace pass over his features.

'You too are in pain?'

'No, but I shall be. The French are not kind to captured prisoners,' Berenger said.

'I will not have my prisoners assaulted needlessly,' the Genoese said dismissively.

'Yes. For certain.'

'I swear it, my friend.' The Genoese waved a hand expansively over the vessel. 'My name is Chrestien de Grimault. You are my guest and friend while you are on my ship, and because you did not choose to fight on needlessly and cause the death or injury of my men, I honour you. While you are aboard the *Sainte Marie* you need not fear. My men will leave you in peace. You can enjoy the journey, and when we deposit you on French soil, there will be a good bed and food. You will not be harmed. I swear this on my son's life.' The Genoese bowed low.

Berenger could not help but give a twisted smile.

'I am grateful, Master, for the honour you do us,' he said. 'Where did you learn to speak English so well?'

Chrestien stood upright again. 'Ah, well, I have plied my trade all about the Mediterranean Sea, and there are many English who still live with the Knights of Malta and who populate the harbours and ports. I have learned to enjoy the company of the English.'

'Yet you take up arms with the French.'

'Ah, my friend,' Chrestien gave a shamefaced shake of his head. 'That is sad, but it is the way of things. Genoa is allied to France, so when the French King asked for our help, we were duty bound to assist him.' He shrugged, and the piratical expression returned to his eyes. 'Especially since he pays us nine hundred florins a month for our service.'

His grin was infectious enough to make Berenger forget his misery for the present.

'That is better, my friend. I will have wine brought so we may seal our friendship. There is no need for disputation amongst friends, is there? We are honourable combatants, and should deal fairly with each other, no? Now, my friend: your name, I beg of you?'

'My name is Berenger Fripper.'

'Berenger? But surely you are a knight, with your warlike appearance and bold attire?'

Berenger felt his mouth fall open. 'No, I'm no knight, only a man-at-arms for a knight.'

'You bear yourself well for a mere warrior, my friend. But no matter. *Wine! I will have wine here!*' he called out. Then, turning back to Berenger, he added in a quieter tone, 'I managed to raid a storehouse before setting sail, and have some very excellent barrels that I think had been destined for a bishop. It would have been a waste, to see such a good wine go down a religious gullet!'

He arrived as dusk was beginning to fall, a fellow of middling height with a round face and grey-blue eyes that sparkled. He was hooded and bent, walking like a man twenty years his senior. For him, changing his gait was a matter of habit when he was walking out amongst the English. The Vidame was too used to concealment to walk normally here.

The light was fading, and the shadows lengthening. It was his favourite time to go for a stroll. At night, men were on their guard, but in the twilight they took less notice of other people, even strangers. For a spy, this was the best time to go abroad.

Their meeting place was a grim little chamber off an alley in what had once been a suburb of the town. He cast an eye about the place as he entered. Old sacking mingled with the refuse of the years, with broken spars, and bits and pieces of frayed rope. A rat's corpse lay partially mummified beside a shred or two of rag. It was a shit-hole, basically. Not his first choice, but it served.

'What happened?' he demanded as soon as the door was closed behind him.

'It wasn't my fault,' the big man said immediately.

'It never is *your* fault, is it, Bertucat?' he said. 'Not even when you go to a private assignation with me and get into a fight!'

'There was an English archer eavesdropping on us. He tried to break in.'

'An English archer? Bah! He would have been out for plunder, that's all.'

'Except he was with the same vintaine.'

'What do you mean, the "same"?'

'What do you think I mean? He serves with Berenger Fripper, the archer they call "Clip".'

'Do I care? If you were caught there it would have endangered me!'

'You don't like me, do you?' Bertucat was a typical product of the streets about Marseilles. A brutish, dim-witted fool, with little to commend him but the size of his fists and his fearlessness in a fight.

'You have no idea what I like and what I don't like. However, I do *not* like the thought of being hanged because you are too incompetent to finish things off! You should have killed the man while you could.'

'And have the vintaine come after his killer? They are loyal to each other in that band – you know that as well as me. Better to beat him up like the thieving scrote he is, and have him thought to have been discovered while breaking in. This way we're safe.'

'I wonder.'

'Why, Vidame? What is it? Worried about your own skin?'

The Vidame heard the sneer. It was tempting to kill the man, but Bertucat was built like a cathedral, massively. He had a thick neck like a knight, and a head that was narrow, as if it had been squeezed into a helmet that was too small. His eyes were brown and bovine, but only in the sense of being like an angry bull's.

However, Bertucat was useful. His unthinking belligerence made the Vidame feel safer. For now.

'What is your news?' the Vidame asked.

'I wanted to make sure you had heard about the vintaine.'

'What of it?'

'They have all been captured. Their ship was taken.'

'What of our friend?'

'He was on the ship. Either he's dead or he's a prisoner too.'

The Vidame swore. 'If he is slain, it will take many months to get another man of his calibre into the English camp.'

'I could do his work.'

'You?' The Vidame was so surprised, he nearly laughed out loud.

It had taken him many weeks to find the right person to act as his spy. Bertucat could not appreciate what it was like, living with the enemy all day long, trying to show friendship to men who were destroying the country like a plague. For such a spy, it was a deadly co-existence. The man had to have had two personalities, two nationalities, two lives. One was that of an Englishman keen on plunder and slaughter, the other was a loyal servant of King Philippe, searching for any means to undermine the English army's attempts to ravage poor France.

Only one man he had ever met could act the part convincingly. The man in question had a French mother, an English father, and had spent his life in both camps; because of this, the Vidame's spy was perfect. He was able to wear his Englishness like a cloak, to put on or take off at will.

Bertucat, by contrast, was a brainless thug, who wouldn't last two minutes. No, the Vidame had to pray that his spy was returned safe and well.

It was early in the morning when the galley negotiated the harbour of the little port of Dunkirk.

'And so, my friends, here we must soon part,' Chrestien said.

Berenger and the others were held on the forecastle under the suspicious gaze of several heavily armed Genoese. In the crow's nest, four men with spanned crossbows kept a close watch too, not that Berenger or the others felt any urge to attempt an escape. There was no point. They could see all the galley's men, over two hundred rowers and shipmen. Those were appalling odds for the ship's surviving sailors, thirty-odd at best.

Berenger smiled at Chrestien. 'I am glad to have met you. You are a kindly captor.'

'And you, my friend, are a most gracious guest,' Chrestien replied. He walked to the wale and stared out at the port in the early-morning light. 'I wish circumstances could have been better when we met. I would have enjoyed your company, had we the time to meet over a mess of food. Perhaps we shall still have an opportunity to share a meal? I will raise it with the keeper of prisoners here in the town. There is much about you I should like to learn.'

'There is little to learn about me,' Berenger said. 'I am only a fighter in the King's host.'

'No, there is more to you than that,' Chrestien said, waving a finger with his eyes narrowed. 'You have been trained in chivalry, that is clear.'

'Well, when we are given into the custody of the keeper of prisoners, I fear we shall not meet again,' Berenger said with regret.

'Nonsense! A good keeper will not begrudge us a conversation or two,' Chrestien said heartily. He clapped Berenger on the back. 'I shall visit you on the morrow. I must first see to my stores and supplies, and prepare the *Sainte Marie* for sea, but as soon as I may, I shall come and we shall find the best inn in the town and enjoy a good meal and some intelligent conversation.'

Berenger smiled but he doubted that the French would be willing to release him.

'Frip, what now?' Clip called.

'We are to be taken to a gaol where we shall be held,' he said without turning.

'A gaol, eh? Well, you know what'll happen, don't you?'

'Clip?' Jack Fletcher called.

'Aye?'

'Don't say it. Just shut up.'

CHAPTER FIVE

Berenger had seen worse prisons. Years ago he had been kept in a noisome dungeon that was perpetually damp. Sitting down made a man's hosen sodden from the ordure. This, in contrast, was a goodly-sized chamber with dry walls and straw on the floor. Two leather buckets were provided for the men, and while they were not enough to cope with the needs of all thirty men, at least they did not have to make a mess on the floor at first. All had been entangled with chains. Manacles and ankle-shackles hindered their movements.

'What do we do now, Frip?' Jack asked.

He had walked over to Berenger, and now squatted in front of his vintener. The other men drew near, shuffling closer, as best they could. Tyler, John of Essex, Clip and the rest formed an anxious semicircle about him. Berenger eyed them all. They deserved better than this.

'There's nothing we can do at present,' he said. 'We just have to keep quiet and hope that the French won't mistreat us.'

Clip nodded mutely, and chewed at a nail. The unaccustomed

silence of the wizened, beggarly-featured man was eloquent proof of his inner turmoil. It was rare indeed that he would not declare the vintaine lost and doomed. His assertion that all would shortly die was an irritating fixture in the men's lives, and this curious silence from him was as shocking as a sudden death-rattle in a man's throat.

'Lads, we'll get out of here,' Berenger said with a certainty he didn't feel. 'The French won't want to upset our King more than they have to.'

'Yes, Frip,' Jack said flatly, and the men drifted away, none of them exchanging so much as a glance, as they selected areas to sit and think over their position.

Berenger stared at his hands. He had them clasped in his lap, and now he willed them apart, but for some reason he could not move them. They were linked as though bound with invisible thongs. He felt a heaviness in his soul. Looking about him in the darkened interior of this chamber, he could see his men and the shipmen from the cog, all still and quiet, apart from one or two who stared about them distractedly as though looking for a means of escape.

They all knew the reality. The English had been here in France for weeks, trying to bring the French to battle by means of *dampnum* – war by horror. They had waged war on the peasants and the poor, burning, raping, looting and murdering over a broad front in order to prove the French King's inability to honour his duty of protection towards his people. The aim was to entice the French into King Edward III's Peace and make them reject their own feeble King. Tens of thousands had been robbed, ransomed or slain since the English had landed at St-Vaast-La-Hougue, and any Frenchman would want to take his revenge. If the roles were reversed, if this were Portsmouth or Southampton, and Frenchmen were captured after raiding in England, Berenger knew exactly how the enemy would be punished. They would be tortured to within an inch of their souls' release, allowed to recover, and then tortured again before finally being executed slowly and painfully in front of a jeering crowd. And he expected exactly that kind of treatment.

His hands were shaking with his rising panic. In his breast he could feel the muscles tightening. Fear was engulfing him. He knew how the French executed people. In his mind's eye he could see the crowd before him as he was led to the wheel and bound to it, while the executioner spat and laughed at him, his collection of sticks and iron bars ready. He would break all Berenger's bones one by one. Fires would be lighted nearby to heat the metal brands to scorch and burn him; pincers would be arrayed to flay him alive . . . the horror of a vengeful death with all its concomitant cruelty.

'Frip – you all right?' John of Essex said quietly at his side. 'We can get out of this, you know.'

'I . . . I am well,' he managed.

'Be calm – for them, Frip. Be strong,' John whispered.

Berenger stared at him, and would have answered, but just then there was a rattle of bolts and the sound of a key in the lock, and the door swung open.

Béatrice was in the camp when she heard that there had been a battle at sea. She would never forget that day. Her morning had started calm and happy, with her helping the Donkey to look after their oxen, chatting and laughing with him and Georges, his new friend. There were always a thousand and one things to do. Ed was keen to help, but he would keep getting under her feet, and whenever she looked at him, he would duck away. She was perplexed. He did not try to leave her, so he didn't seem annoyed or angry, and yet there was that curious shyness. Perhaps he was merely upset because the vintaine had gone away, and he thought he should have gone with them.

From then, her morning soured. Béatrice wanted to get on with things, and the Donkey kept dawdling. And then she suddenly realised what was wrong. She had been standing and stretching her arms after bending for a long time collecting some nuts, and had turned to see him staring at her breasts. Letting her arms fall immediately, she felt the blood drain from her face. She did not see Ed the Donkey, the young lad of whom she was fond. Instead she saw only a man exhibiting the same lascivious desire as all those who had tried to rape her over the last, traumatic weeks.

'What is it? You think you are old enough to bed me, boy?' she snapped.

He coloured a violent puce, span around and fled. Instantly she was struck with shame. Ed was no lustful man desiring her body, but a child on the cusp of manhood, a boy confused about his urges.

'*Ed!*' she called, full of remorse, but it was too late. He was already gone. Georges gave her a black look and flew off in pursuit of his friend, while Béatrice stood, cursing her quick temper. She had made many mistakes in her life, but few as foolish as this, she thought. The poor boy had only snatched a glimpse of her body through her clothes. It was her fault, surely, for giving him the opportunity to view her in that light. She should have been more careful. After the last months she knew how dangerous it was to tempt men.

Perhaps Archibald was right, she thought. Perhaps she ought to leave the camp and go away, far away, and find another place to live. Here, she was a constant source of dissension. Wherever she went she brought arguments and fights. If she could even disturb poor Donkey, it was time to look elsewhere.

There was one man with whom she felt content to discuss the matter. Berenger Fripper. He would be rational and sensible, she knew. She could trust his judgement. When he was back, she would take him aside and ask his advice.

With that, she made sure that the oxen were tethered securely, and then made her way back to their camp.

Archibald was already there, and had seated himself on an old wine cask before the fire. He scowled at the flames thoughtfully, nodding his head occasionally as if to some inner argument only he could hear.

'Archibald! Archibald!'

'What's the matter with the boy now?' the gynour grumbled as the Donkey came pelting down the road, Georges close behind him like his personal spaniel.

Béatrice laughed to herself to see the old fellow looking so put out. 'Donkey, what is it?' she called.

Ed glanced at her shamefacedly, but came to a halt before Archibald. Suddenly, his eyes filled with tears. 'It's the vintaine!' he choked. 'They've been taken. All of them!'

Chapter Six

Berenger and the other captives were shoved and clubbed forward by the town's militia. This gaggle of disreputable brutes had no discernible uniforms, not even the town's crest. To Berenger's jaundiced eye, they looked like men who had been pulled from the fields about the town that very morning and selected for their ability to drive cattle. Either that, or they had been emptied, like dregs, from the lowest dungeon in the town. The one closest to Berenger had a thick beard and a wall eye, but that didn't stop him from aiming blows regularly at the vintener as they marched.

Not that their bullying produced a reaction from the English. The archers and sailors bent under the buffets, and apart from Tyler yelping, there was little sound from them, only the constant rattle of the chains at wrists and ankles. Dogbreath ignored every blow with the stoicism of a saint who can see heaven opening before him. Saint Lawrence ducked, but with his height he was hit more than most. Clip was struck over the head with a ferocity that made his legs crumple beneath him, but Jack Fletcher and John of Essex were near enough to grab an arm each and, ducking from the blows now aimed at themselves, they hurried Clip forwards. He tried to pick his feet up, first one boot then the other, but with the length of chain securing his ankles, he could not bring either foot forward far enough to take his weight, and at the speed with which they were propelling him, he could not move both together. Eventually he gave up and allowed his boots to scuff along, dragging in the dirt.

The room into which they were brought was a broad hall with a stone-flagged floor. On the walls hung great tapestries with biblical scenes displayed, while to the left was a vast, unglazed window that gave out onto a view over the harbour itself. From there Berenger could see the sleek lines of three galleys at their moorings, while barrels of food and drink were brought alongside and stored aboard. It was a sight to tear at a man's heartstrings, to see the possibility of escape so near to hand, yet with no means to achieve it.

There were two long tables set out, and on each were piles of parchments and scrolls, while a small army of clerks scurried about, as busy as rats in a bakery. However, it was not this excited bustle that caught Berenger's attention, it was the five men standing before him.

Two looked like well-fed merchants. One of the pair was a little under five and a half feet tall, with pleasant features under mousy-coloured hair. He looked like a man who was prone to laughter and conviviality, but Berenger saw that he had the thick neck of a warrior used to wearing a steel helm. His shoulders too had the breadth of a man who wielded a lance. He was someone to watch, the vintener decided.

The second merchant had pale brown hair, and a harder expression on his flabby face. Taller than the first, this man was clearly no fighter. He had a paunch like a London banker, and his neck was thick only because of the rolls of fat. As soon as the men entered, he fixed Berenger with a gimlet eye. There would be no compassion from that quarter, Berenger could tell. This fellow wore the look of a man presented with the thief who had taken his purse.

A little apart from these two stood a cardinal, a man with bright, birdlike eyes in a face that smiled all the time – and yet there was no answering smile in those eyes. He was, Berenger thought, the most dangerous of all three men. Nearby was a ginger-haired, bearded man with a ruddy complexion. He stood square and powerful, watching the English with hatred on his face.

The fifth man was a soldier through and through. He was as short as the first merchant, but his hair was thick and fair, offsetting his square, uncompromising face. His shoulders were broad and muscled from holding a lance and sword. On his tunic he bore arms, and Berenger wondered what they indicated. Whether he was an esquire or a knight, the vintener could not guess.

The slimmer, more affable-looking man spoke first. 'You say that these are the devils who have wreaked such havoc? Why they look no more dangerous than drowned rats!'

'*Silence*, Jean de Vervins,' the man-at-arms said. He eyed the prisoners without emotion.

'I caught them in the Channel,' the Genoese said. He had followed in behind them all, and now stood at the side, eyeing them contemplatively. When he caught Berenger's eye, he winked.

'They look like the scum they are,' the ginger man said. Berenger was startled to hear the Scottish accent. He had heard that many Scots fought for the King of France, but he had never met one here before.

'You are English pirates,' the man-at-arms stated. He spoke strongly accented French, and Berenger thought the dialect sounded familiar. Perhaps it was from the north, not far from

Calais? 'You are found to have attacked our lawful traffic on the sea. What do you have to say for yourselves?'

'We are subjects of King Edward III,' Berenger said in the same language. His hands shook as he ducked his head nervously. 'We have not attacked any ships. We were there to guard the King's fleet.'

'Only because your vessel was too feeble to withstand a fight,' the man commented.

The fellow called Jean de Vervins cast a glance around the assembled prisoners and shook his head. 'Count, is it not astonishing? These are the fabled archers – those who are thought to strike fear into the hearts of all France? I find this hard to believe. They look like ordinary peasants to me.'

The cardinal had a high, sing-song tone as though he was singing the Vespers. 'Perhaps these are some of the new recruits who have yet to see battle, my lord?'

Jean de Vervins said, 'No, they have the appearance of men who have been campaigning for months. Look at their clothing, their faces. These are not recent-comers to the fray. These are men who have been living well on French soil for some months.'

'You think so?'

'Why, yes. And we should make use of them.'

'And, how do you propose we do that?' the man-at-arms said with a disdainful sneer.

'As an example, of course, Count. We know that many consider these English to be infused with the powers of the Devil. I say, keep these near at hand to prove that the famous archers are in truth mere clod-hoppers,' Jean de Vervins said, his eyes passing over Dogbreath with every sign of revulsion. 'Can you imagine any man being fearful of such as these?'

'No, we must use them as an example to all who would seek to harm poor France,' the merchant with the hard eyes said. 'Put them to work, improving the defences of our town against their own kind. By their own efforts they can keep us secure.'

'At the expense of the guards necessary to watch over them?' the man-at-arms commented. Berenger had noticed that the man called Jean de Vervins had referred to him as 'Count'. 'No. Better by far that we should punish them and throw them from the walls. We have no need of extra mouths to feed, especially when those mouths will require fighting men to guard them.'

'You would not release them to continue their depredations?' Jean de Vervins declared, and his companion nodded briskly.

'No. We would not wish to have them free to rejoin the English. Kill them one at a time. A daily celebration. We could start with that one,' the merchant said, pointing at Berenger.

Jean de Vervins shook his head. 'Surely we should begin with a common archer and save the captain until last.'

Then the cardinal spoke. He had a calm, contemplative manner, with a faint crease in his forehead as though considering his words carefully. 'No, I think not. I would blind them all and cut off the fingers they use to work their bows, and *then* send them to find their way back to their friends. Perhaps we would allow one of them to keep an eye so he might lead them. A display of our contempt for them would not go amiss.'

The Count drew his mouth into a thoughtful moue. 'Very well. It may encourage the other English to reconsider their actions.'

Chrestien de Grimault took a pace forward. 'I explained to you that I swore to these men that they would be well looked after if they surrendered to me. Not that they would be tortured or executed.'

'Then you spoke without thinking of your rights, Genoan,' the man-at-arms said.

'My Lord Comte de Roucy, I would not wish it thought that I would give my word in a careless manner without honour.'

'Then be more careful with your words in future.'

'Nor would I have it thought that I was so ill-regarded by you and your King that my requests for clemency would go disregarded.'

'In that case, petition the King. However, even if he were to listen to your pleas with sympathy, you would find all dead before you received your answer,' the count said bluntly.

Chrestien de Grimault nodded, his eyes hooded. He didn't so much as glance in Berenger's direction. That was when Berenger knew they were lost.

The Cardinal let his eyes range over the prisoners as the Genoese was stilled. 'Then I shall arrange for a platform to be constructed outside the church. The people can witness the punishment of these men there. It will take a day or perhaps two before we have it completed. Then we can turn them all from the town's gate to wander where they will.'

'Yes,' the Comte de Roucy said, 'but first we need to make an example for the townspeople so that they know we shall defend them against these English fiends. We shall pick two for immediate illustration of our determination to punish all English invaders.'

'My lord Count, my lord Cardinal,' Jean de Vervins said strongly, 'surely you would be better served to wait until the King has heard the Genoese's request? It will not harm your case to offer a period for reflection. Then, when the King has made known his view, you can be assured of not going against his will. I would—'

'You are no longer in favour, Sieur Jean. These peasants are my prisoners to do with as I will. I would not delay their execution even if they were lords and eligible for ransom. No! I will see them die and let all the English know that this is what they can expect!'

Berenger felt a flash of anger on hearing this, and he tried to step forward, but a lance-butt struck his belly and he fell back, gasping. His fear left him as he clutched his belly, glaring at the guard who had hit him. He had an urge to spring and hit the man, but before he could act, two Frenchmen behind him had set their swords to him.

'Him and him,' the man-at-arms said, languidly indicating the young, fair-haired sailor who had wept to see his ship sink, and another, older mariner. The two were separated from the rest by lances and clubs. 'These we shall hang now. As for the rest, take them to the dungeons. When we have time, we shall see to them.'

The younger shipman began to wail on hearing this. Crying out as he saw the others being led back the way they had come, but Berenger had no time to spare for his panic. His own mind was working doubly quickly. There must be some means of escape from here, if he could but find it.

Béatrice felt a violent stabbing pain just below her ribcage, as though her inner being had fractured. 'Did none escape?' she said hoarsely.

'They were taken, all of them. Some were slain and thrown from the boat,' Ed said. 'I don't know who.'

'What will they do?' Béatrice asked Archibald.

He grimaced and said heavily, 'What would any leader do to men such as these? Kill them at once. Hack off their heads so they'll pose no risk in the future. Or, if he wants to make a point, he could mutilate them and set them free to live forever as a reminder of French revenge.'

'No! You don't really think they would do that?' Béatrice wailed. To think that Berenger could be dead or scarred for life was appalling.

Archibald looked at her. His face was torn by grief. 'I know it's foul, maid, but that's the way of things. God willing, they will return. If they don't, He chose to punish them and we will need to say prayers for them. But there is nothing more we can do.'

'You just don't care! You are a *callous* old man!' she said, and turned and ran from his camp, leaving Archibald surprised and Ed gaping.

Still weeping, Béatrice ran along the main road towards the town, and then out to the English harbour to the east.

There was a constant shouting, the rumble of great rocks being rolled into the slings of the vast wooden siege machines, and the occasional slither and crack as an engine was released. When that happened, the mighty weight of rock in the counterbalance suddenly jerked downwards, sending the sling-arm up into the air and freeing the rock from its sling, to hurtle through the sky and pound at the walls or buildings of the town.

She had no eyes for that. Her attention was fixed on the sea that was visible from here. The water was filled with galleys and cogs of all shapes and sizes, but there was no sign of their ship and nothing to show what had happened to Berenger and his men. They had disappeared as effectively as if the sea had swallowed them up.

'Out of the way, you silly bitch!' a stevedore shouted at her, trundling a heavy cart.

She was blocking the only path from the stores to the ships, she realised, but she still spat a pithy curse at him before turning and marching away.

It was strange to feel this desolation about the vintener and his men. She had hardly known them any time, and most of them were not the kind of people she would have looked at before the recent catastrophes . . . but since the disaster of her father's arrest and execution, and then her persecution by the local villagers, she had grown more and more dependent on Berenger Fripper and his men. She had come to respect them – almost to trust them.

And now they were taken, swept away from her as effectively as the figures on a chessboard, hurled from their places by an angry, Godlike hand. Their disappearance served only to highlight her own loneliness and despair.

Seeing another man bearing down on her, carrying a heavy bale of cloth on his head and already beginning to swear, she turned and slowly tramped along the road.

She had no idea where she was going. Her feet bore her away from the harbour and the ships, and out towards the west, where the heights of Sangatte loomed. The road took her over a little bridge, and past the reeds that marked the marshes. All the land about here was boggy. She hated it. It reeked of putrefying vegetation. Yet it had one advantage: no army could pass on this stretch of land. Only the two roads, one heading south, the other holding to the coast, could take much traffic. It was a miracle that the town itself had been constructed. Where had they found the stone for the walls – and who could have realised that this was the one site where they could build? Waves crashed at the shore to her right, and she stared out to sea again, wondering how her friends of the vintaine fared. They could already be dead.

The sound of approaching hooves stirred her from her reverie in time to see a small company of horsemen led by a knight. She looked up into a face that could have been carved from the same stone as the walls that protected Calais. It was the face of a man who could happily exterminate a whole race, if there were profit in it.

Only a few weeks ago she had felt the same. She could gladly have seen all her own countrymen executed, for their deliberate killing of her father, and for the way that she herself had been harried and threatened with rape. Yet now she was coming to feel sympathy for the people who lived about here. They struggled and strove like many others, but they were forced to suffer the depredations of men such as this: a knight with no compassion. Men like this were worse than the bestial men-at-arms who slew for pleasure: men of this sort had no pleasure in their souls – possibly no feelings at all.

She had heard of this man before. Sir Peter of Bromley, once Sir Pierre d'Agen, was a knight banneret in the pay of the English King. Once he had been known as a most honoured knight in the service of King Philippe of France, but he had fallen out of favour, and had come to serve the English against his own King.

It was said that Sir Peter's heart was made of steel as hard and unbending as his helm. He exulted in killing not because he held any particular hatred for his opponent, but because he saw death as efficient. There was no sympathy in him for his victims, only the constant urge to wage war effectively for his new master. And if that meant peasants must die, so be it.

He glanced at her, and as his eyes raked her body, she shuddered. It was like being licked by snakes.

She was tempted to keep walking. To leave this camp, as Archibald had intimated – but if she were to leave, where could she go? She had no friends, no family, no nation.

She was lost.

Chapter Seven

Berenger would never forget the screams of that young sailor as he was dragged away. His companion uttered a few choice curses, mentioning the parentage of the man-at-arms and others as he went, but he was at least able to walk. The other was beshitten before he was out of the door.

'I swore that these men, and those sailors, would all be safe,' Chrestien de Grimault said again.

His voice was quiet, but Berenger could hear the anger bubbling. He looked at the Genoese with sudden interest.

'You overplayed your authority, then,' the Comte de Roucy said flatly. 'You had no right to offer any terms. These are pirates and will be treated as such.'

'Count, I would not have men think I would go back on my word!'

'Then, as I said, in future be more careful about what you promise.'

The Cardinal chuckled. 'Of course, if you are nervous about what they might think of your honour, they will soon have other things to occupy their minds.'

As he spoke, Berenger saw Jean de Vervins' eyes pass over the prisoners. When those eyes turned to him, Berenger felt an overwhelming hatred and loathing fill him. There was no feeling in the Frenchman's eyes, he thought. No compassion, no emotion of any sort. He might have been peering at a turd on the street. And then Berenger saw a sudden flicker. It was tiny – a twitch almost – and yet Berenger could have sworn that the man was winking at him. The moment passed, Jean de Vervins' gaze moved on, and Berenger was left standing bewildered, wondering whether he had seen that or merely imagined it.

Chrestien de Grimault laughed lightly. 'So you are saying that my promise will be ignored, then? That is good. A man likes to know how he stands. You will happily leave me to be dishonoured?'

'Your honour is your concern,' the Count said. Then he turned and stared at the shipman, and his voice became low, malevolent. 'If you Genoese had fought better at Crécy, perhaps we would not now be fighting the English. We would have driven them – and these men – into the sea. So the cowardice of your compatriots has left us in this sorry condition, and these English archers are only alive because of them.'

'My compatriots fought bravely, until they were slaughtered by fools who knew little about warfare and less about their allies,' Chrestien de Grimault said tightly. 'They could not fight the English with their bows, because the strings were wetted by the rain, while the English were killing them with thousands of arrows at every step. And their reward for running this terrible risk? They were repaid by your knights slaughtering them and trampling their bodies into the mud!'

The Count climbed to his feet and hissed, 'You dare speak of them in the same breath as those brave knights? I should teach you the meaning of honour and dignity at the point of my sword!'

'I would be happy to comply. My brave Genoese metal can show you the meaning of—'

'Enough! Count, Master Grimault! This matter is closed,' the Cardinal snapped. 'The battle is over, and there is nothing we can do now to bring back the poor dead souls from the field. Take these prisoners away. We shall see to them when we have erected a suitable structure on which to punish them.'

Berenger and the others found themselves being shoved unceremoniously towards the door through which the two sailors had recently been taken. The door gave out onto a staircase of stone, which led down to a paved yard. Pushed and beaten, they were forced towards a gateway in the encircling wall. From here they could see the church and, before it, a large tree. As they were taken out, they saw two men throwing ropes up to where a boy had climbed onto a strong branch. He caught the ropes and passed them over two projecting limbs of the tree, letting the other ends fall to the ground. Enthusiastic townspeople took hold of them.

The young sailor was gibbering, kneeling and pleading with his hands clasped, while his companion glared at him with contempt. As Berenger and the others approached, their guards stopped so that they could enjoy the spectacle.

Ignoring the weeping, petrified sailor, men grabbed the other man and set the rope about his throat. Then four men hauled him up into the air. His legs kicking wildly, eyes bulging, the sailor slowly throttled, trying with every jerk and lunge of his legs to snap his own neck and bring about a quicker end. But he could not. He was still thrashing, ever more feebly, as the French, joking with each other, tied the second rope about the kneeling man and lifted him still higher, laughing and running away as the man's legs flicked ordure over the crowds with each spasmodic kick.

At the sight Berenger felt sick in his belly. This was not justice, but from the gleeful response of the crowds, he knew that he could expect nothing better when it was his turn to stand on a platform and be blinded and crippled with the others. There would be no sympathy here for the men who had inspired so much fear and loathing throughout France.

A blow in the small of his back almost drove him to his knees, but he stumbled onwards, his thoughts directed at escape.

'Not here, my friend.'

He looked around and found himself staring at Jean de Vervins. 'What?'

'You will have no easy escape here.'

Berenger had the unpleasant certainty that this man had read his mind. 'Who are you?'

'Me? A mere country-living knight, used to life far from the King's court,' Jean de Vervins said with a quiet melancholy. 'I am nothing. But you: you think you can drive a path through all these guards? No, for that you will need a miracle, yes?' Jean smiled sadly, turned, and was gone.

'A miracle,' Berenger said to himself. 'That's all. Just a fucking miracle.'

Sir John de Sully was standing eating his lunch when the gynour appeared in his doorway. Like his archers, Sir John had no chair, only a worn three-legged stool filched from a house on their march, although he was five-and-sixty years old, and had enough wounds to prove that he had never run from a battle.

'Well?' he demanded as Archibald stood, coif in hand, looking nervous.

'Sir, have you heard about the vintaine?'

Sir John was a rural knight from Iddesleigh and Rookford. Whereas many knights were uninterested in their men, the banneret had shown himself keen to look after their interests during the long campaign of recent weeks. His hair might be grizzled, but his eyes were as clear as they had been when he sat on his mount at Bannockburn thirty and more years ago now and witnessed the disaster befall the English cavalry. It had affected him to see the men slaughtered so, and since then he had made every effort to protect his men. 'What about them?'

Archibald told him the news. He knew Sir John would be upset to hear of the loss of so many of his men at one fell swoop – but the knight's rage surprised even him.

'Damn those pirates' black souls to hell,' Sir John swore bitterly, hurling his food from his table. He kicked his stool away and raked his fingers agitatedly through his hair. 'Berenger Fripper is one of the most competent vinteners in the army. Christ's bones, but we could do with more like him. You are sure of this?'

'Another ship saw them being captured by a galley. They had little chance against that when it rammed them.'

The knight clenched his fist and was about to slam it onto his trestle table, when his esquire appeared.

'Sir? I was roused by the commotion.'

'Aye, I daresay you were, Richard. Have you heard this tale about the men with Fripper?'

'That they have been captured or killed, yes.'

Richard Bakere had been Sir John's esquire for six years now; he was a dependable, resilient fellow with a Norman's face and bearing, but without the arrogance.

'It's the worst news of the campaign so far,' Sir John said, and when Richard retrieved the stool, he sat down heavily. 'Fripper was a good man.'

'There is no hope of rescue?' Richard asked.

'The Devil only knows where they'll have been taken. In a galley they could be in any of the river-mouths along the coast here. Were we to ride to their aid, we would not know where to go. It would be futile.'

'If they are lucky, their end will be quick,' Archibald muttered.

'Yes,' Sir John agreed, then sighed. 'I would it were another vintaine, though.'

Archibald nodded, standing quietly until the knight glanced up at him.

'Well, Gynour? Is there more bad news you wish to impart?'

'Sir John, I think I may be able to help with the reduction of the town.'

The knight's attention was taken. 'Oh? How so?'

Richard Bakere had picked up the platter from where the knight had knocked it over, and placed a roasted capon upon it. Sir John took a leg while Archibald spoke, but his eyes never left the gynour's face all the while. Archibald's enthusiasm and excitement were almost palpable.

'We are stuck outside the town. The town has excluded us from their harbour, so that their ships can enter the harbour and resupply the town, and there's little we can do about it. We cannot get to the north of the town to command the harbour because of their weapons on the Rysbank, and we cannot get scaling ladders to the walls to attack the town directly because of the moat.'

'So?'

'I am thinking that we need to prevent ships from getting to the town in the first place.'

'I don't think anyone will disagree with that. You may have noticed that we have been attempting to do just that in recent weeks,' Sir John said, his voice dripping with sarcasm. 'In fact, we have only just lost a number of men because we were trying to protect our own ships!'

'But if we maintain a number of ships at sea to blockade the harbour, and then also position weapons to sink any that pass by the harbour mouth, we will be able to stop any supplies from reaching the town. No supplies means no ability to fight. We can starve 'em out.'

'And what sort of weapon would you install at the harbour mouth?'

'We have nothing here at—'

'Then you are wasting my time!'

'I was going to add "but we do have one at home". I have a great beast that could easily sweep any ship from the sea. It is in England, but if you can arrange for its transport, I will do the rest.'

Sir John put the bones on his plate and studied the gynour. He knew that Archibald was a keen exponent of his new gonnes. Personally, Sir John was unconvinced by them. At Crécy he had seen one blow up, taking an entire team of gynours with it. Bits and pieces of the men were found later, reeking of brimstone as though the Devil himself had passed by and despatched them. Yet the gonnes had done significant damage occasionally, for instance when a sack of balls had hit a full charge of men-at-arms, and the knight knew that a man of war should never turn up the opportunity of learning new methods of attack. If this could help, then it might be worth pursuing.

'Where exactly is this gonne of yours?' he asked, leaning forward.

Berenger saw that escape was impossible.

They were held for three days before they were taken out again. Three days of sitting in their own muck. No one came to empty their buckets, so they overflowed after the first night. The men tried to dam the worst of it with the meagre supplies of straw that lay about the place, but it seeped through, and all of them had it impregnated in their clothing after the second night.

The stench, the lack of light, the manacles and chains they wore – all conspired to sap Berenger's will. Their surrender had been shameful enough for English archers, but now, languishing in this cell, he felt emasculated. As he looked about the faces of his men, he could see that most had given up all hope. Some, like Clip, sat sourly contemplating the ground before them, muttering vile oaths against the fate that had brought them here, while others stared up at the single barred hole in the wall, through which the light entered to illuminate one corner of the puddle of muck on the floor. Jack Fletcher sat with his back to the wall, gazing at Berenger as though with hope. Dogbreath was one of the only men who looked unconcerned. He squatted on his haunches, throwing pebbles at a spider that was scrabbling up the wall.

Berenger looked away from Fletcher. *Hope!* There was no hope for them. They couldn't expect to escape from a place like this, not with the whole of the French army about them.

When he was young, Berenger had lost his parents. The barons had detested King Edward II's adviser and friend, Sir Hugh le Despenser, and bands of men-at-arms had invaded Despenser lands up and down the country, burning, looting and killing. Berenger's parents were slaughtered in the first wave, his father for his loyalty to Sir Hugh, and his mother too. After that, life had lost all meaning and purpose. Berenger could remember it clearly. Only when the King himself heard of his plight and took him into his household did Berenger grow free of despair. He was young, after all. With exercise and work, boys can cope with most disasters.

'Frip?' Jack Fletcher called softly. 'What do we do?'

'Wait,' Berenger said. 'What more *can* we do?'

Clip spat into the pool of ordure and whined, 'They're going to take our eyes! Take our fucking eyes!'

'Shut up, Clip,' Berenger said wearily.

'So, do we just submit to them? They killed the other two, didn't they?' Jack said. 'Shall we just go quietly like lambs to the slaughterman?'

'If you have a better idea, tell me!' Berenger snapped.

It was Tyler who spoke up. 'We have to give them something. Tell them something they want to know.'

'Like what?' Clip sneered. 'Where to get a chest of gold? Where to find wine and food? They have all they need already, you prickle!'

'Then we tell them about the army. How many men there are, where they'll—'

'You want to give away the army?' Dogbreath demanded with a low growl, shifting as if preparing to spring on Tyler. Berenger held up a hand to stop any risk of a fight breaking out.

'No, but if it's something that could help them without harming our friends . . .' Tyler began, but John of Essex cut across him.

'If it'd save our skins, you mean. You'd give away your mother's soul if it'd save you a little pain, wouldn't you?'

'I'd gladly—'

'*Enough!*' Berenger said, standing up. 'We'll give away nothing. Do you really think there's anything you could tell them that would save you? We're English archers. They hate us for every French nobleman's life we've taken. They don't want to negotiate with us. You heard them! They want to make an example of us. There's nothing we can do to stop them.'

Then, just as if the gaoler had been listening, there came the sound of boots marching along the corridor outside. Jack and Clip stood, and Berenger glared across at John of Essex, as though daring him to argue. John said nothing. His head hung low; he was the picture of dejection.

Fair enough, Berenger thought to himself. It was how he felt, too. What a wretched way to end their days.

Chapter Eight

Berenger had thought that they were to be taken straight to the place set aside for their public humiliation, but to his surprise, when the guards took them out into the open air, they did not force them along the roads to the church, but down a dark alleyway and along a wider street to a small door in a great wall. Once through this, they found themselves in a broad courtyard paved with cobbles. They were led up some stairs to a large hall, and in here they found themselves confronted by the same cardinal who had selected their punishment, talking to the same red-headed Scot whom Berenger had seen on that first day.

'You should be gone, Sir David,' the prelate said. 'Godspeed, my son.'

'Thank you, my Lord.' Sir David bowed to the cardinal, kissed the prelate's ring and, with a disgusted look at the prisoners, left the room.

'Now! Is there one among you who speaks French well enough to communicate?' the cardinal asked. He was standing at a large fireplace as he spoke, curling his lip at the sight and smell of them.

Berenger could understand why. They all had the same pale, drawn features and eyes that glittered with an unhealthy feverishness, and their clothes stank of the midden.

'We all speak French,' he said.

'Then know this, all of you: you will *all* be forced to suffer,' the cardinal said. 'You have committed grave acts against the Peace of the King, and for that, the penalty is usually death. You are fortunate enough to have won his lenience, and for that you will live, but only after . . . '

'You have had our eyes put out and hacked off our string-fingers,' Berenger said.

'So you did hear what I commanded the other day.' The cardinal eyed him dispassionately. 'Your men will all be blinded. If you help me, you can be the one to keep an eye.'

'How can I help you?'

'If you tell me the disposition of the men about Calais, that will help. And any news of the army.'

Berenger frowned. 'The disposition of the men? Calais is under siege and our army is strong. What more could I tell you?'

'Which men stand where. Which noblemen lead the forces there. We will win this battle, Englishman. With God on our side, we cannot fail. But I would see it ended sooner so that fewer women and children are hurt or slain. You English trample the poor folk of France underfoot like a peasant stamping on ants, but as the peasant will regret it when he disturbs the nest, you will regret your impudence in coming here to challenge the right of the King of France to command his people. If you wish to keep your sight, I may be able to help you.'

'We will tell you,' Tyler blurted out. 'Ask us! We can help you with any questions you have, and—'

With a loud rattle of the chain at his wrists, Jack's hands slammed into his belly and Tyler collapsed in a heap on the floor, gasping and retching. Two guards set upon Jack immediately, beating him with their clubs, and soon he too went down, writhing as they kicked at him.

'Tell them to stop or you'll have nothing from me,' Berenger snarled.

The cardinal raised his hand and the assault stopped as suddenly as it had begun. 'So? Will you help me?'

'If you swear that we will all be treated equally. None of us to be blinded.'

'No.'

'Then we will not help you.'

The cardinal nodded, then pointed to Tyler, lying on the floor huddled about the pain of his belly. 'Raise him and bring him here.'

Berenger felt alarm surging. 'Leave him, he's only a—'

'Someone silence this fool!' A blow to the back of Berenger's head made him fall to his knees, and he tumbled onto all fours, heaving. The cardinal stood over him. 'I gave you your chance. You will not help me, so you will be blinded like the rest. If this man helps me, he may keep an eye.' The cardinal smiled. 'You should be kind to him, if you want him to guide you back to your heretic friends!'

Berenger managed to swallow the bile that threatened, and sat back on his haunches. As soon as he did so, a guard shoved his staff at Berenger's breast, the blow forceful enough to slam him backwards. While he rolled over to scramble to his feet, Tyler was helped towards the fire by a guard, and stood with his head downcast as the cardinal sipped from a gilded goblet of wine.

'Well?'

'I can't tell you where the men all are. So far as I know, they are equally spread about the town. But if you have leaders you wish to hear of, I'll tell you what I can.'

'Your commander? Who is he?'

'Sir John de Sully, banneret. He serves the King.'

The cardinal nodded and began to ask about the various noblemen who were in the King's army. There was no secret about these men – they all wore their arms on their breasts or shields – and Tyler answered accurately enough. Berenger would willingly have sprung on him and set his chains about the man's throat, but there was little point in winning himself another beating for no purpose. And all the information that Tyler gave was unimportant.

'I have heard of Gascons, too. Are there any knights from Gascony?' the cardinal continued and, as he spoke, Berenger saw that his eyes narrowed a little. 'King's officials? What of Pierre d'Agen and other traitors?'

Tyler answered as best he might, but there was little enough he could tell of the various men about whom he was interrogated. There were some more questions, but the cardinal appeared to have little further interest in them.

'Take them away now,' he said to the guards. Then, in an undertone, speaking in Latin, he called to a clerk. 'Tell the executioner he can take them now. Bring them to the church and start to work on them. All of them.'

Berenger heard the words plainly, and at long last, his mind cleared. 'Archers, *form circle!*' he shouted in English, and the men shuffled or sprang to form a loose ring. '*Jack! John!* With me!' he bellowed, and leaped forward.

The other two were with him, and although one guard realised Berenger's plan and tried to get between them and the cardinal, he was already too late. While Berenger grasped one end of his staff, John hammered at his face with his manacled wrists. The crunch of breaking bones could be heard over the rattle of the chain's links, and the man fell with blood gushing from his nose and brow. Berenger had the staff now, and he grabbed the cardinal's wrist, pulling him away from the fire and hurrying back with him into the circle of archers. He looped his chain over the man's throat and tightened it.

'Kill them!' the cardinal gurgled, but Berenger pulled his chains taught.

'If they come near, I'll crack your neck like a capon's,' he growled. 'Tell them!'

He could feel the man's head move as he threw panicked glances about the room at his men, wondering if any were near enough to save him. Berenger clenched his muscles, pulling his forearm across the cardinal's flabby throat.

'Stand back, you fools! Can't you see he will kill me? Stand back!' the cardinal squawked.

'Archers? We're leaving – now!'

Berenger and his men hurried from the room, the guards pushing and jabbing at them with their steel-shod staffs, while the cardinal screamed abuse at all and sundry. Clip went over, and a guard kicked at him. Enraged, Clip grabbed his foot, twisted and shoved, and the man went down, Clip's boot in his groin. The man squealed as his knee joint snapped. Another lifted his staff to break Clip's pate, but Dogbreath gave a sudden shriek of pure fury and sprang forward, grabbing the man's biceps and headbutting him viciously. When another tried to hit him, Jack dragged Dogbreath out of the way before the blow could strike, and then the archers formed a close wall, fists raised. They might suffer in a fight, but all, apart from Tyler, would prefer to fight than submit to torture and maiming.

The guards were bellowing orders and somewhere a bell had begun to sound. Berenger threw an anxious look about him. Jack was helping Clip to his feet, muttering, 'Should have left him tae me. I'd have taken his leg off, the cowardly prickle!' At the other side of the group, John of Essex had bent his head into an aggressive posture once more. He looked like a man fighting in the ring: focused and determined.

'Archers!' Berenger called. 'We can't fight these gits. We need to get out of here and find weapons; get a blacksmith to take these manacles off.'

'Are you mad?' Tyler shouted, and suddenly threw himself at Berenger, hands outstretched. 'He was going to let us go! Now he'll see us all killed!'

'No, he was going to blind us all. That's what he just said to his clerk over there.'

'You'll get us all killed! I had him listening to me – he would have let us go!' Tyler screamed.

'Jack! Get this tarse-fiddler off me and break his neck if he holds us up again,' Berenger said. Jack grasped Tyler's wrist chains and pulled him away. Then, with the rest of the men, Berenger began to head to the doors.

They were open, and the vintaine poured through, Berenger keeping a firm grip on the cardinal's throat. When the man stumbled, Berenger jerked the chain and the cardinal quickly regained his footing. There was a shuffling and muttering as the archers made their way to the main entrance. There Berenger muttered to Clip, who trotted forward and peered out.

'Clear!' he called back, and the men hurried out, still followed by the guards. The stairs outside were not easy to negotiate with his arm about the neck of the cardinal, but Berenger made it without falling, and soon he and the rest were down at the courtyard area. Here, they marched across, heading for the large gate by which they had entered only an hour or so before . . . but once the gate was opened, there was a shocked silence. Outside, with swords drawn, were more than forty men. Strong, weather-bronzed men with dark hair and good linen or muslin shirts: the Genoese who had captured them on board their ship.

CHAPTER NINE

'A good day to you, my friend,' Chrestien de Grimault said, bowing to the cardinal – or was it Berenger? 'I trust I find you well?'

Berenger felt the cardinal's throat move as he tried to speak. He quickly tightened his grip. 'My apologies, but His Eminence is feeling a little weak. I will speak for him in case he grows more fatigued.'

'I think he grows wearier and wearier,' Chrestien de Grimault said. 'It is undoubtedly the weight of troubles lying on his mind. So many things for him to consider, such as swearing to me that my prisoners would be treated honourably when I first brought them to him.'

'He has ordered us to be blinded and crippled.'

'At the church, it is certain. My man told me earlier that your fate was sealed. I feel sure you would wish to join us for some drinks before any such rash decision could be taken.'

'We're going to the port.'

'A fine idea. However, if I may be so bold,' Chrestien said, and his eyes rose to the building behind them, 'it would be sensible to take your guest away from here. There are many men with weapons who watch your every move with interest. Perhaps we should leave here and find a better place to talk?'

Jack stepped to Berenger's side. 'I don't trust the slimy whoreson, Frip.'

'Neither do I.'

'Master,' Chrestien said with a broad smile. 'I dislike the cardinal there more than anyone. And if I and my men wanted to kill you, we could, with all these weapons. So clearly I do not intend you harm. I suggest a stratagem. You slam the gates and jam them, and then follow me. I shall lead you to the ship, where you will be safe.'

Jack began to speak, but behind them all Berenger heard commands and the pattering of many booted feet.

'Fuck! Block the gates, use anything you can!' he roared, and helped the men pull the gates shut, blocking them as best they could with some wagons and a cart. And then, as swiftly as they could manage, the men jerked and rattled their way down after the Genoese.

The clinking of metal was deafening. From the ship, Grimault could hear it like a satanic percussion all around him as the men lurched clumsily with their hobbled ankles. It was good that they had been shackled so quickly, for most of them had chains between the irons that were considerably longer than they should have been. In Genoa they would have been much shorter, designed to hobble the men and prevent escapes. The French blacksmith was not experienced at making prison restraints.

Chrestien de Grimault stood on his ship and watched as the men arrived – a shambling, ill-stinking mess of men, anxious and fretful. He already had four small oared vessels waiting at the quayside, and two cables holding a small supply vessel had already been slipped. 'Hurry!' he called, beckoning with his entire arm. 'Come! Leave that papal usurer and join us here!

'What will you do, my friend?' he said to himself as Berenger stood staring at him from the quay. 'What would I do? I would tell me to go fuck my mother, and then find a smith who could remove all the metalwork, in case I was the sort of disreputable thief and mercenary who would merely take each of you and toss you over the sheers into the sea. With all that iron, none of you would float – and you know that. Just as you know that if you delay, the cardinal's men will surely come and capture you, and even if you kill the cardinal, you will die. There is no profit in death, my friend.'

Berenger and he stared at each other over the water, and then Berenger snapped a command, and the first of the men began to make their way to the nearer boats. Soon the vintener and the others were helped down into small craft, and before long they were being rowed across the waters to the great galley.

'Prepare to sail!' Chrestien roared. He was still speaking in French, for with so many crew members from all over France, it was easier to use the common language. Besides, as the English began to appear, clambering up the rope ladders dangling from the upper hull, it would make most of them more comfortable. Most Englishmen understood at least some French.

'Welcome aboard my ship,' he said as Berenger appeared. 'Did you kill him?'

'He thought I was going to, but no. I tapped him on the head to shut him up. He'll wake with a headache, but no more. He's lucky. I should have killed him.'

'Undoubtedly. But it would have made my return more problematical,' Grimault said with a grin. 'And now, I think I owe you the services of one of my finest men.'

'Who?'

'My friend,' Grimault said, smiling and shaking his head at the naked suspicion flashing in Berenger's eyes, 'I feel sure you require the aid of my blacksmith.'

He could not make out the Genoese. Berenger stood near the mast, gripping a rope tightly as the waves sucked and hissed at the galley's hull, staring out at the white, gleaming track in the water, trying to understand the man.

When he and the other archers had hurried from the cardinal's hall and straight into the shipman, he had thought they were doomed. These were the very men who had caught him and his own, and it was natural to consider the Genoese their enemies. Yet now they had been freed by the same fellows, and from the chattering and ribald humour shared on board, it seemed as though Chrestien de Grimault considered himself to be Berenger's host: he was treating him as an honoured guest.

The man was there now, up at the rear castle, his eyes fixed on the horizon ahead as though daring it to display some threat to him and his ship.

He was a natural mariner; that much was certain. His legs had the bandy look of a horseman, and remained bent as the vessel moved, one leg straightening more or less with the deck as it rolled beneath him, scarcely bothering to hold onto a rope or spar as he did so. He looked a part of the ship, as much as the mast or the rigging. Where the galley went, so too would Grimault.

Seeing Berenger's gaze upon him, the Genoese gave a broad smile and beckoned. Rubbing his chafed, sore wrists, Berenger waited until the deck was almost level, and then let go of his rope and hurried across the deck, moving crabwise as the prow began to swoop downwards into a trough. He made it to the ladder to the rear castle as the prow rose once more, and had to thrust out both hands to stop himself slamming into the beams. This was no life for a man, he told himself for the hundredth time as he set his boot on the first rung and started to climb.

'Godspeed!' Grimault said with a flash of teeth in his bearded face. 'It is a fine, a glorious day, is it not?'

'It's clear enough,' Berenger admitted.

It was a perfect day for sailing. The sea gleamed like quicksilver, so it was hard to look at it for long. The wind whipped at the back of their heads as they stared forward, and to his left, Berenger could see the coast of France. They had been travelling for half a day now, and the rhythmic tapping and clattering of hammers and chisels striking away their irons had at last ceased. All the men had been released, and although one of the younger boys from the ship's company had complained as the chisel slipped and the bracelet twisted, snapping a bone in his arm, the ship's tooth-breaker and surgeon reckoned it should heal well enough. Worse was the man whose ankle had been deeply gouged when the chisel span from the armourer's hand into his flesh. Luckily it didn't quite shear through his Achilles, but he would be limping for a month with the damage done.

'Do you not trust me yet?' Grimault asked.

'We're alive and free, so I suppose I do. A little,' Berenger said, looking along the hull towards Jack, who stood near the drum. The galley could be called to war at a moment's notice, and the ship taken to battle stations by a simple drumbeat.

'He is well enough there,' Grimault said, and cast a sly look at him.

If there were to be a battle, Berenger wanted at least one of his men there, beside the ship's drum, so that he and his men could swiftly take control and turn matters to their own benefit.

'He doesn't get ill.'

Grimault laughed. 'If we call battle orders, he will be held comfortably, just as you will. You have no need of subterfuge on board my ship. You are our friends. This is a matter of honour with us, you see. We rescued you – we will not wish to harm you.'

'But you caught us.'

'Yes. And I promised that you would come to no harm, did I not? That is why I was forced to liberate you. I was going to break in the cardinal's door to remove you.'

Berenger scowled. 'How did you know we were there? Didn't you go to the gaol first?'

'Yes, of course. But the gaoler had already shown us that you were no longer in the cell.'

'It was good fortune for you to decide to rescue us on the very day the cardinal decided he would see us executed.'

'Ah, perhaps there was some fortune in it.'

Berenger nodded with comprehension. 'The gaoler was bribed to warn you, was he?'

'No, of course not!' Grimault said, scandalised. 'I would not pay another man's servant to break his own oaths. The gaoler was sworn to secrecy. However, his pot boy was not. So, as soon as the gaoler was told, the pot boy came to find me, and naturally we then came to find you.'

'But why?'

'As I said: I promised no harm would come to you.'

'So you chose to come and free us?' Berenger didn't believe the man. 'You are a mercenary, paid by the French. Surely this will damage your reputation?'

'Me? My friend, I own this ship! If the French cardinal wishes to complain to the King, he may do so. I will remind them that I fight under my terms, and if they do not like them, I reserve the right to remove myself. I gave you my word as a man of honour, and that French priest would have dishonoured me. I will not allow that. Not after the last weeks.'

Berenger felt he understood a little better. 'The battle?'

Grimault shot him a look. The smile faded now as he nodded. 'Yes, I speak of Crécy. The French asked Genoa to help in the war against you English, and then, when they went ahead on the battlefield at Crécy and were hopelessly outmatched against your English arrows, the French rode through them and cut them down. I am told that more were slaughtered by the French cavalry than were slain by your companions.'

Two of his friends had been there, he said. One, Iacme, was only a boy, and had fought well for his French masters, but his reward had been an early death at the hands of a French man-at-arms. Chrestien would find that hard to forgive or forget.

Berenger saw his hard expression and said gruffly, 'I was there. I saw the French ride into them.'

Chrestien nodded grimly. 'We know of this. All Genoa will have heard by now. It does not leave us filled with warmth and respect for our allies, to know that they slew so many of us. We will be looking more to our own requirements in the future, rather than slavishly following the commands of the French.'

'Will you come to the English side with your ship?' Berenger asked hopefully. If he were to return to the sea, he would prefer not to have to endure another attack by a powerful craft such as this.

'No, because I have my contract. I will remain true to my word and uphold my honour. I will not overstep the bounds of common sense.'

John of Essex had joined them, and at this he frowned. 'But you are free to go where you will?'

Chrestien nodded seriously. 'Yes, my friend. But who would hire me or my ships if I gained a reputation for running? No man would want to give me a contract if I was considered a turncoat. Nobody likes an unreliable soldier.'

He saw the look on Berenger's face and laughed.

'Come, Master Berenger, be happy! You are free, on a fast ship, heading homewards, alive and well. And if you fear seeing my flag on the horizon again – well, be merry! All you need do is submit gracefully and at speed, and all will be well. Perhaps next time I will take you to another French commander, one in whom I have more confidence.'

'There won't be a next time,' Berenger said. 'By my faith, next time we meet at sea, I will catch *you*!'

Chrestien laughed again, but Berenger was frowning at the sea ahead.

'Where are you taking us now?'

'I cannot go too close to the English, for they will fire upon me and I would not have them injure my men. We shall aim for a place I know. From there it is less than ten miles to Calais. You can walk that, I think, without difficulty.'

'Certainly,' Berenger said, but as he spoke, he glanced to the left and saw another vessel, a small fishing boat with two men labouring away. A flash caught his eye.

It was nothing: only a brief flash behind one of the men, but it was enough to pique his interest. 'What is that?'

'What?' Grimault said mildly, but didn't turn his head. He stared resolutely ahead.

Berenger peered through the slight heat haze. There was so much sparkling where the sun's light bounced, it was like trying to stare into a mass of stars. He looked away, then back; he rubbed his eyes and squeezed them tightly, and then, as the sea shifted and the boat dipped low in the water, he saw it: a mass of ships, tightly packed together in a river's estuary.

He turned away, aware of the Genoese's prattling. Those ships were massing for a purpose, and he was sure that it would bode ill for the English.

CHAPTER TEN

Béatrice returned from fetching food at the market at Villeneuve-la-Hardie, but did not speak to Archibald.

The old gynour had fixed her with a sympathetic eye when she returned three days ago. He understood her. Her despair was bitter, but if the vintaine was gone, it was gone. There was no point swooning and complaining. So, as soon as she got back to his little camp by the guns, she set about making their supper.

She felt sad when she saw young Donkey. He sat huddled, not looking at her, behaving as she would expect a five year old might. Georges tried to tempt him into playing, but Donkey just snapped at him and turned his back. And she understood. He was orphaned, like her. He was young, with fire in his groin like a man, but he had no understanding about the urges that were overwhelming him. Perhaps she should let him have her. They were all outcasts. She had no good name to lose: she was an unwanted Frenchwoman, good only for a quick fuck before slitting her throat. Ed too was worthless, a mere drudge to fetch and carry, of no value whatever, while Archibald was viewed askance because he was in league with the Devil. All knew that: the whiff of brimstone followed him wherever he went. Only those who associated with the Devil could cause those hideous explosions that slaughtered so many. Men had seen him, it was said, at the Battle at Crécy, fighting with the strength of ten when the French threatened to overrun his gonne. No Christian could have done that. He had slaughtered more than a hundred men, it was rumoured.

It was all so much stuff and nonsense. She had been there with him. He did kill a few men, it was certain, but not as many as the archers with their deadly missiles. Compared with them, Archibald was harmless. But no matter: the men looked at him with their superstitions confirmed and enhanced.

'Do you think we'll see Fripper again?' Ed asked, stirring her from her thoughts.

'No,' she said starkly. It was better to deal with harsh truths than try to hide them beneath a coating of sugar. 'The French took them, and will kill them.' She felt a tear start as she said this, and dashed it away angrily. The vintaine was not her family, it was merely a number of misfits and rogues, she thought – and then instantly chided herself. Berenger and his men were better than that. Well, most of them, certainly.

'It's not fair!' he burst out.

She felt her sympathy evaporate. 'Fair? What is fair? I have lost my father, my family, and also my own people! Now we lose the only men I could trust as well, and you say this too is not fair. What is fairness in life? I don't know!'

'I didn't mean, I didn't . . .'

'You didn't think, did you? You lose something and you think the world will end. For me, the world has ended already. Oh, go away! Go and see if you can find Archibald. Leave me alone!'

She marched off to the cart as Donkey hung his head and mooched away after Archibald, followed by his young companion,

Georges. She was about to pour herself a second mazer of wine when she heard strange noises. Peering down the road, she saw a wagon appear, behind which, men and women were being dragged. There were no children.

All about the wagon, men in a mixture of ill-fitting leather and mail prodded and pushed the wailing women and silent, bitter men with the butt-ends of their lances and staffs. The noise continued unabated.

'Will you lot shut up!' the captain cried. 'You think the whole town wants to hear you moaning?'

'Who are these?' Béatrice asked as he drew level with her. He was a man of middle height, with thick, wavy brown hair and eyes that had a gleam of kindness in them, she noticed.

'These? Fine French fillies for our men to enjoy,' the man said with a wolfish leer as he gazed down at her, picturing the delights within her dress.

Reviewing her initial impression of him, she stared pointedly at his face.

He noticed and reddened slightly, clearing his throat. Perhaps he was not so bad, after all.

She said, 'What of the men?'

'Them? They're all from the same place,' the man said. 'Bloody rebels who'd dare take up knives and swords against their King. They don't seem to realise that our Edward is their legitimate ruler. They think they can still argue and reject him, as though he has not been anointed. Well, they'll learn respect.'

'Where are you taking them?'

'The men to the gaol, the women to the brothel.'

She watched as the wagon lumbered on, rattling and crashing along the unpaved roadway, and the sobs and cries of the prisoners could be heard clearly even over that racket.

While she watched, she became aware of someone passing

close to her. This woman was older, perhaps thirty – it was hard to tell, since the lines were so deeply graven on her face and brow – and she walked like one in a daze. She was handsome rather than pretty, but had the kind of elegance that came from good parentage. Her face was oval, and her blue eyes slanted and doe-like, but her thick reddish-gold hair was slathered with mud and muck, and she walked as though the mere action of placing one foot before another was enough in itself to confirm her position in the world.

'Mistress?' Béatrice said hesitantly as the woman passed. She was fascinated by her, and wondered where she had come from. She fell into step beside her. 'Are you thirsty? Hungry? You want something to eat?'

'No.'

The voice seemed to come from a long way away, and when Béatrice glanced down, she saw that the woman had no shoes of any sort, but was padding along gently because her feet were swollen and bloody.

'Mistress, you should come and wash your feet. Come with me.'

She took the woman to Archibald's encampment, and there she bathed the woman's feet in a bowl Archibald used for mixing his experiments. He was scandalised at first, but when he caught a glimpse of Béatrice's face, he said nothing, merely standing aside and sending Ed for more food.

Later, Béatrice coaxed the woman into speaking. She was called, she said, Marguerite.

'My village is destroyed. My husband is dead and I hope my children escaped, but I do not know where they have gone. I have walked up here to try to find them. Have you seen them? They are Georges, Henri and Alice. Georges is the oldest at eleven, while Alice is only five. Henri is eight. My husband and I . . . we lost so many babies in between the three. So many. And now,' she added, her voice trailing away, 'I have lost these too . . .'

She sat on a log, and the tears began to run down her cheeks, but she made no sound. She was too weary to sob or cry.

Archibald had returned as she began to talk, and he silently fetched the woman a mazer of strong red wine. Now, hearing the name Georges, he started. He was about to open his mouth, when Béatrice hushed him with a look. It was the sort of look that could pin a man to a tree at thirty paces.

It was possible that Ed's friend was her son, but the chances of this being the same boy were remote. Georges was a not uncommon name. It would be terrible to raise her hopes, only then to dash them.

'How long ago did you lose them?'

'Two weeks. I have been searching for them, and I've not stopped looking. I do love them, you see,' she said, looking at Béatrice as though seeking reassurance. 'I do love them.'

Béatrice could say nothing. She put her arms about the woman as her own tears flowed. The woman wept for her children and her husband, but Béatrice wept for her, for her children, for her village, and for herself and all France.

CHAPTER ELEVEN

The raiding party they met initially wanted to run them through for practice, but when Berenger and Jack bellowed out their names and confirmed that Grandarse was their captain and Sir John de Sully their banneret, the esquires, who had been seeking a little excitement, ruefully raised their spear-points and trotted away in search of more exciting targets.

It was in the middle of the afternoon when they were finally brought to Sir John. They had slept one night on the galley before Chrestien de Grimault set them down on a sandy shore a scant three leagues from the town of Calais. From there they could see the smoke from the fires rising and drifting out to sea from the English camp. It took them only a little time to reach their comrades.

'We all thought you had died at sea. Many saw the battle,' Sir John de Sully said. He was standing at his table, a smile twisting his mouth while he chewed on an apple. 'Your return was unexpected, but naturally it's a delight to have you back here safe.'

'We thought we were going to die,' Berenger said. He stood

before the knight with his hands in his belt, a new one that he had taken from a stall outside before anyone could stop him. Next, he wanted a sword again, and a knife. Walking about without a weapon left him feeling distinctly vulnerable.

'Your ship sank?'

Berenger grunted. 'The galley rammed us. We didn't stand a chance.'

'And you were captured?'

Berenger told the whole story, and the knight nodded, asking questions occasionally, laughing out loud at the tale of the vintaine's escape, but when Berenger spoke of the fleet in the river, he grew quiet. 'And you are sure of this?'

'Yes, Sir John. I saw them quite clearly. My eyes aren't very good, but I couldn't mistake them. The sun kept glinting on weapons, too. They were not galleys, but merchant cogs in the main. I couldn't count them all.'

'That's surely not possible, though,' Sir John said with a frown. 'We have had raids launched out towards the east several times. The King is determined to keep himself warned about threats, so he has had parties sent on chevauchée, riding out in all directions to see if there are any French forces about. The only men we have found so far have been down to the east and south, but nothing in the estuaries or rivers. He has instructed us to hunt down all enemy ships. We do not wish the Calesians to gain any aid, be it food or reinforcements.'

Berenger considered. 'Perhaps these ships were missed? They were further away, and could only be viewed from the sea, I think. From land they would be hard to reach because of the mudflats and dangerous sands about that part of the coast.'

'I am sure you are right. Did they seem ready to sail?'

'I couldn't be sure – I'm no seaman – but I don't see why they wouldn't be.'

'They must be there to break the siege. Perhaps they mean to sail to Calais with supplies,' Sir John mused. He sat and stroked his bearded chin. 'If they do, we must meet them and stop them. The last thing we want is for supplies to reach the garrison now. That could extend the siege for weeks – or even months!'

Berenger nodded, but from his perspective his work was done. He had passed on his news. 'I must find us all some food, sir. And I must re-arm myself and the men.'

'You all had your arms taken? That's a bad show. Do you have any money for new weaponry?'

'No, sir. But we're owed our pay.'

Sir John stood and went to the door, shouting to his esquire: 'Richard! Come here! Find that useless knave of a clerk and tell him I want money for the vintaine. They need new weapons and armour – and clothes too, from the look and smell of them,' he added with a pointed glance at Berenger's stained jerkin and hosen. 'The old ones need washing . . . or burning.'

Marguerite was alarmed at first when the vintaine returned.

As soon as she saw him, she thought Berenger a grim-faced man who carried himself as if he bore the weight of all his command on his shoulders. The man Jack also rarely smiled, while the others seemed to smile a good deal too much, until Berenger barked at them to leave her alone. Only the ugly one with the horrible breath behaved with anything like civility, rising and offering her a share of his food. The other scrawny one, who she later learned was named Clip, spent his time staring at her body as if he could see through her every item of clothing to her body beneath. It made her feel as though cockroaches were walking all over her flesh.

'Don't worry about him,' Béatrice said in an undertone as she introduced the vintaine. 'Clip is all right, really. He has a kind heart, but he is a man.'

That, Marguerite knew, was the problem for her. She had lost everything, and now she was little better than a whore, fit only for slaking the desires of the men of the army. Looking about her now at the vintaine, she was struck with fear in the pit of her stomach. Here were men who could take her at any moment. All Frenchwomen had heard of the brutality of the English. These were soldiers who had taken nuns, raping them and murdering them for sport; they had stolen children and babies to satisfy their unnatural urges, and even slain and eaten their victims later, so she had heard. Well, if one of these sought to put his hands on her and climb between her thighs, she would cut off his cods!

'You will be safe with these men,' Béatrice said. 'They will not harm you. Trust them. They have protected me.'

There was something in Béatrice's manner that made Marguerite's hackles rise. She was hiding something: perhaps she knew that the men were likely to rape Marguerite? There were tales of Frenchwomen becoming procuresses for the soldiers, finding and trapping other Frenchwomen in exchange for money or food. Perhaps Béatrice was one such? Unconsciously, she began to draw away. When Béatrice put her arm about her, she wanted to pull back and flee, but the other young woman would not let go.

'All is well,' Béatrice said gently. 'Do not be afraid. Come – you must sit down. Now tell me – what were the names of your children again?'

Marguerite blinked, her fears distracted by the mention of her children. 'What?'

'The names of your children? No matter. The eldest – what was his name?'

'Georges. My little Georges.' Merely uttering the name made tears spring into her eyes again.

'It is a very common name,' Béatrice said.

'His father was Georges, too, and his father before him. The family always said that it would survive for as long as there was a Georges in it.' There was a catch in her throat as she added, choked, 'And now all are dead.'

'Mistress,' Berenger said. His expression as he held her elbow was that of a man who had endured suffering enough. 'Mistress, please. Join us and take a little food to break your fast. You look famished. Tell us your story.'

She submitted, taking a seat on a log that Dogbreath set for her, and then accepted a bowl of thin pottage and a spoon. With a hunk of rough bread to chew, she felt she had been given a feast.

'I come from a small village to the south and west of here. It was a good place, but it was burned by the English and I was attacked. I was separated from my family, and could do nothing. I sought for them all over, but could find no sign.'

She heard young voices, and started up, but at the sight of the Donkey, she sank back again.

Dogbreath pulled a face. 'Bastards! There's been too much raping, from all I've heard.'

'A certain amount is good for the men,' John of Essex said.

'But a lady like this? And what of her husband and children?' Dogbreath demanded hotly.

'It's the natural way,' Jack said. 'Men who have been to war need recreations afterwards.'

'I'd fight any poor churl who'd try to take her by force!'

'Oh, aye?' Clip said. 'You'd best prepare yourself, then. There are about ten thousand men here who'd all do the same.'

'Not us, though,' Berenger said quickly, holding out his hand comfortingly when he saw her rising alarm.

Marguerite drank a little of her pottage, then looked about her. To her dismay, she realised that Béatrice had disappeared, and she was suddenly struck with the reality of her position. She was here, hemmed in on all sides by some twenty men, all of them fighters and most of them believing that rape and theft were natural. She cast about her, seeking a route by which to escape, panicked by the thought that she might be about to be assaulted – but then she saw Béatrice.

She was a halfbowshot away, with two boys. One was the lad Marguerite had seen a little while earlier, but there was another boy there, too. Béatrice was talking to him, and then she saw his face turn to her, and – sweet Mother Mary! He looked so like . . .

Marguerite felt a lightness invade her skull as though she was about to swoon, and rose to her feet, swaying, staring, the pottage falling from her grasp. She heard the bowl strike a stone and shatter, and her mind called to her to look down, but it was impossible to avert her eyes from that little boy, the fellow with the tousled hair, who stood gaping, as though he recognised her but dare not believe his own eyes. And then he was running towards her, and she tottered forward a couple of paces and crouched, arms held wide, her eyes blurring with tears as he slammed into her, his arms about her neck, hers clutching him fiercely, desperate not to let him go, her eyes tight shut for fear that when she opened them and looked, she would find that this was another boy, not her Georges, not her son . . . but it was, and her life was suddenly transformed.

'Holy Mother, thank you! Thank you!' she whispered and then succumbed to tears of joy.

Chapter Twelve

At the campfire later that evening, Berenger took in their faces as his vintaine all drank ale or wine, chewing at the gristle in their pottage. After the tribulations of the last days, of having been captured, held in a shit-infested dungeon, threatened with torture, blinding and death, he would have expected some to be affected. Yet now, listening to them, it was as though they had never been away.

'Ach, will ye look at this?' Clip demanded, holding up a non-specific piece of flesh. 'It's just lights and tubes, this. No meat anywhere near it. However do you manage to cut away all the meat and keep only the garbage, eh?'

Archibald's eyes twinkled like a cheery giant's as he rumbled, 'It is a natural skill for some of us, man.'

'As a cook I think you'd make a good poisoner, Archibald,' John of Essex said with a wince.

'Oh, aye, I thought it was the job of the Frenchies to kill us, but any more of your food and we'll all starve to death!' Clip whined.

'No one needs Frenchies to kill us when there is a professional gynour in the army,' Jack said, upending his plate over the grass and emptying the remains.

'I could have added more brimstone, I suppose. Perhaps there was not enough for your taste?' their cook said genially. 'You forget: my brain was designed for mixing powders until they can be placed carefully in a gonne's mouth, rammed back, have a ball or arrow set on top, and ignited.'

'Aye,' Dogbreath muttered, eyeing his food resentfully. 'Happen you should ram this down our throats and save us having to try to swallow it. My pigs had better than this when I was at home.'

'Perhaps I will try that next time,' Archibald said. 'You see, I am good at making things that kill. Gynours like me are rare, you know. You should appreciate me more. Most gynours die young when their experiments grow more confident – and therefore slapdash. Not many live for long after experiencing the effects of too much serpentine powder at close quarters.'

Gonnes were weapons that Berenger still distrusted. It was hardly surprising that so many in the King's army would make the sign of the Devil at Archibald's back as he walked past. Many still held to the superstitious belief that the crack of thunder and flaring gouts of flame, so like to a dragon's breath, were proof of the devices' inherent evil.

Yet it was hard to dislike the man. Archibald went through life like a cheerful mastiff. He expected everyone to like him, and to a large extent, when he sat down with them and chatted on an evening over a horn or two of wine or ale – or his favourite, cider – they would find him an appealing soul with a breadth of knowledge and much sympathy for his fellow men.

It was that quality about him which had persuaded Berenger to deposit his only responsibility with Archibald some weeks ago. 'How's the Donkey, Gynour?' he called.

'Master Fripper, I hope I see you well?' Archibald replied with a grave nod. 'The boy is learning diligently, I thank you. He's proof, were it needed, that the skills of a gynour can easily be mastered by a lad willing to serve his apprenticeship.'

'He is well enough?'

'Aye.'

'And the girl and the new lad, young Georges?'

'They too are well, Master.'

Berenger was relieved. He would not have admitted it to anyone, but he had grown fond of the boy and Béatrice. However, he was alarmed to learn that there was this new woman in the camp now. He shot her a look from under his brows. She looked harmless, but while she hugged and kissed her little boy as though she could hardly believe that he was truly there with her, and only by constant reminder could she ensure that he would not disappear, her eyes were constantly flitting from one man to another about the camp.

'Are you well, maid?' he asked when Béatrice came to his side and refilled his mazer with wine.

She nodded. Always in his presence she was cold and aloof. It was a shame, for she was a lovely woman. Still, it was a mistake for a man to have a woman when he was marching with the banners. Women were a distraction. And this one in particular, he knew, had an inner resolution and resentment that burned all who approached too closely.

'No one offered you an insult while we were gone?'

She hesitated. 'One knight, Sir Peter, makes me fear for my safety. He has no feeling, no heart. I watched him ride off, always coming back with prisoners, and it was as though they were sheep to him, to be impounded and slaughtered.'

'That is how knights are, maid,' he said with a smile. Later he would remember her words and have cause to think about the implications afresh.

Grandarse had walked in while they were talking, and now stood at his side. 'What about you, Frip? How are you?'

'Me? I'm fine.' His attention was still on her, but then he realised that Grandarse was waiting for him to say more. Suddenly, he realised that he really *was* fine. In fact, he felt better than he had for many weeks.

He had served too many kings and warriors to worry about what might have happened. There was no profit in might-have-beens. He was here only for the gold. Once, he would have told himself it was a matter of honour, of chivalry, but when a man had hacked at another, while screaming hatred at his dying face, spittle flying, and then gone to slaughter even more men, there was little chivalry left in a fellow's soul. Berenger sometimes wondered whether there ever had been. He did ask himself whether war and killing was all he would ever achieve. War, to his mind, was a necessary evil – sometimes – and it kept him in bread and ale, but he disliked hearing men elevate it to an art. It was killing. Any butcher could do it.

'You did well to escape the French,' Grandarse commented.

'We wouldn't have done so without the help of the Genoese.'

'Tell me about him again.'

Berenger shrugged. 'Short man, dark hair. Called himself Chrestien de Grimault. He seemed to have the authority of a whore when he was on his boat. Knew his men would do anything he told them. I suppose it's the mantle of command that a shipmaster draws around himself. A shipman has to possess a commanding presence to maintain order on a ship in a storm, and this man had it in buckets.'

'Or perhaps he was a man with a lot of authority,' Grandarse chuckled. He took his seat on a stool and leaned back against the wall, drawing his belt down below his paunch so it didn't cut into his belly. 'You want to know what I've heard? I've heard he's the captain of the French fleet – the most important Genoese in the whole of France. And he let you go.'

Berenger heard the slight note of enquiry. 'What of it? He said his honour was stained by the treatment they were threatening to use on us.'

'But it's odd that the French should have let you get away so easily. Perhaps they *wanted* you to think you were escaping?'

'Nah. They had no thought of that,' Berenger said flatly. 'You didn't see the bodies of the two shipmen they killed.' He shuddered at the memory.

'Well, what other reason could there be? Some might reckon it was a case of "you give us something and we'll let you go" – got me?'

Grandarse was peering at him, the picture of genial good nature, but Berenger saw his eyes glitter. He was watching to see how Berenger would react.

'We told them nothing. Nothing at all. It was because we refused that we were about to be taken away to be blinded,' he said.

'Good! Good. I'm glad to hear it. Then there's nothing for us to worry about. Because if one of your men *had* given away the layout of our camp, the French might realise that we are weak in some areas. They might consider it possible that they could send ships into Calais and ballocks up our siege. They could come and attack us at any time, couldn't they?'

He rose and stared down at Berenger. '*I* don't believe that sort of thing, Frip – you know that. But others may. You keep the men alert, just in case. We don't want any accidents happening to your men here during the siege.'

Berenger nodded as Grandarse left the group, waddling and giving cheery farewells to the rest of the men, but some yards away, Berenger saw him turn and cast a glance his way before disappearing into the night.

There were two things Grandarse would not tolerate: any man who smacked of bad luck who could bring danger to the centaine, and a man who would betray his comrades. Either would be sure to die quickly in the dark of an alley or a low alehouse.

Berenger considered for a moment, then allocated men to keep watch through the night. Although they grumbled, he was insistent.

'I am glad you returned safely,' the Vidame said.

His spy drained his cup of wine and poured another. There was a shake in his hand as he measured out his drink. He pointedly ignored the Vidame's empty mazer. 'I am not only glad, I am astonished.'

They were in a large tavern, with many English archers and warriors drinking and singing, but at the rear of the chamber they had relative peace. Speaking in low voices, so no one could overhear them, both kept watching the crowds for a curious person who might speak of their meeting.

'What is so surprising?'

'They were going to *kill* me, Vidame! How ironic would that be? To be slain by my own people, merely for want of a sign that I should be protected.'

'Is that why you wished to see me?'

'You think I would entrust such a message to a boy?'

'I would hope not. Calm yourself, man.'

The spy stared about him. 'This life is growing too difficult, Vidame. I'm as keen as any to help the King's efforts, but not at the risk of having my own neck stretched.'

'You forget yourself, my friend. The important thing here is the defence of France and the kingdom. Individuals will die, it is certain, but that is sometimes necessary for the good of all.'

'Those are fine words,' the spy said, 'when spoken by the man who takes fewest risks.'

The Vidame smiled and looked at the spy. 'Do you really have so little faith? By my actions I shall be forced to suffer the worst torments the English can contrive.'

'Very well.'

'You do not believe me?'

'I trust you, Vidame. Where would the world be without trust?' the other added bitterly.

'It seems certain that the man from Essex knows nothing that could implicate you. I think we may leave him alone. But watch him. At the first sign of danger, let me know and I will have Bertucat kill him. However, for now I think it is better to leave him to his own devices. We have other things to consider.'

His voice dropped as he spoke. 'It is not only the man from Essex. Your vintener is astute – more than I had considered. He saw the fleet and warned his knight; now, I think, he looks upon our messenger with suspicion. Soon he may cast his suspicions upon you.'

'Fripper? He suspects nothing. He is just worried for the men under him.'

'If he suspects you, he would soon be able to make you talk. I do not want to be implicated,' the Vidame said.

'You will be safe.'

'And then again, the business on which you are employed would suffer if you were captured. We need your talents. We need to know where the blow should fall.'

'First the army needs to come here. The King must bring his host and attack. I will point to the best place for the assault.'

'Good. But the vintener still troubles me. It would be a good thing, were he to die.'

'How? By me? It would be difficult to insert a knife into his back while the vintaine watches!'

'When he sleeps?'

'You do not know the man. He is wary of everyone, as he should be.'

'I understand. However, our messenger has been noticed by him, and we cannot afford to lose the boy.'

'Very well.'

'The English will send a messenger to the north, to warn them of the French ships taking men and arms to the Scottish. With luck the Scottish will rampage about the North of England and visit retribution for the damage done by the English over here. The sooner the messenger gets there, the sooner the English will be prepared. We must have the messenger delayed.'

'I do not understand.'

'Your vintaine will be sent to guard the messenger. I will have Bertucat go to speak with certain friends. There are some here who have friends in England who would not be averse to earning a purse of gold by delaying the embassy, or even killing a man. Look to attacks from other men, and take advantage, if you may.'

'Can you be sure my vintaine will be sent?'

The Vidame leaned back, chuckling quietly. 'The vintaine that miraculously survived capture by the French? The vintaine that managed to win over a Genoese mercenary and take a ride on his ship? The vintener who saw the ships in the estuary and discovered the risk of French ships travelling to Scotland? Which other vintaine would be sent?'

'But the escape was come about by simple good fortune!'

'Yes – but others begin to doubt that. Now many know that the escape of the vintaine was aided by the Genoese. Would it not be amusing if, when I have finished dripping poison into the right ears, many believe this Fripper to be in league with the French himself? We could use our own crimes against him!'

*

The following morning, Berenger woke to find his entire vintaine asleep in the chamber. He rolled onto his back, scratching his armpits and staring at the roof while he gradually came awake. Last evening they had all gone to an inn over to the east, and some of the men had gone out to watch and gamble on a cock-fight that was held in a little arena by a stable. Oliver had lost heavily again, and Pardoner too. Not that they got much sympathy from the others. They were late back and Berenger set Clip to take the first watch.

He had set Clip to the first watch!

Rising, cursing, he went to the recumbent figure in the corner and gave it a kick, demanding, 'Did you wake Jack to take over your watch?'

'Jack was asleep,' Clip yawned. 'There wasn't any point, anyway, Frip. What, do you think some Frenchie's going to sidle up here, half a mile or more into the English lines, just to try to murder us in our beds?'

It was tempting to kick him again – harder, this time – but the eyes of the others were all on him, and Berenger didn't want them to see that he was rattled. He hissed, 'Next time I give you an order, Clip, you had best obey to the letter, whether you like it or not, because if you don't, I'll see you flogged!'

He took a dry crust of bread with him outside and sat on a low wall to eat it, staring glumly at the roadway before them.

A short while later, Jack came outside and joined him. 'It wasn't Clip's fault, Frip. You would have questioned an order like that yourself, you know it. What's it all about? We're in the middle of an army of twelve thousand or more. Why worry about our own sentries?'

Berenger broke off a little more bread and offered it. Jack took it without enthusiasm, studying it for a moment before cramming it into his mouth.

'You remember the night before last?' Berenger said. 'Grandarse came to warn me. Apparently, some think we bribed our way out from the French, using secrets instead of money.'

'They're fucking mad!' Jack blurted out, spraying dried crumbs in all directions. 'You mean some prick's been saying we betrayed our own?'

'And some of 'em would like to come and repay the kindness. So we all have to keep on our toes, Jack. If we don't, any evening one or more of us is likely to walk into a blade.'

'I understand,' Jack said gravely.

'What do you make of the newer guys?'

'Christ's ballocks, Frip, you expect me to comment on them before we've even seen a French horse running at them?'

'We saw them on the ship.'

'It's hard to gauge. John of Essex was mad to get into things, as usual. He's got even less brain than Donkey. Show him a fight and he'll rush to get into the thick of it.'

'The rest?'

Jack puffed out his cheeks. 'Dogbreath could be useful. He didn't look scared and he tried to tangle with the first of them when they came at us. He was knocked down in the first mêlée. Aletaster, I didn't see. Turf was throwing his guts up when the attack came, as usual. Pardoner didn't look too clever – he seemed to get knocked down and he disappeared until the ship was crushed – and then he suddenly reappeared in time to be rescued and captured. I didn't see Saint Lawrence or the others during the fight.'

'So no obvious cowards or fools who could be dangerous?'

'Not that I saw, no.'

'Good. Then we'll stick to them, but we'll have to work them. You know what it's like. Bored archers get sloppy. We need to get them to some butts or make our own. That'll have the advantage of both testing their skills, honing them, and keeping us all away from any mad bastards who think we may be traitors.'

'Right enough. Do you want me to get them ready now?'

'Yes, I . . .'

Berenger was interrupted by the appearance of Richard Bakere, Sir John de Sully's esquire. 'Sir John needs to see you, Fripper.'

He nodded. 'Jack, get on with it. Give them a good going-over. I want to know we can rely on them in a fight. I'll be back as soon as I can.'

When Berenger entered the room, he was surprised to see Grandarse standing at the corner of the chamber behind Sir John de Sully. Berenger felt his hackles rise in warning, but not because of those two. It was the others.

They were not alone. To one side was the slim, elegant figure of Peter of Bromley, the man Berenger knew had been called Pierre d'Agen, with his clerk, Alain de Châlons, and a man-at-arms. Peter of Bromley was just one of many men who had appeared here in the King's army seeking wealth, power, or simply revenge for actions taken by the French, but the sight of him set Berenger's teeth on edge. A man who would turn traitor was likely to find it easy to do so again.

The warlike Bishop of Durham, Thomas Hatfield, was in the room too, with a serious expression on his face, and at his side was the barrel-chested figure of the Earl of Warwick.

Christ Jesus, Berenger thought to himself. *What have I done now?*

The Earl peered at him. 'Fripper, we have been listening to reports. Last night, I had a scouting party ride out towards the estuary where you said you saw the ships.'

'Yes?'

'There's nothing there,' he said. 'They're all gone – *if* they were there in the first place.'

The vintener thought about it. His eyesight was poor, but he couldn't have mistaken those massive shapes, nor the tall masts towering over the trees. 'They were there. I'm sure of it.'

'In that case, someone got a warning to them. The question is, will they appear here soon, and when they do, will they merely replenish the town, or will they come to attack us?'

'They will not be able to assault our positions here on the coast,' Sir John said firmly. The bishop was nodding as he spoke, and Peter of Bromley inclined his head in agreement. 'They must be coming to supply the town.'

'Then we must be ready for them,' the Earl said. 'I have commanded the ships to stand off a little from the coast and when they see the enemy, to attack them at once.'

Berenger was frowning. 'My Lord, do you know when the scouts found the estuary empty – at what hour of the night?'

The Earl turned and an esquire stepped across the room from his post at the wall, bending and whispering in the Earl's ear. 'Apparently it was the second watch of the night. Why?'

Berenger made a quick calculation. 'Even with the still evening, the ships must surely be visible from the coast now if they are coming. They were only five or six leagues from here. If they were to draw out to sea, they must still be visible from shore.'

'So?'

'If no one can see them, either they have taken a most extended route to get here, or they are not coming here at all.'

'You think perhaps they could have gone to hide?'

Berenger frowned, and then remembered the stocky figure with the ginger hair in the cardinal's hall. David, he had been called.

'My lord, what if they were not intending to come here? Perhaps they are sailing to land French fighters somewhere else?'

'Such as?'

'Scotland! They mean to invade the north through Scotland with their allies, to create a diversion that must call the King's men back home to protect the kingdom!'

Chapter Thirteen

Jack watched the men with a sense of glum resignation. 'Archers, *nock your arrows*!'

There was a disjointed ripple along the line as men reached for their arrows. Some had them in quivers, two had them thrust into their belts, while Dogbreath had shoved three into the ground before him, snapping one shaft as he did so. He turned to Jack with a shame-faced grimace, the nock and fletchings in his hand, the splinter with the point stuck in the ground. 'I think there's a rock down there.'

'Be more bloody careful, you horse's arse! Those arrows are all that will protect you and the rest of us from the French army when it comes,' Jack snarled.

After some fumbling, most managed to get their arrows fitted to their bowstrings.

'Archers, *draw!*'

There was a creaking, groaning sound as all the bows along the line were bent, the archers pulling the great strings back until they touched their ears, aiming high at full draw, the yew and strings complaining under the massive tension.

'Archers, *loose*!'

The thrumming of so many bows was like a sudden gale passing through a forest: a susurration of death.

Jack sighed and walked along the line to where Pardoner stood hopping on one leg, his right hand gripping his left wrist, an expression of the keenest agony on his face. Saint Lawrence stood laughing nearby.

'I told you to wear a bracer, didn't I?' Jack said.

'I'm sorry, Sergeant, I couldn't find it when we came out today.'

Jack took his hand and studied his arm. From elbow to wrist the string had scraped all along the soft flesh, leaving a red-raw bruise in its tracks; already blood was spiking from tiny rips in the flesh. 'You'll live,' he said.

'I can't carry on, sir,' the man said, fighting back the tears. 'It hurts.'

'Welcome to the pleasures of a soldier's life,' Jack said unsympathetically. 'You'll go back later, when you've actually hit a target.'

He walked back to his post at the side of the line of archers, calling, 'Archers, *nock*!'

'With this lot, we'll all get slaughtered,' Clip said at his side.

'I don't need any of your cheery comments, thank you,' Jack growled. 'Archers, *draw*!'

'Leave them. Go on, leave them there a while. See which one can hold his bow,' Clip pleaded.

'Archers, *loose!*'

'You're allowed a little fun, Jack.'

Jack sighed at the sight of an arrow all but buried in the soil only a matter of fifteen paces from the line. 'Who was that?'

Horn lifted a tentative hand.

'Go and cut it loose. Don't try to pull it out of the ground;

you'll snap the shaft, Horn. You have to dig out the grass along its length and lift it out,' Jack explained. 'Break it and you'll have to pay for it.'

'Have any of them hit anything?' Clip asked.

'Dogbreath there is not so bad. The rest have hit a lot of field.'

Clip watched the next couple of flights, his face a study of gloom. 'Any chance of moving to a new vintaine?'

Clip walked back while Jack was still exercising his charges at the range, but as he walked, his eyes were narrowed in crafty thought. He was not needed for anything today, and that meant he had time to try scrounging what he could.

Just before they had been pushed onto the ship and sent to help the convoy, he had been out scavenging and, while investigating a little alleyway, trying to capture a chicken or two, someone had knocked him down. This assault by some unknown civilian offended his sense of justice. To have his head broken when he hadn't even taken anything (yet) was not only grossly unfair, but it also left him with a strong sense that there must be something more valuable to protect than mere chickens. Some soldiers had pillaged wealthy manors and churches in this area. Perhaps there was a little store of gold or silver in a house near that alley? It was worth further investigation, if no one was about.

Without thinking, his feet had already bent their way towards the interesting alley.

As he went, he noticed two men walking along in front of him. One was a large man, tall, with massive hands and legs like small oaks. The other was just some scruffy tatterdemalion with a triangular-shaped face, mousy hair and blue, deep-set eyes. He met Clip's look, but didn't appear to recognise him, and he didn't know the other man either, so as they passed on, he carried on his way without any intimation of danger.

Clip reached the alley and stood nonchalantly, leaning against a post at the entrance, idly picking his nose. Inspecting the results on his finger, he looked around him sidelong making sure that no one had seen him, before sucking the contents off his finger and sidling into the alleyway.

The moment he was in the alley, the light was shut out as if a candle had been snuffed. He walked on silently, his attention focused on the bright patch at the end. A chicken wandered into view, unconcernedly pecking at the ground, and he took that as a sign that all was clear. Chickens, in his experience, tended to try to fly away at the least provocation – even the sight of a man usually. He slipped further on, until he reached the very end. He tentatively peered around the corner of the wall. Nobody. He stood silently, scarcely breathing as he strained his ears for any sounds in the vicinity, but there was nothing. All was well.

He stepped out into the yard, but then his heart stopped. The chickens fled squawking, and he found himself confronted by a man. He was broad, like a miller, and had hands like hams.

'Who are you? What do you want here?' the man demanded in a thick Carlisle accent. He was carrying a set of gardening tools, and he dropped them as Clip turned and bolted. Clip would have made it too, as he tried to say later, were it not for the Devil's own chicken that ran under his feet and made him stumble and fall. And then he felt a huge fist on the back of his neck, lifting him like a doll and shaking him.

'You thinking of stealing one of our chicks, were you? I reckon you need a damn good thrashing to stop you from ever coming back here, eh? Right, little man, let's see if a dip will cure you of thievery!' the man snarled.

Clip was relieved to hear that. A dip in the water wouldn't be too bad.

*

When he was finally allowed to leave the room, Berenger stood outside and took a deep breath.

That was one of those moments when he really should have held his tongue. After all, the ships could well have been moved further away. Perhaps the French officers had realised the dangers inherent in trying to break the English blockade, and had pulled the ships away, so that they could be kept safe. But even as he tried to tell himself this, he disagreed.

The French ships were definitely heading somewhere else. Bishop Thomas knew as well as Berenger where they were going. It was clear in his eyes when he spoke: complete conviction – *Scotland*. Still, Berenger should have kept quiet. If people already suspected that he might be in league with the enemy and if he appeared to be in possession of inside information, they would wonder where he had got it from. It was but a short step from that to thinking that he must be a traitor. And in this vast encampment, a man such as himself could be made to disappear all too easily.

Berenger pushed himself away from the shed and walked into the road. It was muddy and befouled with excrement from dogs, horses and men, and he tried to avoid the worst of it as he made his way down the street towards the chambers where his own vintaine was billeted.

The road narrowed, and as he stepped around a large pile of ox dung and over a puddle of urine, he heard a sudden movement behind him.

There was a short splash, and Berenger span on his heel to find a large man confronting him. Berenger's quick glance took in the knife held low to gut him, the dark eyes scowling in a thickly bearded face – and the vintener scarcely had time to register the man's quick look to Berenger's right before instinct made him spring away, just missing the leaden hammer on a long shaft that had been aimed at his head by another man.

He grabbed for his sword, too late remembering that he hadn't put it on in his hurry to respond to Sir John de Sully's summons, and hastily backed away from the two men. 'Who are you?' he demanded.

'We're Englishmen,' the darkly bearded man said. His companion, of slighter build and fairer-complexioned, sniggered at that.

'So am I!'

The man made a feint and tried to punch Berenger, before grinning. 'But you took money from the French. Everyone has heard about it. So we're going to kill you.'

Berenger said nothing, but watched the two narrowly. There was a moment's calm as he moved backwards and the two paced after him, all three crouching, two ready to spring, one prepared to defend himself. As if on a signal, the hammer swung at Berenger's head again, and as it flew at him, making Berenger duck hurriedly, the bearded man slipped his knife out and up, trying to snag Berenger's gut. He missed, and Berenger slapped at the blade with his hand, but then the maul was driving back towards him, aimed at his shoulder, and he had to jerk away even as the steel slashed at him once more.

The lead came close again, but Berenger sprang forward. He grasped the maul's shaft with both hands and twisted, jerking the man across his front. The knife-thrust intended for him found its mark in his opponent's flank, and the man gave a short cry as he struggled with Berenger for control of the hammer. Berenger was not going to let go. That would mean death. He crooked his elbow and slammed it into the face of his enemy, jabbing it at his eyes and nose, hoping to connect and hurt the fellow, but nothing seemed to work. Instead he concentrated on keeping the man's body between himself and the knifeman, until he felt the hammer man lurch slightly: his foot had slipped on a stone. Berenger let him fall, then jerked the hammer forward with all his strength. The maul caught the bearded man full in the face and he staggered back, dropping his knife as the blood flooded his vision. Berenger let the hammer fall on the back of the other man's head as he crouched on all fours in the ordure of the street. The hammer connected with a dull thud, and the man toppled senseless into the filth.

The other was wiping at his nose, which was smashed and flattened across his face. He spat a gobbet of blood at Berenger, and then turned and fled.

Berenger stood a moment, panting as the thrill ran through his body and then left him, leaving him feeling as weak as a deflated bladder. Then, after a moment's pause, he reached down to the hammer man and rolled him over. 'Don't want you drowning before we've asked you some questions, do we?' he said breathlessly.

Chapter Fourteen

Berenger heaved the figure to the edge of the street and left him, slumped and snoring slackly while he hurried on his way. He kept the maul, letting it swing experimentally as he trotted along, until he reached the shed where his vintaine was based – but there was no one there. After a moment or two, he found Archibald by the gonnes, and having secured his help, he returned to the street. The man was still there, and Berenger waited at his side until John, Jack and Dogbreath arrived with the Earl, summoned by Archibald's boy, Ed the Donkey.

'Fetch a bucket of water,' Berenger said to the Donkey.

Ed wanted to demand why he should obey him, but the grim expression on Berenger's face dissuaded him. He walked away at the slowest speed he could to demonstrate his independence, but fast enough to ensure that he didn't earn a buffet about the head. The vintener was demanding too much. And Ed would let him know soon. He wasn't the vintaine's slave, he was apprentice to a gynour. He had more knowledge already about the making of powder and its use than any of the vintaine's men.

Walking back, he saw Béatrice talking to the new woman. He eyed Georges' mother with jealousy. She had taken all of Béatrice's time since she arrived. Now Ed hardly ever had a chance to speak to Béatrice himself. It was a constant source of annoyance.

He saw Béatrice glance at him and smile, and suddenly the sun seemed to shine. He ran to fetch the water, and brought it back to Berenger, who didn't even say thank you. He could cheerfully have tipped it over the vintener's feet.

But just at that moment there was a pause in the chatter. Then, 'Sweet Jesus, Clip,' Berenger said, wincing. 'What happened to you?'

'Er . . . I had a bit of an accident.'

Jack was stepping away. 'God's blood, man! What sort of an accident?'

Ed could see Clip's eyes moving about shiftily. 'I fell into a latrine,' he mumbled.

'How?' Jack demanded.

'Which one?' John asked.

'Who pushed you?' Berenger said with more perception.

Berenger sent Clip to soak himself in the surf and wash his clothes. Meanwhile, he explained what had happened.

Berenger kicked the man's foot. 'Who are you? Who sent you to waylay me? I said, who are you?'

The snoring had all but ceased, so Berenger upended the bucket of stagnant green pondwater over the man's head.

He awoke and sat up angrily, trying to shake the water from his face and hair like a dog leaving a river, but a boot in his chest kept him on the ground. 'What is this?'

'My question precisely,' Berenger said. 'Who are you? Why did you attack me?'

The man's little blue eyes darted around as though hopeful of finding an escape. He was not, Berenger reckoned, as bright as the other fellow. 'I didn't attack anyone.'

With a sigh, Berenger leaned down and pushed the man's head back until the sore patch where the maul had hit his skull touched the stones of the pathway. Then he pushed twice, hard. 'Answer me.'

'Aargh! Stop! Very well, it was Sir Peter of Bromley who told us all about you.'

'I asked who you are, and which centener or banneret do you serve?'

'All right! God shrivel your ballocks! My name is Willie. Some call me Willie Armstrong, others know me as Willie of Durham.' He bared his teeth.

'Very good, Willie. Why did you try to kill me?'

'We know you're a traitor, and we were going to punish you. But touch me now, and Dick will have you arrested under martial law.' He spat at Berenger's feet. 'You can't touch me – not if you want to live.'

Berenger narrowed his eyes. It was alarming to learn that some already viewed the vintaine as treacherous. 'Dick was your courageous friend?'

'You can kill me, but you'll still die.'

'You say Sir Peter told you I was a traitor?'

'Yes. Last night.'

'Why would he say that, Frip?' John said.

Berenger ignored him. 'So you are in his host with him?'

'No, we're from the force with Sir John Cobham. But we know Sir Peter.'

'That can't be right,' Jack said. 'Why would he assume you were guilty of treachery or anything?'

'It's like I told you: Grandarse warned me last night that there could be something like this.'

Jack indicated their prisoner, who now sat up, holding his throbbing head. 'What do you want us to do with that piece of shit?'

'Let him go. He's no use to us.'

'What – not kill him?' Dogbreath demanded. 'He tried to kill you, Frip, after all. We may as well stop him reporting things to his companions.'

'You want to kill him?' Berenger asked.

'Wait!' the man said. 'You harm me and Dick will report you.'

'Oh, as to that,' Berenger smiled, 'my lads will swear they were never here. I was set upon by two outlaws and one of them was killed. That's you,' he added in his most patronising manner. 'You are of no use to us, but we cannot trust someone who might try something again in future.'

'You can't kill me like that! I haven't done anything except try to protect the army.'

'You did it by trying to kill me. I'm happy to return the favour.'

'I may be able to help you.' The man was less cocky now.

'How?' Berenger hefted the maul thoughtfully. It was massy, and with its weight, could easily crush a skull. He let it slap into the palm of his hand, enjoying the wince the fellow gave as he heard it.

'It's not only us think you're guilty. It's the rest of Sir John's men, and Sir Peter's too. It's obvious!' His eyes suddenly widened as Jack's knife appeared in front of him. 'Sir John was the one who said someone should remove you. It wasn't our idea. You need to talk to him. Kill me and you won't make yourself any safer, but if you speak with him, you may. I can help you – I can explain you're innocent too. I can—'

Jack spoke very quietly. 'There's no point keeping him alive, is there? Just let me do him, Frip.'

'Why do you say it's obvious?' Berenger said, ignoring him. 'What is "obvious"?'

Willie was not ignoring him. His eyes were fixed on the blade with terror. A trickle ran from between his legs. 'Someone must be betraying our secrets to the French, and you were all allowed to escape from them. Why did they let you out and then give you a safe passage on a Genoese ship, if you didn't tell them what they wanted to hear?'

'Very good. Let him go, Jack,' Berenger said. 'Willie, if you ever lift a maul or a knife to me again, I'll kill you. No arguing or discussion, I'll just stick you. Understand?' He waited until Willie had given a nod. Then, 'Tell your friends that we're not spies. We're only doing the same job as you. You're supposed to be on our side!'

'You should have let us kill him,' Dogbreath muttered as they returned to their rooms.

'It wouldn't have achieved anything,' Berenger said.

They had left the man sagging like a sack of turnips. He had not believed that they would allow him to live, not after his attempt to waylay Berenger, and after his rudeness about the vintaine. As they walked away, he had essayed a jeer or two, but it lacked conviction.

'I'd have felt better for it,' Clip said. He was still damp after scrubbing himself violently in the sea, but a certain odour continued to surround him. The others avoided him.

'What now, Frip?' Jack said.

Berenger looked out through the open door. 'I don't know. I wish I did.'

'Can you speak with Sir John?' Jack suggested. 'Perhaps he can persuade Sir Peter that he's mistaken.'

'Yes,' Berenger said. He recalled Sir Peter of Bromley's expression in the meeting, he had not bothered to conceal his disgust for Berenger and his vintaine. It was something that Grandarse had noticed too, Berenger was sure; it was no mere figment of his imagination. 'I don't trust him, Sir Peter, or Sir Pierre, whatever he wants to be called. He must have had a reason to accuse us and put us in danger.'

'What, you believe that scrote Willie? Do you really think Sir Peter was responsible for this attack on you?' Jack said.

'I think it's very possible.'

'If there's a traitor, it's more likely to be someone like him,' Clip said unexpectedly.

'What?' Berenger asked with surprise.

'It makes more sense, a nobleman, rather than a churl like you or me. We'd not give away our mates in the line. What archer would betray his friend? But a lord or a knight, well, they only fight for money, when all's said and done. If they were offered enough ...'

'Don't you think that they'd find it as hard as you or me to see their companions caught or killed?' Berenger said.

'Them?' Clip said. 'They are used to fighting each other all the time. And *they* know that if they get caught, they can claim the right to be looked after and just pay a ransom. They value each other's lives, but as I said, they're used to fighting each other. Us? We're just meat to be cut up.'

'I think the Genoese was right,' John of Essex said. 'He gets paid for his work, and that means he is looked on as being worth something. Look at us, we get nothing.'

Jack had listened carefully. 'You're talking shite, man!'

'You really think so?' The Earl lifted his own head to join in. 'Think on this, then: when you and I are standing side by side in the front rank of archers, there's no chance we'd risk each other's lives, is there? But a knight, he'll still go out in front of the rest to show he's not scared. He doesn't care about the strength of the line or his friends, all he cares about is his own personal honour and the money he can win. That's all.'

'You don't know what you're saying,' Berenger scoffed. 'But I still don't trust Sir Peter.'

'What do you want to do about him?' Jack asked.

'Nothing, for now. We'll have to keep an eye on him, though. If he's telling other people that I'm a traitor and deserve to be removed quietly, we'll have to be careful. Tell the vintaine to keep together, Jack. No wandering about alone until we know what's happening.'

'I understand.'

And in the meantime I'll try to raise the matter with Sir John, Berenger thought.

The Vidame slipped along the street with the easy confidence of a man who knew he was safe here. He was almost at his door when a sudden low whisper made him spring aside and reach for his knife.

'It's me – Bertucat!'

'I could have gutted you for that,' the Vidame hissed. His blood was still popping and fizzing in his veins after the shock.

'Then you'd have lost a loyal servant who may one day save your skin,' Bertucat growled. 'You think I like creeping about in the shadows, when all the while you're—'

'Enough!' The Vidame shot a look about him, then joined his servant in the dark doorway of a closed shop. 'What is it?'

'The two lummocks tried to kill Fripper, but he bested them. Next time it would be better to have two men with brains rather than only muscles between their ears.'

'He bested them both? By my faith, I'd have hoped one could spring a surprise on him, let alone two.'

'He's been warned now. The bastard won't be so easy to surprise next time.'

The Vidame nodded grimly. 'Did you manage to speak to your friend?'

'About the messenger? Yes.'

'Before he leaves, make sure he is aware that there will be a bonus if he can remove Fripper. I do not want that vintener to return here. He is too clever by half and will get in our way and make our task that much harder.'

'Very well.'

'And make sure that the man understands one more thing: I do not want any slip-ups!'

Sir John was in his chamber, his whetstone in one hand, a long-bladed sword in the other when Berenger knocked and entered.

'I'm glad to see you. Did Grandarse come back with you?' Sir John asked as he set his sword aside.

'Grandarse?'

'I sent him to find you, Fripper. Isn't that why you're here?'

'No,' Berenger said, 'I wanted to talk because . . .'

'I don't have time. You are to gather your vintaine and prepare to depart. There's a fishing boat ready to take you over the Channel.'

Berenger stared. 'What? Why? Where are we going?'

'You guessed aright when you spoke before Earl Warwick. You were very persuasive – you certainly convinced Sir Peter. The French ships are still nowhere in sight. The view of the Bishop and the Earl is the same as mine: the ships were either to come here, or they were designed to bring succour to our enemies. After all, as you said, the only conceivable place where they could head is Scotland. If they arrive there unannounced, and there are significant troops on board, it could prove a disaster for us. We cannot afford to risk the Siege of Calais, but we must warn the Northern Marches of their danger. You will go with your men to inform them that they are to be attacked, and give them instructions as to how to deploy their men.'

'I see.'

'You will sail as soon as the shipmaster thinks he can safely leave, and when you reach England, you must procure horses and ride north with all haste. The ships left yesterday, so they have some head start on you, but your route is direct. They will have to land in the north, ride to meet the Scottish, persuade them to join in their venture, and then march for the border. That will take them time. With fortune, you will already be in Durham and waiting for them. Is that all clear?'

'Yes, sir.'

'All I want you to do is warn them, then come back here.'

'Sir, all this could be done, and faster, by sending one of the King's messengers.'

'And it will be. You are there to ensure that that messenger reaches the Archbishop of York safely. It'll be on your head if you don't.'

'What do you mean?'

Sir John took a mazer and filled it from a pot of wine. He turned to Berenger. 'There is talk going round that you or one of your vintaine is a traitor.'

'Who dares say that?' Berenger said angrily.

'Sir Peter of Bromley seems to think so. He it was who proposed that your vintaine should be sent. He said that if the messenger doesn't reach the Archbishop, that will confirm many in their opinion that you are not as dedicated to your King as you should be.'

'He says I am a traitor?'

Sir John peered at him over the brim of his cup. '*Some* think so. So do not fail!'

CHAPTER FIFTEEN

They were ready early the next morning. As dawn broke, Berenger was already leading the men to the eastern shores, where Sir John had told him to meet the vessel that was to take them over the Channel.

'Sir John,' Berenger greeted him as they walked into the little harbour.

'Fripper, I hope I see you well. Godspeed with this mission.'

Sir John was not happy to be leaving Berenger like this. It felt too much like throwing a good man to the wolves, but the knight knew that he had little choice in the matter: Fripper had been selected. However, Sir John noticed that Sir Peter had taken a strong dislike to the vintener, and Sir John had no idea why. 'You will take every precaution, Fripper. Look after this messenger as though he possesses your own life.'

'I don't understand ...' Berenger began, but then there came the sound of marching feet and the men all stood up straight in respect.

The King, Edward III, was no youngster. He had been born in

November 1312, but for a man in his middle thirties, he showed little of the paunch most would own by then. His pale blue eyes were restless, as though there were too many other duties which called on his attention. And yet he had come here, Sir John thought. It was a proof of how important the King considered this mission to be.

'Master Fripper,' the King said, walking straight over to Berenger.

Berenger bowed.

'Rise, my friend. We are all comrades here. You have been briefed about this? Good. I would speak with your men.'

Standing aside, Berenger called to his vintaine to listen.

'My friends, you have a most urgent and important task. In the last two days, a fleet of French ships have slipped their moorings and sailed north. There can be no doubt where they are heading: they are aiming for Scotland. They hope, so we hear, to bring fire and bloodshed to the Northern Marches. By these means, they believe they can break the back of our men here in France. Imagine! They think that a campaign of terror on our northern borders will check our advance here, and that we will wish to depart this shore, to defend our wives and children at home. And indeed, if there was a need for us to get back home and see to our families, we would do so. But, my friends, there *is* no need. So long as the good Archbishop of York and others set to defend our realm are given due warning, our English levies will stop the Scottish advance and turn them around, sending those who still have legs to walk on back to their hills and bogs without halting for breath!

'My message to those craven souls who think that any news of an attack in the north must force us to abandon this siege is: *it will not*. For were we to try to escape here, what would be the result? The French army would inevitably attack our rear as we boarded our vessels. The enemy waits only for a moment's weakness. In that instant they will fall on us in force.

'So we must remain here. And remember that the Scottish are a weak force. They do not have the strong men who once could lead them against we English. All you need do is hurry there, warn those who guard the north, and let them battle their foes.'

Berenger watched the eyes of his vintaine as the King spoke, and now that there seemed to be a pause, he nodded meaningfully to Jack, who began to cheer and cry 'Huzzah!' Falteringly, the others joined in.

'And now, I wish you all Godspeed. I pray that you have a safe journey, and that you return here in good time to join in the sack of Calais when we capture the town!'

Aye, thought Berenger sourly. *Unless all goes to the Devil in Scotland, in which case best not to return at all, except carried on a shield.*

The King nodded to the men, and as he left, Jack kept up his frantic applause until Edward was out of sight and earshot.

'Phew, that was rare. Not many have the King himself come to send them off,' Berenger heard Dogbreath say.

'Aye, rare enough,' Clip said, adding, 'but it would be even better if he'd given us a reward for agreeing to help in this way.'

'Ye're always looking to your next profit,' Aletaster said with disgust. 'There are some things that have their own reward.'

'Have their own . . .' Clip's face was a picture of mingled bafflement and disgust. 'Give me one example of a reward that is worth starving and dying for? You can keep it. Me, I'll stick to the clink of cash in my purse and a full belly every time.'

'Besides,' Pardoner said, 'why would the King come here to speak with us unless it was to emphasise how important and dangerous this message is?'

There was a sudden hush at that. Men who, until that moment, had thought only of the wenches and ales between the south coast and Durham, were thinking of all the threats that lay on the open road.

Berenger interrupted their musings. 'There are risks to ordinary travellers, my friends. We, however, are an armed vintaine. How many are likely to try to assault us or block our path? Wherever *we* go, we shall be the more fearsome and daunting. Have no concerns about footpads or those who would like to break your pates. They will walk warily around you.'

He was about to add more, when the messenger himself arrived. He was a slender fellow of perhaps fifteen years, with drab hair worn a little long. Although he had not shaved, like all the other men there, he had only a light fuzz of beard at his jawbone and chin, because he was so young. His pale, greenish eyes travelled over the vintaine with what looked like disdain. He arrived in the company of Sir Peter of Bromley with his clerk and three men-at-arms, as though he did not trust Berenger and the vintaine. His clerk stood and watched Berenger with a frown, as though studying an insect's incomprehensible activities. Sir Peter, for his part, had a fixed glare, as if disgusted that a man of the vintener's mean standing could be permitted to enjoy any status in the army. It was easy to see that he believed Berenger to be a traitor.

He really doesn't like me, Berenger thought to himself. The feeling was mutual.

Berenger shot a look at Sir John, but the knight affected not to notice as Sir Peter approached.

'Sir John, God protect you! This is Master Retford.'

'Glad I am to meet him,' Sir John said, but his tone told Berenger that he didn't mean it. His feelings seemed reciprocated. Sir Peter hardly looked at him, and the glance he gave Berener now was so haughty that the vintener had a strong urge to hit him.

Sir John noticed his expression and Berenger saw a smile chase fleetingly across his face. 'If I may address the vintaine? Thank you. Men, this is Andrew Retford. He is a King's Messenger, and you will guard him with your lives. His message is vital. The whole kingdom's future could rest upon the delivery of it.'

The boy put his left hand on the little message pouch that hung just above the hilt of his sword. It looked as though he was trying to keep tight hold of it and protect it from the coarse group of men set to guard him.

The vintaine looked collectively from Sir Peter to Retford. They were not impressed.

Sir John saw the reception and intervened. 'Men, this lad has to get to Durham. It'll be eight days' travel to get him there. Perhaps you could cover the distance faster. You will have the King's permission to hire mounts on the way at his expense. However, the main point is, you must deliver this boy and his message safely and bring them back here to Calais with any news. Is that clear?'

Berenger glared at Jack and Clip until the two reluctantly nodded and grunted agreement. With them giving their assent, the rest of the vintaine gave their own approval.

'Good,' said Sir John. He then turned and gazed at Sir Peter expectantly, as though politely dismissing him. Sir Peter took the hint, bowing and patting Andrew Retford on the upper arm before striding away with his men towards the camp.

'Master Retford, I wish you Godspeed,' Sir John said. 'You may wish to acquaint yourself with the rest of the vintaine?'

The lad nodded, but Berenger thought to himself that the fellow looked like a rabbit surrounded by the hounds, unsure which way to turn. His eyes went first to the disappearing back of Sir Peter, before returning to Sir John. And although he walked in the direction of the vintaine, he didn't join them, but stood instead staring out to sea.

It left Berenger wondering, *So why does Sir Peter wish me to guard this messenger in particular? And why has he brought the lad here himself?*

He could think of no solution to these questions.

After Sir Peter's group had walked away, the Vidame went and waited for his spy.

It was hard to live as an intelligence gatherer, mingling with those who were his enemy, but the spy appeared to contain himself with skill. He had professed to detest all English, but he had so bound his hatred within him that, to see him, a man would believe him to be entirely devoted to the King of England. His true feelings were kept under the tightest of reins.

'You know your part.'

The spy eyed him. 'This is my life at risk. I will be as careful as I can be.'

'It is not only your life, friend.'

'Vidame, your risks are as nothing compared with mine. If you are uncovered, you will receive a quick decapitation. Me? I'll suffer all the torments of hell a vengeful vintaine can think up. And they will be most inventive.'

'You know to be cautious, then. Good.'

'You look to yourself.'

The Vidame held his anger in check. There was no point in losing his temper with the spy. He did, as he said, run the higher risks.

'Godspeed. I wish you safe passage. And remember your orders.'

At the third hour of the day, when the men filed past him to the plank that gave access to the ship, Berenger realised that Grandarse had appeared at his side. Sir John saw him and took his arrival as proof that it was time for him to leave.

'Godspeed, Vintener. I will be praying for your safe return,' the knight said. 'And right swiftly, too.'

'I'll hope to be back very quickly, sir, thank you.'

He watched as Sir John walked away between the barrels and bales left on the harbour, dodging the stevedores as they tramped back and forth, the heavy sacks and baskets bowing them so they could scarcely lift their heads to see before them. 'Well?' he said to Grandarse.

'I heard today you were set upon, Frip. It's a bad business when a man can't walk to his home.'

'We found out who they were,' Berenger said.

'I know. Interesting that the men were from Sir Peter.'

'Do you think he has something against me?'

Grandarse looked at him owlishly. 'How so?'

'The men who attacked me swore they were from Sir Peter. It is plain as the beard on your chin what is going through his mind. He has started to raise the idea that there could be a spy. Do you think he really believes there's a traitor in the vintaine?'

'What do you think?' Grandarse asked slowly.

'I think it's a load of ballocks! Look at my boys: Clip, Jack, the others. Apart from the eight new lads we've had to take on board, the vintaine has been fighting for the King for longer than that pretty popinjay Peter! Why in God's name should we listen to what he says or thinks?'

'Because, Frip, you moon-addled gull, the man has the ear of the King and his son. What Peter of Bromley thinks today, the King will be thinking tomorrow. It's the way of these royals: they make their choices about advisers, and you won't change them. If Peter of Bromley is pissing sweet nothings about some hairy-arsed vintener who's got a traitor in his ranks, the King will believe him. Oh, he may try to ignore it for a day or so, and then he'll try to find arguments against it, but with a man like Sir Peter, persistent and consistent, the King won't be able to argue too long. Confusion and focus.'

'*What?*' Berenger said.

'Aye, Frip, I may be an old fart, but I know some things you never learned for all your cleverness. Like: if you're a king, you have people mithering at you all day long. You have peasants pleading for alms, merchants haggling for custom, priests demanding plots of land for new churches or abbeys, pleaders asking you to look at their poor clients' claims – and advisers advising. All through the day. You get a moment or two for every decision. Is it any wonder you start to rely on the men you think you can trust? Is it any surprise that so many decisions could be better made by a poxed whore from the Winchester stews?'

He spat accurately at a stick, making it jump. With a satisfied belch, he hoicked his belt northwards again and went on: 'Aye, Frip, I've seen it often enough. Best, usually, just to keep your head down when this kind of ballocks is going on. Leave politics and all that shite to the arses who can actually win power for themselves. For you an' me, it's enough to know that at the end of the day, you're still around with a pot of ale in your fist, a good meal inside you, and a strumpet to fondle. Because the alternative means rotting under the ground, and that's not much fun, is it?'

'No.'

'So ride like the Devil for the north and show you'll do all you can to serve the King by protecting his interests, and then hurry back so you can prove you're not interested in running away. Up and back, swift as you can.'

'Grandarse, did you see the messenger we're to protect?'

'The boy? Yes.'

'Why such a youngster? Who is he?'

'You'll need to find out for yourself. I don't know. But you'd best make sure the little prickle makes it back here safely, too.'

'Yes,' Berenger said. But even as he spoke, his mind was moving in a different direction. 'Grandarse, there is another way to look at all this.'

'Is there? What? How?'

'What if Sir Peter was secretly intending to lead the King into an impossible position, perhaps even into a trap, so that he could turn his coat to the French and act the traitor? Perhaps he would try to alienate the King from his own troops. He might begin by sowing discord and disaffection with me and my men. Tarnish our reputation with the King. He must know the King respects us. If he could damage us and make us seem treacherous . . .'

Grandarse scoffed at that. 'You think one vintener is going to harm the army? Surely you don't reckon you've such a strong reputation that your death or humiliation will affect the course of the siege?'

'No, of course not, but if he could sow enough discord within different vintaines here, he might bring about dissatisfaction with the leadership of the army – and that in itself could lead to barons deciding to desert the King. Whatever he says about me or the men, he could well be saying about others too. He could even imply that venerable centeners were as guilty, couldn't he?'

Grandarse stopped and stared. 'That booger!' He gazed into the distance with a frown creasing his brow. 'Look, Frip, you give the Scotch bastards hell, and come back safe. And whatever you do, don't lose that poxy git of a messenger.'

CHAPTER SIXTEEN

As the little ship made its creaking, complaining way over the water towards England, it was hard to concentrate, between Clip's loud grousing and Turf's regular retching over the side.

Berenger watched the messenger.

Master Retford had a nobleman's natural arrogance in the way he stood slightly apart, one hand resting on the hilt of his sword, while the other clutched at a rope, but his youth was clear in the way that his head snapped around at every sudden noise. When a rope parted with a crack like one of Archibald's gonnes, the boy looked as though he might have broken a bone in his neck, his skull revolved so speedily. No, the arrogance was a show. This lad was scared: perhaps because he was taking part in his first major task for his lord and King? Or was it because he had been warned that the mission on which he was engaged was dangerous, and the men with him could be traitors? Either way, Berenger knew he would have to be careful.

When they were almost halfway across the Channel, he walked across to the messenger and said, 'Master Retford. A word.'

'Yes?'

The lad was no older than fifteen – sixteen at a pinch. For all his attempts at youthful cockiness, the eyes told a different story. His attention moved from Berenger to Jack and the others and back again. There was an anxious set to his brows, and his fingers seemed to clasp the rope with a drowning sailor's grip, but he still managed to curl his lip as though he was as ashamed to be confronted by a mere churl as any nobleman would be.

Berenger led him to the prow, where they would have some privacy. 'If I'm to get you safely to the north, I need to know a little about you. Are you trained in how to use that?' he asked, nodding to the boy's sword, which hung close to the little message pouch.

'I've had a good education,' Retford said defensively.

'But can you use a sword?'

'Yes.'

'On horseback?'

'I don't think . . .' he began haughtily, then caught sight of Berenger's steady gaze and reconsidered. 'Yes, I can,' he said.

'Good. And you are used to riding long distance?'

'Of course.'

'How far in a day?'

'Often twenty miles.'

'A King's messenger will manage thirty-five in a day, same as a messenger on foot. We won't have time for niceties. If we're to get the message to Durham in time to prevent the Scots from launching their attack and laying all the north of England to waste, we'll have to travel as fast as possible. That means sore buttocks and thighs and riding for fifty miles a day, if we can. I want to get to Durham in six days – that is my aim.'

'I can do it.'

'I hope so, boy.'

Retford bridled, as Berenger had intended. 'I am no *boy*!' he hissed. 'I am a *Nuncius*, a Messenger to the King! You will treat me with respect!'

His hand strayed to the little leather message pouch again as though he expected to have to defend it from Berenger.

Berenger rolled with the ship as the prow pointed down into a trough. As it emerged, the deck was flooded with water for a moment, and he felt his boots slip on the wet decking.

'Until you show me what you're made of, you'll be *Boy* to me. I'm your senior by more than double your age, and I will not take orders from you. You, on the other hand, will do everything I tell you, because if you do not, you may bring danger to my men. I am responsible for seventeen men here, all told, and I won't have their security put at risk because of your foolishness. Their safety means more to me than yours, because they and I have fought many times together, and I know they'll risk their lives to protect me. That demands my respect. You, on the other hand, are simply a boy with a message to deliver. Well, my men and I can deliver your message *with* or *without* you. You are dead weight, until you prove otherwise. I daresay you were born to a free man, and you were taken on by the King's Household some time ago when they needed a runner to deliver orders for the baker to make more loaves, or the huntsman to prepare the hounds for the King's pleasure. And now you have your more important message to deliver. That is fine, but do not mistake – or overestimate – your significance in this.'

He turned and was about to leave when the boy spoke.

'I have been warned about you. Your threats don't scare me, Master Fripper! Just remember, I have my sword at the ready at all times. If you try to kill me, you will live to regret it. My Lord Peter of Bromley will know whom to blame if any hurt comes to me.'

Berenger eyed him musingly. 'Boy, if you bring danger to me

or my men, I will slay you myself, orders or no. Apart from that, I will guard you well enough. We aren't footpads here.'

'For certain,' the boy sneered, peering at the vintaine. Pardoner and Oliver had joined Turf at the wale and the three could be heard groaning and spitting even over the noise of the waves slapping at the hull. 'No felons in your vintaine.'

Later, as he rolled himself in his blanket to sleep, already halfway to London, Berenger remembered that look and his words. It almost sounded as though the lad knew something about the men that he didn't. Of course, the boy could have meant Berenger himself. That would explain Sir Peter's look, too, if he felt that Berenger was a traitor. It would explain the two men trying to waylay and kill him, too.

But it could also relate to the older members of the vintaine; if any were a traitor, Berenger would be willing to wager that it was Tyler. Mark Tyler, who had stirred up enough trouble for four men in the last month, and who had been willing to trade his person for news of the army in Dunkirk. Certainly Retford's look and tone told of a conviction that someone in the vintaine was guilty of treachery or some other heinous crime.

Berenger wondered whether Tyler's behaviour could have blinded him to another's evildoing. In his mind, he reviewed the men. Saint Lawrence was clearly incapable of committing a crime, as was the Pardoner. For his money, he considered that Horn, Turf and Wren were similarly unlikely felons. The Earl, Dogbreath and Aletaster were more likely. He would say that any one of them could have been a felon. As for the older members of his vintaine ... well, Clip was more trouble than a gaggle of whores. Come to that, Oliver or any of the others could have given offence. Especially adventurers like John of Essex.

It wasn't surprising. When the King decided to send his largest ever army into France, he had collected together all the men he could find. Some were volunteers, but many were the dregs of society, men who had crimes to hide from, men who had committed adultery, runaway priests and monks, pimps, tricksters, draw-latches, robbers and cut-purses. It took all kinds of men to fill an army. And some, of course, were convicted felons who had been offered a pardon for their service. The fact that Andrew Retford had thought about things showed good sense, in that he appreciated the risks of such companions.

Then Berenger reconsidered. Perhaps it showed nothing of Retford's thinking, but more about Sir Peter's. If the knight wanted to harm the reputation of Berenger's vintaine, it would be easy to instil in Retford a belief that the other men with him were guilty of unimaginable crimes. If Retford survived and made it back, he could boast about his skill and guile in fooling the men of the vintaine who were out to destroy him; if he did not return to Sir Peter, the knight could easily allow it to be known that he had never trusted the vintaine from the outset. Either way, doubt and suspicion would lurk wherever the vintaine were to go. More men, like the two who had set upon Berenger, would be sure to try their luck. There would be nowhere safe for them.

If only he knew why Sir Peter had decided to mistrust them!

He curled up, trying to push his misgivings away. Surely the good knight Sir Peter was only doing the best he could for the King. He was the King's friend, after all. And the King was no fool. Had he not recently trounced the French armies at Sluys and Tournai, at Crécy, and even now at Calais? King Edward III was an astute warrior and judge of men. If he were not, he would hardly have gathered about him the strongest, brightest and boldest men in all the kingdom.

Even a king might make a mistake, Berenger reminded

himself. He had enormous regard for his monarch, but the King was still only a man.

Berenger would be on his guard, but more importantly, he would keep on guard for Retford too.

Four days later Clip's nasal whine woke Berenger. 'Get on, Jack!'

'I'm only saying,' Jack said in his imperturbable manner. 'It's clear as day to me.'

'Ye've got to be joking, man. This – a holiday? My arse is as flat as that oatcake!'

'You're too scrawny to complain about a flat backside,' Jack said.

The Earl was lounging with an elbow resting on a tree. 'Perhaps all this riding is a little hard, but I prefer it to running the risk of a lance in my belly.'

'A good point,' Jack said. He flipped his oat cake over to cook the other side on the stone by the fire.

It had been a principle of Berenger's from early on to see to it that the men had oat cakes to break their fast of a morning. During the wars in Scotland he had seen how each Scotsman would carry a small bag of oatmeal and mix this with a little water to make their cakes to eat each evening. But for him, it was more important that a soldier had something to keep him walking all day, and a couple of oaten cakes were filling on an empty belly.

'When I think of a holiday,' Clip said wistfully, 'I think of the hog roasting in the great hall, and good salads, and the wenches all dancing like wayward sluts, and the ale tasting of strong malt and flavoured with honey, and the bonfire outside, and dancing out there as the stars glitter overhead, while men wander off with their sweethearts and . . .'

Jack's ribald laugh interrupted him. 'What? Go on – what then?'

'You with a sweetheart! How much did she cost, Clip? Did you pay for the night or only by the spurt? She'd have cost you less that way by far!'

'Damn your soul, Jack Fletcher, you ruin anything!'

'Never a good story though, Clip. Go on – make up some more!'

Clip ostentatiously turned his back on his comrade and spoke to Saint Lawrence and Turf. Horn, Dogbreath and Aletaster all appeared as he spoke.

'It was a lovely manor, when I was a boy. The famine had passed through the year before I was born, and took both my brothers as well as many of the other youngsters in the vill, but at least it meant that there was food for all. I had a happy childhood there.' A chuckle from Jack made him spit: 'At least I knew my parents!'

'You knew your mother,' Jack said. 'And a man or two!'

'Are you saying I'm a bastard? At least I was born that way. I'm not a self-made man like you!'

There was a moment's absolute silence, like the calm before a storm; the men all stared, waiting to see the first blade flash in the sunlight, while Jack and Clip remained utterly still. Berenger saw the messenger sitting a short distance away from them, apparently petrified with fear. He clearly expected the two to explode into violence at any moment. Then Jack nodded and slipped a knife from his belt.

The new recruits moved away slightly, their dazed expressions reflecting their trepidation. Even the Earl glanced anxiously at Berenger, but he only watched the oat cakes cooking, unconcerned. The tension mounted as the new recruits stared at Jack. Only Retford stood back, giving himself space, and his hand strayed to his sword's hilt.

Under their fixed gaze, Jack eyed his blade, testing it with his thumb. Then he shot a look at Clip's back, before sliding it under his cakes and flipping them over.

'Is me bleeding cake ready yet?' Clip demanded.

'Come here and breathe on it. All that hot air and ballocks you're giving us, you might make it cook faster.'

'I don't know why you bother eating. You must know we're all going to get killed. The outlaws and felons around here are the most dangerous in all the lands.'

'Oh?' Berenger called and rolled from beneath his blanket. 'Where are we then, Clip?'

'Three days north of London, Frip – didn't you know?'

'Felons grow worse the further north a man travels, then?'

Clip ignored him, picking up his oat cake and hastily blowing on his fingers. 'Roast your prick, Jack, you could have told me it was burning hot!'

'Sorry. I had thought you could still use that space between your ears for something. I suppose your skull's only fit for a hammer, eh?'

Berenger stood up and wandered over to them, scratching and rubbing his face. 'If you look at him, you can see that other people have been using him as a mallet for ages. With a face like that, it's hardly surprising!'

The newer recruits began to talk again and Berenger could feel waves of relief waft about their camp.

'Try not to increase their tension too much, you gits,' he muttered as he took a cake.

'Only giving them a basic training in being a soldier,' Clip said. 'And they'll all be killed in the first battle anyway.'

'Don't start, Clip,' Berenger warned.

'He's not wrong, though,' Jack said more quietly. 'The Aletaster may be big, but Christ Jesus, he's slow. Dogbreath would survive by breathing on his enemy, and Saint Lawrence may live. He has a good reach with his height. But the rest? We'll need to make sure they get some more training in before they go into the line, Frip.'

'When we're back in Calais we'll plan to give them some weapon practice then,' Berenger said. 'How were they with bow and arrow?'

Jack shook his head. 'I've never felt so threatened in my life.'

CHAPTER SEVENTEEN

It was late in the morning, almost noon, when it happened.

Berenger was riding up at the front of their group, with the others straggling in a line behind. At his side, Retford had begun to open up a little. After so many days in the company of the men, the messenger was more inclined to laugh and joke with the rest of the vintaine. He even unbent so far as to share a song or two as they rode.

It was not easy riding here. They were into a landscape of rivers, thick forests and small, granite houses. Vills were few and far between, and the people they saw were unwelcoming and mistrustful. Still, Berenger was content to be making moderate progress. The horses were being forced to work hard, and he was aware that soon, they would have to change them for fresh mounts. It should be possible, he thought, if there was an inn on the way, but if they failed to find one today, tomorrow they would need to rest their beasts more. As it was, they were dismounting regularly to help the horses.

'How do you know Sir Peter?' he asked Andrew Retford.

'He is a great leader of men. I am proud to know him,' Retford said with a flash of his earlier arrogance. Then he slid a look at Berenger. 'His esquire, William of Windsor, came to my town when he was heading for London one day, and saw me playing. He offered me the chance to go with him, and which boy wouldn't want to join an esquire? My father had been wondering what to do with me, because I had no skill with my hands, and no one wanted me as apprentice, so it seemed a good notion to put me with him and see whether I could learn the martial arts.'

'How long ago was that?'

'When I was six, so almost ten years ago.'

'You have enjoyed your service?'

'I would say yes, mostly. William of Windsor is a hard master, and he believes in teaching with a staff or a rope's end, but he is pious, so it is to be understood. He mortifies his own body as much as he does anyone else's.'

'But your esquire is now in the household of Sir Peter of Bromley?'

'Yes. My master was in the service of the Lord of Bromley, but when he died a year and a half ago, and Sir Peter was given the manor, my master and I joined his retinue.'

'Is it a good manor?'

'It's wonderful! The orchards are full each autumn with apples, plums and pears, and there is a separate nut garden, and roses and other flowers lend their fragrance all through the summer, and the house is magnificent and strongly defended, with a great wall set about it, high and with marvellous gates that would keep out even the—'

He stumbled to a halt, and Berenger could guess why. It would be treason to suggest that a property might be held against the King.

'Are there good estates to go with it?' he asked tactfully.

Relieved to be diverted from the dangerous line he had taken, the boy replied enthusiastically, 'Why, yes – the manor has many vills within it, all the way from . . .'

There was a sudden hiss and clatter. Berenger instantly slashed his reins over the rump of his mount, bellowing at the top of his voice, 'AMBUSH! Archers, *string your bows*! Jack, Clip, Oli: into the bushes and flank them. Earl, you stay with the new boys! Andrew, get back to the rest!' He flew back to meet with the others. A whirr and thud told him that an arrow had missed its mark and hit a tree nearby, and then he was sliding from the saddle, grabbing his bow as he went, stringing it with the speed born of long practice, and grasping a handful of arrows from the quiver at his saddlebag.

'With me!' he cried, and plunged into the woods.

He moved forward at a crouch, pushing the ferns and bushes aside with his bow, eyes fixed on the taller trees, warily watching the upper branches, aware too of the trunks in case an arrow was being aimed around one.

A prod in his back, and he turned slowly to see Jack touch his lips: *quiet*! He held up four fingers, jabbed upwards: four men in trees overhead. Berenger nodded, but frowned; he couldn't see anyone in the trees. He watched as Jack took a short detour to an oak. There he stopped, gazing intently overhead, and then, apparently satisfied, he nocked an arrow and leaned around the side of the tree. He drew and loosed in one easy, fluid movement, returning to the protection of the trunk even as Berenger heard the wet, unpleasant sound of an arrow striking and piercing a man's body. There was an exclamation, more a sob than a cry of pain, and Berenger heard something large falling through branches until it landed on the ground with a loud thud.

Berenger turned to Clip, but he had already moved away and stood behind another large tree. As Berenger watched, he nodded to Jack, and both turned, drew and loosed, and a yelp let Berenger know that another man was either hit, or severely startled by the nearness of a shaft. He rose and peered above him. There were two or three men still up there in the trees, but he hadn't seen them. It was a proof of how poor his eyesight was grown, the fact that both of his men had seen their targets, but he had not. A movement, and for a moment he thought he was a target, but then he saw it again and realised it was only a branch waving in the wind.

'Ready?' he called.

'Three, two, one . . .' he heard Jack count, and then two more whistling arrows were sent on their way. Jack's found its mark, and Berenger suddenly saw a man thrown back clutching at his breast, where the fletchings of an arrow-shaft had appeared. Clip's arrow had missed its mark.

'Two more!' Jack hissed.

But he was wrong. Even as the three made their cautious way forward, there came the sound of ropes and men sliding down, and then a loud crashing as their attackers blundered away through the undergrowth.

'Missed them,' Jack said, disappointed.

'Only the last pair. You haven't done badly, Jack,' Berenger said. He was stepping forward to where the first man had fallen from the tree. It took him a while to locate him, for he had tumbled into a mass of ferns and nettles, but then he saw a crushed section of plants and found the body just behind it.

The man was only young. Not yet in his middle twenties, at a guess. His pale brown eyes had remained wide open. A fly was already feasting on his left and Berenger waved it away with disgust before closing the dead man's lids. He hated to see flies on the dead. It reminded him that soon afterwards they were likely to be crawling over his food.

'Bring the others here,' he said.

When they had been gathered, he pointed at the body. 'This is the sort of danger we're exposed to now. We need to keep an eye on the trees as well as the bushes. If one outlaw gang can try to attack us, so can others.'

'Sir,' said the Pardoner, 'I'm sorry, but was it a quick death for him?'

Berenger glanced down at the head lying so nearly parallel to the body's shoulders where the neck had broken. 'Oh, yes. I think so.'

They were passing through a great plain two days later, and the lack of any apparent danger had affected all of them, making them relax their guard. That was when the next attack took place.

One moment they were riding moderately close together, and the next, a horde of men sprang out from nowhere, surrounding them all.

'*Back!*' Berenger screamed at his men. 'Jack, Clip – swords!'

There was no need for his order. Already he saw Clip's long-bladed knife flashing, and his horse was kicking and trying to escape. Meanwhile, Berenger himself had enough on his hands, with three men all clad in fustian and green riding straight at him. They tried to grab him from his horse, but then resorted to hacking and stabbing at him with a hatchet and two short swords. He was glad that none of them had a polearm. At close quarters like these, a man with a lance, or even a staff, could turf a man out of the saddle with ease. It was bad enough trying to block the men as it was. Their blades rose and fell, and it was only good fortune that led to the horse turning at the exact moment that one assailant was trying to hack at Berenger's leg. The blow went wide and struck the thick leather saddle instead. Swearing and cursing, Berenger crouched and aimed a cut at the man's head. It connected, slicing a thick swatch of scalp away, and the other men fell back, suddenly aware of their own danger. It was enough to give Berenger time to spur his petrified mount away from the scene.

He rode away, and as soon as he was safely distant, he pulled his bow free again. His mount was panting and whinnying, and when he looked, he saw that a long flap of flesh had been sliced from the beast's shoulder. He dismounted and strung his bow, pulled an arrow from his quiver and sent it into a man near Clip. The next he aimed at a man attacking the Earl, and that man also fell, but then he waited, the third arrow nocked and ready, watching the men fighting. There were some thicker-set fellows not far away, and he kept a wary eye on them, but they appeared to be watching just as he was, and not attempting anything.

However, there was no sign of either Horn or Andrew Retford, and he cast about anxiously for any sight of them. Jack's words came back to him now: that the men were not capable of defending themselves against a determined foe, and although he bitterly regretted not having been able to give them more training in the use of their arms, there was nothing to be done about it now.

A man stood, slamming a fist into the face of the Pardoner, and Berenger drew his bow. As the Pardoner slumped to the ground, his attacker lifted a dagger to stab him. Before his blow could fall, the shaft struck him under the armpit and disappeared. The whole of the clothyard had pierced him so that the shaft had flown through his body, pulling him away from Pardoner and leaving him squirming in the grass.

Clip and Jack were done with their assailants already, and were joining the other men. Berenger was sad to see the little man they had called the Wren suddenly jerk as a sword opened his throat wide and his blood sprayed thickly over other fighters, but he looked to be the last man to die. Then, with the ever-present threat of Berenger's bow, Jack's sword or Clip's long knife, the outlaws took the line of least danger and fled the field.

Andrew Retford lay panting in the long grass. He had been dragged from his horse early on, and stood up to draw his sword only to feel someone punch him in the back. When he turned, he found his legs were weak, and now he lay with a sense of faint puzzlement at the constriction in his chest. He could hear water from a small stream gurgling and chuckling merrily nearby, and his chest was making similar noises. There were loud cries and bellows from his friends. They would come to him soon, he was sure, but just now he was mostly aware of how his lungs seemed to fill with water. He felt as though he was drowning.

The grasses here were very long. As he coughed he could see them over him, their seed heads pale amber-coloured against the grey of the sky. Somewhere overhead he could hear a bird singing from a tree, and there, far off in the sky, was a buzzard, soaring easily. He could almost sense the wind under its wings, the feeling of joy in its heart. He remembered sitting under a tree back at the manor, looking up through the branches and seeing a hawk in the sky high overhead. It looked so free, so careless, that even as a youngster he had felt a pang of jealousy . . .

There was a quick pain in his chest, and Andrew Retford was free to fly at last.

Chapter Eighteen

Clip saw a body on the ground. It was an outlaw, and he thrust twice to make sure of the man before looking for others. The vintaine were all standing and panting, the sudden explosion of excitement and terror giving way to the lassitude that always assailed new recruits after their first battle. Clip himself could still feel the thrill coursing through his veins. There was something magnificent about surviving. Every time, life felt sweeter. The fact of living when others were dead made existing more precious.

He dropped and felt over the man's body. His purse held some coins, but not many. Still, better a few than none at all, he reflected. The man had a knife, too, stuck in a sheath about his neck. Clip pulled the thong from over the corpse's head and slipped it over his own, along with the little stone to whet it.

A snap of a twig, and Clip started up. Ahead, creeping around a bush, a man was staring at him. The face was familiar, with deep-set eyes in a curious, triangular-shaped face, but Clip couldn't tell where he might have seen him. Perhaps he had noticed the outlaw during the battle. In any case, the man was thirty paces away, and Clip had neither a bow and arrow to kill him, nor the inclination to run after him.

'Oh, just fuck off,' he shouted, waving an arm. The man gave him a thankful look, ducked, and bolted away like a startled rabbit.

'Wanker,' Clip muttered, and went on to the next body.

'Frip?' Jack said. 'You're not going to like this.'

'What?' Berenger made his way through the long grasses until he was at Jack's side, but then he stopped and stared at the body at their feet. 'Oh, shit.'

Clip was with them a moment later, whistling tunelessly through his teeth. The whistling ceased. 'Fuck! How did he die?'

There was no wound on his breast. 'Help me roll him over, Jack,' Berenger said. Then, 'That's how.'

'A stab wound in his back. That's not good,' Clip said. 'Ach, the poor bugger caught it when he was trying to run away.'

'He didn't get very far,' Jack mused.

'What was he doing over here anyway?' Berenger wondered. 'I didn't see. I was too busy with the fight.'

'I saw him being pulled from his horse, and then others crowded round to get at him,' Jack said. 'After that, I had to look to myself. Those bastards seemed to spring from nowhere.'

'They managed to kill the one man we were commanded to protect,' Berenger noted.

While the three were studying the body, John of Essex appeared. 'What's this? Oh, he's dead is, he? Should never have been sent. He couldn't handle a knife or sword to save his life.'

He stopped when he noticed all the others staring at him. 'What? It's the truth, isn't it?'

Berenger turned back to the corpse at their feet.

John of Essex peered down. 'What killed him?'

'He has a stab wound here,' Jack said.

They studied it, John of Essex craning his neck to view it from above. 'That looks like a dagger,' he said.

'Thank you, John, I think we realised that,' Berenger said with heavy irony.

'It's got the diamond shape.'

'Yes,' Jack said.

'One strike only,' Berenger said. 'And it looks like it was a downward blow. You can see where the blade moved here. The killer must have hit the shoulder-bone or a rib, and that sent the blade sideways.'

'He wouldn't have known much about it, anyway,' Jack said with rough kindness. 'It must have punctured his heart or lungs. That's what comes from running away.'

Berenger nodded. But in his mind's eye, he remembered Clip and Jack's bickering from the other day, when Retford alone of all the new recruits in the vintaine had stood his ground and not retreated nervously. The idea that he would turn and run was not credible.

Of course, someone in the outlaw gang could have slipped behind him and stabbed him – but the vintener could not help but wonder if Sir Peter was right.

Was it someone from the vintaine who had killed him?

'That was a nasty little skirmish,' the Pardoner said, and shivered.

John of Essex grunted. 'You think so? Nah, I've seen worse brawls after a good market-day football match where I come from.'

Berenger didn't look at him. They had brought the three bodies to lie in a row at the roadside: Horn, Wren and Retford, all with the same sad emptiness. Alive, the men had possessed vitality, and their spirits had given them strength and poise. Without the guiding soul within them, they were mere bags of bone and meat. Wren still wore a look of surprise, which could almost have been amusing, but for the eruption of blood that had smothered his breast and hosen. Horn looked dreadful. A war hammer had ended his life, the spike punching a hole deep into his skull and killing him instantly. Retford, by contrast, looked almost peaceful.

'We'll take them with us,' Berenger decided. 'It isn't far to York.'

John of Essex looked around at the empty countryside. 'Is there any point? We may as well . . .'

'They will receive a proper burial,' Berenger said firmly. As he spoke, Jack Fletcher stepped near to him. Jack had received a nasty cut to his brow that had left him with a bloody face, smeared where he had tried to wipe it away. It lent him a demonic appearance as he gave John a warning look. John glanced at him and submitted.

The ponies had scattered. Although they could not find one of them, the rest were discovered huddled anxiously in a little copse where a stream passed, and they were soon gathered together again. Wren's, when they threw his body over her back, became skittish, rolling her eyes and jerking her head at the stench of blood. Eventually Berenger snapped at the men to move the body to a different mount and put a live rider on her, and at last, shivering fearfully, she allowed Jack to soothe her. Berenger's own horse had to be slaughtered. The cut to her shoulder had gone too deep, and they had no time to try to let the wound heal. Already the flies were feasting when Jack took a poleaxe to her.

At last Berenger and the remains of his depleted command mounted their beasts and set off.

'Frip?' Jack said after a little.

'Yes?' Berenger didn't turn his head. His eyes were flitting from bush to bush, hedge to hedge, tree to tree as he sought any sign of a new ambush.

'Retford. Are you content about his death?'

'Content? No! I wanted to bring him safe to the Archbishop. Of course I am not pleased that I have failed in this, no.'

'I meant, his death.'

'What?' Berenger turned to him irritably. 'What is that supposed to mean?'

'I was talking to Aletaster, and he said that he saw the Saint and Retford run together. Yet the Saint now denies it.'

Berenger shrugged. 'Perhaps Aletaster was mistaken, or Saint and Retford only appeared to be together. You know as well as I do how a man will see one thing under pressure, when something else entirely happened. I've known it myself.'

'He was convincing.'

'So?'

'I just think we should keep an eye on the Saint. Perhaps the rumours of a spy were not so wide of the bull's eye, after all.'

Berenger turned his attention back to his study of the scenery. 'Keep your eyes on the Saint then, but watch all the other newcomers too. I don't know that I trust any of them yet. And I certainly don't care for Tyler. He's a more likely candidate than the others.'

That was a thought: he had made the comment from a simple dislike of Tyler, whom he had mistrusted ever since the long march from the coast to Crécy. Tyler had, so he suspected, tried to cause friction between Berenger's men and others in the King's army.

'I'll do that,' Jack said. 'You still don't trust him, then.'

'Would you?'

As they rode away, the man with the triangular face wiped the dirt from his brow and gave a sigh of relief.

That had been close. When the scrawny one had seen hm after

the fight it had felt like his heart was going to stop. The little prick could have easily killed him, or at the least summoned his comrades.

It was fortunate that Clip had not recognised him. He had feared that Clip might while the two of them stared at each other over the greensward. Clip had followed him that day back at Villeneuve-la-Hardie. It was his mentioning Clip to the heavy-set Carlisle man that had led to Clip's unpleasant immersion in the latrines. But perhaps that soaking had led him to forget the man he had followed. The vision of a great brute from Carlisle had entirely overridden his memory.

It was late the next afternoon that the vintaine reached the walls of York.

The city lay in the countryside like a great cancer, under a black fog of smoke from all the fires. Grey moorstone walls, lightened with occasional splashes of ochre or raw, red stains in the stone, encircled it. From their approach, Berenger could see the towers of the great church and spires of lesser churches, while outside the walls, suburbs of wattle and daub buildings had been hastily thrown up, some straggling as though for comfort up against the walls themselves.

He led his group along the road to the gates, and in beneath the vast gatehouse, and up along the street behind. It was narrow for the main street in such a large city: barely wide enough for two carts to pass, and Berenger and the men were forced to sit and wait impatiently when two sumptermen fell to arguing in the middle of the street. Overhead, the buildings jettied out, leaving only a narrow sliver of sky, and that, Berenger could see, was as grey as a slab of stone. Bad weather was on the way or he was a Gascon.

'Move yourself!' he called at last, irritated by the delay. At once he became aware of the attention of several people. Two were the sumptermen, one of whom cursed Berenger before realising that he had a vintaine behind him and swiftly buttoned his lips. But another group took notice, a half-dozen men with polearms and the tatty remnants of uniforms.

One, clearly their captain, eyed Berenger and the others with scowling interest before wandering over. He had a crop of black stubble sprouting on his jaw, a broken nose, and an overall appearance of competence with the weapons in his hand and at his belt. 'What are you doing here?' he asked.

Jack turned his mount and stared at the man, waiting for Berenger to comment.

Clip snorted, hawked and spat. 'Aye, we've ridden all the way up here to save the prickle, and now he wants to arrest us for it?'

'Silence, Clip,' Berenger said.

'We'll all get killed by our own, is all I'm saying,' Clip said, unruffled.

'Master, we are here to see the Archbishop with an urgent message from the King.' Berenger held up the message purse he had rescued from Retford's body.

'What's that?' the watchman demanded, pointing at Retford's body slumped over a pony.

'We have been attacked by felons. They killed three of our men. We need them buried.'

'The Archbishop doesn't demean his office by things like that.'

'Did you not hear me? I have messages from your King. Lead us to the Archbishop immediately.'

After a certain amount of reluctant arguing, the man finally agreed and took the vintaine towards the great cathedral church, but on the way Berenger saw a rough board hanging over a doorway, with a picture of a ferocious-looking wild boar painted on it. 'Jack, take the men in there and wait for me. I'll be back as soon as I've passed on the message. Hopefully then we can escape back south to sanity.'

Jack nodded, and after Berenger had paid one urchin to take the reins of two of the ponies with their cargoes of Wren and Horn, he followed after the watchman with the reins of the pony carrying the body of Retford loose in his hand.

He left the bodies on the ponies as he entered the cathedral's close, and soon he was at the Archbishop's hall.

'You have a message for me, I think?' the Archbishop said.

William de la Zouche was no doddering fool. He was the latest in a line of intelligent, strong men from his family, and political manoeuvring was in his blood. He waited while Berenger kissed his ring, and then nodded. 'You are from the King?'

'Yes, my lord. The King's message was being brought to you by a companion of mine, Andrew Retford, but I am afraid he was killed when my party was attacked.'

'When was this?'

'A day and a half ago. We were waylaid by two groups of men, but the last killed three of my vintaine, including Retford.'

The Archbishop took the small rolled vellum and read it quickly, a frown puckering his brows. 'This says that French ships have sailed for Scotland, and that you saw them?'

'I did, my lord.'

'Then speak! When did you see them – where – how many were there? Tell me everything, and speak quickly! We have just heard that the Scots have broken over the border and are heading towards Carlisle.'

CHAPTER NINETEEN

Archibald worked at his gonne, cleaning the inner barrel with a lambswool swab soaked in oil. Standing in a muddy field waiting for something to happen, he was as content as a man could be. He had known muddier fields and filthier weather. However, it was important to keep the two boys busy. Georges and Ed needed constant supervision when they hung around too close to the powder, and when they had no work to do, he was worried about what they might get up to. An army was not a safe place for lads of their age.

His ruminations were interrupted by Sir John de Sully, who appeared with his esquire.

'Master Gynour, I hope I see you well?'

'Aye, I am well indeed, Sir Knight. Just seeing to my little toy here.'

'You spoke to me of a larger beast that you could use.'

Archibald set down his swab and turned to face the knight. 'Sir?'

'We can send a ship to fetch it. When could you be ready to sail?'

'Any time now, sir.'

Sir John nodded. 'You will sail to fetch it and bring it back here to set it up at the harbour mouth and destroy all ships trying to force their way to the Calesian harbour.'

'I'll need more powder, too,' Archibald said.

'Bring all you require.'

'One thing: I must have men here to guard the gonnes and the powder while I'm away.'

'I will set guards myself,' Sir John promised, and soon afterwards took his leave.

Archibald picked up his swab again, whistling happily. The knight was obviously one of those who held a superstitious fear of Archibald's trade. No matter. He was confident of his own unique expertise.

'Donkey!' he bawled as he swabbed.

Ed and his new friend appeared.

He would leave the boy behind, he thought. Béatrice would be able to look after the guns with Ed's help. Especially now that Marguerite and Georges were here as well.

'You may not realise it, you scruffy little churls, but you are looking at the man who could just be the saviour of the siege here. Me and my little toys will help to end it quickly – and in our favour!'

'We'll all get killed,' Clip droned. 'Why is it always us at the sharp end?'

'Shut it, Clip,' Jack said.

'It's fine for ye to tell me to shut it, but what'll happen when you're in the front line with ten thousand hairy-arsed Scotch bastards running at you with their pikes ready? Ye'll change your tune then,' Clip said with satisfaction.

'If you don't shut the fuck up, I'll throw you at them to carry their points,' Jack said nastily, 'and then I won't have to listen to your moaning and maundering.'

'Oh, aye. That'll help you. And how will ye fight without me? It's me has given you the backbone to fight,' Clip boasted.

'Sweet Mother of God,' Jack said, rolling his eyes.

'Give it a rest, Clip,' the Aletaster put in. 'You think we want to listen to your constant blather?'

Jack turned to him and gave him a cold look. 'Have you stood in a line yet? In battle? Then keep your trap shut. Clip has fought more battles than you've . . .' his face twisted. 'I was going to say, than you've had hot meals, or you've drunk ales, but neither would be true for a fat git like you, would it? Until you've held your place in the line with the others and pricked your targets as they run at you, and fought them off with your axe or sword, you keep your gob shut and your thoughts to yourself.'

'That's right,' Clip said happily, grinning malevolently at Aletaster.

'*Shut up*, Clip!' Jack said.

'Why do I care? You'll all get killed,' Clip said.

Berenger grinned to himself as he jogged along. He had been given a fresh pony by the Bishop, and now he and the rest of his vintaine were riding to the muster at Richmond.

'I can't listen to Clip for another minute. If I hear that we're all going to die one more time, I'll kill him myself,' Jack said savagely.

'You'll have push past me to get to him first,' Berenger said.

'What do you reckon to this, Frip?' Jack asked a moment later.

'What, the muster? The Scots have seen their chance. King Edward is wallowing in the mud about Calais, so King David thinks he can carve out a chunk of the North of England for himself. It'll be the same as the Scots always do: they'll ride fast and steal all the cattle, sheep and plunder they can get their hands on, and then run before we can catch them.'

'So you don't think they'll be in the mood for a fight?'

'They haven't wanted to fight us since Hallidon Hill, have they? No, they are in it for all they can snatch,' Berenger said dismissively. 'I've fought against them before. They rarely risk an actual battle against us, because they know they'll lose. They don't possess the equipment and armour that we have.'

'Aye, that's true,' Jack said with every appearance of satisfaction.

The Earl had been listening. Now he urged his pony forward to join in the conversation. 'There is one aspect that gives me pause, I fear,' he said. 'The ships that you saw, Vintener: I've heard it said that the French could have sent men to aid the Scots in an attack. If so, surely our King must draw his men away from Calais. He could not suffer an army to trample over his northern marches.'

'What do you know of the Scots and French?' Jack scoffed. 'You're only a rich boy from London.'

'How do you make that out?' Earl asked.

'Your accent, your behaviour, everything.'

'You are from London, aren't you?' Berenger said.

'Yes. I am from the city. My father was a goldsmith, but he never really got on with others in the trade, and so although I was apprenticed for some time, it wasn't a job I felt comfortable with. It was the way he was treated, I suppose.'

'What happened to you?' Berenger said.

'I was in London last year when the riots started. You remember that – when the apprentices went on the rampage? It was something to behold. I was with them, and it meant I got in with a crowd of rebellious fools. But the real fool was me. I trusted them, but my trust was misplaced. There were two or three ringleaders, and they had great ideas when they were drunk. Talked about all kinds of nonsense, including, I'm afraid, capturing the

Mayor of London and tarring him because of his treatment of apprentices. But what I didn't know was, one of the men coming up with these ideas was himself a paid employee of the Mayor. So when I agreed, I was arrested and thrown into the gaol at Newgate.'

'I've heard of that,' Jack said, nodding. 'Not a good place.'

The Earl shuddered briefly. 'There, you speak the truth. It was a hell-hole if ever there was one. And I was going to be forced to stay there a long time. I had lost my apprenticeship after that, so I volunteered to join the King's army when I heard that I would be pardoned if I did. So here I am.'

'You look as though you are too old to have been apprenticed recently,' Jack said suspiciously.

'At Newgate, you grow old very quickly,' the Earl told him.

'That doesn't explain why you think you know so much about Scotland,' Jack said.

'All I know is, when we were at Calais, I heard someone talking about the French. There were rumours that they were supplying the Scots with armour and weapons in return for them attacking England. The Scots are always happy to fight, but they want to fight on their terms. This time, they want money and the chance to kick the English King while he's away.'

'You heard all this at Calais?' Berenger said.

'Everyone was talking about it. I'm surprised you didn't hear.'

Jack and Berenger exchanged a look. Soldiers were always talking to each other, most often to complain and bicker, but occasionally one or two could pick up a nugget of decent information. Perhaps this was accurate.

'I don't know,' Berenger sighed after a while. 'I have a feeling that the ships may not even have been heading to Scotland. They were probably supply ships and the French wanted to replenish them to break the siege at Calais. For all we know, they may have attempted to get to the town while we've been travelling up here. That would be ironic.'

They reached Richmond the following day. Berenger and the men were eager to find a place to sit and rest while they waited for news of the French, but before they could take their ease, the Archbishop sent a man to them.

'You are Berenger?' he enquired. 'The Archbishop has asked that you come to see him.'

Berenger left the men, telling Jack to see them quartered and fed, and followed the messenger. He found the Archbishop prowling in his tent like a great cat. He looked up with a scowl as Berenger entered, and then resumed his slow pacing.

There were four other men in the room: two knights and two clerks, one a personal secretary to the Archbishop, the other a harried-looking man who dealt with other administrative matters for the Archbishop. As usual with such a senior political figure, all the time while Berenger and the others were talking, a constant stream of men were passing in and out of the tent, bringing messages to the harassed clerk, who then passed some to the Archbishop for his approval. Berenger had to listen carefully. All present spoke in the harsh, guttural dialect of the north. To his ear, they sounded like the Scots themselves.

'Vintener, these are Sir Henry Percy and Sir Ralph Neville. While I am Warden of the East March, my friends are commanders of the northern armies and responsible for the defence of the kingdom. You will tell them all you have said to me.'

Berenger quickly retold his story of the ships. Before he had finished, Percy was already talking. He was a heavy-set man of average height, with thick thighs and shoulders, as befitted a man who had spent his entire life battling with the Scots on the borders. His fair hair and pale grey eyes gave him the appearance of a genial nature, but that was belied by the sharpness of his tongue. The Percys had ruled Northumbria since the Conqueror's time, protecting their lands from Scottish invasions too often to count. While some men were keen to avoid fights by paying the 'black rents' – money to ensure that their farms and estates would not be despoiled – the Percys preferred to take to their horses, sword in hand, and attack those who would seek to rob them. This Percy was cast in that mould.

'So you tell us that the French may have sent ships to Scotland. Why so? To tell them to assault us, to pay for them to attack, or to provide them with equipment to help them attack?'

'I would consider all three most likely.' This was Neville, a man some ten years older than Percy. He had brown hair turning grizzled, and a square, rugged face. His beard was thick, and he scratched at it as he spoke like a man unused to the feel. 'The French no doubt demanded that their allies should attack at once.'

'The King will not wish to send back even a portion of his men, no matter what,' Percy said.

'Of course not!' the Archbishop exclaimed. 'And nor should he.'

'It would help to know what the Bruce intends,' Neville said.

'He intends to bring about bloody disaster on the North of England,' Percy said with disgust. 'He would see it laid waste. He's already ravaged all the farms from Durham to the March. No freeman will go there now – not with the risk of losing wealth, cattle and life.'

'Then we must gather our strongest force and make our way to meet him,' the Archbishop said heavily.

'Aye, but we needs must gain information. How many men does he have, how does he array his fighters, are they fed and healthy, do they have enough horses and ponies . . .'

The Archbishop was approached by his clerk and bent his head to listen as the clerk spoke quickly. 'I see. Sir Henry, Sir Ralph: we have an informant! A man has just arrived and has asked to speak with us. He may be able to help us.'

'Bring him in,' Sir Henry said.

A short while later, the tent's flap was opened and Berenger grasped his sword as he recognised the smiling face of Jean de Vervins.

'He's French!' Berenger blurted out.

'This man,' the Archbishop said, 'has come over with the ships you saw. He can tell us all about the ships, the Frenchmen with the ships, and the weapons. *And* he can tell us all the Scottish dispositions.'

CHAPTER TWENTY

Ed was glad to be left behind. There were some new guards set about the place, mostly foolish men who ruffled Ed's hair and embarrassed him by joking about his age and height whenever they had the chance, but so long as Béatrice didn't see, he didn't care.

He was enjoying his time with Georges, although the boy was oddly quiet on occasion. Well, Ed had lost a father and family when the French attacked his town, so he could understand how his friend might feel. Georges was lucky that he and his mother had been reunited. There were plenty of lads who had lost their families and never found them again, and many whose families had all been killed.

Not that Ed was overly worried by Georges. He spent most of his time helping Béatrice. He carried the heavier buckets for her, he lit the fire for her, he inserted himself between her and the barrels when they must be moved, anticipating her every move so as to save her efforts. And when he was not working with her, he shot sly glances at her. He loved the line of her throat when she sat at her ease, the way that the sunlight played about her eyelashes, the little dent in the left of her brow where a scar marred the perfect symmetry, the swelling of her breasts – oh, how he would like to rest his head there! But his love for her – and he knew it was love – was not mere foolishness or lust. It was almost religious. He revered her in the way a priest adores the Blessed Virgin. She was, to him, feminine perfection. And he wanted to possess her.

Georges had no idea. He was too young, and Ed dare not confide in him, but he was sure that Marguerite had noticed his infatuation. She smiled at him in a sad manner, as though thinking that he could never aspire to Béatrice, but Ed knew differently. He could win her heart – he *would*! One day, she would recognise his love for what it truly was: the wholesome affection of a mature lover. And on that day, she would come to him.

'Donkey? Are you awake?' Georges called to him.

Startled, Ed felt embarrased when the two women looked over to him. He reddened in an instant, before grumpily going over to Georges and almost snarling, 'What?'

His friend stared at him. 'Is something wrong?'

'Look, you wouldn't understand,' Ed said, but then, glancing at Béatrice again, he felt he could not keep his secret any longer. He had to tell someone, or he would burst. 'Look, it's just that . . .'

'What's that slimy little fucker doing here?' John of Essex demanded. 'We ought to rip his balls off as a reminder of our time in Calais!'

'I am only here to help,' Jean de Vervins said. His slim features wore that cheerful smile again, the one that made Berenger want to punch him.

'You only ever wanted to make money out of people,' Jack said coldly. 'Don't think we'll trust you.'

'I don't care whether you do or not. The main thing is that the Archbishop values my assistance. I have proved myself to be very useful.'

'Oh? And what have you been doing then?'

'Since seeing you in Calais, my friends, I journeyed with the ships you saw and I have been living with the Scottish. They appreciate the help of people, after all. They know that all France is on their side.'

'And that means you too, eh?' John of Essex thundered. He leaped to his feet and would have thrown himself at the smiling Frenchman, had not Jack and the Earl grabbed him and held him back. 'Let me get to him! He would have seen us executed, damn his soul!'

'That is true. But now, you see, we need to work together. You may not like me, but I can at least help you and the others,' Jean said. 'My information is very important.'

'More to the point,' Berenger told his men, 'we have orders to protect him. I don't like it any more than you do, Jack, but the Archbishop is convinced that this man is going to be useful to the campaign.'

'Did you tell him what this prick tried to do to us?'

Berenger didn't answer. There was no need. He had expostulated at length when he had been told to protect Jean de Vervins, but all to no avail. 'They don't give a damn. As far as they're concerned, the only thing that matters is that Jean survives until the battle – and there will be one. We're to pack and leave as soon as possible.'

'I'll rip his head off his scrawny shoulders,' John of Essex snarled. 'What? You want us to protect this piece of shit?'

'We have no choice, do we, Frip?' Jack asked.

Berenger sighed, shaking his head. 'No choice at all, no. The bastard has us by the short and curlies. After the death of Retford, we can't take any risks. You hurt Jean, or let someone else hurt him, John, and I'll personally castrate you. We can't lose him as well.'

'Well, that's just wonderful!' Clip said. He had been listening carefully as the others argued. Now he tipped his head to one side and eyed Jean with distaste. 'So in order to save ourselves from an accusation of spying, we have to protect a spy.'

'Ah, but at least I am a spy for you. I am on your side,' Jean beamed.

'At the moment,' Berenger said grimly. 'But if I think you've turned to work for the French against us again, I'll cut your head off before John can get to you.'

They were mounted and riding again that same afternoon. The muster had quickly gathered together all the spare men from Cumberland, Lancashire and Northumberland, although the men from Yorkshire had not reached them yet. The Archbishop was keen to get moving as soon as possible, and he sent messages to the Yorkshiremen to march straight to Durham and meet him there. It was at Durham, Berenger learned, that the English were determined to stop the Scots.

'They have already despoiled the lands all the way to Carlisle, where the populace have paid the Scots their black rent,' Jean de Vervins told him.

One of Lord Neville's men was riding nearby. Hearing this, the lanky youth with a shock of brown hair laughed. 'The men of Carlisle told them to fuck off and leave them alone!'

Jean de Vervins nodded, but without humour. 'Before that, they laid siege to Liddell Strength for three days. Sir Walter Selby was there, and on the fourth day, they took the place. King David has always hated Sir Walter, because he promised to serve the Scots but then reneged and submitted to King Edward II, our King's father. Since our King took the throne, Sir Walter's remained utterly loyal.'

'But the Scots took the place?' Jack asked.

'They destroyed it. King David had the two sons of Sir Walter brought before him and had them strangled in front of their father, before killing him too – unshriven.' He said slowly, 'I was there. I saw this.'

'Whatever he's done, he'll pay for it,' Berenger said, 'just as I will, and you too, Jean. But to kill his boys and then him – that speaks of a cruelty beyond belief.'

A short time later, Jean spurred his horse to go and speak with another vintaine of men, and Jack leaned over to Berenger.

'That man Jean brought this news to the Bishop? He is a spy for England now?'

'That is what he says. Perhaps he always was.'

John of Essex, who was close by, said, 'I would never trust a spy. After all, who can tell when a man of dishonour is likely to change and spy for your enemies again?'

The noise of the men marching, the plodding steps of the ponies and hobelars, the squeaking and jingling of accoutrements and harnesses, of thousands of swords rattling in cheap sheaths, the clinking of mail coats and armour, built to a cacophony in Berenger's ears as he and his vintaine jerked and rolled towards Durham. All the way, the vintener was thinking of Jean de Vervins. The man was dangerous, he knew, but there was no way of telling just how dangerous. He had no loyalty to the Scottish, so far as Berenger knew, but he was born to a family in France, and surely he must feel *some* loyalty to his King?

After witnessing the depredations of the English army in France, it was very unlikely that any Frenchman would change his allegiance. All along their route to Paris and thence up to Crécy, the English had burned, looted, pillaged and raped. Even a Frenchman with water for blood would find it boiling to see the damage the English had inflicted. It was hard enough for Berenger. Whenever he saw a dead child or woman, he'd think it could have been his daughter, his son, his wife lying there in the dirt, surrounded by the charred timbers of a home. He was glad on those occasions that he had never married, never fathered his own children. If he was French, he would not allow a day to pass before joining the French King's armies to avenge those sights. Was it really possible that Jean could view the slaughter and devastation with equanimity? Perhaps he sought only to line his pockets? After all, a man who delivered his own countrymen and their allies to the King should be handsomely paid. But assuredly, a treacherous mercenary like that would find judgement in the afterlife.

'You do not like me, do you?' Jean said now, seeing Berenger's eye light upon him.

'It's not my place to like or dislike you. I have been ordered to protect you.'

'You should be glad of my aid. I saved you in France, you know.'

'I saw you. I heard you. What was it you said? We needed a miracle to escape?'

'And I provided it. I spoke with Chrestien de Grimault and showed him how he could recover his honour by saving you and the others. It was, I think, a flash of genius.'

'It had more to do with the man's chivalry. He was honourable. He wouldn't change sides for money.'

'You think so?' Jean chuckled softly, but then his tone hardened. 'My friend, this is a matter of war, not honour. Do you think there is honour when you are looking at a butchered family? When you see a mother, raped and slaughtered before her husband and sons? When a man has to witness three, four, five men raping his daughter? No, there is no honour in war – not for peasants and free men. Only death. Chrestien is a mercenary like me. He takes his ships wherever the money is best, and he delivers victory to the men who pay him. Occasionally he sees fit to take a different path to his rewards. That is what he did for you. But do not make a mistake. We are all the same.'

'I am *not*!' Berenger spat. 'I fight for my King!'

'Would you be here, if you were not permitted to take plunder? Would you be here if you did not see a way to make more money in six weeks than you would make in a year?' Jean de Vervins sneered. 'No, you are no different from me. And you know it.'

CHAPTER TWENTY-ONE

They halted at Barnard's Castle, a mingling of men, carts, ponies and horses. Knights bellowed at esquires, esquires shouted at yeomen, and everyone shouted at the boys.

To Berenger it looked like a miserable kind of place. He was used to the lush greenery of the south, but here all looked bleak and grey, with flurries of fog moving all about as if it was a city of wraiths. The superstitious notion was enough to trigger a physical reaction: a shiver ran down his back. He pushed the idea to the back of his mind. The vintaine had more to worry about than some figment of imagination. There were real soldiers out there, somewhere ahead of them. And from all he had heard, it was a large force the Scottish had sent.

As he rode onwards, Berenger frowned to hear a shrill cry. It came from behind a low wall, and he turned to investigate, but a couple of men-at-arms blocked his path.

'I'm a vintener with the army,' he said. 'What's going on?'

The older of the two, a man of around thirty with a thin face that carried a woeful expression, said, 'We've been told to keep people away, sir.'

'What is going on?' Berenger repeated. 'Come, answer me!'

'They caught a Scotsman. They're questioning him.'

Berenger stared at the man, and then, as another scream tore through the air, he rode on towards the sound. The two guards lifted their lances as though to prevent him, but the mass of the vintaine was with him, and the two were forced from their path.

It was too late to do anything for the lad. From his face, he might have been only twenty, and from his build, he had been both fit and strong. Now, as Berenger reached him, the last breath rasped from his ravaged throat.

The men at his bloodied torso shrugged and wiped their blades clean, pushing aside the strips of flesh they had flayed from his stomach and breast as they packed their bags.

'What were you doing?' Berenger demanded, and the two gave him a look much as a butcher would give an ox. One was sallow and older, clad in leather and linen, while the other looked a simple boy with a cast in one eye and a curious way of holding his head, as if he had been injured and never fully recovered.

The older man said, 'We were questioning him. He was one of the Scotch murderers and we were told to get all we could from him.'

'Except he didn't know anything,' his partner said with a giggle.

'And he told us that before we started!' the other one smirked.

Berenger felt his anger mount. He had seen death in many forms, but the sight of this body, lying broken and savaged like this, was worse than seeing a wild animal's victim. He opened his mouth to curse the torturers both to Hell and beyond, but before he could do so, he heard his name being called.

'Vintener Berenger, to me!'

He turned to see Sir Henry Percy waving at him. Nothing loath, he left that ugly scene, and as he passed the vintaine, he muttered, 'Jack, keep the men all together and wait for me.'

'Yes, Frip.'

Berenger kicked his pony into a trot. 'My lord, did you know what they were doing there?'

'The two executioners? Aye. We found a scout and had to learn what he knew.' Henry Percy gave him a quick once-over. 'Master Fripper, I know damn all about ye, but I do know of Sir John de Sully, and I trust him. I believe he is yer master?'

'I serve Sir John, my lord, yes.' Berenger was still shivering from the sight of the boy's body. The way the men had torn the flesh from his body, the way . . .

'Then I can trust ye. The fact is, most of the experienced men aren't here, man. They are down at Calais with the King. He has taken the best of all fighters and commanders wi' him, and we have been left with the dregs. Ye can see that for ye'self.'

Berenger said nothing. Percy was gazing around with the eye of a professional warrior, assessing the men all about him. His tone was not that of a man complaining, but of a commander taking stock.

'You fought under the King at this place called Crécy?'

'Aye.' Berenger took a deep breath and forced himself to listen.

'How was it?'

'We fought hard for our victory, but it was a powerful proof of the King's strategy. We were greatly outnumbered.'

'Where were you placed?'

'On the left flank. He had archers and gonnes set out at either side, men-at-arms on foot between them. Before us all we had dug many pits to trip their mounts and make them stumble or fall, too.'

'So the French charged the men, and were destroyed by the archers before they could come to blows?'

'For the most part, yes. They only managed to reach us after the failure of many charges, and then they were hampered by the bodies as much as by our pits.'

'Right. Ye know yer part. I'm giving ye a new post, man. My captain has fallen from his mount. The brute threw him and he's broken his pate. Christ's Saints may know whether he'll heal, but I don't! Pick yer best man and make him vintener. I'm making ye captain, and giving ye the command of the archers on my flank. Don't make a ballocks of this, man. Ye hear me? We'll either win a glorious victory here or be slaughtered, and be sure, these Scotch gits won't help ye up if ye trip. I've been fighting wi' them a' my life, and they'll cut their own hand off at the wrist, rather than help an Englishman.'

'Yes, my lord,' Berenger said. He looked about him, stunned. He had not expected to be given a new post. To be made captain was far beyond his expectations.

'Like I said, man, don't fuck this up! Now, get to yer men and . . .'

Just then, a rider appeared, whipping at his horse as he thundered through the mists, and only when he was in the thick of the Archbishop's army did he appear to notice the men. Berenger could see his startled expression as he took in the sight of the troops all about him – but then he looked at the Archbishop of York's banner, and the banner of Ralph Neville, with its gules and a saltire argent, and the blue lion rampant for Henry Percy – and the rider seemed to sag in his saddle as he realised that he was at last safe.

'My lords, the Scottish are approaching!'

Within an hour, the army was formed into three battles, with archers on either flank, and the long columns began the last march.

'It's all right for the captains,' Clip moaned. 'Ye'll have the pick o' the plunder, won't ye? We poor whoresons'll get nothing but a knife in the guts.'

'The poor man who stabs you will lose his blade, Clip,' Berenger said. 'You're so full of bile and piss, your blood will eat away any metal before you could die. You're safe from all danger, man.'

'D'ye think so? Well, *I* think it's more likely the lot of us will die. We're all marching to our graves,' Clip said cheerfully. 'Aye, well, it's been good to know ye, Frip. When I get to Heaven, I'll look down on ye, and think, *Aye, he was always a little chilly. Poor man'll be warm enough now*.'

'I could have you flogged for insolence. Don't forget I'm a captain now,' Berenger laughed.

'Oh, aye, a captain, eh? Remember you'll have to organise all these losers now,' Clip said sagely.

John of Essex was looking about him. 'There's some handy fellows here,' he said thoughtfully.

'Do you think we can make enough of them into archers, though?' Berenger mused. 'Jack, you're vintener here. Send men to speak with all the other vinteners and bring them to see me. I need to find out what sort of fighting men we have.'

'Yes, Frip,' he said, and hurried off.

'Do we know where we are going?' John of Essex asked.

'It's only a few miles to Durham. I think that's where the Archbishop intends to meet with the Scots,' Berenger said. 'We'll be there tomorrow, and then we'll see what's happening.'

'What is the news of them?' Jack asked.

'We know the Scots spent four days taking Liddell when they slew Sir Walter Selby and his family, so they're not in a hurry.'

'Why? Usually the Scots will ride fast and steal what they can, won't they?' Jack said.

'Yes,' Jean de Vervins said. He had joined them and now stood nearby. 'But this time they are not here for plunder and theft alone. They are trying to force the King to send troops away from Calais. Perhaps they think he will raise the siege? Even if he only sends a portion of his men, that would make it easier for the French to break the siege. The longer the Scottish take, the happier they'll be. It will give time for King Edward to send more men.'

'But when we were trying to tempt the French to attack us in France, we sped along in a fine hurry,' Clip said.

'We wanted to do as much damage as possible to show the French that they could not rely on their own King to defend them,' Berenger said. 'The faster we went, the clearer it became that their King must come and stop us. Here, the Scots want time for the news to spread so that King Edward must choose to split his forces.'

'Will he?' the Pardoner asked.

Berenger glanced at him. 'What do you think? When has our King worried about distractions when he has his mind fixed on a goal?'

'So the King will stay at Calais? He won't come to protect the north? You mean we're all there is to stop the Scots?' John of Essex asked, aghast.

'Never mind about the Scots,' the Earl said, gazing around with distaste, 'my concern is all the uncouth fellows on our side. This mass of stinking, hairy humanity is terrifying enough!'

'So, you are enjoying your new duties?' Jean de Vervins asked later.

Having spent the last hours with the vinteners of the archers on the flank, Berenger was returning tired but reassured. This force would acquit themselves with honour, he thought. All were heading now to where the messenger had said the Scots would be found, while scouts were riding in all directions to track their enemy.

Berenger held his gaze for a moment longer than necessary. He saw again Dunkirk and the two English sailors' bodies kicking and thrashing as they slowly had the life throttled from them, and if he could, he would have happily taken his dagger and plunged it into the Frenchman's breast there and then. 'You're fortunate to be alive now,' he said. 'I wouldn't lift a finger to help you if I could avoid it.'

'Such a sad position to be in – to want to see a man dead, and to be forced to keep him alive,' Jean de Vervins chuckled to himself. 'But make no mistake. When you were told to keep me alive, it was for a worthwhile reason. I will be valued above all the men in this army if I succeed. Indeed, your King would value me above all the lands about here.'

'You? What service can you give our King?' Berenger scoffed.

'You would be surprised. There are opportunities for a man like me.' Jean de Vervins leaned back in his saddle and surveyed the road ahead. 'Look at all this land here. It is verdant, yes? With animals, with good husbandry, with men, it will bring in a fortune. But allow war to rear its head, such as now – and look about you! Where are the peasants? All have fled, taking their belongings, their cattle and sheep with them. And as a result, this land is valueless, because the peasants are not here to work it. So, war destroys not only all in its path, its *rumour* alone destroys.'

'What of it?'

'I am working against the French. Wherever the French expect to have income, I will help destroy it. With no money for the peasants and townspeople, there is no tax. With no tax, the French King has no income, and with no income he has no army, no friends, no supporters – *rien*! All that, I provide for your King. So that, when he wishes, he will be able to march about the whole of France as his own Kingdom. I will give that to him.'

'You're talking ballocks,' Berenger told him, but there was something about the easy confidence of the Frenchman that inspired belief.

'No, my friend. Within a few months I should have conspired to give your King at least one city, and such a blow to the French Crown that the King himself must be toppled.'

'Why?' Berenger asked.

'What?'

'I said: *why*? Why do you do this. Is it only the money?'

For a moment Berenger saw an expression of hatred fly across the Frenchman's face.

'Never mind why. It is enough that I do it. My duty is to provide cities for your King, and your duty is to guard me so that I may do so swiftly and without trouble.' He spurred his pony and rode on.

Berenger looked after him thoughtfully. He had seen that expression. Fleeting though it had been, he was certain that it had not been directed towards the English or the French.

It was a very personal self-loathing.

CHAPTER TWENTY-TWO

It was infuriating that she continued to treat him like a foolish child – or worse, like a younger brother.

Ed the Donkey felt particularly aggrieved that day, not because he had been given too much work to do, which was his usual complaint when Archibald was about, but because Béatrice had told him to go and 'play' with Georges. *Play!* As though he was nothing more than a child. After the last month, she should realise that he was a man, a fighter in a man's world. He had seen men killed on the battlefield, he had seen Jack and others use their long *misericorde* daggers, the 'mercies', to put injured men out of their pain – yet she still looked upon him as a mere boy.

'Have I upset you?' Georges said. He had that look of anxiety and fear again.

'No. I just wish she understood that I'm not a kid like you,' Ed said without thinking.

He wished he could take back his words as soon as he spoke. Georges' eyes brimmed, and his lip began to quiver as Ed's words sunk in. Guilt made Ed vicious.

'See? I can't even speak to you without you bursting into tears. Cry baby!'

Georges turned away, and Ed tried to catch his shoulder, to apologise, to say something kinder and more sympathetic – but the younger boy snatched his shoulder away.

And then he stopped. Ed saw him looking at someone in the crowd. A man was standing there, a cleric, who smiled at them and came over. He gazed from one boy to the other with eyes that seemed all-knowing. 'My sons, this is not the time or place for a quarrel. Come, shake hands, and promise me that you will be bosom companions. If boys like you cannot be friends, what hope is there for the rest of the world?'

Ed took the hand he proffered, and kissed the ring. Georges did the same, with more eagerness.

'That is good, my young friends. I shall pray for you and watch over you both,' the cleric promised.

'*Up*, you lazy, whoring sons of dogs! Stop dreaming about your sluts at home – you have work to do. Up!'

Berenger strolled about the archers. Most were already awake and stowing their blankets, donning satchels and hats, scratching armpits and groins, and the air was full of the sound of men coughing, hawking, spitting, cursing, groaning and occasionally barking orders.

There was a small cask of wine in the cart provided for the vintaine's use. While the smell of the oat cakes cooking rose, Berenger filled a wooden mazer and he went to squat near the men.

'You still come to talk to your old companions, then, Frip?' Tyler said. He was sitting on a saddle on the ground, whittling with his knife at a long stick.

'Captain Fripper to you, Archer!' Berenger said coldly, then grinned. 'Jack, how are the new ones getting on?'

'They all got a decent night's sleep. I made sure they woke in good time, too, so they should be fine.'

'Right. I've been thinking. When we go into the line, I will be in the middle of the archers, but I'd like you to take the vintaine out towards the far flank. Listen out for my orders and repeat them as loudly as you can so that the archers all about us hear. With luck, we'll be able to give commands efficiently enough.'

'How do you think we should dispose the new men?'

'I'd keep them at the front until we see how they respond. The last thing we need is to have some fool release his bow into our front rank just because he let his nerves get on top of him. Better to keep them for'ard and have them shoot directly at the enemy. We know our old hands will be able to control themselves and their arrows. We need to keep them safe.'

'Aye.'

Berenger didn't add, but he knew Jack was thinking it too: having the new recruits in the front would provide a protective wall of weaker fighters when the hand-to-hand struggles began. The experienced archers would be protected for a while by the novices. It was better to sacrifice a number of those than valuable, battle-hardened warriors.

A fine mist was wisping about the trees as the men finally kicked over the morning fires and prepared to march. A horn blew, then two more, and men began to mount their beasts and prepare for the morning's journey.

'Where to now, Frip?' Jack called.

Berenger was sitting beside Jean de Vervins once more. He waved a hand as the columns of men began to trudge onwards. 'Where do you think? To Durham!' he called.

The mist was thickening nearer the river, and as they passed by that morning, Berenger grew worried in case the men at the back decided to run away. Desertion was always a problem for any army, but for a force like this, when the weather gave such a perfect cover, many would be tempted to flee. No one could be thought a fool for trying to make a run for it and escape death. Berenger trotted back a short distance and cast a look over his shoulder. He could see a winding line of men on foot and on horseback, plodding onwards with their heads down for the most part, but now and again he saw a man whose gaze had strayed to the bushes and trees and who, when Berenger caught his eye, shamefacedly looked away.

Muttering a curse under his breath, Berenger rode back along the line of archers to where Jack sat uncomfortably on his pony. He had never been a natural rider.

'Jack, bring the vintaine with you. I want you at the rear of the column.'

'Why?'

'Too much risk of losing men in this weather,' Berenger said.

Jean de Vervins had overheard. 'You don't trust your own men, Captain?' he sneered. 'What does *that* say for the courage of the English soldier?'

Berenger didn't answer that, but commanded, 'You stay here, Vervins – right here in the line,' wheeled his pony about, and led the way.

They pulled the vintaine out of the line and trotted back to the rear, where they reformed. 'Keep an eye on your own men, Jack,' Berenger added quietly. 'We don't want to lose any of them either.'

'You can leave them with me,' Jack said.

'I'd best get back to that damned Frenchman,' Berenger said reluctantly. He already missed his own vintaine. Having command of the whole mass of archers on this side of the army was a shocking promotion for him. Back here with his own, it felt as though he had returned to the cradle of his family. Least of all did he want to spend time with that repellent fool Jean de Vervins.

'Go on, Frip. Godspeed!' Jack chuckled.

Berenger cursed him mildly, and was about to spur his pony, when he heard something behind him. 'What's that?'

'Nothing, Frip.'

'I heard harness, I'm sure,' Berenger said. 'Some fuckwit deserter's wandered right back into the column.'

'We'd have noticed a deserter,' Jack argued.

The fog had been bad, but now it was thinning slightly. Peering back through the mist Berenger could see the shape of a man. 'There he is, the arse.'

He had lifted his reins to slap his beast's rump, when he saw that the one man had become several. It must be the Yorkshiremen who had missed the muster at Richmond, he thought, and was about to say so to Jack, when something else caught his attention. There was something odd about the riders' saddles and equipment. Perhaps Yorkshiremen rode in that loose manner, he thought . . . and then he saw a look of horror on the face of the two leading riders, and realised who they were. Raising his hands, he bellowed at the top of his voice: *'Archers, string your bows!'* and with a quick blast on his horn to warn the rest of the army, he drew his sword and prepared to fight.

The Scottish army had found them.

Berenger was aware of Jack at his side, and wanted to tell him to get back with his command, but then he recalled that he himself was responsible for all the archers. He shouldn't even be here!

As the first of the riders thundered towards him, Berenger ducked under the swinging blade aimed at his head. His own blow went wide, but then the second man was on him, a thickset, ginger-haired brute with bloodshot blue eyes and a heavy beard. He carried a war hammer and aimed it squarely at Berenger as his little horse sprang forward. Berenger spurred his pony to slide away to the left and heard the hammer head whistle as it flew past him – but then there was a third man before him, a young fellow, half Berenger's age, with the dark hair and grey eyes of a Celt and a crazed smile on his face. He hefted his sword like a man cheering on a companion in a race.

Behind him, Berenger heard the first familiar cry: 'ARCHERS! Archers, *nock*! ARCHERS! Archers, *draw*!'

Berenger had only a moment. As he approached this fresh enemy on his right, he lifted his sword blade high to block the lad's and then, hauling on the reins, he stopped his own mount and brought his mailed fist down and slammed it into the fellow's face with all his strength, feeling the satisfying snap as the nose and two teeth broke. And then, all at once, he felt a blow on his helmet. The world span, and he almost fell from his mount. He slumped – and then he heard a loud scream, and saw that Dogbreath had ridden to his side. He blinked, woozy and uncomprehending for a moment, while Dogbreath shrieked and whirled, crazed as a berserker of old, his sword and a dagger spinning and creating wild patterns in the occasional flashes as sunlight tried to force its way through the mists.

Then there was a scream of wild men, and two more Scottish warriors were galloping towards him. Berenger could only watch, the blood pounding in his veins as they approached, but before they could reach him, there was a fierce bellow of '*Saint Denis!*' and Jean de Vervins thundered past. An arrow took the first Scot, and Jean rode straight for the other, his sword gleaming. It struck, and the Scot's horse was rearing, blood pulsing from a great gash in its neck. Jean gave a short backhanded slash, and the rider disappeared.

Berenger saw him thrust and parry with another Scotsman, the blades moving so swiftly that Berenger couldn't follow them, and then he seemed to come back to life. He saw that his sword lay on the ground near his pony's hooves. He climbed down, picked it up and clambered back into the saddle, just as a mace was aimed at his head. He ducked, the mass of spikes missed him, and then he was seated again, and he gave a bellow to his men to call them back.

'With me! Dogbreath, Sir Jean! With me!'

He saw Sir Jean de Vervins, who glanced back as though uncomprehending, but then he nodded and clapped spurs to his mount.

'To the trees!' Berenger yelled. Ahead, all he could see was a rippling line of silver, and he knew what that meant. A line of archers were drawing, and any moment, those sparkling points would hurtle upwards and towards them.

'The trees!' he roared again as he saw the sudden disappearance of the arrow-tips. They were flying already!

He lashed his horse, urging it to greater efforts, even as Sir Jean, crouching low, overhauled him and entered the little copse.

Berenger reached the trees as the first of the screams broke out behind him. Dogbreath was at his heels.

Turning, he saw that the man he had punched lay on the ground, dazed, while all around, horses stamped and pawed the air, maddened by the sudden violence. And then there was a hideous pocking noise as arrows stabbed down from the heavens, followed by agonised shrieks. Horses whinnied, thrashing and rearing, and men cursed and wept as the clothyards pinned them to the ground, some receiving four in as many breaths. Men rolled feebly in the attempt to free themselves, one man crawling away sobbing as the shaft that had penetrated his belly snagged the ground beneath him.

More Scots were riding up now, and he heard Jack's call: 'Archers, *nock*! Archers, *draw*! Archers, *loose*!'

A whistle and whoosh of finest goose feathers, and it was like watching a scythe taking the tops off a field of barley. One moment, five men-at-arms were riding at full tilt towards the English, and the next, all were gone. The arrows had all found their mark, and a heavy arrowhead with a yard of ash behind it was enough to penetrate any mail at this range. Each rider had three or more strike simultaneously, and all were hurled from their steeds, one to be dragged away screaming, his foot entangled in the stirrup.

More had appeared: a fresh group of pikemen, with their captain on a great charger. A flight of arrows, and the destrier plunged to the ground, throwing his rider, who landed heavily on his head. Berenger could hear the crunch of breaking bones over the rattle of the armour. The men after him were cut down as they ran, groups of two, three or four surviving and trying to force their way onward, until only one remained. As a kindness, he was pierced by five arrows all at once and fell only a few yards from the line of archers.

Berenger waited for the next eruption of Scottish men, gripping his sword with a fist that now shook as though he had the ague. He stared at it with incomprehension for a while. It seemed curious that he should have this feeling now that the fighting was all over, but then a bleak reaction set in. He had acted like a fool, drawing steel against God alone knew how many men, while his own men needed his direction and support; he could have been slain in the first moments. It was pure good fortune that had kept him unhurt. Apart from anything else, an English arrow could have found him in that mêlée.

He thrust his sword back into its sheath and bellowed, 'Don't loose! Hold your arrows! Jack? It's me, Berenger Fripper! I have Sir Jean de Vervins and Dogbreath with me!' He waited until he heard Jack's answering bellow, before urging his pony forward into the open once more.

The ground was littered with the wounded and dead, at least a hundred men all told. Some few lay with terrified eyes, contemplating the imminent sight of the angels of Heaven, but more squatted with fury in their eyes, watching the approaching English with hatred.

Archers had already unsheathed their long knives or swords and were moving among the dead and injured, stabbing all to make sure of them and despoiling them. More than one archer earned himself a new pair of boots that day, and several acquired a new sword or mace.

The man Berenger had knocked from his horse was on all fours, panting and spitting. When Berenger reached him, the fellow lifted his sword and waved it in his direction, but one eye was already closed, and the other was narrowed with the pain. Every movement must have cost him dear, Berenger thought.

'Put it down, boy. You'll get yourself killed.'

The lad peered at him, his sword slowly lowering. And then, through his mashed lips, he managed a hoarse, 'Who are you?'

Berenger stared. It wasn't that the boy had shown an interest in him. It was that he had not used the harsh, guttural language of the Scots.

The boy was French.

Chapter Twenty-Three

Henry Percy and Ralph Neville had been fascinated by the French youth when Berenger managed to bring him to them.

'Set him down there,' Neville said when Berenger reached him.

The boy had miraculously been missed by the arrows plunging into that small field in the mist, but with the blood and snot smearing his face he looked in a worse state than many of the men who had died.

'What is your name?' the Archbishop asked in French. All the nobles and most of the clerks were perfectly familiar with the language. He stood before a trestle table on which many papers lay. 'You know that we can find out all we wish about you. Better to tell us now without forcing us to extract the information.'

'I am Godefroi de Valmet,' he answered after a moment. 'I come from near Laon.'

'I know the land there,' the Archbishop said pleasantly. 'It is good country for wine.'

'Yes, my lord.'

'What were you doing riding up on us? Did you mean to attack us?'

'No, my lord. I was riding with William Douglas. We were on our way back to the main army after a reconnaissance.'

'Can you find your way to the main army?'

'Yes.'

'Is it commanded by the King of Scotland – David Bruce?'

'Yes.'

'Where does he intend to attack next?'

A flare of animation lit the lad's face. 'He rides to Durham to take it. He has a huge army: two thousand knights and fifteen thousand footsoldiers!'

'So many?' Percy said, but there was no wonder in his tone, only satisfaction. 'This will be a victory worth recording, then.'

Godefroi stared at him. 'You cannot win! You have only a fraction of his men. Yours are all about Calais.' This last with a blaze of enthusiasm.

'Aye, well, we will show ye what English blood and bone can do,' the Earl said imperturbably.

'You will have to call men from Calais if you want to save your land. We are come to lay waste all the country as far as London.'

'Ye won't pass us.'

'You do not realise your danger,' Godefroi said with contempt.

'There's only one thing ye need worry about. I swear, if ye go into battle against us, ye will die. Our army is a match for anything to come out of Scotland.'

'You should be measured for your coffin.'

Percy smiled easily. 'We'll see. After the battle, I'll return home to me wife. Ye'll be sad to see the Scottish crushed.'

The Archbishop held up his hand. 'This is havering. God Himself with His saints will decide the battle. Just as He did at Crécy.' He studied Godefroi for a moment. 'You will ride back to your main army with a message. I will send a herald with you, and you will deliver the herald to the King of Scotland. We shall await his answer.'

After the fellow had been hurried away, the Archbishop looked about him. 'Well?'

Percy snorted. 'Yon little prickle has scarcely more than the sense he was born wi'. But no matter. It's enough. The lad confirmed what Jean de Vervins told us. We know the size of the fight now.'

'Aye,' Neville agreed. 'But we have to show we have the right of it.'

'Yes,' the Archbishop nodded. 'We have to ask them to leave the country and cease in their depredations, otherwise we shall be forced to bring them to battle.'

Berenger felt his mouth falling open. 'But why? Shouldn't we just bring them to battle now?'

'Och, we can no' do that, Captain,' Percy said. 'This is the March. We have the right of it, but to go at 'em without the courtesies could make us look like we were in the wrong.'

'How can that be? They're in England, stealing and killing!'

'Don't concern ye'sel'. This way'll make it neat and proper, that's all ye need to worry about.'

A herald arrived, and the Archbishop and Sir Henry gave him the form of words. In a moment or two he was out and running for a horse.

Percy turned to Berenger. 'Ye did well to form the archers and hold back Douglas's men.'

The Archbishop grunted. 'And now we'll all have to do as well. The army will march with the Sheriff of Yorkshire on the left flank, I will take the middle battle, and you, my Lord Percy, will take the right. We will march to the town now, and when we find a suitable location, we will attack these sons of dogs. And may

God grant us the victory we deserve against these insolent invaders.'

Berenger left the pavilion shortly after that. Outside, he saw the herald pulling on gloves with a distracted air, while a groom of ten or eleven years hurried to fetch him a horse. Berenger was sorry for the man. He could imagine what was passing through his mind. It was nothing to do with the actual message that he was to deliver – that would be memorised already. No, it was the thought of the reception he might expect. The Scottish King had a reputation for chivalry and being honourable, but he was, when all was said and done, a warrior at the head of some of the most barbaric fighters known to Christendom. It would be no surprise if some of the more hot-headed amongst them thought it would be amusing to send back their own message in explicit form, by returning the herald's head in a sack, or perhaps every part of his body disassembled in a barrel of salt.

'Your horse, sir,' the groom said, but when Berenger looked up, the boy was not bringing the herald's mount. This was the mount for Godefroi.

The Frenchman stood with his mouth pressed into the vambrace protecting his forearm. The coolness of the metal against his damaged lips must have been soothing. Seeing Berenger, he drew his lips away and stood haughtily.

'I'm sorry about your teeth,' Berenger said.

'I will live, which is better than some can say,' Godefroi replied. His voice was muffled from his damaged mouth, but he unbent so far as to duck his head as though in appreciation of the comment, although his face did not ease its rigidity.

'Why are you here?' Berenger asked.

'I am an esquire. It is my place to fight for my King no matter where he sends me.'

'You were sent here, then? Were you on the ships?'

Godefroi glanced at him. 'What ships?'

Berenger explained about the ships he had seen in the mouth of the river.

'Ah, yes. We brought good French armour and swords for our Scottish friends. King David was glad of them,' Godefroi said with a note of pride. 'I was responsible for bringing them and for asking King David to enter England.'

'To distract King Edward and force him to send men back here.'

'Of course. He will have to do so.'

'I don't think you understand the balance of power here,' Berenger said.

He could not help but admire the martial spirit of this French esquire. Godefroi was very similar to young warriors the world over. He was so convinced of his own ability and strength that he paid little attention to the merits of others. He was young and keen and he felt his cause was just – and since his cause was just, he thought his comrades would be as filled with warrior-like ardour. But Berenger knew only too well that ardour alone was not enough. Supplies were important, and the support of companions, but the most important aspect for any army was the training of its men. And England had been training for war every year since Edward III took his throne.

'Balance of power?' the Frenchman said scornfully. 'We know more than you could imagine!'

'You know what happened at Crécy?'

'A rabble of Genoese bowmen failed us. They turned and ran, to their shame, and in so doing, they spoiled the charge of French chivalry so that many knights and men were injured or killed.'

'No. The Genoese were failed by their bowstrings. When their strings became wet, their bolts would not reach the English lines, but our bows could reach far beyond them. They were horribly pricked by our arrows, and then ridden down by the front line of your knights. And those same knights were slain before they could strike a single blow.'

'So you say. But the battle was a matter of good luck. We shall see who will win the battle for Durham.'

As the herald's groom appeared, Godefroi mounted his horse and waited politely for the herald. Then the two rode off into the gathering gloom.

Berenger watched him go with a feeling of sadness. He rather liked the fellow, but he had a strong presentiment that he would not speak to the young esquire again.

Chapter Twenty-Four

'I fucking knew it. They brought us all this way just to throw us in the front line again,' Clip whinged.

'Shut up, Clip,' Jack said.

'We'll all get killed.'

'Shut up, Clip.' That was Saint Lawrence.

'I'm only young, me. I don't need all this walking and fighting,' Clip grumbled.

'Clip?' Aletaster said. 'Shut up.'

'I'm just telling the truth, that we're all going to—'

'Oi!' The Pardoner stopped and stared at him. 'If you don't shut up, I'm going to sit on your head until you do. And I have a magnificent fart brewing, Clip: when I let rip, you'll suffer, so bloody shut up!'

'I was only saying.'

'Shut up!'

Berenger had placed himself and his old vintaine near the middle of the archers on the right wing. He listened with half an ear, noting that his vintaine showed no signs of concern at the coming battle, while the newer men's anxiety was apparent in their voices or their silence. For all present knew that battle was inevitable and inescapable.

He pulled off his dented helmet and rubbed the swelling on his scalp. It hurt like a bad burn, and although the local barber had offered to bleed him, he had refused. He needed all the concentration he could muster for the coming fight.

After the skirmish yesterday, the herald had been sent to the Scots, where he received a reply both curt and brief. Once the Scottish had heard from his French victim, King David would be sure to want to attack. The idea of taking on a force only one third or one quarter the size of his own would appeal to any warrior. Certainty of victory counted more than notions of chivalry. Chivalry was for knights – a series of rules so that the rich and brave could expect to buy back their lives, were they to be captured. Berenger had no doubts about his own fate if he was captured by the Scots. It would involve a blade and he would have his bleeding at last. Well, he reflected, it would at least take away the pain of his head wound.

Certainly the English had not slowed in their advance, and last night they had sheltered, shivering, on the plain to the south of Durham. The weather was dry, but now, in the middle of October, it was so chilly as to leave a man quaking all night under his blanket. Berenger had woken feeling forty years older, trembling like a man in a fever until a cup of strong wine mixed with hot water managed to send some warmth to his extremities. Still, as he mounted his pony and stared about him at the mess that was an army on the march, he felt another shudder pass down his spine.

It was a sight to send a thrill into the most unresponsive heart. All around him, men packed away their belongings, boys brought up the ponies while yeomen rubbed down and saw to the feeding of the men-at-arms's beasts, warily attending to highly-strung destriers that would be more than keen to bite a groom. Campfires were extinguished with the last of the water from cooking pots, and men wandered about, chewing the rough breads made by the bakers overnight, as they threw on their baldrics or tugged at their warbelts. Archers checked the sheaves of arrows on the carts, some eyeing the sky for rain, before taking their bowstrings and pushing them into their shirts against their skin, or shoving them beneath their caps to keep them dry.

The army was moving urgently now as the sun crept higher into the sky. The squeak and rattle of cart and wagon did not quite mask the sound of hooves and boots. On the men marched, all of them aware that they must soon go into battle.

Most there were levies called to serve – both young and old. Percy had been gathering a force from his lands to take to Calais, but the men from Yorkshire and those from Neville's lands were less young and eager, not quite so ready to be thrust into the front line of a battle gripping a lance and hoping that the point would rip into a destrier's breast before the rider's steel could reach them. That was no surprise to Berenger, for he had stood in the line himself often enough.

'You all right, Frip?'

'Captain Frip, Jack, if you don't mind,' he grinned. 'Just looking at the men we're fighting with.'

'They'll be fine.' Jack cast an appraising eye over them himself. 'These ones look hoary and hearty enough. And I'll warrant that Sir Henry Percy knows how to place his men. After all, he was bright enough to promote you.'

'I hope I don't show myself incompetent,' Berenger said, voicing a fear that was ever in his mind.

'You won't. We've done this before, Frip,' Jack said sharply. 'Just remember Crécy, and keep your head. We can't afford to have our centener lose faith in himself.'

Berenger gave a dry smile. Crécy had shown what Englishmen could do with their bows. Tearing apart the French cavalry charges before they could fully form and slaughtering them far away before any Englishmen could be hurt. 'Hard to believe that was only a few weeks ago. Let's hope this goes the same way.'

'It will. We'll pick the best piece of land and defend it.'

'Aye.' That was all they needed to do: so long as they reached the battleground before the Scots could take it and force the English to attack.

But when they reached the most likely place for their defence, Berenger felt his heart drop.

'Oh, *shit*, Frip,' Jack said.

On the hill before them, the Scots had already taken their place. The English would be forced to attack them.

'Ballocks!' Berenger said.

'I telled ye – we'll all be slaughtered,' Clip called in a slightly quieter voice.

'Fuck *off*, Clip!' Jack growled.

'Form battles!'

Berenger remained on his horse while the footsoldiers nearby relinquished their mounts and passed the reins to the waiting boys. He had already told Jean de Vervins to stay back with the baggage. He had lost one charge already when the King's messenger died. He would not lose this one. Each lad, whether nine or thirteen, took five or six mounts and scurried back to the rear of the battles where the wagons were all set out in a ring. The horses and ponies were brought inside the circle of wood, the boys standing with their beasts and waiting for the summons that would indicate a rapid advance and charge, or an ignominious flight.

From his vantage point, Berenger could see the ground clearly. The Scots had drawn up into battle formation on the hill opposite, and the English were bellowing at their own men, pushing the recalcitrant troops into three battles across their own hill. Sir Henry Percy was pointing and speaking with his captains, while his deputy, Sir Gilbert Umfraville, stalked about the place roaring commands at the centeners and others.

These men were all veterans of the fighting along the Marches – Northumbrians with calculating expressions tightening their faces as they watched the Scots, fingering their weapons with the manner of men long-used to war.

It struck Berenger suddenly that these men were not like him. He had taken to fighting when he was a young man, and then it was in order to support his King. But his King, Edward II, had been deposed by the arch-traitor, Roger Mortimer, and sent into captivity. Afterwards, Berenger had helped take the man who had been King to Avignon, and then joined him on the long journey to Italy. On his return, he was accused of treachery, and it was only the sudden overthrow of Mortimer's tyranny that saved him. Since then, he had been a warrior, always seeking the next battle to bring in a little more money. Perhaps if he had settled down, he would have been able to escape this life, but he had never found a woman with whom he could make a home and a new life. There had never been the opportunity.

These men were different. They were farmers, peasants, smiths, carpenters, tradesmen of all kinds, and yet they were English enough to grasp a sword or axe when their lives or homes were at risk. All over Northumbria, men like this worked hard to make a life for themselves and their children, and every so often the Scots would invade and slaughter, and rob, and rape and burn, until there was nothing left. This land was emptying not only because of death, but because the men who lived there were weary of constantly striving to keep their enemies at bay. And now these same men were here with their weapons in their fists, determined to keep what was theirs, and to punish those who sought to take it from them by force.

Berenger had a sudden sense of awe for these hardy, valiant men.

Summoning the vinteners, he gave them their dispositions. The archers would extend beyond and forward of each side of the three main battles of fighting men, like horns on either side of a bull's head, so that they could loose arrows forwards or, as battle was joined, into the flanks of approaching Scots. The vinteners all appeared to understand his commands, and he formed a healthy regard for them as they all marched back to their men. They knew their jobs here.

Back at the line, he saw three priests galloping towards the army. A rider stopped with Sir Henry Percy, and began to expostulate, pointing back the way he had come. Berenger could see, in the distance, the great mass of Durham Cathedral, and for a moment he wondered whether the priests were calling on the army to fall back that way. He prayed, if that was their aim, that the Archbishop and other commanders would pay no heed. The worst disaster for any army was to fall back; it would inevitably be slaughtered while running.

Yet a short while later, the rider rode away, and there were more horns winded and shouting. Slowly, under Umfraville's command, the army began to march on.

'Frip, we have to move!' Jack was calling.

The vintaine was all about him now. Their cart, full of bow staves and sheaves of arrows wrapped in canvas bundles, each carefully separated to protect their fragile fletchings, was being pulled by three men now that their donkey had been taken back to the ringed camp of wagons, and as Umfraville stood pointing and shouting, the archers began to move along the brow of the hill. Berenger soon saw why.

On the shoulder of the hill, the English had an unimpeded view of the Scottish dispositions. The enemy were formed in a similar three-battle formation, but where the English had space for all their men, the Scottish were constrained into a smaller area. On their own side, Berenger saw that the English site was protected by a pair of deep valleys, one at either side, that would prevent any attack other than directly up the slope before them. Meanwhile, opposite, the Scots had taken a position with stone walls and ditches. Any assault from there would be broken. It would be like Halidon Hill again, Berenger thought to himself exultantly.

He dropped from his pony and passed the reins to a waiting boy before walking to the front of the archers.

'You all right, Frip?' Jack asked.

Berenger stood staring over the ground before them. The Scots were waiting at the hilltop. Faintly on the wind Berenger thought he could hear their taunts and jeers, and every so often blades waved and flashed in the sun. It was nothing. The usual ranting to build their spirits while they waited for the real onslaught to begin.

'We'll all die,' Clip said.

Jack said nothing, but his open hand smacked hard across the scrawny archer's pate.

'Ow! What was that for?' Clip demanded angrily, a hand to his head.

Jack ignored him. 'Frip, do you want us to lead forward?'

'Yes. Take a few paces in advance of the three battles,' he agreed. 'The archers must form two blades, one at either side. Then, when the Scots run at the men-at-arms, our storm of arrows will lance into them. We shall keep them assailed from both sides.'

'They're all dismounted,' Aletaster said.

'I'm sorry, but I'm really scared,' Pardoner said.

Berenger glanced at them. The fat man was sweating. Two streams ran from under his hat down each temple and formed greasy drips at his chin; Pardoner had a wide-eyed, terrified expression and he shivered like a mare with a wound.

'It's normal,' Berenger said cheerfully. 'We fight on foot, the same as our ancestors did. There's no point in a knight mounting and charging the enemy, not when it's the Scots and they have their lances. They'll set the butts of their weapons in the ground, and any horse riding into them will be impaled before the knight can strike a blow.'

Aletaster nodded doubtfully.

'Aye,' Clip sniggered, 'and it means the lazy bastards can't just run away, either. They're here with us, whether they like it or not.'

'You always have to bring things down to your level, don't you?' the Earl murmured.

Saint Lawrence gave a short laugh. 'It's all he knows. When you're in the gutter, all you can see is arses above you!'

Berenger smiled to himself. If even the newer fellows were capable of joking at Clip's expense, it boded well for their ability in a battle.

'Are you all well?' he called.

There was a chorus of more or less positive cries. Pardoner scowled and fingered his blade. Dogbreath was sucking at a tooth, while John of Essex ran his fingers through his hair, staring over the battles to their left, then peering ahead, evaluating, assessing and calculating. Berenger had the impression that John of Essex would soon be a military commander again, so long as he learned to control his warlike ardour. He was quick to see an opportunity, and he could read the land, too.

'Keep it careful, Jack,' he said quietly. 'Place the newer ones to the front, and let the old lags keep them in line when necessary, and for God's sake muzzle Clip, if you bloody can. If I hear him say he's going to die today just once more ... I'm likely to run him through myself!'

He was about to return to the middle of the horn of archers, when he suddenly noticed a face and glared. 'What are you doing here, Jean?'

Jean de Vervins smiled and pulled off his bascinet, the tippet of mail lifting off with it. 'God give you a good day, Master Fripper.'

'I said, *what are you doing here*?'

'I will stand here in the line. What, would you have me wait at the wagons with the children and the women? If I am to die, I will die here with a weapon in my hand, fighting alongside the brave men who dare challenge this invasion.'

'You were to be kept out of harm's way,' Berenger rasped. 'Jack, get someone to take him to the rear where he can't get under our feet.'

'Do you want to protect me, or ensure that I'm not a danger to you?' Jean de Vervins asked mildly.

'I want you out of the way. *Now!*' Berenger said. 'I was grateful to you and to Dogbreath when you saved me, but I cannot have you here. If I am worrying about you, it will impair my judgement.' He was about to hurry to the middle of the line, when Tyler called out to him.

'Do you want a messenger? It makes sense for you to have someone who can take your orders to your men up and down the line.'

Berenger gave him a long stare. 'The day I trust you is the day I deserve to be hanged.'

He detailed Clip and the Earl to take the Frenchman away.

CHAPTER TWENTY-FIVE

The men were ordered and bullied into their lines, their captains fearful of a sudden attack while they were still preparing themselves. They formed their battles and took up positions over their hill, and when all were ready, an unearthly silence fell. Berenger walked to the front of the archers and stood there watching the Scots with narrowed eyes. He wished his sight was as sharp as it had been in his youth.

'What are they doing, Jack?'

'A few look like they're arguing, perhaps demanding that they should be given the honour of being first to tackle us.'

They could see how small the English force was, but it was clear that the Scots were being restrained. Too many memories held them back: Dupplin Moor and Halidon Hill served to dampen the ardour of the leaders. They knew the effect of massed English archers on an attacking force.

Berenger nodded to himself. The Scots were in for a long wait if they wanted the English to attack first. He turned away – and then gaped. 'Look!' he said to Jack. 'Have you ever seen so many flags?'

The great banners of the Archbishop, of the Percys, the Nevilles and Umfravilles, the flags of the Sheriff of Yorkshire and John Mowbray, stood fluttering in the breeze, but behind them were more. Flags and banners flew all over the English fighters. It made the army look twice or thrice its actual size, and as Berenger watched, his heart swelled with pride. This was a battle the English were going to win.

But only if the Scottish could be persuaded to attack. It was due to the strength of the English archers and their tactics, that no army could hope to attack without suffering massive losses. The downside of this advantage, also proved over many years, was that if the enemy refused to attack, the two armies could stand for hours or even days, without coming to blows. And then, overnight, the Scottish would depart the field, leaving the English feeling deprived of their victory.

As the two watched, a group of three priests appeared bearing a huge crucifix, which they carried to the front of the middle battle near the Bishop and his flag.

'That's better,' Jack muttered sarcastically. 'I like to think of dying under a cross – because some donkey-swyving arse of a priest has got in my way in the middle of a hand-to-hand fight, and tripped me at the wrong bloody moment!'

'Ach, let's get at these Scotties,' Dogbreath said impatiently. 'This waiting's pointless. I want to get in there among them!'

'You go up there, and they'll kill you before you reach within fifty yards of them,' John of Essex said.

'We should take the fight to them,' Dogbreath insisted. 'This is cowardly, standing here and waiting like little virgins too nervous to lift our skirts.'

'You can think what you like,' the Earl said smoothly. 'Personally I am happier here, waiting, than walking into their weapons.'

Tyler grimaced. 'I don't like the waiting either, but I'm happier to use my brain than run up there.'

'You lot are all mad,' Dogbreath said. 'I want to get this over and done with.'

'So do we all,' Berenger said.

'If they don't move soon, we'll have to make 'em,' John of Essex said thoughtfully.

'And how do you think we should do that?' Tyler said with scorn dripping from every word.

'Send some archers forward and loose a few arrows into the mass of them. That should persuade them to get a shift on. They're just playing it safe up there like a bunch of silly cunts.'

'We'll wait until we have orders,' Berenger said sharply, but he eyed John with a renewed respect. There was sense in what he suggested.

The Scots were playing music, with pipes and clarions blaring, and drummers beating their skins for all their worth, but the battles were not so well organised as the English ones, Berenger thought. With his eyesight it was hard to tell, but he fancied they were more densely arrayed. 'Do they look as though they're squeezed together?' he said to Jack.

'Yes – far too tightly,' Jack responded. 'I don't think they'd survive long, were we to do as John suggests. A few arrows loosed into them would soon give them so much ginger, they'd have to charge. It wouldn't take much.'

Berenger looked over to the left, where Sir Henry Percy and Umfraville stood sharing mazers of wine, and made a decision. 'Earl, come here. You are to run to Sir Henry Percy and say I think we should send some archers ahead to try to tempt the Scots out of their positions. I want to take five vintaines within bowshot to see if we cannot persuade them to move. Go and tell him that. And hurry!'

The Earl nodded, and ran at a trot along the front of the army, while Berenger set to studying the Scots once more. He was sure he was right, and that the Scots had been packed so closely into their narrow position that it would prove enormously hard for them to swing their weapons.

'Frip?' Jack called softly, and Berenger turned to see that Earl was already back, beaming from ear to ear.

'He said, "Sting the bastards till they get off their backsides and do something," Fripper.'

Berenger looked at the distant men and grinned. 'About fucking time!'

Calling to his commanders, Berenger explained their plan before hurrying back to his old vintaine. He wanted to leave from the ranks of his friends. He took with him a third of the archers from the wing, grabbing a bow from a cart as he went. It was a good, heavy yew bow, with a slight knot near the grip, but nothing to worry him, and he strung it quickly before snatching up a sheave of arrows and throwing it over his shoulder.

'Archers! We're going to within bowshot to tease the Scotch bastards to leave their hill. We have to approach, sting them hard and fast until they howl, and then run back to our lines. Do you understand?' he shouted.

Jack thrust a fist clutching a bow skywards and the archers gave a roar of approval, although Pardoner and Oliver in particular appeared less enthusiastic than others.

Berenger felt his blood roil like fire as he roared: 'Archers! Forward!'

There was no cover here, no hope of moving without being seen. Berenger strode purposefully onward, without glancing around. All he cared about was the group of Scots before him. He could make out the fluttering of flags, but could not tell what symbols they held.

'What do you reckon, Jack?' he asked as they passed maybe eighty yards.

'A little further, Frip. We want the men to be able to see their quarry.'

'Good. Give it another twenty paces.'

'That'll do fine.'

Berenger felt the old tingle in his breast as he stood there, confronting the enemy ahead.

From here he could see them, if indistinctly with his poor sight. Row upon row of scruffy men, their weapons ready, some waving them in the air, others crouching low, fists clenched, to roar defiance like wild beasts. Some with bascinets, some with simple steel caps, many with mail twinkling in the sunshine, while others appeared to be wearing little more than quilted jacks and felt hats. They exuded a ferocious mixture of bloodlust and excitement, with men thrilling at the thought of destroying another English army. Too many had heard of the disaster of Bannockburn. It was before Berenger's fighting time, back in 1314, but it was a battle that still rang down the decades: a story of victory and glory to all Scots, and one of disaster and horror to the English. The Scots had tried to emulate that battle ever since, but the English had learned from their mistakes and now they could hold their place against the Scottish on any battlefield. Today, so long as they could acquire the tactical advantage of the land, and could wait until the Scots attacked, the English should win. Their archers would make sure of that.

'That's the idea, anyway,' he muttered, and then held up his fist, shouting: 'Hold!' He turned to Jack. 'What do you think?'

'We're near enough to see their eyes!' Clip said and spat. 'What, do you want to get near enough we can count their teeth?'

There came a sudden roar. Berenger looked up. Over at the other flank, the archers from Yorkshire were already engaging with the Scots. He could see them bend their bows, leaning back, letting their arrows fly high, high overhead, so that they must plummet down into the midst of the Scottish horde.

'Archers! Archers, *nock!*' he bellowed. 'Jack, if we don't make them fear our sting, they'll rush at us all the sooner! *Archers, draw! Archers, loose!*'

He felt it again, that wonderful thrumming that ran through his entire body, from his loins to his shoulders, as the bow came to life. Drawing a mighty bow gave a man a sense of power unlike anything else Berenger had experienced. It was almost like the thrill of sex, one moment the anguish of muscles straining to hold a string at full stretch, each part of his body as taut as the bones within, and then the exquisite release, when for a second every particle of his body was relaxed, and he could see his arrow soaring away and then plummeting down into the mass of the enemy. Not men, just an amorphous collection of bone and muscle and blood, all baying for him and his men.

Jack was already bellowing the commands. Berenger saw him draw, the other bows straining in unison, the arrows pointing up, ready, then the ripple as the bows straightened once more, hurling their long missiles up and away towards the men on the hill.

Five flights they loosed, then one more, and Berenger saw gaps opening up in the Scottish lines. He saw the little puffs of blood as arrows slammed into bodies, the rage building as the men stood impotent while death rained upon them, and he saw that rage growing, fed by the resentment and horror of death dealt at such a distance, until at last the cup of their endurance was overflowing. That was when the Scottish began to run straight for him and the others.

'Archers, *nock* . . . *draw* . . . *aim* . . . and *loose!*' Jack cried, and then Berenger bellowed his own order: 'Back! Back! Back to the lines!' and they were hurtling, pell-mell, over loose stones and slippery grass, running for their lives, running as they had never run before, more than one dropping his arrows and bow in the mad flight, not stopping until they had reached the safety of the lines . . . and at last they heard the friendly bawling of the centener Berenger had left in charge, and they saw the bows bending, the arrows rising, and with a whistle and a hum they flew overhead before pelting into the bodies of the Scottish pursuers.

Berenger stopped, panting, to watch as the rest of his command returned to their posts, and nocked an arrow in readiness while he gazed at the Scots, choosing a target. There was a man in heavy armour, he saw, and he drew his bow fully, aiming carefully – and loosed. The arrow flew perfectly true, and he heard it strike with a sound like a hammer on an anvil. The man stopped in midflight, his head dropping uncomprehendingly before two more arrows struck him, and then he was seen no more as the Scottish ran over and past him.

'Loose at will!' Berenger cried, and he drew and released as quickly as he could, the blood thundering in his ears as the Scottish came nearer and nearer, until there was no point, and he drew his sword, waving it over his head: 'Archers, *draw steel!*' He sprang at the first screaming madman – a black-haired rogue with the face of a felon – who swung a sword at Berenger's head. He slipped to the side, blocking with his bow, and the string parted with the sound of a gonne firing, but then the man had pushed past him and was stabbing and slashing in all directions. Blood spattered into the air, and Berenger felt it hit his brow and cheeks, and he thought it might be Jack – but then he saw Saint Lawrence stagger away with a great gash in his face that laid it open to the bone . . . and then John of Essex was there, and he blocked the Scot's next wild cut with a blade that rose and turned, and as it turned, the point slipped through the Scot's defence and slashed into the soft flesh under his arm. John stood still, watching his enemy, and then he pressed hard, once, and the blade slid into the man's breast.

'Frip! Behind you!' someone shouted.

Berenger turned and saw the mass of Scots running at him. He just had time to clamber to his feet, throw away the shattered remains of his bow, and grip his sword in both hands when the first screaming hordes crashed into the line of archers.

He was clutched at the back and flank by other archers, all gripping swords or long knives, and they clung together as the Scottish tried to shove them over. Every Englishman had an enraged Scottish face before him, and as great mauls, maces and axes whirled and crashed into them, there was no escape for anyone here. It was a brutal fight, but simple. Kill or be killed.

Berenger bellowed to his men. 'One! Two! *Push!* One! Two! *Push!*' and they thrust forward with each command, trying to unsettle the Scots and force some over, if they could. He could see nothing but the face or two faces in front of him. Beside him, above him, behind him: nothing existed. His entire universe was before him and beneath him; a claustrophobic existence of foul breath, of blood, of shit. He stabbed, slashed, felt his blade strike something, someone, felt the spatter of warmth, and pushed on again; the line began to give, and he pushed more forcefully, bellowing. He saw a man go down before him, and stamped with all his might on the fellow's body, desperate to prevent a sword opening his entrails from beneath. A blow was aimed at him, and he caught a reek of foul breath, and instantly it brought Dogbreath to mind, but then he had another face in front of him, and this time he couldn't protect himself from the blade that crossed wildly in front of him, and he felt it hit his cheek, dragging hideously across his face to his nose. He jerked his head aside before it could stab his eye, and lashed out madly with his sword, which hit his attacker in the mouth. He wrenched it, ripped it aside, and the man's face disappeared. Berenger bent his head, snorted, hawked, spat blood, stamped down again, ducked as a war hammer came near, felt the shaft crash into his shoulder – the head miraculously missing him – and felt his left arm fall dead with the shock. He punched forward with his sword and the blade caught something, but now his vision was blurred with blood from his opened cheek, and he had to wipe it, but he couldn't lift his left hand, and he dared not use his right.

He swung and stabbed, ducking as he became aware of weapons heading towards him. His world, their world, was all here. There was nothing outside the pain, the stench, the fear, the horror: no sun, no sky, no pleasure, no joy, no love, no comradeship – only the unrelenting reality of death.

A shriek, a stumbling shove, and he was down, scrambling to be out of the line where any man could kill him in an instant, thinking him to be a foe. He scurried between legs like a rat running from the dogs, but then he collapsed. He was too exhausted to continue. With the blood running down his chin, he sank to the ground.

Death would have been a mercy.

Chapter Twenty-Six

Berenger felt himself being lifted and rolled out of the way, and when he could at last look around groggily, he saw that the battle was continuing. At his side, Jack and Turf were panting.

Jack snapped, 'Keep him here, Turf. Don't let him go anywhere!' and then he sprang back to the hacking, frenzied mass of fighting men.

Berenger could see that where there had been a thick group of English archers, now there was a much thinner line, spread more widely. He could see their backs, with many figures wearing tan, russet or green jacks quilted against sword blows, while a few wore steel helms or mail. There was a continual clatter of metal striking metal, of shrieks and screams of agony, or of fierce joy, and the rumble of voices bellowing at each other. He looked on as a man walked backwards from the line, only to stumble and fall and lie still. Another turned, and Berenger saw the hole in his brow as he toppled softly to the ground, eyes wide. Three Scots appeared in the gap where the two had been, but they suddenly fell, pierced by several arrows, and the gap became sealed with more Englishmen. And then there were more men arriving, rushing to the aid of the archers: fighters from Northumbria with grim, resolute expressions, men who had fought the Scots before for the security of their ancient lands, and who now took up arms again with fierce determination to remove the threat of raids once and for all.

Exhausted archers fell back as their places in the line were taken by fresher, keener fighters. The weary men strolled a short distance away to fall down and pant after their exertions.

Jack was one of the last of the vintaine to return to Berenger's side. He peered at his captain with an air of concern, but then shook his head. 'Your looks aren't improved.'

'And there was me thinking that a rakish scar would bring the wenches flocking to me.'

'Aye, well, at least it covers the worst of your ugly mug,' Jack said.

Turf, meanwhile, was gaping at the seething mass of fighting men with a look of near panic.

'You all right, mate?' Jack said, not unkindly.

'Saint Lawrence is dead. I was trying to fight, but being small I couldn't quite reach, and this sword came at me, and he grabbed me and pulled me to safety, but then a sword hit him on the head and he fell.' Turf's voice broke. 'He was smiling at me when he died. I couldn't do anything to save him . . .'

Jack suddenly slapped Turf hard on the cheek. The sound was loud enough to make several of the other archers turn and stare, but Jack kept his eyes on the short archer, hissing, 'Keep that to yourself. There are many other good men here who've died. You won't help any of them by blubbering like a girl. For fuck's sake, get a grip!'

'Yes, Vintener.' The man was instantly calmer.

Jack looked about him. 'How many casualties?'

'I'm here,' Dogbreath called.

'I'm all right,' the Pardoner said.

The Earl held up his hand and nodded, as did Oliver and the others.

Clip was his usual bitter self. 'I was out there, stuck in the front, and none of you bastards bothered to come and get me, did you? Oh, no. It's all very well to look to me when you need something, but when I'm in danger, you'll all leave me alone to suffer in silence and—'

'Silence?' Jack guffawed. 'That'll be the day.' Then: 'Hold!'

They heard a bellow, a cheer, and then a rumble announced a change in the battle.

Jack was on his feet in an instant. 'Archers, *quick!*'

He pulled out his sword again and set off towards the line. The fighting men were swaying, pushing, shoving, hacking and stabbing with vigour still, but as Berenger looked, he could see that they were advancing. The Scots must be giving way, for the lines were unmistakably moving forward, and as the men thrust and shoved, the carnage became more clear. On the ground, littered thickly, severed limbs and dreadfully slashed and damaged bodies had stained the ground red with gore.

'*Push!*' Jack gave a mighty roar, and he and the others took their place behind the lines, shoulders to the back of the men before them, legs straining, boots slipping and sliding on the blood-wet grass.

Berenger spotted a leather bottle. He grasped it, pulled the stopper free and took a deep draught of water. It was warm and brackish, and tasted of the pitch used to seal the leather, but it was the most wonderful drink he had ever taken. It flowed through his frame like an elixir, bringing refreshment to tired muscles and renewed life to his mind. His face hurt so badly, it felt as though a mule had kicked him, but the stinging was somewhat abated as he stood, swayed a little, shivered, and then set off towards the fighting line.

'Wait! Frip, Jack said you—'

'Fuck Jack and fuck the Scottish,' Berenger said bluntly and threw himself at the line of struggling men. 'Archers! Archers, one, two, *heave!* One, two, *heave!*' he snarled. It hurt like hell. He almost expected to feel his head explode with the effort, but the call was taken up by other men. A man glanced over his shoulder, saw Berenger's bloody, ravaged face behind him, and blenched at the sight, before pushing onwards with gusto, probably more to get away from the demonic-looking archer behind him than from any desire to rush back into the fray.

The tide was turning now. Berenger was not the only man to see that. The archers, reinforced by the Northumbrian levies, were taking the ground. The Scots had been fighting at the same place for an age, and now those who were uninjured were weary to death of the constant ferocious assault. Weakened by lost troops, they were bone-tired, thirsty and growing desperate. It was clear that they were being forced backwards, and while they knew that they must endure, it is one thing for a man to *know* he must continue, and another to persuade fatigued arms to lift a heavy weapon and strike for the thousandth time, or to tell legs to hold position when a solid, teeming mass of enemies are hell-bent on driving you off with regular ramming movements.

At first, one or two men fell back, some too whipped even to defend themselves as the English blades stabbed down into their bodies, while others began to withdraw; and with every man who turned and ran, the line was weakened as though it had been depleted by ten. It took one man running to dismay five or six others from near his position, and when twos and threes began to turn and flee, more and more felt that their cause was lost.

And then their army broke en masse, and the remaining

Scottish fled as one. Tripping and stumbling, they raced over the fields which they had crossed so enthusiastically only an hour or two before, passing the dead bodies of the men who had been picked off by the English archers, some throwing down their swords that they might run the faster, others falling flat and leaping up and bounding away like the deer of the Scottish hills, filled with the terror of men who sought to escape the fate that pursued them.

The English archers sank to their knees as the enemy before them ran, but Berenger remained on his feet, the sense of elation intoxicating him like strong wine.

Looking to his left, however, he saw what the others had not: the battle in the centre was as vicious and dangerous as their own had been a moment or two before. 'Archers! Archers, *nock your arrows!*' he bawled, feeling the life flooding back into his body as the thrill of continued battle ignited in his soul.

There was a scurrying of men hunting for weapons. Most had dropped their bows in the madness and now they picked up any stave they could find undamaged amongst the bodies littering the ground. A few found arrows: Berenger saw Jack and another vintener sending boys hurrying back to fetch sheaves from the carts.

'Archers, *loose at the enemy*!' Berenger shouted, pointing.

Singly, then in groups, arrows rose into the air and curled lazily down towards the scrambling, fighting mass. A full fifty to eighty each minute, lifting and then falling, looking no more dangerous than drops of rain splashing down on the men, but these drops were deadly, bearing sharpened steel points designed to puncture the strongest armour and pin a man to the ground.

'Archers, *to me!*' Berenger cried at last, when the arrows had done their work. It was time to finish things.

He had found another sword – his own he had lost in the

mêlée – and lifted it high. There was a slither of steel as the rest of the archers drew their own weapons again; he waved his sword once and plunged forward, towards the Scots.

There was about sixty yards to cover, and Berenger ran as fast as he could, hearing only the rattle and curse of the men fighting and dying. Behind him, screaming and shrieking like so many banshees, came his archers and the rest of the Northumbrians, and as they approached, Berenger saw the Scots nearest turn haggard faces to this new threat. Then with a high, keening ululation, Dogbreath pelted past him, eyes wide and staring, a sword gripped in each hand, mouth wide in a demonic rictus. He was first to hit the Scottish.

The archers crashed into the line with a breaking clatter like storm waves striking a pebbled shore, their axes and mauls beating at the Scots. Berenger found himself at the point of a dagger of men that had stabbed deep into the Scottish flank, and now he was holding his sword two-handed and dealing death with a raging determination he had never known before. He swung and chopped, lopping off a hand, then thrusting at a face and feeling it give as the blade pierced bone and slid on inwards. His blood pounded and roared until he could hear nothing else.

There was no exhaustion now, only the will to finish this butchery as soon as possible.

Suddenly there was a clear space before him, and he saw that many Scottish lords had formed a defensive ring about one man – their King. A banner fluttered overhead, and he saw that it held the lion of Scotland. He trampled bodies underfoot as he approached, and saw before him, as part of the ring, the Frenchman with the mashed face who had been sent back to the Scots with the herald. The lad stared at him with stark horror in his eyes. This was his first battle, and he had seen too many die already.

His face and his horror cut through Berenger's exultation. He felt drained, as though the whole weight of the fighting had suddenly struck him with full force. His head was a ponderous weight, as though his brain was turned to lead, and he let his sword-point drop.

The boy seemed to understand him, or so Berenger thought. A wakening gratitude came into his eyes, but even as Berenger thought he might surrender to him, a scream came from his left. He saw a group of knights with maces, axes and war-hammers leap forward and beat at the nearer Scotsmen. And then, in their midst, he saw a man-at-arms with a sword. It was Jean de Vervins.

Berenger wanted to go and remonstrate for his breaking into the battle, but even as he considered ordering the Frenchman back, he realised that Godefroi had seen Jean too. The two gazed at each other, Jean's face turning a ghastly white. He looked utterly benumbed to see his countryman on the opposing side of the army.

A bellow went up, and Berenger saw a Northumbrian knight suddenly hurl himself through the circle and grab at the Scottish King. King David punched him in the mouth so hard Berenger saw the blood fly, but it was to no avail. The knight lowered his head to protect himself from the King's assault, and bore him to the ground. There were howls of rage and delight on all sides, but the King was hustled away by four men-at-arms, and the Scottish realised that their cause was utterly lost. The English pressed forward on three sides now, and Berenger felt himself shoved aside as Sir Henry Percy and Umfraville and their bodyguards beat their way forward.

'*No!*' Berenger cried, but it was too late. The young Frenchman was clubbed in the face by a mailed fist and fell instantly. Berenger wanted to go to him, but before he could do so, he saw an English spiked war-hammer fall. The pole-axe impaled the Frenchman's skull, and Berenger saw his eyes widen and fix as the knight wrested it free, jerking the dead youth's head this way and that to remove it. Then the tide of the battle passed on and forward, and there were no more French or Scottish alive anywhere near.

Berenger went to the body and knelt beside it. 'I'm sorry,' he said hoarsely, but he could feel the guilt pressing on him even so. He should have saved this boy. He *could* have saved the boy, if he had been a little faster.

That was when Berenger Fripper, captain of the army of the north, vintener in the King's host, began to weep, hating the battle, this war, these men, but most of all, hating himself.

Chapter Twenty-Seven

He had no idea how long he remained there, kneeling on the damp grass.

The blare of a horn jerked him from his reverie. From his position beside the Frenchman, Berenger could not see the sudden charge of the English, nor the way that the Scottish broke and ran, but he could feel the difference in the line as the dwindled English battle stopped pushing and cheered. There was a renewed series of horn blasts and bellowed orders from throats already parched and raw from rasping out commands, and horses were brought up: great destriers, the chargers of the men-at-arms, which stood pawing at the ground, tossing their heads at the reek of blood and death.

All about him on the field, men were pulling off their helmets and rubbing sweat-soaked hair. Knights, esquires, men-at-arms, freemen and peasants had laboured on this field harder than most would work in a week. Arms were sore and muscles tightened with over-use, and men sagged or slumped to the ground as the realisation struck that their efforts had won them the victory. Already Clip and some other archers were ransacking the bodies, snatching a ring here, a bracelet there, a dagger or a jewelled belt. Occasionally the injured owner would feebly demur, but then the pillagers would give a quick jab with a dagger and the objections would soon cease.

Feeling like an old man, Berenger rose to his feet and gazed about him.

Over at the left flank, the Scots had already fled the field, and the only men still refusing to submit were the middle of the Scottish battle. This group was fighting still as they retreated in good order, even after the loss of their King and commanders. The depleted force gathered together more tightly, but that only made them an easier target for the bowmen who still had their weapons and some arrows. Boys were darting in amongst the dead and wounded, collecting all the undamaged arrows they could find and passing them to the archers.

Back at the wagons, the first knights and esquires were already mounted and making their way forward at an easy canter. Berenger saw the horse of Umfraville taking a wall like a light rounsey with a child on its back, rather than an armour-clad beast bearing a knight encased in steel. Umfraville rode with his lance high, until he approached a Scot, when the lance-point dipped to spear the man. The lance rose with the horse's momentum, the squealing body also rising high, only to be flicked aside as the horseman cantered on. It was as though the horse and rider were a machine, working as steadily and stolidly as a watermill, regardless of the body that squirmed and wriggled in its wake as a moorstone millwheel. Then he was on the Scottish battle, and even as he rammed his way through, three other men-at-arms, then a fourth and a fifth, then still more, poured into the Scottish line, stabbing, slashing, their mounts trampling, kicking and biting.

That was the last Berenger saw. He looked down at the Frenchman again and sank to the very depths of despair. He was aware of an exquisite hatred for the Scots. If it were not for their intolerable greed and unjustified disputes, all this could have been avoided. Thousands lay dead here, and to what purpose? It was senseless savagery.

He saw a small group of Scots running around, away from the horses. Some were running straight at the English, disorientated after the battle, confused by terror.

'What are you doing? Are you mad!' Berenger cried. He was surprised how weak his voice sounded to his own ears, but then they were ringing still to the clash of weapons and bellowing voices.

'Let me take them,' Jack said. He had appeared at Berenger's side and the vintener stared at him uncomprehendingly for a moment, but then he understood.

'It looks worse than it feels. I'll be fine, Jack.'

His comrade nodded, and then, as the Scots came closer, Berenger tried to call to them, to have them drop their weapons and submit. One man, he saw, heard his words, but instead of agreeing, the fellow bared his teeth and rushed at Berenger with an axe held high overhead. Four arrows slammed into his breast and throat, and he was almost lifted from his feet by the terrible power of the clothyards.

'Enough!' Berenger cried, but too late. The arrows flew fast, and before Berenger could stop them, all the Scots were sprawled on the ground, so full of arrows they looked like nothing so much as so many hedgehogs.

'Are you all right, Frip?' Jack said.

His concern was plain. 'I am fine. Fine.'

'Well, God has blessed us, Frip. We have a great victory today. Are you sure . . .'

'Go. There are men to be put out of their suffering.'

Jack nodded. John of Essex was a short distance away. He looked at their vintener. 'I'll go, Jack. You stay with Frip.'

'No. Both of you go. I'll be fine.'

The rest of the day was spent in despatching the wounded while the knights and other men-at-arms chased the remains of the Scottish army over the fields, in and out of the walls and ditches, and up almost as far as the March itself.

But Berenger took no part in the hunt or the pillage. He found a wagon with a pot of wine on it, and sat with it until Jack found him, and took him, singing a sad song, to see the physician.

Berenger looked about him as Jack helped him towards the barber. The field was covered in bodies, and the grass had the oily, scarlet sheen of congealing blood. As they approached the makeshift camp beside the wagons, he saw the Frenchman's body. It was already almost naked. The armour had been stripped from him, his weapons taken, and even his shirt and braies were gone. Only a neckerchief remained about his throat. Berenger's eyes remained on him as he was led past the wagons and over to a trestle table where the worst of the wounded were being seen to by Gyles of Healey, or 'Tooth Butcher', as the men knew him.

'Shit, man, you picked your fight with the wrong fellow,' he said, his face twisted in concern at the rip in Berenger's face.

'Yes. Can you fix me up?'

Wordlessly, Tooth Butcher took his arm and made him sit on a stool while he hunkered down, his fists on his thighs as he stared at Berenger thoughtfully. 'Aye, I can make it a bit better, but it won't be easy. You'll owe me after this,' he said at last.

He went to his leather bag and dug around inside it. There were several tools there. He brought out some pincers, two shears for cutting hair, some pliers for extracting teeth, and then a roll of canvas. Bringing it to the table, he unrolled it and contemplated the array of needles. 'Now, I'm no saddler, laddy, but my needlework has been said to be as good as the best harness-maker in London.'

'Who said that?' Jack asked.

'Me.'

Berenger left the barber a half-hour later. The fellow took regular swigs from a leather jug while he worked, but Berenger was past caring, and shared the strong ale. He had a feeling that if one of them stayed sober the after-effects would be less traumatic, but since he was already full of wine, the thought did not linger. Soon his face felt as though it had been skinned and rasped with a file, and perhaps burned with red-hot brands. On the way back to his men, he was vague about the direction and had to rely on Jack's patient ministrations to return him safely.

The archers had gathered over to the right of the main battlefield, away from the blood-slaked area where only a few hours ago they had scrambled and fought. Now they were sitting in distinct groups. Berenger walked among them, muttering a word or two of encouragement, resting his hand on the shoulder of a boy who sat huddled, his knees gripped tightly with both arms, his head all but concealed behind their ramparts, eyes wide and unblinking with shock. There were always those who could not cope with the foulness of battle, Berenger knew, but that boy's expression hit him harder than most. It reminded him of the fear on the face of Godefroi when he died. There was something unutterably sad about the death of youth or the shattering of youthful spirits.

With Jack aiding him, he uttered words of praise or support as he saw fit until they reached his own vintaine.

'I looked after you well enough before,' Dogbreath said, peering at his face. 'I didn't hardly need to bother, did I?'

'Aye, well, they tried, Frip, eh?' Clip said. He had a dirty cloth wrapped about his shoulder, through which the blood was already seeping. 'Yes, they tried to kill us, but our luck hasn't run out yet.'

'Your luck never will,' the Earl said. 'The Devil himself doesn't want you.'

'That's true,' Dogbreath said. 'He thinks you'd bring the tone of the place down.'

John of Essex chuckled along with the rest as Clip swore at the pair of them, but then looked at Fripper. 'What do we do now, Captain? Do we stay here to support the Archbishop and his men?'

'No. We have to return to the siege,' Jack said. 'We have a duty to be there.'

'Aye, we should be first at the plunder,' Oliver said. He licked his lips. 'Furs, gold, silver, women and wine, eh? What more could a soldier want?'

'We'll be getting none of that,' the Pardoner said. 'We've been away too long.'

'That doesn't matter,' Jack argued. 'If we are there for the end of the siege, we will have the right to our share.'

'Do ye remember so little?' Clip said. 'When we took all those cities in France on the way to Crécy, we were the ones sent on to guard and keep watch, while all those who did nothing for the battle helped themselves. It'll be the same this time, you hearken to my words: we'll do all the work, and they'll send us to the hardest places, and then some other bastards will take the credit *and* the profit.'

'Well, Fripper?' John of Essex said again. 'What will we do?'

Berenger closed his eyes against the hideous pain of his cheek and nose. It burned, as though someone had branded his face. The stitching pulled as he tried to speak.

'Tonight I will take some more wine, and then, if I can, I will sleep,' he mumbled. *And*, he added to himself, *I will try to forget*.

Chapter Twenty-Eight

He was woken early the next morning and was already up when Sir Henry Percy came to see the men. One of the new recruits had died in the night, and Berenger was looking down at the lad as the priest spoke the *viaticum* over his body and muttered his way through the *Pater Noster*.

'Captain, I hope I find ye well? Yer face shows you were at the forefront of the battle.'

'We were. My men fought well,' Berenger said. He wanted to say, *they fought like barbarian savages*, but what would be the point?

'We destroyed their army, captured their King, killed or captured some French knights fighting with them, and took Douglas, three Earls and more than fifty other barons and knights. Hah! We were chasing them all the way to Corbridge. Damn their souls, but they could run!'

Berenger nodded wearily. 'Does that mean that they are defeated for long? Will they recover their strength soon?'

'Nay, man. They are a spent force now. We'll have guaranteed ten years of peace on the Marches. They'll take that long to replace all the men we've killed. What of your men?'

'Among the archers, our losses were few. I lost some in this vintaine, but in general our losses were light.'

'Ye've had a bad battle though, man. I can see that.'

In truth, the baron himself looked thoroughly unwell. He was pale-faced, and although his joy at the victory could not be mistaken, he coughed a great deal and his head hung low. Berenger thought he looked very haggard, like a peasant who has worked long hours in the fields, or like a man about to suffer from a fever.

'My battle was not so bad as that which others suffered,' Berenger said.

'Well, ye've earned a rest.'

'We must return to the King,' Berenger said. 'I swore that I would bring news of the French to you, and that I did, but the King will need to know what has happened here.'

'Then I'll wish you Godspeed, Master Fripper. For my money, you've earned the rank of captain in the battle yesterday. You did well to rally the archers after the first arrows stung the Scots into retaliation. Without that effort, they could have overrun us all, or the Scots could have waited and forced us to try our luck against them. *That* could have been disastrous.'

'Sir Henry, the young Frenchman who was slain in the ring around their King . . .' Berenger started, but then he didn't know how to finish. What could he say? The poor boy was too young, he wanted to surrender, he wanted to return to France to woo a woman or two, to grow old with his grandchildren on his knees, a loving wife at his side?

'The youngster? Aye. I saw him. It was a shame to see the young scamp killed, but that is war.'

'Sir, would it be possible to pay for a stone for his funeral?'

Sir Henry looked at him for a moment. 'This was the same

youth ye caught in the rearguard action the day before the fight, was it not? Aye, man, I'll gladly put some money together for a stone. I feel sorry to see a fine, proud fellow like that die so young.'

'I thank you, Sir Henry.'

'And now, man, ye should get some rest. Ye look as though ye'll need it.'

Jack asked quickly, 'Sir, will Fripper be taking all his vintaine back to the south?'

'Well, man, my Lord Neville was to send three thousand to the siege. It seems his men are not badly required up here now. I see no reason why Fripper here and his vintaine shouldn't go with them. And if Fripper is content, I'll give order that he's to be the captain of the archers. Would that content ye?'

Fripper tried to smile, but the scabs of his wound made him wince. 'That would indeed, my lord.'

The journey was long and uncomfortable, but Fripper and the men made their way in stages until they had passed the great wen of London and could catch a ship to France.

He stood on the quayside at Calais with the first groups of archers, listening to their banter.

'Doesn't look as if they've stirred their stumps, does it?' Clip said. 'The minute we left, they must've put their feet up and had a rest.'

'You would expect them to have broken into the town by now?' the Earl asked languidly.

'I feared they might. I want me share of the winnings. What, would ye have the bastards get in and snare all the best prizes?'

'There aren't likely to be too many prizes here,' Jack said. 'The best things will have been moved before the full blockade worked. The gold and silver would have been boxed and sent by galley to be placed in safekeeping. The furs and rich silks may still be there, a few of them, but the rest?' He threw his cupped hands up as though tossing handfuls of flour. 'Poufft! Gone!'

'What would you do now, then?' Clip said, unwilling to surrender his dreams, but always ready to learn from another seasoned campaigner.

'Me, I'd leave this eyesore and work my way down the rivers towards the richer little towns. You could take a town with a small force, and rule it like a lord. That would be fine work. To have a little place all of your own, tax all the people, maybe set up your own tolls outside the town, and take a share of the money from travellers passing by.'

'And have the French King breathing down your neck inside a week?' the Earl said with disdain. 'I can think of faster ways of having my neck stretched, but not many.'

'Are you as big a fool as you look, then?' John of Essex asked. 'You think the French King has men to spare just now, with his main town on the coast being held ransom? And if it were not just me, but four or five groups of men had the same idea, we could take over a county, perhaps. Capture a bigger town and the area all about it, and form alliances with the men in other towns. Man, it would be easy!'

Jean de Vervins was nearby, and now he joined in the discussion. 'There are indeed rich towns in France. You are correct, my friend. Look at Champagne, for example. There are magnificent places there. Many. I would think of one such as Laon. That would be worth some effort.' He spoke with a curious twist to his mouth, as though he had seen a joke that was hidden to all the others.

'What do you know of such places?' Berenger demanded.

'I know all the Champagne area. I was born there, and I've spent many happy hours riding about the land,' Jean de Vervins smiled.

'When we were fighting up at Durham, I saw you in the middle battle. You were there, fighting, although you'd been told to stay back.'

'Yes. The fighting was already mostly done, and I thought that since the men had been striving so hard for three hours of the day, I with my fresh arms and unweary muscles could do some good.'

'The French fellow saw you – the youth called Godefroi whom we caught. He recognised you – why?'

'You mean the man we caught after I saved your life, Vintener?'

'That doesn't answer my question.'

Jean's eyes narrowed, and his expression reminded Berenger of a man who was hooding his thoughts.

'Do you know who Godefroi was?' Berenger persisted.

'Yes. He was a messenger for the French King, up in the north to exhort the Scottish to fight. I was on the same ship as him, travelling to Scotland.'

'He was a messenger?'

'Of course. He was to give messages to the Scottish, and then fight with them to encourage them in their campaign. According to the French, my own task was the same. If one of us were to die, the other would survive, you see.'

'And you succeeded?'

'My interest lay in delaying the army so it would do less damage. I believe I succeeded. You know the little tower in Northumberland – Selby's? Well, Selby had sworn fealty to King David some years ago and it made the King angry to see him so content in his English castle. So I suggested that the insult to his honour should be razed, just as the castle should be laid waste.'

'Godefroi was convinced that there was no chance the English would hold back the Scottish invaders,' Berenger stated. 'Why would he have been so certain of that?'

'Perhaps he merely considered that with King Edward here in France along with all his army, the Archbishop and his allies could not hope to hold the March against such a strong foe as the Scottish.'

'And perhaps he had been misled by someone.'

'What do you mean?' Jean enquired mildly.

Berenger wasn't sure himself. The idea that this man Jean de Vervins could have been a spy for the English was curious enough, but was it any more preposterous to think that he could have been serving *both* sides? Or that he could have served one side, but appeared to serve both? Perhaps he had convinced the French and Scots that he was on their side, while in reality he was helping to destroy them?

It sickened Berenger. He thought of Godefroi's face again, seeing that moment when the pole-axe broke into the boy's skull and his eyes died, as though his soul was no more than a candle-flame to be snuffed. It was one thing to know that a man had died in a fair battle, but quite another to think that he had died because he had believed in a lie told by a man pretending to be a friend who was in reality determined to see his destruction.

'I serve your King,' Jean de Vervins said, and this time he smiled.

Berenger could happily have smashed that smile with his gauntleted fist.

The Vidame was definitely not expecting to see the huge figure of Bertucat approaching him openly in the town, and he felt his anger flare.

'I have to speak to you,' Bertucat mumbled, and was gone.

The Vidame caught up with him further into Villeneuve-la-Hardie within sight of Calais' walls. The artillery was loosing stones at the walls in a steady barrage, the huge wooden structures swinging around, the slings releasing their vast weights into the sky, tumbling and spinning lazily until they slammed into the walls with a hideous impact. If a piece were to hit a man, some were large enough to cut him in half. As it was, the smaller pieces could inflict severe injuries.

'What is it?' the Vidame hissed as he came closer. He was tempted to pull out his knife and stab the fat man where he stood.

'Jean de Vervins,' Bertucat said flatly.

'What of him?'

'He was on the ships going to Scotland to help advise them of our King's support. I've been waiting at the docks to learn what happened. It's not good news.'

'Tell me!'

'I overheard some of the messengers coming back. There has been a great victory – our allies were crushed. There will be no more support from Scotland. The English even captured their King. He's been hurried away to a safe prison.'

The Vidame felt as if he was holding his breath at this appalling news. He wondered whether God truly had moved to support the English. They seemed invulnerable. He had a sudden sense of impending disaster. France, it seemed, was deserted. She was alone, desperate and bereft, while the English stamped on her and trampled her into the mud.

'There's more,' Bertucat said. 'Your spy has returned and says he must speak to you. It is urgent. He said he has seen Jean de Vervins.'

'Good. Did Jean have any news?'

'You don't understand me. He saw Jean because Jean is a traitor. Jean de Vervins has become an agent of the English.'

The Vidame's voice shook. 'My God!'

Turning, he stared at the walls of the town. They looked impregnable, but even as he watched, a rock struck the parapet of the nearest wall and knocked off two castellations. It looked like the beginning of the end for the town. For the first time, the Vidame began to suspect that Calais might fall. And if Calais, why not Rouen, or even Paris?

The Vidame felt weak and lonely. If Jean de Vervins had double-crossed them, whom could he trust?

Chapter Twenty-Nine

Berenger's face was itching. Tooth Butcher had come with the army from Percy, and now appeared to have adopted Berenger as his own personal experimental patient. Every few days Berenger would see him in the roads and he would peer closely at his stitching with every sign of satisfaction. No matter how often he heard the barber tell him to leave it alone or he would scratch it into gangrene, he could not help but worry at the edges of the bloody clots.

'You've seen gangrene, haven't you, Frip? It's a horrible thing. Eats away at you under your skin. And it all comes about, I reckon, because of daft buggers like you, who keep fiddling with your scar, and before long you'll have killed off the skin and got yourself diseased. You do that, and I won't be answerable. It'll be a coffin for you, and that's the truth.'

'As a barber, you are good; as a bone-fixer or hacker off of other men's limbs, you are competent, I'll give you that. But when it comes to things like this, you have no idea how greatly it plagues me! I *have* to scratch to get some relief!'

'It's your life, Fripper. And I'm not your mother. Just don't come running to me when you find that your face is falling off and you're being eaten away from inside, that's all I'm saying. Got that?'

Berenger took his advice and tried to keep his hands from his face – but Christ's cods, it was difficult! On an evening like this, when the bitter wind was blowing, shrinking a man's balls to the size of acorns, it was even harder. The chill seemed to inspire the scar tissue to produce greater heat in comparison. The worst of the scabs had fallen away, but the feeling of tightness, and the sense that inside the wound there was a scrabbling of insect feet trying to escape, was utterly maddening.

Things were not eased by the discussion he was forced to have with Sir John and Sir Peter of Bromley. Sir Peter made it clear he thought the full responsibility for the death of the messenger lay at Berenger's door, and insisted that Berenger was demoted; no longer a captain, but merely a vintener again. He had demanded that Berenger be reduced to the rank of archer, but there Sir John drew a line. He threatened to take the matter to his friend Prince Edward, and on hearing that, Sir Peter reluctantly backed down. Sir John was known to have the Prince's ear.

In those times, the only ease Berenger knew was when Béatrice took to caring for him. For the first few days after returning, when it felt as if he was going to have to scratch the whole of his face away, he was soothed by her soft hands. She draped cool cloths over his wound, murmuring gently to him all the while. When he opened his eyes and saw her face, he was struck by the compassion there. It was like looking into the eyes of a nun, or even the Madonna herself.

Marguerite too was kind to him. For a woman who had suffered so much at the hands of the English, she worked like a saint. Every so often, he even thought he saw a little smile begin at the edges of her mouth, as though she was not tending him from duty alone, but from a sense of personal gratitude. Not that he had done anything for her. She had come here because Béatrice and Archibald had invited her and her son.

Today, his wound was painful again.

'Bad, Frip?'

'I'll live, Jack. Is there any news?'

'Only that Sir Peter's been given a bollocking by Sir John. It seems he blamed you for everything, from the death of the messenger to the bad harvest last year!'

'I don't trust that man,' Berenger said.

'I think you'll find he views you in the same light,' the Earl commented from near the fire.

'If he were a spy, he could have spread news of our journey to Durham,' Berenger said grimly. 'He could have betrayed any of our missions.'

'So could another,' Jack said reasonably.

'He's a knight. He comes and goes on raids all the time.' Berenger was thinking of what Béatrice had told him – that Sir Peter was often out, away from the siege. That would give him time to leave messages with others – messages that could be passed on to the French commanders. Sir Peter was only a recent turncoat, when all was said and done. What if he had never genuinely changed his allegiance? Besides, Béatrice detested the man and Berenger trusted her judgement in many matters.

'What of it?'

'Just warn the men to keep their eyes open where he's concerned. Sir Peter of Bromley may have forgotten he's supposed to have changed his allegiance.'

It was mid-November, and the weather had grown steadily worse. The huts of their wooden town had become islands. The roadways between were filled with mud and puddles, reeking as middens overflowed and human waste lay in the streets. Any grass that had once filled the lanes was long gone, and the place had become infested with rats and wild dogs, both species slinking away warily when humans came close.

It was the rats that had led to the men coming out here today. They had some small dogs with them and had been trapping all the rats they could find. Now several sacks' worth were moving and scrabbling as the men began to heft them. The vintaine had cleared a space, lining it with close-fitting stones to make a small arena, and now the men emptied the rats into it. The creatures ran hither and thither, and Grandarse stood booming out his appreciation of the sport to come.

Three small dogs, yapping and barking enthusiastically, were held in sight of their prey while men wagered coins as to how many each dog would kill; when all the bets were taken the dogs were released and thrown in amongst the rats.

So far, the men had been sitting outside Calais for two and a half months. Berenger and his vintaine had at least been able to get away for a while, even if it had involved putting their lives at peril, but for the rest of the army, the dampness and monotony, with the ever-present risk of fever and death, was wearing all the men down. It was partly in order to counterbalance their demoralised state that Berenger had suggested the rat-catching. It certainly had an impact on the men in his vintaine.

'Get that one, you poxed little wimp!' Clip shouted in disgust as his terrier bounded over one rat and missed another. 'What is it with you? I'll bloody kill you meself if the rats can't be arsed!'

'Ah, did your special little doggie miss again?' the Earl enquired with spurious sympathy. 'Let me see, what did you call it?'

'I think he called it the Berserker, didn't he?' the Pardoner grinned.

'Someone or something's berserk, I will agree,' the Earl said.

'Look at that! Mine has the big bastard by the throat!' Aletaster cried.

'Your little one is being played with,' Dogbreath muttered. 'If I was in there, that one would have been first to go.'

'If you were in there, my friend, the rats would all have fled from the stink,' the Earl said.

Dogbreath turned on him, snarling, and would have leaped upon him, but Berenger was glad to see that the Pardoner and Clip both took a shoulder each and heaved him back to the entertainment. The vintaine's survivors were melding well into a unit.

Berenger watched as a terrier snapped a rat's spine. One bite, a jerk of the head, and the rat's back was broken. It dangled limply, one leg pawing at the ground as it was dropped, and the dog ran to its next victim. A snap, a shake, and another died. It was like watching a hunt – when the alaunts and hounds ran to a fox or a hart, the leader of the pack snapping the spine and killing so swiftly. Few men could kill so cleanly, he thought. Some did: he knew an expert warrener who would catch his rabbits, softly stroking them as he disentangled them from his nets, deftly calming them until he quickly broke their necks. They died without fear at his hands.

Not all these rats did as well. Running wildly in their panic, they were hunted down by the vintaine's terriers. One rat, he saw, was flung high into the air, and he watched as it flew up – but as it fell, his gaze remained fixed on the distance.

'What's up, Frip? What is it, man?' Grandarse demanded.

'*Archers!*' Berenger bellowed. '*Archers, to arms!*'

'What the fuck's going on?' Clip said.

'French ships! They're resupplying the town!'

The Vidame was in his tent when the doorway was opened.

'I am glad to see you here,' Jean de Vervins said. He wore an ingratiating smile on his face.

The Vidame drew his lips tightly over his mouth. 'And I you. I heard you were serving with the English against the Scots.'

'Yes. It was an interesting little engagement. Quite lively.'

'May I offer you wine, Sir Knight?'

'No, I thank you,' Jean said. 'I merely wanted to come and find a friendly face.'

'You can always rely on me,' the Vidame said. 'After all, when we renounced our vows to King Philippe, and became servants of King Edward, we burned our houses and vills behind us.'

'I did not,' Jean said with a trace of asperity. 'Mine were all stolen from me before. When the King took my enemy's part, that was when I was forced to choose a different route. He betrayed me, just as he did you, too.'

'He betrayed us all,' the Vidame said. But in his heart he was screaming at Jean de Vervins that there was only one traitor in the tent.

As soon as Berenger had spotted the ships, the men had scurried away from the rat-killing, apart from Clip who leaned down, quickly cuffed his losing dog, and grabbed their arms and bows and arrows. With Georges, whom they had adopted as the replacement for Donkey, to push their cartload of arrows, they hastened to the docks and boarded a fishing vessel.

Casting off, Sir John and Grandarse had to threaten to kill a member of the crew to persuade the shipmaster to take them to the midst of the French ships. As soon as they drew near, the archers began to loose their arrows. Some sailors could be seen leaping from the rigging as arrows ripped through sails or struck, quivering, into masts and spars, while many lost their grip and fell screaming to the deck beneath. One man was hit and fell, only to strike the wale with such a loud crack that Berenger could hear it from his boat. The man had surely broken his spine, and started to shriek with every movement of the ship, unable to free himself.

Sir John stood at the prow, his sword drawn, yelling with rage at the ships moving before him. 'Aim for that one!' he bellowed, and the shipmaster turned her prow towards the vessel indicated, but before they could reach it, another was close to ramming them. 'Mind that!'

As the ship turned to save her hull, Sir John roared at the men to get grapnels and draw nearer to this new target, but although some archers kept up their practice, to aim and loose from a rolling, bucking deck was no easy feat. Many arrows flew too high, and as many ended up planted in the hull of the ship. Few indeed found their mark, and as they worked, so did the French sailors, hacking with swords or axes at the grapnel ropes as soon as they landed. One parted with a great crack, and the men holding it were thrown backwards as the rope flailed. The rope-end knocked another man senseless, opening his brow to the bone from temple to temple.

A shouted command, and suddenly crossbow bolts were coming at the English. Two archers were hit and collapsed, while another had a bolt through his thigh. He kept on loosing his arrows, but Berenger could see he was weakened. Later they realised his artery had been severed, and he died of blood loss.

Berenger grabbed a polearm and began to use it to keep French sailors away from the grapnels, before leaping up onto the wale. At his side he saw Sir John jump lightly into the enemy vessel and begin to attack the French with his sword. With three sweeps of his blade, Sir John had cut down two men, and now already Jack was at Berenger's side with an axe and poleaxe, and Clip was near, loosing more arrows and dropping more Frenchmen. There came a bellow, and a Frenchman darted forward to loose a crossbow bolt. All the men instinctively turned, and as they did so, two more French shipmen pelted forward and hacked away the remaining grapnel ropes. Now there was only Sir John, Berenger and five men left on the ship, and the whole ship's company of Frenchmen began to press upon them urgently, striving to force them into the prow itself, where the boarders' movements could be restricted and they could be picked off one by one. A crossbow bolt flew into the face of one of the archers – Berenger didn't have time to look down to see who it had hit – and then they were rushed. The French came at them en masse, and that was when Berenger was struck on the left shoulder, making him cry out. Once more, his arm fell dead at his side. For a while he thought it was a sword blow that had cut off all sensation, but then the feeling returned with a vengeance, and he had to grit his teeth against the pain.

They fought on, weary but determined, as the French tried to force them into the sea, or at least just kill them all. And then, when Berenger felt sure that he was at the uttermost limits of his own strength, there came a juddering crunch in the timbers at his feet, and he was almost thrown to the deck. And joy of joys, suddenly he saw that it was their shipmaster with his humble little fishing boat, and the deck rang to the clatter of English armour as the men sprang over the sides and attacked the French from behind.

Yes, it had been a success against that one ship. That was itself good. But the rest of the ships had got past and revictualled the town.

'We cannot go on like this!' Sir John said as they disembarked.

'We could mount siege engines to sink their ships, sir,' Jack suggested.

'Archibald would be happy to test his gonnes against them,' Berenger put in. 'Although whether he would hit them at any distance is another matter.'

'Don't ever let him hear you question his machines,' Sir John joked, but then continued more seriously, 'This siege is sapping our army. With all those ships getting through, we'll be here another three months at least – all through December, January and February. My armour will have rusted to dust in that time.'

'What else can we do?'

'Break this damn siege!' Sir John grated, and in the grey morning light, he stalked away in the direction of the King's pavilion.

Chapter Thirty

Sir John de Sully looked exhausted already when Berenger saw him the next morning. The knight had been up all night, first with Berenger's archers and then on the ship, and his efforts had taken their toll.

The vintaine itself was weary, after sending flight after flight of arrows into the ships sailing into the harbour, but today they had a little respite. They stood on the shore and watched while Archibald's gonnes thundered and roared – and achieved spectacularly little. Sir John, furious to see so many ships making their way for the harbour, had commandeered another small vessel and tried to get to them to sink some, but it was already too late. He had spent all the early hours trying to clamber from one ship to another, but beyond gaining a fresh scar on his right cheek, his attempts had all failed.

'You should rest, Sir John,' Berenger said. 'You look worn out.'

'Nonsense. Never felt better.'

Berenger grinned to himself. Sir John was unfailingly cheerful – a trait that could never be underestimated in an army.

'How about you?' Sir John asked kindly.

Berenger gave a dry smile and flexed his arm.

Earlier in the summer, he had taken a crossbow bolt in the flesh of his upper torso, and the muscles had never fully healed, and then during the vicious fighting outside Durham, the maul which had struck him hit near the same place. Fortunately, he had been wearing his padded jack, and that, along with the mail on top and the tippet of his bascinet, had deflected much of the force of the blow. Even so, it was a cruel injury. Sometimes he thought it hurt more than the wound on his face.

'I feel as if a horse has kicked me,' he said.

'At least you have been persuaded to keep your helm on your head,' Sir John said.

'Yes, sir. After this Scottish cut, I felt my luck was running out. Besides, a helm is less annoying in this temperature. It's much worse in the middle of the summer, when you can scarcely breathe with it on.'

'Aye. True enough.' Sir John was gazing back out to sea. Now that the sun was thinly penetrating the heavy clouds that lowered overhead, the battlefield of the night before could be seen clearly.

'What now, Sir John?'

'We have to do more to stop ships entering the harbour. Archibald swore his gonnes would stop them, but they are as much use as throwing shit at the French. They achieve sod all!'

'He does his best.'

'Well, his best is not good enough. We need to come up with something else.'

He was exhausted, but it had been exciting to see the battle, Ed thought. He had been at the gonnes with Archibald when the ships had appeared, but once the vintaine was sent to a ship to pursue the French craft, Georges had been left behind. The younger boy and Ed took the opportunity to run to Archibald's emplacement and see the gonnes fire.

Archibald had made a comfortable fort on the northernmost tip of the east shore, and the two gonnes were resting on great oaken trestles, pointing directly over the entrance to the Calesian harbour, towards the Rysbank. There, Calesians with crossbows and small gonnes tried to blast at him, but since he could call on a vintaine or more of archers to guard him, he and Béatrice could work without fear of being hit. The crossbowmen were not foolish enough to put themselves to the challenge when so many archers could rain down missiles on their heads.

The roar and flame of the gonnes discharging was enough to send Georges squeaking and weeping to the back of the bunker at first. The two shots were so loud, he thought his ears must be destroyed. A gout of flame, and then the slamming concussion hit, as he saw the enormous blue-black smoke launching towards the ships in the harbour. He felt a mixture of horror, terror and exultation all rolled into one.

Ed saw his initial shock, and put his arms about him. After witnessing ten or more discharges, he gently pulled Georges away from the cannonade.

It was then that he saw the cleric. The man was standing nearby, his rosary in his hand and an expression of deep sadness in his eyes. Ed was sure that the man hadn't noticed the two boys, but he felt Georges stiffen momentarily and then he shot a quick look at Ed, as if wondering whether he too had seen the man. But Ed took no notice. There were clerics and soldiers all over the town of Villeneuve-la-Hardie.

One more made little difference, so he thought. But when they had moved away and left the gonnes some way behind, he was aware of Georges turning and staring back towards the man again. But when Ed looked, the cleric was gone.

Weeks passed, but the determination of the English to break the deadlock was never stronger. After the last convoy had managed to break into Calais with their supplies, it was clear that the town would be able to survive well beyond Christmas and into March 1347. But even with the new town being built all around Calais, none of the English wanted to remain there longer than necessary.

The members of the vintaine were as cheery and enthusiastic as only English soldiers can be.

'Look, Frip, the poxy water's frozen again,' Oliver called.

Clip sneered unpleasantly. 'Stick your head in then, and talk. With all your hot air, you'll soon have it boiling.'

Even Jack chuckled at that. Then, 'Oliver, why are you bothering our captain with that? You know he's an ideas man. He can't deal with detail.'

'Because I'm fed up with being stuck in this shit-hole and want to get back to England, to a real alehouse with English ale that hasn't gone sour or salty being brought over here.'

'You should be grateful. It takes away the taste of the rotten meat,' the Pardoner said.

'We'll break the town before long,' Berenger said.

'How?' the Pardoner said rudely. 'Are we to cut the ice into the shape of rocks and use the stone-throwers to fling them over the walls so we may freeze the townspeople to death?'

'No,' Berenger said. 'For some weeks there's been a plan to assemble ships here – I'm told they're on their way. We'll have more than fifty fishing boats and all with ladders pegged to their decks. The King's had all the carpenters he could find in the South of England working on them for the last month, apparently. With luck, when they arrive we'll be able to scale those walls and take the town.'

'Scale those walls, eh?' Jack turned and stared in the direction of the town, where the great walls reared high over the shacks of Villeneuve-la-Hardie. 'They're the best walls of any town in France, they say.'

'Yes, but even the best walls can be taken by a few determined men,' Fripper said.

'So long as we're here to protect them,' Clip said. 'You wouldn't get me up a ladder on a ship.'

'The ladders won't all be on the ships, I expect,' Berenger said. The thought of using a boat as a base for a ladder did not appeal to him either. 'But once we're in the town, all this nonsense will cease. The French can come and knock on *our* door for a change.'

'Aye,' Clip said. He pulled a face. 'So long as they don't seal us in there like we're trying to do with them!'

Clip need not have worried.

Berenger was grim-faced as he passed along the line of his archers. The Donkey was at the cart again, helping to show young Georges what was needed. Berenger wanted to give them a smile as he passed, but he couldn't. His face felt like it was on fire, and he could only wear a fixed glower. It felt as if he had a scalding flame licking all the way from his ear to his nose and beyond, and he felt close to screaming because of it. The pain was constant, nagging at him no matter what he did all day. It kept his expression harsh and unrelenting, and he regretted it when he saw Georges recoil, but there was no time to spare for a young lad's finer feelings.

'Frip?' Grandarse called as Berenger approached.

The older man was leaning against a wooden pavise, drinking

from a massive leathern jug. 'Are ye ready, Frip? By God's tears, if this works, we'll be in the town this very evening!'

'*If* it works,' Berenger grunted. He had little enthusiasm for the idea.

'Don't look like that, man! Anyone'd think you were being sent up there on your own to take the town's defences,' Grandarse chuckled, then his smile vanished and he bellowed at a hapless archer chatting to a companion, 'Hoi – you! String your bow! You won't do much good from here without a stave to send missiles against those French bastards, will you, you idle git!' Turning to Berenger again, he confided, 'You've got to keep on top of these daft beggars. Most of them would prefer to be in a tavern than earning their spurs.' He took another long pull at his jug.

'Yes,' Berenger agreed, but in truth he was barely listening. He felt peculiar. His face was tormenting him, the wound pulsing and thundering with every step he took or word he spoke, and meanwhile his shoulder was thudding dully. The maul-strike had not been strong enough to damage any bones, but the muscles from his collar bone to his shoulderblade had been mashed and his left arm was still all but useless.

'Show a little enthusiasm, man,' Grandarse said, this time with an edge of seriousness. 'Remember, you're the leader. Your men need to see you happy and confident, or didn't I teach you anything?'

'Yes, Grandarse,' Berenger said. 'You told me to shine like the sun before your men, and then fart in their faces.'

'Aye, well, the farting you do later, when it seems safer. But keep 'em lean, keep 'em mean, keep 'em keen – that's the way. Just like a guard dog. Ah, they're going.'

At the sound of horns being blown, ships appeared, sailing around the point and into the waters between the Rysbank and the town. In the foremost vessel, Sir John de Sully stood with his banner flying: a series of bars gules on an ermine shield, the little black marks showing clearly. They came on, steadily, over the next half-hour of the sun. Berenger could see the change in shadows as the ships began to approach their target.

As his eyes followed them, he caught sight of Sir Peter. The knight stood watching him from further down the bank, his clerk at his side, two men-at-arms from his household just behind. Sir Peter made no attempt to conceal his surveillance.

Grandarse roared: 'Archers, *nock*!'

The ships were sailing slowly but steadily, and then, as they came opposite Berenger and his archers, the vessels turned towards the walls of the town.

'Archers, *draw*!'

Berenger turned his attention back to the town. All along the line of the wall, there were shouts and screams as the ships dropped anchor and lashed themselves to the shore or to ships alongside, and then the first of the scaling ladders were hoisted and rattled to the side of the mighty walls.

'*LOOSE!*'

The arrows sped to the walls as the first heads appeared. Some ducked away, but two or three were struck. Then Englishmen were clambering up the ladders as the vessels beneath them moved in the water, rocking on the waves. Over to the left Berenger saw a ladder begin to slide sideways, the men at its top clinging on for dear life as it continued, gathering speed. It crashed into the neighbouring ladder, and the two went over together, the men clattering on the rocks while their ships bucked beneath them. It made Berenger's belly roil to see so many men dying so needlessly.

Sir John was halfway up his ladder when a rock hurled by a Frenchman struck the head of the man above him. That man immediately dropped, and when he struck Sir John, the knight's legs were ripped from the rungs. He fell, but only a few steps – but above him now, three rungs of the ladder were gone. The heavy rock had smashed them in passing. Sir John had to clamber back down to the ship, unable to use that ladder now, but he was soon organising his men, and passed to the next ship in the line, which was bound to his own. Yet before he could reach that ladder, boiling oil had been poured from the walls, and a flaming torch was dropped after it. Instantly great black clouds of smoke were rising from the ship, and struggle though the men might, they could do nothing against the flames. The ship was evacuated.

Sir John de Sully coughed and spluttered as a thick fog of smoke smothered him. He could feel the filthy smuts in his eyes and clogging his lungs as he chopped at the ropes holding this ship to the others. It was vital that they took this ship away before it could spread fire to the others. While some ladders had been taken out of the ships and set to rest on the rocky shore beneath the wall, much of the space was filled with huge boulders and rocks that made siting a ladder safely quite impossible. The men scrambled about, but most had to rely on the ships to give them the platform they needed.

He rushed to the next ship and the men helped heave the burning vessel away. Overhead he heard the shouts and commands of the French, but that was soon overwhelmed by the sudden whistling of hundreds of arrows passing together. It was like a massive flight of swans, he thought, but then he was at the next ship and clambering up the slick rungs. A man above slipped and landed on top of him, and he fell a second time, winded, staring up at the men on the walls. One, he saw, was sticking two fingers up at him. The French would routinely cut the fingers from an archer's hand, but Sir John neither noticed, nor cared. All he knew was that his backside hurt abominably, and that his mouth tasted of soot.

Grabbing his sword, he stood and glared about him. Men were still trying to climb, but the French had the upper hand. One man, he saw, at the far side of the ships, was smothered in boiling oil, and for some moments he ran about the ship, shrieking in anguish as the oil flayed the flesh from his body. A merciful comrade slew him with a blow from a poleaxe. Just then, more oil was ignited in a great roaring *whoosh* of flame that Sir John could feel from where he stood. He had to turn and cover his face.

'It's no good!' he bellowed. 'Stop the attack! Shipmasters, unbind the ships and weigh anchor! We can do no more here!'

He had to shout the command three times, and then blow a blast on his horn to get the attention of the shipmen and fighters, but at last they heard and the attack was called off, to the hilarity and jeers of the guards on the walls. He could hear them shouting abuse, and it was enough to make him want to turn back. Perhaps if they were to concentrate all their energies on one small section of the wall, take archers to focus on the wall at either side and keep defenders at bay, perhaps then they could take that small part, and use it as a bridgehead, bringing up more and more men ...

No. That too must fail, he thought. There was nothing they could do. It had to be a case of slowly starving out the garrison and population of the town. There was no other way.

Berenger allowed his bow to drop. This fight was over. But then, as he turned away, he saw that Sir Peter was still standing and observing him.

It made the vintener feel deeply unsettled.

Chapter Thirty-One

All through December and January the assaults continued. King Edward III was hungry for victory and needed to lance this boil. Although Berenger agreed with Sir John about the strategy of starving the inhabitants, it was clear that there would be no relaxation in the constant attempts to take the town by force.

More and more men poured into Villeneuve-la-Hardie, and not only soldiers. To support the artillery, large numbers of carpenters were brought across the Channel, and they began to construct more stone-throwing machines, while Archibald was delighted to be given ten more monstrous gonnes, and as many barrels of powder as he could store. His serpentine was carefully placed away from any risk of moisture damaging it, and the gonnes kept up a steady, if unmelodious cacophony. It all added to the unreality of the situation.

Jean de Vervins walked about the town with a growing feeling of impatience. To his mind, this siege was pointless. There were far better things for him to be doing.

Ever since the day that his King had humiliated him at the field outside Paris, allowing Henri du Bos to vanquish him with an unfair attack, Jean de Vervins had been desperate for revenge. He had broken away from his home, from his former loyalties, from all that had defined him – and now he was doubly a traitor. Not only had his French King not comprehended the depth of his rage at the humiliation, Jean de Vervins had covered his tracks so cleverly that the fact of his treachery had not been noticed. Using him to pass messages to King David in Scotland had cost the Scots their lives, their army, their future. All because of him, Jean de Vervins. And next he would begin to bring the battle home to the King of France. He would bring the battle to Paris, or near enough to cause despair at the royal court.

All he needed was to hear from his friend Gauvain de Bellemont about progress at Laon. As soon as the merchants and town's guilds were prepared, Jean would be able to bring a small force and take the town. After that, all the towns of Champagne and the lands up to the Flemings would convert and take oaths to support England. No one trusted the French King to be able to defend them now.

How *could* they trust him after the military disaster of Crécy?

Berenger thought Jean de Vervins was a mere turncoat, a man determined to win payment for his loyalty: a *mercenary*. He was much more than that. Jean was the man who could bring about the ruination of the kingdom of Philippe de Valois.

Jean was unique.

It was in the night that the fever took him. Berenger had enjoyed a good meal of pottage with some salted beef, and was sitting back with a horn filled with cider, when the first sensations of something being not right began to assail him. He blamed the meal. Salted beef was heavy on the belly, and it was quite a hot food for a man who was naturally a little melancholy, as a physician had once told him. He wished now that they still had the services of the leech who had joined them on their journey to Crécy, and who had nursed so many of the vintaine back to full strength on that march when wounds threatened to carry them away; however, he had left before they reached Crécy. His skills had been seen and appreciated by the Earl of Warwick, and with the offer of a vastly better purse, he had reluctantly left them.

But now Berenger felt he could really have done with the man's expertise. He decided to take to his palliasse.

Later, he could recall certain things. But of the following week, he would only ever have a sketchy memory. He had lain, so they told him, in a muck sweat, shivering and complaining while the scar on his face glowed like a branding iron in the forge. It took all the efforts of two women to keep him cool and quiet, and even when the fever was over, he was left feeling like a piece of metal after the smith has pummelled it on his anvil.

Later he remembered only snatches of those days. He knew he had looked up and seen the Devil overhead, and tried to beat at him with his hands; he remembered the two women's faces looking down at his with such sweetness in their eyes that it made him want to weep; he woke once and saw Marguerite sitting at his side, her head resting on the wall, her face pale, her mouth hanging slackly open, and he thought she must have died, but then he realised she was only sleeping. When he did finally waken fully, he could see from Marguerite's pallor that she must have spent many hours in that room with him, washing, feeding and soothing him. As he looked at her, she stirred, and her eyes opened and met his. For a moment, he saw in her eyes a pure joy, as though his recovery was the greatest gift she had received, and then she slowly rose. She was exhausted, her feet leaden, her every movement slow as she walked to him and helped him drink a little. Then she bent and touched his brow with her lips, like a mother kissing her child. It was only fleeting, and then she was gone. It was a relief to him to see her go to her own palliasse, lie down on it and fall into a deep, natural sleep.

Berenger watched her. Her breast rose and fell and she rolled, her head cradled on her arm, breathing quietly. She looked as beautiful as the Madonna, and he felt a quickening of his heart, but he closed his eyes and turned away. She was married; he was a soldier. Life was complicated enough.

Grandarse came when Berenger was recovered, and told him how the siege had progressed while he was laid up.

After more attempts to assault the walls, the English had surrendered to reality and decided that it would be better to fully surround the town instead, and starve the people of Calais into submission. The first stage of this strategy was to remove the Rysbank, a long bank that protected both the harbour and the town itself from attack. The English were determined to take this, and several assaults had been launched, all so far to no avail. However, with the arrival of the dire winter weather, that was less of a concern. The French would be unable to supply the town until spring at the earliest. The Channel was vile in such weather, and the English themselves had to rely upon supplies being brought overland from the Fleming territories.

At last, as weak as a newborn kitten, Berenger left his bed to hobble about the place. He felt as though his bowels were constantly in danger of voiding themselves. Marguerite was always on hand to lend him an arm to lean on. She had become indispensable to him, even as her son had become essential to the vintaine. He watched her covertly as she went about her business, cooking, washing and generally helping Béatrice with her duties, and every so often he would catch the Donkey's eye and thought he could discern a note of reproval there. What the hell. He was a boy. He didn't understand anything.

It was well into January before he felt as though he could hold a sword again. Even then, his left arm was still badly injured.

'I might as well have it strapped to my chest for all the use I can make of it,' he grumbled to Jack.

'We could always ask the barber to remove it for you. I daresay some of the men would do it for you,' Jack said, eyeing it quizzically. 'I could do it with an axe, if you want.'

'Fuck off.'

The sight of the cleric was unsettling to Ed. There was something about him that put his teeth on edge.

Georges clearly knew him, but wouldn't say much about it, except that the man had been helpful to him when he had first arrived in the camp. Even when he had said that much, Georges seemed to grow ashamed, or upset. It was natural enough. Ed remembered a little about the time when his own parents had died. For a long while after that he had felt quite guilty. There was something about being alive when they had died that made him feel some kind of responsibility, as though it was in some way his fault that they were dead. He could all too easily imagine that Georges felt a similar guilt for the death of his own father and family, but Ed thought he might be feeling even worse. His mother had not died. Georges should have remained close by and searched for her, rather than running off and joining the very army that had killed his father and the others.

Why *had* he joined the English? It was a thought that kept popping into Ed's head, and for some reason it happened more and more on days like this.

Ed had spent the morning with Béatrice, helping her and Marguerite as they looked after Berenger. The man was still very weak, although gradually he was coming back to life. Ed was relieved to hear that Berenger was fretting at being kept to his palliasse. That sounded more like the man he knew, and if he was honest, he was sick of seeing Béatrice go to him each day and mop his brow, feed him his broth or pottage, help him to a chamber pot, or any of the other hundred and one little tasks that she performed for her patient. Ed did not like to think of her soft, gentle hands on Berenger's body. *He* wanted to feel her fingers on him, and to be allowed to run his hands over her . . . but it was foolish to think like that. It was only torturing himself.

Today, hearing Béatrice and Berenger joking and laughing in the chamber, and Marguerite's quiet chuckle, infuriated him. Ed was not prey to jealousy with most things, but he craved Béatrice's company. However, even if she were to leave Berenger and sit with him, Ed knew that he'd be so tongue-tied that he would become flushed with embarrassment and resort to silence, hoping that she would guess the depth of his affection and respect for her from the tormented expression on his face. He had a horrible conviction that she wouldn't.

Torn between the wish to remain near her and his frustration, he left the rooms and walked out towards the port with Georges. It was here that they saw the cleric again.

The fellow always smiled, Ed noticed, but like so many of the other men, he smiled with his mouth only, not his eyes or heart.

'I hope I see you well?' the cleric said, addressing them.

'Yes, Father,' Georges replied.

Ed was silent. He saw how George's face changed when he saw the priest. His eyes lit up, and he looked like a boy who could see his own salvation. The cleric took his hand and patted it, and glanced enquiringly at Ed as though expecting him to come closer too. Ed felt like a dog being called to its master, and that made his anger boil. He'd had enough of being bossed around by Berenger. It seemed to the boy that he spent his entire life being told what to do – by his vintener, by the men of the vintaine, by Grandarse, by Archibald, by Béatrice – by *everyone*! Well, he wasn't going to do as he was told any more. Not by the archers, not by this priest.

'My son, you are unhappy,' the priest said.

'So?'

'Come, let me pray for you. I can soothe your troubled breast.'

Ed glowered blackly at him. 'You can't help me.'

'The Word of God will help any child.'

'I am not a child!' Ed spat. 'I'm a man in the King's army!'

The priest gave a condescending smile. 'Of course you are.'

Georges sniggered.

Ed had been patronised by many other men in his short life, but he was old enough now to recognise and resent it. He stared wide-eyed at the priest and Georges, and then stepped away.

'Boy, come back here!' the priest said sharply.

Ed shook his head and turned his back.

'Boy! You will come to me.'

'Go swyve yourself!' he shouted and continued on to the port.

There were running steps behind him, and Georges caught his sleeve. 'Wait, Ed, please. Wait.'

'Go back to your great French friend,' Ed snapped.

'What? No, come back with me to the priest. He is an important man, it won't do for you to annoy him.'

'I don't care about him. I'm going to watch the ships.'

'You won't come back?'

Ed ignored him. At the harbour a great cog had arrived and was disgorging barrels and bales of essentials for the men. Ed sat on the quay and threw stones at a large pebble.

The cleric had insulted him. *No one likes me*, Ed thought bitterly. *They'll make the most use they can of me, and then ditch me*. He loved Béatrice, but deep down he knew he didn't stand a chance of getting her to lie with him. She would never be his wife.

If he was honest, she only thought of him as a younger brother. Well, he'd show her. He'd do something to make her respect him. Make her love him as he loved her.

Berenger enjoyed his period of convalescence. He walked a great deal around the new town as it grew up about Calais. Soon the walking was not enough. It was true that he needed exercise, but he needed peace too; he had no wish to return to war, not yet. He still felt weak from the fever, and in the cold and damp of a coastal winter, that weakness was set to grow. Still, the ministrations of Béatrice and Marguerite were gradually reducing as his health returned, and now that he was able to get up from his bed for several hours in a day, he was glad to go outside for fresh air, and to sit by the fire in the evenings, chatting with the other men.

'Donkey, what's the matter with you?' he demanded one day when he saw Ed sitting with his customary brooding expression.

'Nothing.'

'It must be a big "nothing",' Berenger said kindly, 'for you to have a face blacker than those clouds.'

Ed did not respond.

Berenger decided the boy needed something to do. A lad of his age needed to keep his hands and mind busy. He would speak with Archibald and see if the gynour could sort something out for him.

It was late in February when Sir John de Sully came to see him.

'How are you, Fripper? I was worried about you,' he said, entering Berenger's rough shack and sitting on a long stool.

'I am well enough, I thank you, Sir John. It was an unpleasant few days.'

'I once had a bad fever. I thought it would take me away at first. By the end, I was praying that it would. There is nothing so debilitating as a disease; it is one of my abiding horrors, that I should be taken away by one. Far better for a knight to be killed by a quick stab of a lance or a slash of a sword. Quick and clean.'

'Yes, sir.'

'I am not, however, come here to talk to you about your fever,' the knight said.

'Would it ease your throat to have a sup of wine?'

'Some wine would be most pleasant, yes, I thank you.'

When Berenger was sitting and both had taken sips of their drinks, Sir John cast a look at him from under lowered brows. 'This siege is going to endure a while longer, Fripper. The French are still sending ships to revictual the town, and there's little we can do to stop them. There are simply too many of them, and the galleys guard them well.'

'It is not the season for war at sea.'

'No indeed. This siege is set to last at least another four months by my reckoning. Another four months of this, eh?' he sighed, looking about him at the room. Water was leaking in from a hole near the middle of the roof. Puddles had formed in the packed earth of the floor, and the hearth itself was damp. Starting a fire in this weather was always hard.

'We are losing too many men to fevers,' Berenger said sombrely.

'So anything we can do to bring about the end of the siege would be welcome. There is one thing that could be tried.'

'What is that?' Berenger became alert.

'The Duke of Flanders was killed at Crécy. His son is only sixteen years old, and has inherited a large territory. The taxes of that land support the French Crown, but so do the ports. Philippe needs Flanders to remain loyal. However, the Flemish do not want to be allied to France. The merchants and townsfolk all prefer to align themselves with us.'

'I see,' Berenger said thoughtfully, wondering where this was going.

'We need to take offers to the Flemings to persuade them to renounce their French overlords and come to join with us. What can the French give them that we cannot? The Flemings would be doughty comrades. My messenger must be someone who can be trusted, someone who can keep his men under control, and most of all, someone who can see to it that the message is delivered.'

Berenger felt his stomach contract. 'This is too great a task for me, Sir John, I—'

The knight held up a hand to silence him. 'No, Frip, you fool. Not you. Listen to me. The main task will be, apparently, to deliver a message to the Flemings. Another will do that. However, a second job will need to be undertaken: to travel to Champagne and safely deliver a certain man . . . and then bring him back in one piece.'

'I don't think I can do that,' Berenger said. 'I am too weak still.'

'This will be quick and easy, I hope. Champagne is over on the other side of Arras. It should not be a difficult task. You'll have to keep away from French troops, and avoid large towns. But we can give you all the men and provisions you could want. Only you must deliver this man to Laon.'

'Laon? I've heard of that place,' Berenger frowned.

'It is a good little city, I think. But the main thing for us is to persuade them to come over to our King. If we can do that, we will have driven a spike into the French King's strategems.'

'Who is this mysterious man? Do I know him?'

'You do. It is Jean de Vervins.'

The Vidame sipped at a cup of strong wine, his eyes wrinkling with delight as three men regaled him with stories of their travels and courage in the face of adversity, but when one mentioned the coming journey, it took all his efforts to control his features.

'To Laon? But why should the King want to send men there?' he said lightly.

'The King's new friend, Sir Jean de Vervins, he says towns in that area are so scared of the English that they will transfer their allegiance to King Edward,' one of the men explained. His features were bloated and red with wine and food, and the Vidame despised him for his gluttony, but such were the men he must deal with.

'Is that so?' The Vidame took another sip of wine and drawled, 'It would be a dangerous mission, surely, to travel all that way into enemy country?'

'Not for Englishmen,' the man said. His companions hooted with laughter. 'We have Sir Walter Manny, Sir Thomas Dagworth and thousands of others. Each of 'em's more of a man than ten Frenchies! Hah! We'll ride to Laon as if we were on a day's casual touring about the King's Forest.'

The Vidame left them a short while later and walked thoughtfully towards his rooms. He had relinquished his tent as the weather grew less clement, and while the rooms were more comfortable, there was the disadvantage that when he wanted a secret meeting or needed to discuss matters in confidence, he must keep a wary eye on those who might be watching to see who visited him, or listening at a doorway.

He must send news of this latest mission – but at the present time he had no means. Yet he would have to do so somehow, or watch as a ring of cities fell to the English without an arrow being loosed or sword unsheathed. There was no doubt that terror of the English had grown massively since the disaster of Crécy.

There *must* be a way to get news to France . . .

CHAPTER THIRTY-TWO

A triangular face, mousy-coloured hair and deep-set eyes.

There weren't many men who had that kind of look about them, Clip thought. He was walking near the alley where he'd been attacked when he saw that face again, and this time he recalled precisely when he had seen the man. It was when the vintaine was attacked and the messenger was killed. *This* was the man he had allowed to go free after the fight.

Shit, the bastard's one of the outlaws, he thought and stopped dead in the lane. In order to create the appearance of nonchalance, he leaned against a post from which a pig's body was hanging, the hind legs spread wide while a butcher eviscerated the innards. A fleck of blood landed on Clip's shoulder and he irritably flicked it away, glaring at the butcher, who met his gaze with a shrug and made no attempt to stop spattering him with more gore.

Clip walked away, some ten paces behind the man he was following. To his surprise, the fellow paused, glanced about him and then darted into the alley, making his way to the yard where Clip had been beaten up – where the Carlisle man had pushed him into the latrine. Making sure that no one was following him, Clip went warily up the narrow alley again, his ears straining for any sound that could herald danger.

He stopped halfway along, still listening intently. Somewhere a door slammed, but he could see nothing ahead. He crept along a little further. Nothing again.

He reached the end and peeped out around the corner.

'My son? Do you want something?'

A cleric was sitting on a simple wooden bench, his hands concealed inside the sleeves of a heavy robe like a friar's, and he smiled affably as Clip entered the yard.

'No, Father. I was just looking for a . . .'

The sudden movement warned him. Perhaps it was the effect of being attacked in here before, but his senses were screaming at him even as the man sprang out from behind him. He had been hiding in a doorway, and as Clip spoke, he tried to cut him with his dagger.

Clip leaped to his right, and the blade sliced through the air. Pulling his own blade from its sheath, Clip saw that his attacker was the man with the mousy hair. He must have realised he was being followed and slipped away as Clip entered the alleyway. Clip made a quick feint. The man's footwork was neat, speedy, definite, as was his attack when it came. Clip blocked his forearm, made a lightning stab into his knuckles and heard the man curse as Clip's knife sheared through a tendon.

'Want some more?' Clip asked breathlessly.

There was a sudden step behind him and he moved, but not fast enough this time. A blow caught him on the left shoulder, and he whipped round to find the priest before him. Even in the midst of battle, he was unwilling to kill a priest. However, his lips pursed with anger, he lashed out twice; both times, his fist smashed into the priest's face. Then once more: this jab with stiff, straight fingers to the man's neck. The priest fell, gasping for breath, his nose broken, choking through the blood in his nostrils and the constriction at his throat.

Clip was already whirling as he fell, and thus avoided the stab that would have punctured his kidney. Crouched, he was ready to thrust or block again. His opponent, the man with mousy hair, licked the blood on the back of his hand and eyed him doubtfully. Clip made a feint to the left, then stabbed immediately to the right, and the man retreated. Once more, a quick stabbing, and the fellow drew back. This was too easy, Clip thought. He stabbed again, and the man suddenly lurched forward, knocked Clip's knife aside and thrust at his neck. Clip jerked away, but the knife nicked his ear even as the man's fist slammed into Clip's eye. He reached up and blocked the man's fist with his forearm before the attacker could pull his hand back and cut his throat, but even as he did so, the man threw his left fist straight into Clip's nose. There was a crunch and Clip felt his balance wobble, but as he went backwards, he kicked up with all his strength. His boot caught the man's cods, and he gave a howl even as Clip stumbled over the priest, who was on all fours trying to rise. Clip glared at the priest and punched him again.

'Fuck you! Stay down, Father!'

The priest collapsed, but Clip was up again, and now the man with the mousy hair was crouched, retching in a huddle of pain. Clip walked over to him and kicked him, once in the flank and once in the head.

'Try to waylay an archer, would you?' he panted, and grabbed his chemise. He pulled the man to him and held his knife to the man's eye, hissing, 'I ought to blind you!' He studied his attacker carefully. 'It *was* you! You were one of the bastards tried to kill us in England.'

'I was only doing what *he* told me!'

'Who?'

'The priest there – Father Alain.'

Clip turned and stared at the priest. 'Why?' he demanded.

'How the fuck should I know?' the man said. He was trembling, his hands still on his cods as though preventing them from falling away.

Clip stared at him, then in a flash he snapped his head back and butted the man as hard as he could. He fell back and Clip dropped him. It was tempting to go and stab the priest there and then, but Clip did still have scruples when it came to killing a man of God.

The outlaw saw Clip's stern expression, and tried to push himself away, moving in an ungainly fashion. Blood was running from his left eyebrow where Clip's butt had broken the skin, and his eye was already swelling quickly.

Clip knelt at his side and pushed his knife up inside the man's nose. 'I don't want to hear anything more about you trying to harm archers. In fact, if you dare to assault me or any of my friends, I'll hunt you down and cut your balls off – after I've marked you by cutting your nose here.' He sawed gently until the blood ran down his blade. 'You understand me?'

'Yes.'

'And if you hear anything about that prickle priest wanting to attack me again, you'll let me know, won't you?'

'Yes.'

'Good.' Clip stood up and walked away, back to the alley. As he passed the priest's body, he gave the man a hefty kick. 'That's for trying to waylay me, you arsehole.'

Jean de Vervins watched as Berenger Fripper approached him, with Sir John de Sully following a pace or two behind.

Fripper's face was as black as the clouds on a thundery day, and there was a set to his shoulders that spoke of approaching violence.

'You want me to take you to Laon,' he said tersely, 'Why?'

Jean glanced at the knight behind him. 'This is not to be discussed, Sir John. You know that.'

'You're talking to me, you French turd!' Berenger snarled. 'Answer my question!'

'Sir John—'

'It will save a lot of time if you do as he asks.'

'This whole matter is intended to be confidential, Sir John. I have been given a task by your King because I have ideas that will hopefully bring this war to an end and to his benefit.'

He saw with pleasure that as he spoke the vintener seemed to swell like a pigeon about to issue a challenge. He must be used to being bested by men with greater wit. Besides, the archer was in no condition to argue or attempt to berate him. The fellow was in a terrible state. Everyone had heard about his fever. Coming on top of his wounds, it was scarcely surprising that he should look so emaciated and enfeebled.

Jean was just considering shouting at him, when he was surprised by the foul little man springing forward and giving him a sudden blow that all but knocked him over.

'I *said* I want to know what you're doing!'

Jean felt his anger rising like water boiling in a pan. Lowering his head like a bull about to charge, he stepped forward, placing his hands on Berenger's chest – but the archer lifted his hands between Jean's and knocked them effortlessly aside. Berenger's leg went behind Jean's, and the heel of his hand slammed into the point of the Frenchman's chin. Jean felt the swift tearing at the hinges of his jaw, then the click as his teeth met, and his head was thrust back. He was bent backwards over Berenger's leg.

Teetering, he was forced to grip hold of Berenger's belt, spluttering with anger.

The vintener was glaring down at him. 'What are you doing in Laon? This is the last time I'll ask. If you don't tell me, I will not go, and I will not release any of my archers to join you either. So *speak*!'

Jean tried to pull himself up, but the archer unhooked his fingers and let him fall.

'Sir John? I demand that you force this man to release me and stop his interrogation!' Jean snapped.

'Oh, I have no control over the good vintener,' Sir John said, and he idly whistled a gavotte.

Jean de Vervins stood up and brushed himself down. 'I am distressed to think that my honourable attempt to help you could be so completely misinterpreted,' he said through gritted teeth. He wondered whether he could draw his knife and throw it into the archer's shoulder. Or perhaps just attack him and give him an equal scar on the other side of his face? It was more likely that the man would best him, though. Jean reminded himself that he had been considering how puny the man looked after his illness. It was always a mistake to underestimate an enemy.

'I know Laon,' he said. 'I know many men there – merchants, burgesses, barons – all are weary of the war. They have seen English might at first hand. Is there a noble family in the whole of France which has not lost a father, a brother, a son? Your men rampage over the country, killing and burning, and the people are heartily sick of it. It would take little for the populace to rise against King Philippe. After all, what does he do for his subjects? He fights the English on land and at sea and loses, or he sits back and does not fight, and watches you walk away with everything. The people have had enough. Now, if I were to go and speak to the local inhabitants there, and perhaps say to them that they could rely on the English not only to come and protect the city, but also pay for the pleasure of their comradeship, that would bring about a better resolution of affairs. If Laon cedes, a city right on the edge of the Île de la Cité and Champagne, what would that do to the resolve of other towns? And if you had just succeeded in bringing the Duke of Flanders into King Edward's circle of friends and allies, what then could we not achieve? It would mean a whole series of cities taken from the French King. Take away his cities and you take away much of his money. Without money he cannot maintain an army or indulge his whims to engage in war.'

'You know local people, you say?'

'I have many influential friends in that region of France.'

'Why are you prepared to do this, then?'

Jean fell silent. He eyed the archer, wondering. There had been a time, when they had first met, when he would have trusted this man, but now Berenger was shown to be too full of his own importance. As though a mere archer – albeit a vintener or even a captain – could begin to comprehend the scope and majesty of Jean's plans.

'Well? I'm waiting. Why?'

'I have good reasons. My *own* reasons.'

'*What* reasons?'

Jean de Vervins felt his own rage rising. 'King Philippe, the Valois, embarrassed me. *Me!* I was his most loyal vassal, but he betrayed me. I fought for him and served him well, but he repaid me with dishonour. You understand? I was fighting in a tournament, and when my opponent unhorsed me, the King gave him all I own. Not only my horse and armour, but he wished to take my castle too. I will not accept a theft that beggars me, just to enhance the prospects of a silk-clad popinjay! So I say, *fuck* Henri du Bos, and *fuck* King Philippe de Valois! If they want my castle, they will need to take my life first!'

He stared fiercely at Berenger, his eyes brimming with tears. Perhaps it was that, rather than his story, which convinced the archer. Suddenly the vintener nodded as though to himself, and put out his hand to grip that of Jean de Vervins.

'Good,' Berenger said simply. 'We'll need to prepare, then.'

Chapter Thirty-Three

Berenger was in a foul mood as he stalked away from Sir John, the knight's last words still echoing in his ears.

'I know you don't like him. I don't trust him further than I can throw him myself, but be that as it may, we have a duty to do all we can in the King's cause. With the Flemish cities on our side, this move could have a great impact on the conduct of the war. It is worth our while to exploit any plans Jean brings to us.'

'He is a traitor,' Berenger scowled. 'I saw a Frenchman in the battle near Durham who recognised him – and I am sure that he had been feeding information to the Scottish. If he will betray his own, how do we know he won't betray us?' It was true that the Frenchman had saved his life, but that was not enough to silence his fears.

'As to that,' Sir John said heavily, 'it comes down to money. The man is insatiable for gold. If we provide it, he will remain loyal.'

Berenger snorted. He had heard of such men before. 'We know what Jesus thought of those who were dedicated to money. Would you *buy* a mercenary to serve under you? Would you *pay* a man to stay here under arms because he had a contract?'

'I detest mercenaries, Frip, and under normal circumstances. I would have nothing to do with them. However, these are not normal circumstances. These are truly exceptional times, and we needs must bend with the wind or we will be broken. The King respects this Jean de Vervins, so we must do all we can to assist him. That is all.'

'That is all,' Berenger repeated to himself as he entered his hut.

'Frip, I have some news,' Clip said as he saw his vintener.

'What now?' Fripper said tiredly.

'The clerk to Sir Peter tried to ambush me.' Clip quickly told his story.

'Shit! So Sir Peter's tried to get me killed and now he's started on you too,' Berenger said.

'Be fair. Clip *was* there to rob them,' Jack laughed, and Berenger surprised himself by laughing too.

'What did the knight want?' the Earl asked.

Berenger's amusement dissipated like morning mist. There was a barrel of ale at the far wall, and he went over and filled a drinking horn before sitting down on a bench and casting an eye about the chamber. It was a rude hall, but it was at least theirs. His feet were sore from being perpetually wet, his mouth was gritty from mud and dust, and the place had so many leaks and draughts, it was little better than sleeping in a field, but for the moment at least, it was home. He had no wish to leave it. Not if it meant riding over the countryside for miles, the target of every French hunter of ransom or bounty money.

'I'll explain later. For now, fetch John of Essex, and bring me the rest of the vinteners. Tell them I need to talk through a special escapade with them. First, I've got to see Grandarse. Where is he?'

'In the tavern up at the harbour.'

'I'll be back as soon as I can. Get the vintaine together and have them wait for me here.'

The Vidame would see Clip would suffer for his assault! That pig's turd wastrel had fought like the devil! If the Vidame had any authority, he would see Clip die slowly. The King's torturers would bring all their inventiveness to bear.

But just now there was a matter that gave him pause for thought. That man, Clip, was one of the vintaine under Fripper. If Fripper's men were to escort Jean de Vervins – may his soul rot in hell for all eternity! – the Vidame could not go with them. That little fight had ruined his opportunity of joining the party. Someone else must go and warn the people.

There was only one man he dared send. The spy.

Berenger found Grandarse standing in the inn. He had that beatific smile on his face that said he was not on his first drink of the day, nor his last. When Grandarse had an opportunity, he would always stick with the rough ciders of any town. He reckoned they kept him regular in all things.

'Eh, Fripper? Come in and try some of this. It'll put hairs on your chest.'

'No doubt,' Berenger said. 'Grandarse, I need to talk to you.'

'Oh, aye? The captain needs to speak to me, does he? Come on, lad. There's a quiet place over there.'

Grandarse led the way to a bench that consisted of a plank laid across two barrels and evicted the two men already drinking there. One wanted to dispute Grandarse's right to throw them off their table, but his companion recognised Grandarse and saw in Berenger a figure of alarming authority. It was the sight of his scar, Berenger told himself. It would always be a source of alarm to those who didn't know him.

'Aye, so what is it, then?' Grandarse said, planting himself on the board over a barrel and taking a long swig from his jug of cider.

Quickly Berenger explained about Jean and the idea of leading him and others across Flanders and down to the city of Laon. 'I don't trust the fellow, Grandarse,' he concluded.

'Oh well, as to that, who would you trust, man? True, he's a little shit who'd sell his mother for one groat and an evening's whoring, but in this army there are many more who'd do the same.' His eye took on a reflective look. Berenger was sure that he was calculating the potential value of his own mother, were she still alive. Grandarse shook himself, coming back to the present. 'You mark my words, more men will be coming over here just for the money. What is the point of coming all this way just because your master decides it's time to win his spurs? Better to make sure you fight because someone's going to reward you with wine, ale, food, and money – and the chance to spend it. Why should men slog their guts out to work for a master and risk their lives, all for this notion of "service", eh?'

'I've been told to take some archers with me.'

'What? You're to go to an obscure little dump you've never heard of, to defend this prickle all the way, and then give him an armed guard in the place once you get him there? You'll need more than one vintaine. And how long will you stay there with the men? Will it be a day? A week? A month? You'll have to have enough men to afford to lose a few. Go to a city and try to occupy it, and you'll soon find that half the place doesn't want English soldiers there. The other half won't mind them so long as they have money to chuck around, but when the money runs out, they won't want you either. So you'll have some on your side at first, but when you've nothing left to bribe 'em with, they'll all hate you.'

'God's ballocks, it's a mess,' Berenger muttered.

'Aye, but there's potential too. There could be some lively little French maids in there, eh? A wriggling handful with a smile saying, "want a feel of my French fancy"! Oh, aye, I could manage a little of that.'

'What do you mean, you could *manage* it?'

'What do you think I mean, Fripper, you empty-pated son of a dollypoll! I'll come too. You can't be trusted on a job like this. Nay, I'll bring my centaine. You'll need at least seventy or eighty men to hold a city, and more to help in Flanders. Aye!' He stood and belched, then grimaced for a moment. A thunderous noise heralded his breaking wind. 'Aye, come on, Frip. Get a grip. We have men to find.'

When Fripper and Grandarse returned to the vintaine at Fripper's hall, the place was almost full. Grandarse told Ed to run and bring four other vinteners, and when he had returned with them, the room went quiet while Berenger outlined what he had already told Grandarse.

'Keep all this to yourselves,' he finished. 'There are men in the camp who wouldn't object to making a little money for themselves by selling this secret, even if they were in on the journey themselves.'

'You think one of my men would be thick enough to give away news like this when it could lead to him being ambushed and killed?' said a wiry vintener from Lincoln called Paul.

'I think most archers are so dim that if you whacked them in the head with a poleaxe you'd be hard pressed to hit a brain,' Berenger said smartly. 'However, there are many who will assume that just because they have a few drinks in a tavern with someone, that fellow must be a comrade and reliable, when all the time their drinking companion might be more of a friend to their enemy than to them.'

John of Essex snorted and leaned back against the wall. 'Well, when do you want to leave?'

'How many of you will come with us?' Berenger asked, looking around at the men.

Paul grimaced. 'What do we get out of it?' he asked. 'If I tell my lads that we're going, when they know that this place is likely to collapse soon, they'll tell me to swyve a goat and refuse.'

Sitting next to John, a shorter man called Adam, who might have been Grandarse's son from his belly and chins, agreed with this. 'Speaking for mine, they'd be more likely to tell me to swyve myself – and then threaten to cut my ballocks off. Why go riding off on a wild-goose chase when there's all the plunder they could wish for right here, without any need for getting frozen stiff and sleeping rough?'

Grandarse glowered around the room. 'You think to tell them? You have less between your ears than I have in my arse!'

'That's likely true,' Paul said, and the room burst into laughter as Grandarse patted his buttocks with an expression of benign contemplation and muttered, 'You could be right there, son!'

It was good, Berenger saw. The sudden humour had released some of the tension that had built up. Now the men relaxed a little.

'We're to be sent off in a couple of days, apparently to take messages to the new Duke of Flanders, but in reality we'll be riding for the town of Laon because it seems that the place is ripe to fall into English hands. That, at least, is what the King's informant tells him.'

'Who is this informant?'

'You will learn later.'

'And if we're going to this town, Laon,' said Adam, 'will we be travelling secretly? I don't like the thought that we'd be going into Flanders with the entire countryside knowing what we're up to.

We'd be the target of every ransom-hunter in France – and most of the executioners.'

'I agree,' Grandarse said, standing and hoicking up his hosen, which had fallen below his belly once more. 'And now, you idle gits, get your gear packed and ready. We'll leave as soon as we can. No sense in hangin' around, eh?'

Berenger watched the men as they all shuffled to their feet and made their way to the door.

'Well, ye bum-faced old bugger, what's the matter now?' Grandarse said. 'I got them all on your side, didn't I?'

'Yes. But it doesn't change the fact that I still don't trust that Frenchman.'

Grandarse eyed him for a moment, then sat down again. 'Listen, Frip, and listen well. This Frenchie, is he a fool? Is he moonstruck? Does he strike you as the sort of man who'd willingly risk his own life for nothing?'

Berenger shook his head.

'Then think on this, man. If it's a gamble, and there's a good reward in it, then he might take a chance. If it's a good wager and the risks are small compared with the winnings, then fine – but if it's all t'other way round . . . aye, man, he wouldn't do it. So, what you have to ask ye'self is, where's his advantage in betraying you? Does he think that the English are losing here? Does he think that the next time the French army meets us, they'll slaughter us all? Could he think that, after the last few years of English victories? No, so it's not that. So perhaps you're thinking he could betray you in Laon, and sell you to the French King, because you have such a great value? Or me? Aye, man, the two of us together, now that would fetch him, what – a couple of pennies? Nay, there is no value in us, nor even in the sixty men we'll have with us. However . . . if he does win over this town, and because of that, the next town, or three, fall to our good King Edward – why then, he could count on an excellent profit! Perhaps he wouldn't even have to lie or cheat again, and he could retire to a nice little vill with his own manor, to while away his final days thinking about all the enemies he's made and being visited by the ghosts of the men he's killed, until he's gone fully mad, eh?'

'I know. I just thought . . .'

'Aye, Frip. That's your problem. You keep on thinking, thinking, thinking. Don't do it, man. Leave the brainwork to them as have the mental powers for it. In fact, leave it all to me, eh?'

Grandarse stood and slapped Berenger on the back. 'But for me to think properly,' he said, hitching up his hosen again, 'I do need to have sustenance. So I'll let you buy me a cup of sack or a quart of ale for giving you the benefit of my experience.'

Berenger nodded with a grin and joined the centener crossing the floor to the door. However, they had not yet reached it when Paul threw it open.

'So, were you just blowing smoke in our eyes, Fripper?'

His tone was not unfriendly, but there was some edge to it.

'What do you mean?' Berenger said.

'This horse-crap about going away secretly! I expected this sort of joke from you, Fripper, but not from you, Centener. You should trust your own vinteners.'

It was Grandarse's turn to look blank. 'Eh?'

'This mission – to go to Flanders and then Laon. You could have told us we were to travel with the King!'

Chapter Thirty-Four

Packing their bags took hardly any time. All the archers were experienced in travelling and carrying as little as possible. Berenger had his satchel filled in short order, and then it was only a case of rolling up his blanket and cloak, and shouldering them. He threw a quick glance about his room, and then went out.

'You are leaving?'

He had not thought of the two women. Now, seeing Béatrice, he smiled and walked over to her. 'Not for long. We're being sent into Flanders,' he said.

'Is that all?' Marguerite asked, looking anxious.

'We will be back before long.'

'What of us?' Béatrice asked.

'You will be safe with Archibald.'

'I don't want to be with him,' Marguerite said, and to Berenger's confusion, she began to weep.

'What is the matter?' he asked.

Béatrice gave him a scathing look. 'What do you think? She is here, in an army of men who have murdered her husband and children, and now you are abandoning her here with only a gynour to guard her. She is still not used to the noise of the gonnes and the smell of the powder.'

Berenger had not considered that. It was true – Béatrice was the daughter of a man who had made powder for gonnes, and she was used to it. But for another, like Marguerite, it was not so easy. Even Berenger was uncomfortable, being around it. How much harder must it be for a woman like her? he asked himself.

'What would you have me do?' he asked Marguerite.

'Take me with you. You will have need of a boy like mine. Take us both, and we will help you.'

Berenger scowled at the ground. 'I don't know that you will be safe with us. Surely you would be better off here?'

Béatrice snapped, 'Are you taking the Donkey?'

'Well, no. He's Archibald's servant now, and—'

'So who will you have as your boy for the vintaine?'

'I suppose we'll take Georges, but—'

'So you will take this woman's son, but leave her behind? After all the others in her family have died?'

Berenger opened and closed his mouth three times while he tried to get his mind around this latest conundrum. 'You think we should take her as well?'

Béatrice flung her hair back, scorn in her eyes. She forbore to respond.

'Yes, of course we should take her as well,' Berenger amended. He looked from one woman to the other with the hunted look of a man who knew he had lost. 'Yes, well. If that is what you wish, Marguerite? Yes. Of course.'

Then he walked away, trying not to hurry.

The town was full as the English army rode in through the main gate.

Berenger was on the flank with his vintaine, riding to the rear of Sir John de Sully and his esquire, behind the fluttering banner that was now, after months of campaigning, showing distinct signs of wear.

The army had been instructed to polish all their armour and smarten their appearance as best as they might, before their arrival here at Berghes, in the south-west of Flanders, and for the most part the men had succeeded. They all gleamed in the sunlight. Even the white tunics had been beaten and pummelled into cleanliness, and the men looked fierce and warrior-like as they marched along the roadway. Berenger could feel almost proud of the martial air they struck.

King Edward had brought a large contingent with him. From where Berenger sat, the men snaked around the roadway behind him. There must have been a thousand men or more, he guessed, with two hundred men-at-arms, the rest mounted archers. A very strong force for a king visiting a potential ally, but this ally had proved reluctant. The camp followers straggled behind, but he had kept Marguerite and her son up with the archers. He felt happier keeping them in view. As he glanced at her, she caught his eye. He saw her sudden smile, and looked away quickly. He had too much to do to allow himself to be distracted by a trim figure in a skirt, he told himself.

On the way here, Jean de Vervins had explained much about this visit. Apparently, since the death of the Count of Flanders's father on the field of Crécy, there had been extensive efforts to bring the boy to heel.

'At first, it was the French King. Philippe wants Flanders to renew its pact with France and the French Crown. They need the towns and cities, rebellious though they be. And our King wants Flanders too. He travelled to meet with the Flemings late last year, in October, and the burghers agreed to formalise a treaty with

England. To confirm that, our King has offered his own daughter to seal the pact. And the young Count has agreed, but yet he prevaricates about dates, and who should be present, and whether it's legal yet, and any other reason he can bring to mind.'

'Why is he being so difficult?' Clip asked.

Jean gave him a long, hard stare. 'Did you not hear how his father died? Would you marry into the family that had caused the death of your father?'

'That is one thing,' Sir John said, overhearing them, 'and the other is, this is a young lad. He's what – fifteen, sixteen? I dare say he's wary of marrying any woman he hasn't seen. I would have been at his age. And what does he get from it? An alliance with King Edward is not to be sniffed at, but a fellow of his age is entitled to be somewhat callow.'

Jean looked at Berenger and shrugged expressively.

'You don't think so?' Berenger asked.

'His father was held at the court by his people because they had so much power over him. Now, if this lad agrees to a contract with our King, he will still remain under their power. The French King might help the Count to squash those who would hold him back. Philippe knows the quality of the people, and also knows where the Count's own loyalties lie. I wonder whether the boy is reluctant not from his age but because he knows where the true power lies.'

'How do you know all this?' Jack demanded.

'I am keen on the study of politics in my own lands,' Jean said. 'I have an interest, you understand?'

'Perhaps,' Jack said.

And now they were here, in the heart of the town where the Count was waiting for them. If Jean de Vervins was correct, there was little reason to be anxious. The young Count might be reluctant, but all his advisers and most of his people were enthusiastic supporters of the English rather than their French overlord. At the mere thought of a potential fight, Berenger felt the dull ache in his shoulder again. His scar was healed perfectly now, but his shoulder appeared to have acquired the ability to warn him when rain threatened or when the wind was about to change. He felt as though it could also act as an advance warning against riotous crowds. True, all about him he could see people smiling, waving and shouting support, but he had seen crowds change mood in an instant. The London mob was only one example. Every city and town had its own mad gangs.

The King rode at the front of the army. From here, Berenger could see how his hair moved, bright and golden, like the mane of a lion, and he rode slowly, with the precise stateliness of a lion, too. Like a lion, he was the lord of all he surveyed. He had beaten the French King and the greatest army in Christendom, and even now his army laid siege to a strategically crucial town with impunity while the French King cowered and permitted the English to do whatever they wanted in what he called 'his' lands. The appearance of Edward III demonstrated his might, his honour and his prowess. He was a man whom none would dare refuse. How could they, when he held the power of life and death in his royal hands?

At the doors of a great hall, which Berenger later learned was the main guildhall for the town, stood a large crowd of finely dressed townspeople. Silks and expensively embroidered clothes showed the wealth not only of the individuals, but of the town as well. Flags hung from upper windows, and more fluttered from lance-points in the hands of the militia in the streets. It was a scene of enormous grandeur and of civic pride. The town was revelling in the honour done to them today.

The King rode up to the hall and inclined his head. That was when Berenger saw the Count of Flanders: a lad of middle height, with a sharp eye and proud demeanour. The youth was not unhandsome. He bowed while the people twittered and tittered, yet Berenger noted that there was no submission in his eyes. And then, while the crowds applauded, Berenger noticed the Count moving perceptibly away from his group of advisers, as though he wanted nothing to do with them. Soon the King, with his senior knights, with Sir John and others, dismounted and went to be greeted by their hosts, who escorted them into the building.

Berenger saw a scruffy street urchin who appeared at the edge of the crowds and stared at the men, before throwing a look over his shoulder. Following the direction of his gaze, Berenger saw a cloaked figure pointing and jerking his head. The boy went up to Jean de Vervins even as Berenger felt for his dagger, but all the boy did was to reach up and whisper something in the Frenchman's ear.

Jean de Vervins immediately wheeled around and strode away.

'What's going on? Where are you going?' Berenger demanded, but the man was already gone.

CHAPTER THIRTY-FIVE

The town was much like a provincial French town, Jean de Vervins thought as he hurried down a street. Narrow lanes, wooden buildings jutting out overhead, blocking off much of the light, the occasional board to indicate a special trade conducted within, and plenty of smells: those to tempt a jaded palate, those to tease the senses, and more than a few to repel.

Outside a butcher's, surrounded by squabbling curs, a boy was cleaning some ox-bowels and flinging the faeces into the kennel that ran down the middle of the street. Next door, the tavern-keeper was loudly berating the boy and his master for befouling the entrance to his tavern, but it was clearly a dispute that had lasted for many years. The boy took no notice, and when the tavern's host made a threatening movement as though to go and clip him about the head, the butcher appeared in his doorway, a long, bloody knife in his hand which he whetted with a stone tied to a thong about his neck. He said nothing, but the other man turned and stamped back to his tavern.

Jean stood and studied the lanes. He could see a cloaked figure in a doorway. With his belly feeling strangely empty, he went to the tavern and followed the tavern-keeper inside.

Within it was dark and gloomy, not the kind of drinking hall that would usually appeal to Jean, who was fastidious in his eating and drinking habits, but it smelled well enough of fresh straw. He felt it to be tolerable.

'A pint of wine,' he said to the host, who stood behind a simple bar, glowering at the world. 'Your neighbour is a man of little civic pride,' he added conversationally as the man reached to a barrel and opened the tap into a jug.

'That fellow possesses the brains of an ox. He's a brute and a bully.'

'Such men are all too common in these uncertain times,' Jean sighed, gratefully taking the wine.

'You are not from this town,' the tavern-keeper said.

'No, I come from further east, originally.'

'It is said that the King of France will soon have to give up his overlordship of Flanders. What do you think?'

'I think that the French will hold on to whatever they think they can,' Jean said diplomatically. 'But the English King has a mighty army, and a reputation for skill at warfare. I would not gamble on the French.'

'But France has the mightiest army in all . . .'

'*Had*. And only in terms of numbers. King Philippe has many knights and barons, dukes and counts, but how many fighting men? After all, you Flemings showed the world at Courtrai that men with pikes and lances can beat even the most determined horsemen. England has knights, but King Edward's knights fight alongside their men, on foot. I have seen them. They are terrible.'

'You are with them now?'

'No!' Jean laughed. 'I joined their party because it was sensible to travel with so mighty a band, rather than put myself at the risk of footpads and outlaws, but I am not a part of them. I travel on southwards to the land of my fathers.'

As he spoke, the tall, cloaked figure appeared in the doorway. The man pulled off his outer garments. Beneath, he was a cadaverous-looking fellow in the dark attire of a pleader at court. He gazed about the room before making his way to the bar, nodding to the tavern-keeper. 'A pot of wine, friend. I would gladly wash away the dust and dirt of the road. Jean, it is . . .'

Jean shot him a look, and his friend subsided. 'Messire, would you like to sit? My arse is sore from the miles here from Calais.'

His new companion assented and they were soon sitting at a bench, and speaking quietly so that the tavern-keeper might not hear them.

'How go things?' Jean asked.

His friend, Gauvain de Bellemont, sipped the wine and grimaced. 'I hate cheap rotgut. My belly turns to acid when I drink this sort of piss.'

'And?' Jean asked with poisonous politeness.

'It all appears to be going in our favour. I have spoken with the town's leading merchants, and they are supporting the move. The feeling is that good King Philippe has lost his grip. No one can forgive him for refusing to join battle with the English. All those frightful campaigns that King Edward led over French soil, polluting it with the blood of nuns and of monks, slaughtering all who crossed his path, all those terrible chevauchées, and not *once* did our King dare to make a move to stop him! Is it any surprise that waves of sedition are even now lapping at the walls of major towns? And then to lose at Crécy! It was the most catastrophic disaster ever to strike France. And all because of King Philippe.'

'What about the town's watch and the garrison?' Jean wanted to know.

His friend sat back contemplatively, replying, 'They will do as they are told. For the most part, they are all local men, and will obey the town's council. If the guild goes with us, the people will too.'

'What now, then?'

'I have a messenger,' Gauvain said, sipping and grimacing once more. 'He took the message to the English King as soon as he could. He arrived at Calais a day or two ago.'

Jean de Vervins gave a fleeting scowl. 'I have heard nothing of a messenger yet. I have prepared the way, but I expected your man to arrive sooner than this. It is cutting the cake a little too finely. You are sure he left on time?'

'I was there when he left. He was grumpy about the journey, but he understood the urgency. You should have no concern on that. Still, if you prepared for his message, the timing is less important. Are men to be sent to Laon?'

'Yes. I have arranged for eighty or more,' Jean said thoughtfully. 'And yet, I would have expected him to have arrived *before* I left Calais. Certainly I would have expected him by now.'

They rose and walked to the door. As they left, Jean de Vervins cast a frown at his companion. 'Who is this messenger?'

'Just a smith from Metz. But he has his own grievance and is a keen supporter of us. He was born a Laonese, and he wants to return to his home, but he cannot do so under the King of France. I have explained the law to him,' he added smugly. 'He knows that Laon will allow him to go home if the city changes allegiance, and he will be keen to have this come about. He badly wants to see his wife again and will be as persuasive as he knows how in demanding that the town goes over to King Edward and renounces King Philippe.'

'You have no doubt, then, that the people will follow us when they hear the proposal?'

'No. They should do.'

'*Should*?' Jean allowed his tone to become tart. 'I should prefer more certainty.'

'Then you needs must live with dissatisfaction, messire,' his companion said curtly. 'You will not have certainty. We live in dangerous times, Jean, and that means we live with risk. The rewards will be great, but there is a rule in gambling: for the highest reward you must wager against the greatest risk. I risk all in this. *All!*'

Jean nodded. Gauvain de Bellemont was always nervous. It came from his job as an advocate in the Parlement in Paris. He patted his friend's arm. 'Do not fear. I already have the men to come and aid us. With a hundred English archers at our back, the whole city will soon submit to the inevitable. And then, afterwards, we can look to other cities in the area, and as more and more accept the fact of King Edward's reign, his most trusted advisers and confidants will reap the greatest rewards. We are looking ahead to a glorious time, my friend.'

'That is the one hand of the scale,' Gauvain said. He held out his hands, palms uppermost as though weighing an argument, but then he drew his right hand down and his left up and looked at Jean. 'But on the other hand, we have the risk. And the risk is, being flayed alive, broken on the wheel, and quartered. If we fail, my friend, do not wait to be discovered. End your life immediately.'

Jean would come to recall those words.

The spy remained in the doorway as the two men hurried along the street.

He had heard their discussion at the entrance of the inn. So there was a smith from Metz who would take the demand to Laon: *surrender to the English and see the rewards you will win.* Yes, he could all too easily imagine that.

It was with a spring in his step that he bent his way back to the vintaine. Now he knew about this smith, this messenger from Metz, all he need do was ensure that the French got to learn about him too.

Simplicity itself.

Berenger waited with Grandarse outside the hall. With the King's personal bodyguard and the knights all inside, there was no need for still more men, and the vintaine had dispersed to the small taverns about the square. It was unlikely that there was a single hall in the whole of Berghes that could accommodate all the English.

'Eh, I could just about eat a horse and come back for the rider,' Grandarse muttered.

'If we were to wander off to find a meal—' John of Essex began, but Berenger cut him off.

'Not now. You stay here with us. Can you not sense the atmosphere?'

To him, the growing danger was tangible. Yes, there were plenty of smiling, happy people, but there were many others who showed distinct animosity, and he kept catching glimpses of men on rooftops. He knew that although riots often started in the streets when apprentices with a grievance, usually drunk, started to run amok, for a serious battle the first place to look for danger was on the roofs, with men hurling bricks or rocks at the poor devils beneath. He had experienced enough of that in the last year, when they were marching down to Paris.

'The place looks quiet enough,' Grandarse grumbled. 'All we need is a good pot of cider or something to wash down a meal of fresh bread and a capon or two.'

Berenger looked down at Marguerite. She had unconsciously moved closer to him. It gave him a quick sense of warmth in his breast to see that she trusted him so much. Sensing his gaze, she looked up at him. A hand rose to a stray wisp of hair and tucked it away. She coloured slightly and averted her gaze. He felt a tingle of pleasure to see her reaction.

'We will stay here then, Centener, while you go and look for it,' he said, his eyes still on her.

Grandarse glared at him mutinously. 'Ye're not Captain any more, Frip.'

'But I will remain here nonetheless.'

'Aye, have it that way if you insist,' the other man muttered. 'Ach, but there was a nasty shop back down the way there, with a table full of the best breads you could hope to find. And a maiden at the counter with a wicked gleam in her eye. She'd be a good one to snuggle up to on a cool night like tonight will be.'

'Then she'll never know her good fortune in staying at the shop today and not missing Grandarse of the giant tarse!' Berenger said with a grin. His eyes were still scanning the rooftops. So far he had seen little to alarm him, but that didn't mean they were safe. His senses were on full alert.

'Where did you disappear to?' he said when he saw Jean de Vervins approaching.

'Me? I went to find a glass of good red wine, Vintener. Why, did you miss me?' the man sneered.

Berenger was about to give him a piece of his mind, when the doors to the hall suddenly opened and the King came out, followed by his guard. Sir John de Sully came behind looking about him warily. He shot a look at Berenger, who shook his head to show he had seen nothing to cause concern. Soon all the townspeople were gathering, and Sir John made his way to Berenger.

'Gather up the men and prepare to leave,' he said. 'We are to ride to Laon.'

Archibald was delighted to hear that the English had at last taken the Rysbank. Now, with fifteen labourers, he was setting out a new fortification on the sands.

It was not ideal. Every trench that was dug quickly began to fill with water, but for all that, he had designed a strong little fortress. The gonnes would sit on large wooden rafts, secure behind a broad rampart strengthened with timbers taken from the woods at Sangatte. Behind the rampart, Archibald would be able to stand and fire the gonnes at any ships attempting the harbour both as they sailed towards Calais, when they entered the narrow way between the town and Rysbank, and when they attempted to moor. All the while they would be under his gonnes and running the risk of being hit.

He whistled as he worked, occasionally pulling off his worn leather cowl and wiping away the sweat, for the weather was surely turning at last to spring.

'Are you full of sack, that you stand there instead of working?' he bellowed.

Ed the Donkey was peering out over the embankment, a frown marring his brow. 'I'm sorry, Gynour. There's a man there. I don't like him.'

'Where?'

'There, the priest.'

Archibald tensed, then stared intently. Once, Archibald had been a monk, but had run away. Now he had a permanent fear of being captured and taken back to be punished. Still, this man did not strike him as an immediate threat. 'Him?'

'He was watching you when you had the gonnes at the other end of town, and now he's back here again. I don't like him. He was keen to speak to me and to Georges before, but now he always seems to be hanging around nearby.'

'Well, then, boy. We shall have to keep an eye on him, won't we?' Archibald said pleasantly.

The spy was back at the tavern with the archers before they were called to regroup and prepare to leave. He drained the cup of wine proffered to him, and hurried to the horses.

He had passed on his message. The King of France would be warned. This foolish enterprise of capturing Laon would be stopped before it had started.

CHAPTER THIRTY-SIX

Staring down at the city of Laon, Berenger wondered what their reception would be like. He expected it to be less enthusiastic than the cheering crowds at Berghes.

It had taken them four days to cover the distance, making more than thirty miles a day. Berenger had installed Georges on the wagon that his vintaine used for their heavier belongings, their food and sheaves of arrows and spare bow-staves. Marguerite was fitted on her own small pony. Luckily much of the landscape here was flat, and with little in the way of obstacles they could make good time without overtiring their mounts.

The sense of being hemmed in on all sides at Berghes had made Berenger uncomfortable, and to be back in the open, with clear views of the land all about, was a joy. He even found himself whistling as he rode along.

'You seem happy, Fripper,' Sir John said.

'Well, the sun's out, true, I'm warm enough, I'm dry, and I know there's food in my bag. Why should I not be happy?' Berenger said, smiling at Marguerite.

'The sun is out, but clouds are gathering, I think,' the knight replied gravely. 'We are a hundred men, all told. And we're being sent to support a city when it tries to defend itself against the might of the French army. They have siege engines, weapons that can destroy walls, they have miners to tunnel beneath the towers and undermine them, they have . . .'

'I am aware of all this, Sir John. But for all we know, this city will fall into our hands with ease, and then we can return to our friends at Calais.'

'Perhaps.'

Berenger looked across at him. The knight was serious, as though he was aware of dangers that Berenger could not conceive of. 'What is it?'

'When the King spoke with the Count of Flanders, it was clear that the little shit won't forgive us for the death of his father, although it was his father who attacked us at Crécy! The man died honourably enough, but his whelp doesn't want anything to do with us. He made that plain. King Edward was at last persuaded that polite blandishments wouldn't serve, so he showed his own mettle instead: told the boy that without signing and sealing their contract and agreeing to demonstrate that commitment by marrying Edward's daughter Isabella, he could find himself deposed by another more warlike fellow. The boy eventually agreed, and also said he would lead an army into France in support of the English.'

'Then why do you sigh?'

Sir John glanced around. Grandarse was chatting to John of Essex and Jack about a woman he had known, while Jean de Vervins was at the rear, laughing uproariously at some sally of Pardoner and the Earl. The knight turned back to Berenger. 'I dislike it because the boy was forced into it. You didn't see the way his eyes glittered. Full of malevolence, that fellow, or I'm a

Cornishman. He was forced to give his word about betrothing Princess Isabella, in front of the men who represented Ypres, Bruges and that other town . . . Ghent. Yes, he was happy enough to give his word in front of them, but I'd trust him about as far as I'd trust Tyler.'

'What can he do? The people of his main cities demand that he obeys them.'

'That is more than half the problem. He is not allowed to go for a piss without men watching to ensure he's not trying to escape. He is in the same position as poor King Edward, the King's father: when he was mistrusted by all his barons, they set spies on him. Every member of his household was removed and replaced, and he knew he had no one in whom he could confide. And what happened? He fretted at the shackles holding him until he decided to throw them off, and England was left with years of struggle and bloodshed. Putting a proud man under constant surveillance will lead to him doing something drastic to release himself from his captivity.'

'You think he will attempt that?'

'Think? No, I am certain of it! He's a young man, a nobleman, and in his eyes, he is being held back. His inheritance was the control of his lands. Instead he is forced to submit to the English Crown, and if he marries the daughter of our King, he knows full well that he will lose all independence forever.'

Jean de Vervins was a short distance away.

'You don't trust him, do you?' the knight said.

'No.'

'I heard he saved your life, however. Surely that is enough for a man?'

'If you recall, until the fight outside Durham, he was the sworn vassal of the French King. He lied and fooled all his companions there. And now he is here, leading us to . . .'

'To a glorious coup, perhaps.'

'And perhaps not,' Berenger said.

'No. He may be a traitor, leading us into a trap.'

'Is there anything we can do about it?' Berenger had paused and was staring at the city ahead.

'Us? No, nothing.'

'Then we might as well enjoy the weather while we can,' the vintener said easily, and persuaded his pony to trot onwards.

They were a half-mile away now. Berenger stopped and looked back at Grandarse, who he belched and waved a hand airily. 'You tell 'em, Frip!'

'Archers! We are here to work with the local people to make their city safe from French attack. In a matter of days they will declare themselves in full support of our King, and will renounce their own cowardly monarch, Philippe. They will need our help to keep the city calm, and to help hold it in case of a siege. But we aren't strong enough to hold it against the will of the people. You understand me? This is not a city we have conquered. We haven't had to bring scaling ladders and ropes to take the place. We are here as comrades, and you will behave in like manner. No brawling with the people, no fighting, and above all, no raping or murdering! Any man found to have committed rape will be castrated and then hanged. Any man found guilty of murder or theft will be hanged. These people are our friends and we will not have that put at risk. Do any of you have any questions?'

There was a low rumble of denial.

'Good. Now, archers! Onward!'

Gauvain de Bellemont had ridden hard and managed to reach Metz before dark on that same evening. First, he needed to rest, and then he would speak to his messenger about the arrival of the English. After that he would hasten to Laon, so that the city could be prepared. Colin should be back by now, and he wanted to speak with the smith and make sure that the English King's reaction was favourable.

Colin Thommelin, a rough man with the build of a greyhound, was about thirty years old, with a face square as a block, small, suspicious eyes and a permanently sullen expression. It was an embarrassment to acknowledge that he hailed from the same native city as Gauvain. But where Gauvain had moved to Metz in response to preferment from the Crown itself, Colin had moved there more urgently as a result of a slaying after too many cups of wine. It was one of those everyday little matters: Colin had insulted a man, the man had remonstrated, knives were drawn with the courage and enthusiasm of men well into their third pints of wine, and a little later there was more than wine spilled on the floor.

He had never conquered his aggressive nature. It was common enough with all men, it was true, but Colin Thommelin should have learned to control his rages and anger better, or conceal them beneath a calmer exterior. The problem was, he had never learned common courtesy. He had lost his first wife, but he still had two sons, and he could have found a new woman to warm his bed, had he displayed even a little commonsense. But the man lacked all charm. He was a *forgeron*, a smith of sorts, and that was what he would remain. A man who lived alone with his sons, who went to the wineshop every evening and stayed while he had money; a man who had no ambition and no hopes of advancement.

And yet, the man had a use. He was, like Gauvain, from Laon, and he was the ideal messenger. Smiths could travel easily. That was why Gauvain had chosen him to take the letter that Gauvain had painstakingly written out with his companions in treachery.

Treachery! It was a harsh word. Connotations of fire and agony came with it. To be judged a traitor would result in the most painful of deaths, that was certain. Still, with Colin delivering his letter, Laon would soon become English territory, and Gauvain could return to his ancestral home with the knowledge that his life would become secure. The English were always generous with their payments to men who aided them, and no one could aid them more than he who gave them Laon and the cities of the region. Colin knew that he was barred from Laon while the city remained under the suzerainty of King Philippe, but once it became English, he could appeal to King Edward for his conviction to be quashed. His only wish was to return to the city where he had been born, and this was his means of achieving that.

Gauvain entered the city as the bells were pealing, and slowed at the sight of a party of watchmen marching along the roadway ahead of him. Idly, he followed them, walking his horse homewards. He would go there first, and rinse the worst of the dust from his face, brush some of the mud from his hosen, and once he had partaken of a little food, he could go to speak with the other merchants of the city and let them know that the English were on their way. There would be celebration at the news, he was sure. Everyone had been working to this end for so long, and now their plans were coming to fruition.

A spark of anxiety flashed in his breast and he almost lost his footing in fear. A man laughed at him, telling him to mind his step on the loose cobbles, but it was not that which had made him trip: he had distinctly heard one of the watchmen mention his name. Gauvain slowed and listened intently as the men continued. The sergeant of the watchmen was giving orders: they were to break into the house of the lawyer, three men at the front, two at the back in case he tried to flee, and capture him.

'You know what you have to do. That letter tells us what's been happening here.'

It was only then that he saw the familiar shape of Colin

Thommelin up there with the watchmen, and he suddenly realised that if Colin could gain his pardon from the English King by helping bring about the delivery of Laon, he could expect at least a pardon from King Philippe for warning him about a plot to hand the city over to the English. So that was why his messenger had never reached the English King. He had not tried to. Instead he had taken Gauvain's letter to the French King.

'Shit, shit, shit,' he murmured to himself as he turned along a separate street. His horse was reluctant, and tried to jerk his head free of the reins to hurry to their home and a manger of good hay, but Gauvain smacked his rump and spurred him until the recalcitrant beast complied.

'I have to warn them,' he said to himself, but that was a secondary consideration. Right now, he had to protect himself. He must escape.

He had a friend in Reims. That was where he would go. He would be safe there.

CHAPTER THIRTY-SEVEN

Riding beneath the gates of Laon, Berenger felt a fleeting horror and shuddered. It was an age-old terror of buildings looming overhead. Once more he saw in his mind's eye missiles being flung down at him from rooftops, rocks and arrows crashing and clattering all about him. He saw old friends, and witnessed them die once more. It was a momentary thing only, but it was powerful. Fighting in towns was petrifying. In the open country, you saw your enemy form, you saw them prepare, you heard them attempt to put the fear of death into you as they roared their battle cries and rattled weapons and shields long before they were ready to advance. Arrows, bolts, lances, all could be observed and avoided as best one could. But here, in a town, a man could walk about the streets only to be seized from behind, or have a rock fall from a roof without warning. A man must be wary of all around him, before and behind, but everything above as well. And riding under a city gate like this merely added to the sense of trepidation that infused his spirit.

'Archers, *keep together*!' he called over his shoulder as they entered the streets, and then, 'Marguerite, stay close to me.'

There were people everywhere, and while they did not look entirely welcoming, nor did they look dangerous. No city liked to receive as guests a hundred or more soldiers, after all. Soldiers were a threat at the best of times, and usually an impediment to business; even if these men were not here to cause trouble, their demands for food and drink would themselves be an annoyance, if not worse. Yes, Berenger could all too easily understand the reluctance of the people here to greet their visitors with joy and open arms, but he was reassured by the lack of displays of anger or rejection. Rather, he thought, the people here showed bemusement and surprise – and something else.

'My friend, you do not need to worry,' Jean de Vervins said. He had gained in confidence, the nearer they came to the city. 'We are safe here. Trust me, this is my city. These are my people. As soon as my friend arrives, we shall declare our change of allegiance, and then watch the other cities in this area fall to our King!'

'Aye, that's right excellent to hear,' Grandarse said. He was puffing and panting after the unwelcome exercise. 'But do you think before anything else we could talk about where we'll be staying? I could do with a chance to shut my eyes and have something to fill my belly before I do anything else.'

'No. First we see to the horses, Centener, and then we think about ourselves,' Sir John said disapprovingly. 'Master Jean, I want stabling for all the mounts, and I want it close together. I don't wish to see them spread all over the city. We must be able to get to them in a hurry, if need be. Our own accommodation must be together and close to the mounts as well.'

'I am sure it will be ready.'

'Who should be welcoming us?' Sir John said.

'If we continue on this road, we shall soon be at the cathedral. I expect we shall be met there,' Jean said.

The city was built on top of a ridge, and with the massive

cathedral towering over the whole area, it was a strongly defensible position, Berenger reckoned. 'If there are even a few hundred men prepared to secure these walls, we'll be safe,' he said to Sir John.

'Yes. Even a matter of a few hundred,' he agreed, but there was a flat tone to his voice as he looked about him, gauging and assessing as he went.

It took but a short while to push their way through the crowds thronging the streets. It appeared that they had chosen the very same route as all the other people in the city that day, but soon they reached the mighty bulk of the cathedral with its two enormous towers.

'How does it stay standing?' the Earl remarked, gazing up at it.

'You think God would let it fall?' the Aletaster said.

The Pardoner sneered, 'You haven't heard of all the cathedrals in England where the spires fell?'

'Perhaps this is God's country, then,' the Aletaster countered.

Berenger didn't speak. He had seen too much death, murder and horror in the last year to think that there could be anything about this country that God liked.

'Where are your friends, Jean?' he said. There was no apparent threat, but he didn't like the fact that they were still out in the open with a vast crowd of people. 'You said they'd be here.'

'And here they are,' Jean said with a touch of smugness. He waved his hand and Berenger saw three portly gentlemen hurrying towards them. 'My good friends, burgesses all: Simon, Paul and Alan. My friends! I am overjoyed to see you! Have you all in place? Did the messenger arriver?'

'But I thought he would be with you?' the first said.

'No, he was sent before us,' Jean de Vervins said, and for the first time Berenger saw a slight crease at his brow as though he was concerned. This was surprising news to him.

'You think the man could have been waylaid?' Berenger asked.

Jean de Vervins shook his head. 'He was only a lowly fellow. No one would give him a second glance.'

'Unlike your warriorlike party! You have been travelling long. We should bring your men into the hall and feed them,' the merchant added, eyeing the mud-spatters on the men's hosen and tunics.

'There you speak good sense!' Grandarse exclaimed. 'Where is the stabling? And then, lead me to the table, my friend!'

The English archers were all treated to a good meal that evening. Even Tyler, who could usually be guaranteed to complain about any billet, was quiet in the face of the feast provided. And since more men had been expected, the quantity was more than enough.

'How many are there of you?' one of the townspeople, a man with lank fair hair and greenish eyes, asked Berenger as he helped himself from another mess of thickened pottage.

'Archers, five vintaines, so about a hundred men all told,' Berenger said.

'One hundred? Is that all?' the man said, his face falling.

'Have you seen what one hundred English archers can do in three minutes?' John of Essex demanded. 'All releasing four or five arrows in each minute, covering a field with arrows that can pierce any steel?'

'So many?'

'And more,' John said smugly.

'But if there were a thousand men attacking each side of our town,' the man said with a frown, 'you would have five and twenty to each wall, and your hundred would look sparse.'

'We don't lose our battles,' John said.

'Good,' the man said, but as he turned away, Berenger saw his concerned expression.

He was right. One hundred men to protect a town this size was far too few.

After even a cursory glance at the walls, it was clear that this city held a magnificent position over the surrounding countryside. Even a determined attack by well-trained English forces would find this one a hard nut to crack, Berenger told himself. The land fell away from the walls, which were massive, and the town had an excellent view over all the lands hereabouts.

'Any French force would come from those directions?' Berenger asked, pointing to the roads south and west.

A merchant, Simon de Metz, had joined Sir John, Grandarse and Berenger at the wall. Simon answered: 'Yes. Most probable is the western road.'

'Do you have any idea how many men will gather to attack us?'

Jean and Simon exchanged a glance. Again, it was Simon who responded. 'No, I do not know.'

'So we don't have any idea whether it'll be the full force of the French army or a posse?'

'No, we do not know,' Jean said. 'But so long as we can count on the people here, we should be safe enough.'

It was their first full morning. Most of the archers had fallen on their mats last night, the instant the drink ceased to flow, and many were mooching about the city now, suffering the effects of last night's indulgence. Meanwhile, Berenger and Grandarse felt the need to check the town's existing defences. Sir John had already sent a vintaine to the west in order to sweep around to the south, patrolling the countryside in search of forward parties from a French force, just in case.

'The walls are strong for the most part,' Sir John said, 'but *there* and *there* are patches of disrepair. How about the population? Are the people for us?'

It was Jean who smilingly answered, 'But of course! You will be their liberators.'

Berenger returned to his lodging with Grandarse, and both settled at the table silently as they broke their fast.

'You too?' Berenger said at last.

'What?' Grandarse said.

'You're not comfortable, are you?'

'I don't know what you mean, man. Never been happier in a billet.'

'No, nor me,' said Berenger, smiling up at Marguerite as she brought in loaves of bread and a board with a cheese.

They had almost finished their meal when the clamorous tolling of a bell made both leap from the table and rush outside.

Berenger stared first towards the church, then down the road, to where a bedraggled group of men were hurrying up the street as fast as their exhausted legs would carry them.

'Shit, Grandarse! It's Paul's vintaine,' Berenger breathed.

CHAPTER THIRTY-EIGHT

Their tale was soon told.

'We were riding down the road only a couple of leagues from here, Sir John, when we rode straight into a sodding great force of militia. At least two thousand of them, I think. There was no time to string our bows or anything. It was a straightforward bal-locks of a mess! Before we knew it, three men were down, and Paul was one of the first, with a bolt through the head. It was all we could do to pull the men out and get back here.'

'Were they chasing you?' Berenger asked.

'They're coming, yes, but they're still over a league behind us, I think. We rode fast, but they have wagons and carts, and we slowed them anyway. I took the boys to a little copse, and we used our arrows from there for a while.'

'Good!' Grandarse said. He looked to Sir John, who was stand-ing absorbing the news.

'You only lost three?'

'Four in all, sir. And two won't be fit to hold a bow or sword for a week or two.'

'Right, Grandarse, you will need to appoint them a new vintener.'

The older man nodded. 'I'll put John of Essex in charge. He's a good commander.'

'Tell him not to bugger off on any more private ventures, then,' Sir John rumbled.

'Yes, sir.'

Jean de Vervins looked distraught. 'How can we hope to hold this place?'

Sir John set his head on one side. 'You asked us to come here, man! We are still a strong force.'

'But against twenty to your one?'

'We also have the townspeople,' Sir John said.

Jean looked away. 'Some, perhaps.'

The Earl and a few of the vintaine were listening. At that, he gave a hollow laugh. '*Some*? That does not exactly inspire confidence, does it, not when our lives are at risk.'

'Be quiet!' Sir John snapped.

'He's right, Sir John,' Pardoner said. 'How can we be expected to guard the walls about this town? We'd be spread too thinly to guard even a quarter of the walkways.'

'Many of the citizens would no doubt come to our aid,' Jean de Vervins said.

'*Many*? What is that supposed to mean?' Now it was Sir John interrogating Jean de Vervins. 'Enough to guard a whole wall or two? Speak!'

'I had hoped to have more time here, to persuade others to our cause,' Jean de Vervins said, his voice thick. 'But this has all happened so swiftly. We have had no opportunity to speak to people. Some are already saying they should arrest you and your men, to save the city from the King's vengeance.'

'You asked us to travel all the way here and now you say we

can do nothing?' Berenger said angrily. 'What is it you expect from us?'

'If he's right, we should get out of this poxy town and hurry back to Calais before that city falls and we lose all the pickings inside,' Grandarse said.

'Is that what you think?' Berenger asked. 'That we should flee?'

'You cannot prevail here, if the population rises against us. They'll know that if the army arrives, it'll be only a matter of time before the city is taken,' Jean de Vervins said.

'So, there is indeed little point in our remaining here,' Sir John said.

'For safety, I can give you another, more defensible place,' Jean said slowly. The panic was leaving him. Yes, this city was impossible to hold with so few men, but there was always his own little castle of Bosmont. He could take the English there, perhaps, and with these men hold the place. Otherwise, the first thing the French would do would be to capture it and he would have lost his inheritance – and that would be a bitter pill indeed to swallow.

'Yes, there is a place we can go to, and then the English army can come to our aid, with good fortune.'

Grandarse was seated on his mount by the time Berenger arrived in the main square with Marguerite straggling behind him. 'Make sure your boy is on his cart,' Berenger told her curtly and went about the men, checking they had their equipment ready for a swift departure.

Sir John was already wheeling his horse about, his esquire Richard faithfully responding and bringing his own horse into position as though the two men were preparing to mount a charge immediately.

Berenger felt the mood of the men about him, and suddenly he realised that the city itself wasn't threatening towards the archers; rather, the population felt threatened by the arrival of the English. They must know that the presence of English archers would surely precipitate a tumultuous reaction.

Grandarse suddenly dropped from his saddle and hurtled into a wine-shop. He was soon out, bearing a heavy goatskin. His horse was reluctant and peevish, and retreated before him. 'Come here, you old sow,' he shouted.

Marguerite was back in a moment, her eyes wide with terror.

'Is the boy with the cart?' Berenger asked her.

'Fuck!' Grandarse said as he struggled to get back into his saddle, while his horse moved skittishly.

'Yes,' she answered.

'You look alarmed, maid,' he observed.

'The people ... two of them spat at me,' she said, her eyes welling. 'They said I was a traitor and would be punished.'

Grandarse's foot missed the stirrup as he again tried to remount. 'Christ's ballocks!'

'We will soon be gone from here,' Berenger said trying to conceal his own concern.

'I hope so.'

Seeing a nervous watchman hurrying up the roadway, Berenger asked him, 'How far are they?'

'They will be here before noon,' he said. He was a large man with protuberant eyes that looked close to tears, and a huge belly that put even Grandarse's to shame. The mound of flesh under his chin wobbled as he spoke – the skin looked as smooth and soft as a baby's.

'Then, Sir John,' Berenger said, 'with your approval, I would send a vintaine of archers to engage the French. They can hold up the advance while we leave.' When Sir John nodded, Berenger turned back to Jean de Vervins. 'Where is this place?'

Jean answered dully, 'A castle, not terribly far. A day's ride at most.'

'And you are sure we will be welcomed?' Sir John cut in.

'Oh, yes. I can personally guarantee—'

'How did the French hear about us so quickly?' Sir John interrupted.

Jean held out his hands, bewildered. 'I have no idea. My friend was arranging matters for us here – a lawyer. I saw him in Berghes before we left, and he seemed confident that—'

'Was there another who could have given away our plans?' Sir John rasped. 'We are clearly betrayed.'

Berenger threw him a look. His suspicion of Sir Peter of Bromley was growing into a certainty: the man was a traitor, his act of changing allegiance merely a ploy to gain the trust of the English.

'Gauvain is no fool! He gave a letter to an accomplice to take to the King at Calais.'

'Yet no such letter arrived,' Sir John noted.

'He gave his letter to a fool who got lost,' the burgess Alan said. He was fretting as he stood. 'Friends, we should not be here. This must lead to a catastrophe. What will happen to my children? My wife? Oh, dear God!'

'Shut up,' Berenger said. He had a duty to his men, above all. 'Jean, you said that the city would rise in our support. Now you say it will not?'

Jean shook his head. 'The plot was to begin to gather up all the supporters of King Philippe, and hold them. That way we would control the finances and military, but now all that is but a dream. The populace may help us, but if many refuse, well, we are lost.'

Alan wailed, 'We are lost! Lost!'

Berenger said nothing, but John of Essex, who had already dismounted, took a cudgel and brought it down on the back of Alan's head. Alan's eyes rolled up and he crumpled. 'Sorry, but he wasn't adding anything to the discussion,' John said.

'We must ride to Bosmont. It is my own castle,' Jean said. 'We can hold that. Then people will come to us and support us under the flag of your King.'

'Sir John, for my money we are too few,' Grandarse said. He had managed to haul himself back into his saddle, and now sat there, red-faced and blowing. 'With only a hundred men we can't man a castle. We need food and drink to keep a stronghold for any length of time.'

'You may be right, Grandarse, but we will need to look anyway. If we take over a castle here, it will force the French to contain us with a force that will otherwise go to Calais, so it will be worthwhile. Have the men prepare to move off. And now,' the knight continued, 'Jean, tell me all you can about this messenger of yours.'

'He is a reliable friend, a lawyer named Gauvain de Bellemont. I have known him for years. Only a few days ago I met him in Berghes,' Jean said with a frown. 'He was about to leave then. Did they catch him? Has he been here yet?'

'He may still be on the road,' Simon said. 'Perhaps he was held up?'

'But the men of the King of France clearly know about your plot,' said Simon de Metz, eyeing Alan's protrate form, and glancing at John warily.

Berenger noted that this was now Jean de Vervins' plot, not Alan's. Jean also noticed, from the filthy look he gave his confederate.

'So, as we expected, news of our arrival has precipitated a reaction,' Sir John said. He pulled down the corners of his mouth so that it appeared like a drawn bow. 'It changes nothing,' he concluded, 'other than to increase the urgency of our actions.'

'But you don't understand,' Simon said. 'Our city here is not ready! The walls are in disrepair, the populace has not been fully brought over to our side. We must have you send for the rest of your army immediately. We need a much greater force to protect us. Bring us into your King's Peace and save us!'

'I understand your concern,' Sir John said, 'but our King is fully engaged at Calais. He will not dissipate his forces into little packets here and there. If you are to keep this city and protect it, you must rely on your own abilities and skills. We shall ride to Jean's castle.'

'You will desert us?'

Sir John stared at the man. 'If we stay here, you will die. Our presence will cause a battle, and if we are forced, we will fight to the last man. Do you think your city can cope with that? No? Then you had best ride with us if you do not wish to be captured by your King.'

Gauvain de Bellemont had ridden hard all the way to Rheims and now, under the protection of his new clothing, he felt invisible as he walked about the city. He stood now in the great square before the cathedral, and stared up at the building filled with a sense of confusion at the latest turn of events.

It was bizarre. The act of treachery in which he had indulged would certainly lead to his destruction. All he had built in a lifetime of study and sheer hard effort, was now lost. His family, his properties in Laon and Metz, his treasure, all were gone. It was hard indeed to believe that he had suffered such a catastrophe, but there it was: he would be fortunate to escape with his life and the clothes on his back.

A woman stopped him. 'Excuse me, Brother. Please, I must speak my confession.'

'Madam, I am sorry,' he said, trying to hold his frustration at bay. This was the third woman today, in God's name! Was the entire female population of Rheims so sexually incontinent that they must confess their sins to any passing man?

'Brother, I am desperate for your help.'

'Woman, please, go to your priest.'

'But he knows me! The shame! Brother, you *must* hear me.'

A watchman was observing them with interest and unconcealed amusement. Gauvain set his teeth. 'Yes, of course. But where can we go?'

'We can sit by that wall,' she said, pointing to a bench. 'No one will interrupt us when they see me talking to you.'

'Very well,' he said moodily. It was his own fault. The idea of putting on a Carmelite's robes had seemed inspired at the time. Only now did he see the disadvantages.

They went and sat, and she began to speak. At first, Gauvain's attention was split as he tried to keep an eye on the watchman, but surreptitiously, for fear of exciting the man's interest.

'So, Brother, I was drinking with my brother-in-law and sister, and although I knew it was a terrible thing, I was horribly drunk and all excited, and when Hélène passed out, well, I had to ease the itching in my groin, so I went to Jacques, and ... and ... what I did then was ...' and she whispered in his ear.

Gauvain snapped his head away, threw back his hood and stared at her. 'Woman, that is disgraceful!'

'Hush,' she entreated. 'That is why I had to ask you to listen to my—'

'Christ's bones!' he cried. 'You think I want to listen to this sort of filth? My God, you are a shameless slut – a wanton of the worst sort. Words do not do justice to ...'

He fell silent as he became aware that not only the woman, but the others all about him in the street, especially the watchman, were observing him and hanging on to every word.

'You should, er ...' What kind of penance should he give her? To have done that to her brother-in-law, while her own sister was vomiting and drowning in her sleep ... the woman was a disgrace. But he had no idea how to give her a punishment. What form should it take? A hundred *pater nosters*, two hundred? A thousand? And the watchman was staring at him now, a doubtful expression on his face.

'Begone! You are innocent in this,' he tried desperately. 'Go to your priest and tell him that you were tempted by a devil and that he must pray for you.'

'But you are a monk, Brother, and if I tell him this story, he will be always on at me to go and swyve him. I know what he's like!'

'You must go,' Gauvain hissed, but already it was too late.

The watchman, his suspicions fully roused, was purposefully making his way across the square towards the couple. Panicked, Gauvain shoved at her and she fell on her rump with a squawk. There was a moment's hush, as though the whole world was holding its breath, and then Gauvain began to run, the robes flapping wildly about his ankles, until he was forced to lift them, like a woman hurrying after a mislaid child.

There was a street, and he dodged down it. The crowd parted as he flew past as though inspired by some celestial hand to make way for this Man of God. A loose cobble almost made him tumble to the ground, but then he was back on his feet and hurtling on again, the blood pounding in his temples, the air rasping in his throat, aware of light-headedness and a sense of near suffocation as he tried to breathe faster and faster with this unaccustomed exercise. He could feel the strain in his chest as he began to labour up a slight incline.

Risking a glance over his shoulder, he saw that his pursuer was flagging. *Thank God*, Gauvain thought, and turned back round – just in time to see the cart being thrust into his path from a side-alley.

He could not hope to stop. Holding out his hands, he tried to halt his onward rush, but the cart's movement prevented his manoeuvre from working. One fist missed the cart altogether, while the other was caught on a plank, and he felt the splinters stabbing viciously into his palm. Then his hip struck the wheel, and the wheel ran over his foot, and then he was spinning and the cart carried on, but he was falling and looking up at the cart, and his head struck the ground with a crack that made him think he must have broken his pate, and for a moment or two the world lost focus and he was only aware of the pain in his flank and hand and head.

But a moment later, the angry and reddened face of the watchman appeared, and as the man's sword rested on his belly to hold him there while his pursuer panted and coughed, Gauvain suddenly realised again how grim was his peril. He tried to rise, but a boot caught his chin, and he fell back, spitting out a tooth and groaning with the pain and the grief.

CHAPTER THIRTY-NINE

It was a relief for Berenger when he and the other men finally left the city.

His ride under the gatehouse was once more filled with the anticipation of danger; at any moment, he expected to find that the gates before them were shutting, those behind already bolted against them, trapping them – and that the citizens were all overhead on the inner walls, ready to rain down rocks and arrows on them. To his enormous relief, none of this happened. The people of Laon were as worried about the presence of the English as they were about being besieged by the French. It was the inevitable horror of the labouring classes throughout the centuries. Soldiers came and went, but the poor folk were always the lambs, doomed to be fleeced and slaughtered – no matter who the enemy.

As soon as they had made the decision to leave, two men were despatched to tell the outlying vintaines to prepare to depart. They had hurried back in short order, with the news that there was no sign of an army approaching yet, but that meant nothing. When the French did arrive, the English needed to be well away from here.

'It's really not far, Sir John,' Jean was saying as they left the curving walls of Laon and took the road east. 'We ride five leagues east, then another five north – and then we will be there. It's a good castle, you'll see. Strong, well-positioned, and sufficiently distant from here for us to feel secure, eh?'

Grandarse was riding a few horse-lengths behind Berenger, watching and listening. 'Aye, Frip. D'ye see what I said, eh? Right dangerous mess, this. We'd have been better staying at Calais. Still, once we've made it to Jean's castle, we can see what pickings there are about the place. Maybe a little manor or two to visit, and some plate and silver to take away with us? That would serve us well.'

'The main thing is to patrol the countryside,' John of Essex said. 'We must know when the French are getting within a few leagues so we can be ready for them.' He had joined Berenger, and his vintaine was riding in a parallel column alongside Berenger's.

'Aye, that would help,' Grandarse said, but Berenger could see from the look in his eye what he was thinking: it would be safer still to be as far from Bosmont and Jean de Vervins as possible when the French did arrive. No English archer was welcome in France, especially not since Crécy, when so many noble lives had ended at the point of an English arrow.

'Look at them,' Mark Tyler said disgustedly, pointing to the huddle of merchants riding a little to their left. 'What good will any of them be, Frip, when we get to the castle? They can hardly hold a staff, let alone a sword.'

'They may show some courage,' Berenger said shortly. 'As matters stand, we couldn't leave them at Laon. They would be killed for certain. Better to keep them with us.'

'Why?' Tyler grumbled. 'So they can eat our food?'

'I was thinking more because we can find out where they keep their money,' Grandarse said comfortably.

'And I was thinking that the King might be unhappy, were we to mislay his allies,' Berenger said.

'He won't miss allies who failed to achieve the one thing he wanted,' John commented.

'He'll miss any who have money and who could prove useful in the future. Look at Jean de Vervins himself,' Berenger said. 'He's hardly the sort of man I'd expect our King to take to, but he seems to have wormed his way into the King's favour. Not that it will necessarily continue when our King sees that he's failed to bring in Laon. Still, he could work to the King's benefit, if we can keep this castle of Bosmont secure and him with it.'

Grandarse eyed him doubtfully. 'You think so?'

John of Essex was gazing about them as they rode, staring at the verdant pastures and the crops just appearing through the crust of the soil. They were passing a hamlet now, and in it were several pleasant houses and farm buildings. Horses and cattle grazed, and there was a bleating from over a hedge that spoke of lambs.

'Someone will have to go to the King, to bring him up to date with developments,' he said. 'Not I, though. I'll be staying here as long as I can.'

Berenger sighed as he recognised John's expression: it was that of an English soldier who could smell, all about him, the sweet odour of plunder.

Archibald finished ramming the ball up the barrel, and threw himself over the parapet behind his safety ramp. In front he had caused some pavises to be built – large shields of wood so that he was safe from bolts and arrows aimed at him from the town's walls as he worked his gonne. The clatter and thud of missiles hitting the pavises had grown to be a constant background noise, rather like the clatter of hail against a shingled roof.

He aimed along the length of the barrel, then used a heavy, lead-filled wooden maul to hit the breech.

'You need to clobber that harder, if you want it to hit something, don't you?' a sentry asked. He was new here, and hadn't worked with Archibald for long.

Archibald threw a meaningful look at Ed. Even the boy had not been as slow as this. 'I clobber it hard to move it. As I hit it, the barrel turns,' he said. One day, he would have to give some thought to an easier way of shifting the barrel. Perhaps putting it on a wheel, instead of a sledge or raft? He could have it on a trailer, but the massive shock of the detonation would shatter any wagon at the first shot.

'That'll do it,' he said to Ed. The Donkey was hardly listening, he saw. Instead, he was peering over the parapet towards the flats west of the town. 'Hey – Donkey! Shift yourself!'

The boy scurried down to the wooden boards at the bottom and ran to the brazier at the farther end of their trench. Here he grabbed the long coil of string Archibald had made, and thrust its end into the fire. The match blackened and singed, and Ed blew on it to keep it glowing, while Archibald tipped powder from the flask about his throat into the little hole. He stoppered his flask and reached for the match. 'Stand back!' he shouted, and shoved it down.

Béatrice, watching from the powder store, saw the high, inverted cone of smoke as the first powder sizzled in the vent, but then there was the brief pause – the tremble, almost – and the roar as the gonne belched out its flames in a thunderous cacophony.

Archibald danced around at the breech end, shouting, 'Did I hit it? Did I hit it?' as the smoke rolled greasily around. Gradually, as it cleared, and he could see again, he was struck by the sight of a cog bucketing in the sea at the harbourside. As he watched, he saw a new hole in its planking, and the cog began to move more sluggishly in the water, gradually tilting, while shipmen ran aloft on the ropes to try to release the sails, but all to no avail.

'Look at that!' Archibald cried triumphantly. The unmistakable sounds of rending wood came over the water as the vessel's planks and beams began to break apart, torn asunder by the weight of the cargo inside.

But Donkey wasn't watching. His attention was still fixed on the other bank of the river.

'What on earth is it, boy?'

'It's that priest again. He's spying on us, as he was before.'

Archibald poked his head over the parapet and stared. 'Then we must do something about him, mustn't we?'

The little castle of Bosmont rose on its own modest hillock in the bend of the River Serre. Standing on the eastern edge of the river, it loomed over them as they approached. Berenger considered it as they trotted up the narrow pathway.

With a gatehouse that had a strong, square gateway with a drawbridge, three small towers to protect each corner, and one larger tower that was also the donjon, all mounted on a rough outcrop of rock, it looked strong enough to survive an assault by even a very numerous army. The side facing the river was safe enough. Although it had no precipitous cliffs to deter assault, Jean said that the ground near the river was marshy and very damp, therefore unsuitable to position men, let alone siege engines.

'And if you look behind the castle, there are woods. It would be extremely difficult to form a body of men at any distance from here in that direction,' he said smugly. 'If a man wishes to take my castle from me, he will find that I am a tough opponent!' And he slapped his fist against his breast as he spoke.

Sir John nodded. 'I require you to guide me all about your

territory. I must view the lands and see where to place men to warn us of the advancing forces.'

Jean nodded. 'I will come myself.'

'Good. I shall take a cup of wine first and we must water the horses, but then I will want to get moving. We may have little time.' The knight spurred his mount and rode on ahead, eyeing the road at either side for points of ambush.

'You love this castle,' Berenger noted.

'Of course I do! It is mine – my birthright. I have little enough left, after my King's betrayal.'

Berenger had the good sense to hold his tongue as they rode the last yards to the castle's gates.

Jean said bleakly, 'If it were not for King Philippe's intolerable desire to honour those whom he loves, I would still be with him, you understand? I am not a natural traitor. It goes against my nature. But when he broke his oath to me, I could not maintain my own oath of fealty. What is chivalry, if the lord will not honour his part in the bargain?'

'What happened?'

'I was a knight in his service. In the first months of war, seven years ago, it was I who raised the army from local settlements, and we rode into the lands all about Chimay and put Jean de Hainault's men to flight. Those were glorious days, those. Plunder, and the joy of battle and seeing your foes flee before you. But then, the Hainaulters returned the favour, and we were forced to run here, to my castle, where we could lick our wounds and prepare for the next fight.'

They were riding under the gatehouse now.

'So,' Berenger said, 'what made you turn against the King?'

'I told you. Philippe de Valois wanted to honour his friend, Sieur Henri du Bos. So Henri and I were to joust at Paris. And when the day came, the King commanded me to lose. Henri tilted well, and he could have beaten me in a fair fight, but I had no choice: I had promised to lose. It was a moment of utter horror, for of course I would have to give him my armour and my horse, my noble destrier. But du Bos did *not* unhorse me. I refused to be bested and lose everything. The King was furious and ordered me to submit my horse and armour because I had cheated. It was nonsense. I had stuck to the code of chivalry as a knight must. So instead of obeying, I gathered my possessions and left Paris that same afternoon, resolved that I would have my revenge on the knight and the King. I went straightway to the coast. I was determined to go to Edward. I exchanged messages with your King, who was pleased to accept my offer of support. And now, after my efforts in Scotland and in Laon, when he hears of my plight, he will send more men to support me. It is one thing for me to fail to win over the populace of Laon, but another for him to allow me to lose my castle. He would not want to see me suffer in that way. My humiliation would reflect badly upon him.'

'Don't forget, the King has other matters on his mind,' Berenger cautioned. 'With the siege of Calais uppermost, and the marriage of his daughter to the Count of Flanders, there is plenty to occupy him.'

'This is important though, no? He will see the importance of supporting me and saving my castle. It will become a small *bastide* in the heart of France.'

Berenger said nothing. He had his doubts. There were times when Edward of England could be thoroughly helpful and generous, but when he was at war, he became focused on that, to the exclusion of all else. But perhaps Jean was correct. After all, the King had sent men down here: a token force, granted, but a force nonetheless. And he was concentrating all his efforts on destroying the French, which was the reason for his daughter's marriage: to ally the Count of Flanders to his cause. If he could see this little castle as helping his cause, perhaps he would consider sending support troops.

He looked about him as the archers dropped from their horses, rubbing sore backsides and thighs, complaining as only English archers would, about the heat, and their thirst for women and wine, preferably at the same time, and he felt that they might be able to hold this place.

Yes, they just might.

'Gauvain de Bellemont, you have been found guilty of conspiracy to treason, of conspiring to overthrow the community of this city, and of plotting with confederates to bring the town under the control of the treacherous Sir Edward of England. You are sentenced to life imprisonment.'

Gauvain had been captured in Rheims, and brought here to Laon in the afternoon of the same day. This trial was a surprise. He had not expected to survive so long. But the officials here had declared his sentence, and it would be a thoroughly hideous existence. He had seen the gaols here and at Metz; the ones at Laon were more comfortable than those at Metz – the innermost rings of Hell would be more comfortable than *them*. They were wet, with green slime on the walls where the poor light at least permitted some colour to be observed, and with a stinking stream that flowed along the middle of the floor, full of turds. When the rains came and the stream rose, men sleeping on the floor could be smothered in fecal deposits floating in the floodwaters. At least Laon had a bucket.

He was hustled from the officer's hall, and out into the sunshine. Here he was chained and locked to a cart for the shameful ride to the prison. He was forced to sit facing backwards to emphasise his humiliation. As he waited for the cart to start on its journey, he saw people gathering, unsmiling, hostile. He had been promised incarceration, but these good citizens did not approve of such an easy escape for him. He had been willing to put their lives at risk, after all. If he had succeeded, he would have allowed English soldiers into their city. Colluding with the enemy to give away their city, he would have carelessly sentenced many of them to their deaths.

They knew that. And now they wanted their revenge.

'Driver! Carter!' he shouted. 'Take me to the gaol, I beg!'

There was no sound, and when he looked over his shoulder, he saw that the carter was nowhere to be seen. This was clearly a spontaneous mob, desiring to show him their contempt, and the carter, fearing for his life, had fled.

'You're all brave enough now, I see,' he shouted. 'You'll come out to show your courage now, eh?'

He could see the first men and women hefting stones. At the sight he felt his bowels loosen and he could not hold his bladder. All his powers of persuasion failed him now as the trickle of pungent urine ran down his hosen, and he began to sob. He wanted to shout for the official, to plead for his life, but when he glanced at the steps leading to the hall, he saw the man standing at the top of them, watching silently. He obviously knew all about this gathering – had probably organised it. An extra punishment for the man who would have seen the city laid waste and besieged. The man who would willingly have seen the official himself slain.

A howl of rage, a roar of disapproval, a woman screeching at him . . . and then a heavy stone crashed against the side of the cart near his left forearm. He stared down at the mark on the wood where the stone had struck. It had left a massive dent. The wagon shuddered as another rock hit the cart-bed on his right side, and then a cobble smacked into his knee and he screamed.

He screamed for a long time, until the last rock crushed his skull and he could scream no more.

CHAPTER FORTY

The castle was a secure, comfortable group of buildings huddled inside the walls. True, it had been designed some decades before, in the happy days when it was common for men to bed down with their lords in the same building. Nowadays, with guards loyal only for as long as they were paid, it was more normal to keep the guards separate from the lord and his family. Too often had mercenary guards turned traitor, despoiling and murdering their own lords, Berenger knew. But for all that, it was warm and cosy, and Berenger could see why Jean de Vervins was so fond of the place.

Sir John had ordered that the men should be sent out in regular two-vintaine patrols to spy out the land, both to find out when the French army was approaching and to seek out good places for ambushes or attacks.

Leaving Marguerite and her son at the castle for their safety, Berenger had taken his vintaine to the north, in a sweep roughly a league away, when news came to them of Gauvain's death.

They had been riding gently that morning in deference to Berenger's fragile mood. He had a splitting headache, a queasy stomach, and a trembling sensation in his hands and legs. In short, he was badly hungover. As the two vintaines rode past deserted farmsteads, his mood was not improved by the sight of the columns of smoke rising on all sides.

He had known that the vintaines which had come this way yesterday had returned laden with plunder, but to see the results of their efforts was shocking even to him. Berenger had seen many examples of rape and slaughter in his time. The roads to Crécy were filled with the wounded and the dead after the army had passed by. Yet to see this carnage on a smaller scale was somehow more distressing.

'Pointless waste,' he muttered.

Jack was riding nearby, his eyes on the hedgerows and any other places that could possibly conceal an ambush. 'Why does he do it?'

'Jean de Vervins has no brain, but seeks to profit from the distress of others. He thinks King Edward will come here to rescue him. The fool is turning every peasant against him.'

It was unnecessary. There was no need to bring war to these peaceful, flat fields. Sir John and Grandarse had no desire to draw an army towards them any sooner than must inevitably happen, but this kind of wanton destruction was bound to lead to exactly that: a retaliatory raid by all the forces available to the local men.

'Stupid, stupid, stupid,' he grunted as another spasm made his stomach send acid into his throat. He grimaced at the taste and bitter sting, and took a sip of water from his leather flask. It didn't help, just as his chewing a hunk of dry bread had not helped earlier. It just made his belly rumble and complain still more. He thrust the cork back into the neck with excessive force and almost broke it.

'Rider, Frip!'

He looked up in time to see a man cantering towards them. He wore a russet tunic and his green cloak snapped and jerked in his wake. Berenger said, 'Archers, *keep your eyes open*!'

The fellow was only young, but was plainly no fool. At the sight of the archers, he slowed and came closer at a trot: brisk enough, but wary.

'Sir, are you English?'

Berenger grinned sardonically. The fact of their bows should have been confirmation enough. 'Yes. And you too, from your voice.'

'I am. I'm looking for the castle of Bosmont and Jean de Vervins or Sir John de Sully.'

'You're three leagues from it. If you want, we can take you there.'

'Good. I've been riding for the last day without pause. I'll be glad to reach the place at last.'

'You have urgent messages?'

'That useless prickle, the Count of Flanders, has escaped – and some think he could be heading this way.'

'But he was to marry the King's daughter,' Berenger said.

'Aye, he was. He's kept the King and all his entourage dangling in Flanders these past weeks with the constant promise of compliance, but now he's flown the coop and all we can do is curse him! Unless, of course, he rides straight into some of our own men.'

Berenger scowled. This was terrible news. He had thought that the Flemings were all on the side of the English, and if their leader had left, what would happen to the rest of the country?

'Does that mean the people will side with their Count?' he asked.

'Hah! After he fled, his brother tried to raise an army.' The messenger fell into step with the vintaine as they began to make their way back to the castle. 'The people heard of his plans, caught him and executed him. The Flemings want their freedom and they can see themselves getting it from King Edward.'

Berenger nodded, and questioned the messenger about all the activities in Flanders and at Calais.

'There is little enough to tell about the siege,' the man said when he had told of the fighting to the north. 'The French are desperate to have supplies arrive, but we have tightened our fist about the place. They won't be getting any more food in there, or I'm a Saracen. The last attempt left them with three of their ships destroyed; after that the rest turned tail and fled.'

'That is all to the good,' Berenger said. 'So long as the siege lasts long enough for us to join in again. Otherwise my men will string me up for allowing Sir John to bring us all down here. The rewards will be much better in Calais!'

But he didn't relish the thought. He had not forgotten his feelings at the sight of the dead after the battle outside Durham. The young Frenchman who had been poleaxed in front of him still returned to him in his dreams. It was part of the reason for his drinking: not only to help him alleviate the pain of his wound, but also to help him forget that young face.

Perhaps he had seen enough of war, he thought.

Archibald was scurrying around the muzzle of his great gonne like some sort of demented ant, Béatrice thought as he darted hither and thither, swabbing, drying, filling it with powder, tamping it down, rolling a ball of stone into it, ramming it home, and then clambering up the slope to the vent.

She was watching from the west of the town. There was a stand of trees and bushes here that had so far miraculously survived the depredations of soldiers desperate for firewood. It was here, so Archibald had said, that the man kept appearing, watching over the town and Archibald's gonnes. She was to see if she could work out who he was, and bring news to Archibald without running any silly risks. But so far there was no sign of him. She could see much of the shoreline from here, and the first of the moats and walls encircling the town, but the only fellows hereabouts were soldiers and tradesmen plying their wares.

Up at the gonne's little fortress she saw a sudden jet of smoke rise vertically. There was a blast of flames from the muzzle, and the thick column of smoke belched forth, dissipating as it reached halfway across the moat, the thick roiling blackness looking like smoke from the Devil's own furnaces. From this distance she could understand why men looked upon Archibald's devices as hideous machines of Satan.

A loud crack, and the rock flung from the gonne struck a wall and shattered into a thousand shards. The wall, however, showed little damage, and she bit her lip worriedly. Archibald was so convinced that his great tubes would devastate buildings and walls, and yet his greatest gonne had achieved little more than to pepper the town walls with dusty marks where his stones had smashed themselves to smithereens.

And that was when she saw him.

The priest stood a few yards from her, staring over at Archibald's fortress with a look of quizzical disgust as he chewed at a honeyed lark. Then he turned away and began to walk back towards Villeneuve-la-Hardie. Béatrice waited a moment before setting off in pursuit.

'Good!' Grandarse roared as he saw Berenger and the others pass under the gatehouse of Bosmont Castle. 'Thank God's mercy that you got back in time. They'll be here in another hour of the day.'

'What? Who will?' Berenger asked.

'The poxed French, Frip, you lummox! Pay attention, man! We've been expecting them at any time, haven't we? The manky gits who live in the area seem to have got it into their lice-ridden heads that we're unwelcome here. The Bailiff of Vermandois, the Count of Roucy and all the people from Laon and hereabouts are on their horses and riding straight for us, if the scouts can be believed.'

'Shite!'

'Ach, don't be such an old woman. This castle is strong enough. Look at the size of it. We can stick twenty men on each wall and still have a vintaine free to boil oil and bring it to the walls. Right.' He pointed to another vintener. 'Lance, you keep your men down here in the court. I want you to boil the oil, so get the fire started. You'll have to bring the oil to the gatehouse and anywhere else the enemy choose to attack. Fripper, take your men to the wall over there.' He indicated with a jerk of his thumb the wall to the west, nearest to the stables.

Berenger lifted an eyebrow. 'You've changed your tune. At Laon you were all for riding away without hesitation.'

'Aye, well, that was a city with enough men *inside* who hated our guts. Here, we can fight without having to watch our backs every moment of the day.'

While Grandarse continued bellowing orders, Berenger took his vintaine to the wall.

'How long do we have?' the Pardoner asked, gazing anxiously at the flat countryside.

'Long enough,' Berenger said soothingly, with a confidence he didn't feel.

If he was right, and there had been a traitor who had sold them to the French, he swore he would find the man. Not that it should prove hard. He was convinced that Sir Peter was responsible for their precarious situation here. He had tried to have Berenger killed, and then had his own clerk set an ambush for Clip. Jack was right, that Clip was there to forage or thieve what he could, but surely the clerk had laid a trap for him? Although why anyone would want to catch Clip was beyond Berenger's comprehension!

He glanced down at the river flowing sluggishly past below them, and was struck with the uncomfortable conviction that the people of this land would *never* allow them to stay. If the castle had walls ten times the height of these, the citizens of Laon and elsewhere would want to attack it, even if they had to use their bare fingers to pull it down. The English had, as he had reflected only a few hours before, brought unity to everyone here by the scale of their murderous depredations.

Now they would likely reap their just rewards.

CHAPTER FORTY-ONE

The mysterious man was not heading to a church but straight around the town and down towards where the vintaine had been based, Béatrice saw. She continued after him, stopping when he did, keeping her eyes on him all the time. Archibald had said that he was interested in the man, and she owed Archibald a great deal.

It was past the stores that she saw him glance over his shoulder. His eyes passed over her indifferently, as though she was not there. Then he continued onwards. Béatrice was puzzled by his apparent disinterest. She knew that she was attractive enough to be desired by most men. After all, on the way to Crécy she had been almost raped by a priest and others, a total of three times in as many days. Yet this man showed no reaction to her at all. Was she being followed?

She made a decision. A man beside her was innocently studying trays of wilting salad leaves and parsley, and she suddenly slapped his hand with a fierce exclamation as though he had been fondling her arse. The fellow snatched his hand back, turning his shocked face to his wife, but Béatrice was already off.

Picking up her skirts, she ran up the road towards her target. When she was almost upon him, she suddenly span on her heel and sure enough, saw a large man with black hair and grim features running after her. She quickly slipped away, darting down an alley, turning to the right, then right again, following her senses until she found herself back on the main street again. The two men, she saw, were holding a heated discussion at the mouth of the alley down which she had just run, and now, with a quick look about them, they strode off.

Béatrice followed them.

'We can see them!'

It was a youth who called from the top of the donjon, and Berenger looked up automatically to see in which direction the boy was pointing. It was roughly south-west – along the line of the main road from Laon, unsurprisingly – and Berenger set his face into a scowl of concentration as he stared that way, trying to make out anything. His wound stung and the old ache in his shoulder returned, but he stood unmoving.

'You have sharp eyes!' Sir John de Sully said, glaring into the distance.

'There they are, Frip,' John of Essex said suddenly.

Berenger nodded, although he could see nothing. And then, gradually, he began to discern a smudge on the horizon. At first he thought it could be smoke from another burning village, but it did not rise in the still air as smoke would, but stayed low, close to the ground. It was the dust from thousands of tramping feet.

'Shit, there's a lot of the bastards,' John of Essex said musingly.

'We can hold the place, with luck,' Berenger said.

'We would do better with some more men,' Jack said.

'Eh?' Grandarse joined them, and stood behind them now,

peering at the blur of approaching men. 'More men? What, do you think we don't have enough here?'

'We'll all git slaughtered,' Clip called.

'Shut up,' Berenger and Jack shouted together.

'Aye, well, don't blame me when you're lying dead in the gutter,' Clip said cheerfully.

The men were silent for the most part as they waited, wondering how many soldiers the enemy had mustered. Sir John arranged for boys to bring buckets filled with water for the men sweltering in their leather and armour. The men thoughtfully pulled belts tighter, or toyed with the fletchings on their arrows, all lost in their own private reveries. Berenger had fresh biscuits brought to them, but few had any appetite. Ale was appreciated, though.

One who was completely unmoved by the approaching force was John of Essex. Berenger saw him eyeing the landscape all about rather than the force gathering before them.

'If you're looking for support hereabouts, I don't think you'll find any,' the vintener said.

John smiled. 'I don't expect to. But I was wondering where they would be likely to attack first. If I was them, I'd come right here, I reckon. There's more space out there than on the other sides of the castle.' He peered down at the base of the wall. 'They can bring scaling ladders up here without too much trouble. I think this is where we'll need to concentrate.'

Berenger followed the direction of his look. The land looked rough and broken with clitter lying all about. 'I checked there, but the ground's very hard to cross. Trying to run across those rocks and stones would be tough.'

'Perhaps, but remember – this lot are mostly peasants. They're used to moving over rough land. You wait and see.'

Berenger shrugged. The mass of men could be clearly

discerned now: a few, no more than two hundred, were wearing tabards with arms he didn't recognise, but which must surely be the insignia of the Count of Roucy. For the most part, there was no way to distinguish the men from a rabble of peasantry. A few had steel helms on their heads, some even with mail tippets, but for the most part they looked like toilers pulled straight from their fields. However, that was little consolation. A trained, experienced group of warriors like those under Grandarse could tease victory from even the most unfavourable situation, but this army looked moderately competent and, when combined with the advantage of overwhelming odds, that would count for a lot.

Berenger began to feel a sinking sensation in his belly. He eyed the weaponry on display, and saw many peasant tools converted for use as weapons. There were axes, picks, and a variety of polearms, generally with a large sickle-blade or billhook thrust onto a long stave. They looked very agricultural, but then, as he reminded himself, a sickle could take a man's head off quite as efficiently as a sword.

'Archers, *prepare your bows*!' he bellowed. The French were only a matter of a hundred yards away now. Soon Berenger saw that all the bows were strung and ready, many of them with an arrow nocked. Clip was eyeing the field with an appraising eye, Jack peering as he tried to make out the best targets. Mark Tyler was near an embrasure, crouching low against the threat of a crossbow bolt. John of Essex stood unconcernedly as though invulnerable to danger.

While the majority of the French stopped and stared at the castle, a small party spurred their horses forward and rode up to the gate. In the lead was a tallish man with dark hair and a square face with a pointed chin. He sat on his horse like a knight, and his breast bore the same arms that were on the tabards of the men behind him.

'I wish to speak with Jean de Vervins,' he said flatly in French.

'I am here,' Jean de Vervins called from the gatehouse. Sir John de Sully went to join him.

'I am the Comte de Roucy. You know me, Jean de Vervins. I am come here with the Bailiff of Vermandois and the community of Laon to arrest you and punish those who would lay waste to the farmlands all around. You will come down to the gate and open it.'

'Go fuck your mother!' Jean shouted. 'If you think you can take my castle by storm, then give it a try! And now begone, before I tell these good English archers to send some arrows towards you.'

'Your plot has failed. You can have no success with Laon or the other cities here. Your conspirators are dead or arrested. Gauvain de Bellemont was slain by the people of Laon because of their hatred of him and his attempt to sell them and their city; his son Guyot is in prison and will remain there for the rest of his life. Your friend, Colin Thommelin was a loyal servant of the King. He took his letter to King Philippe, as a good, dutiful subject should, so the whole of your scheme is known. He shall be given a great reward for bringing your shameful treachery to the King's notice.'

'I don't need to listen to this!' Jean spat.

'The English brigands here will also have to submit to the people of Laon. Resist and none of you will survive to return to your homes. All will be slain. I call on you to surrender now before any more are injured.'

Grandarse spat over the wall with contempt.

Sir John de Sully said, 'We are English. We do not surrender.'

Jean de Vervins leaned forward at the wall, and bellowed, 'None of us will surrender to you! If you want to save lives, then leave my castle immediately. If you lay siege to us here, we will kill as many of you as we can until you decide to give in and return to whence you came!'

The man nodded. 'Very well. I have your answer. Good. I will see you hanged, Jean de Vervins, for the traitor you are.'

With that, he wheeled his horse about and he and the others galloped back to their men.

As Béatrice ducked into a doorway, out of sight, she saw the two men pause before walking boldly along an alley between two houses. She followed them over to the lane and stared down it. At the far end she could see chickens scratching at the dirt and pecking. She looked at the house, but it was closed up. After a moment's thought, she walked down to the house opposite, and knocked on the door.

A young man opened, his face breaking into a smile at the sight of her. 'Maid?'

'I was trying to speak with the cleric who lives in that house,' she lied. 'Do you know his name?'

'You wanted to speak with him and didn't know who he was?' the young man teased her.

'I think he beat my brother, and I want his name before I tell my father,' she said.

'I see. No doubt your brother was being cheeky or foolish and deserved it, eh? Boys will be—'

'Do you know his name?'

'Yes, of course. He's Father Alain de Châlons. He is the clerk to Sir Peter de Bromley, who lives there in that house.'

Chapter Forty-Two

Grandarse pulled Berenger aside.

'What do you make of that then, eh, Fripper? Sounded to me like the Frenchie wants to get out of this without too much fuss.'

'Well, he would,' Berenger said. His attention was still on the Frenchmen outside the gates. There was a certain amount of shouting and running around.

'There is another thing though, Frip. He reeled off all those names – Gauvain and his son and that. Sounds to me like the whole venture has gone tits up. There's little advantage to us or anyone else in staying here to be massacred.'

'We should be able to hold the place.'

Grandarse nodded sagely. 'Oh yes – we should. Now,' he turned and faced the besiegers once more, 'let me think ... All we need is some artillery, and maybe some more men. Of course, having only about a hundred men is good, because it means we can count on plenty of space to swing our blades, but there is the little problem of them having several blades to every one of ours.

Look at them, Frip! How many men do you think they have against us, eh?'

'They do have more than us.'

'*More*? I don't know if you noticed, Frip, but they have what looks to me like a thousand, perhaps more. More than ten men for every one of ours. Yes, our lads are competent, but we cannot win a siege like this. Look, we have the men in here from Laon, and Jean too. We could let them have the castle and the men they want, in exchange for our freedom, couldn't we? Eh? They'd have to agree to let us walk out with all our weapons, but that should be reasonable, don't you think?'

'I think we would be ridiculed if we were to try it,' Berenger answered. 'What would Sir John say? I think he'd refuse.'

'Perhaps he would. But it's surely worth trying. We'd survive to fight another day.'

Berenger caught a movement from the corner of his eye, and shouted: 'They're at the foot of the wall here. Archers, *prepare to defend yourselves*!'

Under cover of the parley, a couple of score of men had made for the woods at the edge of the river, and now they were dashing at full tilt along the rough ground, just as John of Essex had predicted. They bore heavy scaling ladders, and already the first two ladders were rising into the air.

'Archers, *hit the men with the ladders*!' Berenger roared, and in a moment three arrows were winging their way towards the men at the nearer ladder, but all missed, over-striking. They were enough to terrify the French, but not to dissuade them.

'Aim low! Aim low!' he cried. 'They are below us, don't forget. Adjust your aim.'

Two more arrows flew, and one struck a man at the next ladder, who immediately began shrieking like an injured rabbit, and soon the archers had their mark and were sending regular flights at their targets.

A group of French fighters, screaming and shrieking to keep their morale up, ran into a hail of arrows and were flung to the ground, writhing as they died. Only after twenty-three men had been killed, and many others injured and helped from the field, did the French cease their reckless attacks. They withdrew to a safe distance ... and soon afterwards came the sound of splintering wood and hammering. When they returned, they were carrying strong pavises, constructed from cart-beds, that would protect two or three men. With these they ran safely to the walls again, but once at the wall they were at the mercy of the archers once more. The English arrows would penetrate an inch of good oak when sent from a strong bow, and now most passed straight through the pavises as though the wood was little stronger than parchment.

Once more the French withdrew, and this time they remained out of sight while they considered their next assault.

Mark Tyler stood at the edge of the walkway, peering down with a curled lip as he aimed and loosed. Berenger drew his own bow and felt the tension first in his shoulder, then in his face as the scar seemed to surge with heat. He loosed, feeling the bow's lurch as the string ran along his bracer, and saw his arrow fly straight and true into the thigh of a man-at-arms at the edge of the woods. Another man darted out to help him to safety, and two arrows narrowly missed him, although one did pass through the arm of the already injured man, making him howl afresh.

That was their problem, Berenger knew. While they had plenty of arrows, the archers must make each one count. There were simply too many Frenchmen surrounding the castle for them to waste a single one. While in a battle, archers could depend on being able to rescue arrows from the field, but, here, all arrows loosed were arrows lost.

They would need to be more careful or this siege would not last long.

At his post on the wall, the spy reflected that this was the third time he had been forced to fight against his compatriots on the side of his enemies. It was galling to think that, as soon as the French under the Compte de Roucy entered the castle, he would become just another victim of their savage vengeance.

He drew his bow and loosed at a man running to the wall. The fellow was struck in the thigh, and hobbled his way back to the French lines.

Yes, the only way for the English to leave the castle alive would be if a truce was agreed. But how could a man guarantee that? And Jean de Vervins would never surrender. He knew what would happen to him, were he to do so.

A plan began to form in the spy's mind.

As his men kept up their steady effort, Sir John walked amongst them, offering them encouragement and support. There were a series of sudden attacks, but each was quickly beaten off. Berenger could see that the French numbers were not showing against the professionalism of the archers. If the attackers had been experienced at warfare, the outcome would have been much less certain, but these were men who only that morning had been labouring in their fields. When a few arrows hit their friends, the others would tend to withdraw rather than remain and sustain the attempt. English soldiers would have behaved with more commitment, unconcerned by the injuries of others, aware that the best way to keep safe is to end an attack as swiftly as possible – and press home with utmost energy.

The walkway on the wall was full of men. Berenger had to push past archers leaning over and loosing arrows. The Earl turned to him, his usually laconic face stern, next to Dogbreath, who seemed to be panting like a hound. Pardoner was further along, near Tyler, and both were drawing and releasing as quickly as they could nock their arrows.

He made for the northernmost point of the walkway, and there he pointed out two more men, and as he saw Jack and Clip turn and target them, he felt his foot slip. There was a moment of sheer panic, and then he was falling, staring up at the wall as he hurtled down to the ground inside the castle. A mere moment, but it lasted for a year: an age in which he had plenty of time to see the faces of Tyler, Pardoner and Grandarse staring down at him.

He tried to twist, but there was no protection from the jarring agony when he struck the roof of the stables only some six feet below; fortunately the thick straw thatch broke his fall well. For a brief instant he thought himself safe, but then, with a mighty crack, the timbers gave way and he was falling again, his head striking a rail as he went.

Hitting the hard-packed soil of the stable, he felt the breath slammed from his breast. For a long while he could only lie, winded, as the ghastliness of his situation was brought home to him. He attempted to move a leg, but pain exploded in his brain and he gave a long, shuddering gasp.

And then he was falling again, into what felt like a narrow well with no bottom.

'*Fuck my old boots!*' Grandarse bellowed, staring down as Berenger disappeared through the roof. 'John! Oi, John! Fripper's fallen from the wall, and he's landed in the stable. Get him out, man!'

John of Essex stopped supervising the oils in their great vats and ran for the stables. Inside all was mayhem, and he had to push past startled horses and ponies to get to the place where the roof had collapsed. Spars and planks lay haphazardly all over the floor, and amidst the mess of straw, thick, dried ferns and maddened horses, he could see the vintener. The sun's shafts falling through the hole in the roof were thick with dust from the dry vegetation, and John began to cough as he hurried to the prone figure. 'Help me!' he bawled, and began to cast about for a means of carrying Berenger from the room.

A short while later, he and one of his vintaine left the stables, the two carrying a broad trestle-table top with Berenger lashed loosely to it. They were only a few yards from the entrance, when there was a scream, and Marguerite rushed to John's side, staring down at Berenger's bleeding face.

'Mistress, away, if you please. I have to get him indoors to safety,' John said.

'Bring him to the hall, where I can tend to him. No – now!' she added, as she saw his eyes move to the walls once again. John glared, but nodded to the other archer, and the two carried Berenger inside as she had commanded.

'Look after him well,' John said threateningly, but there was a series of shouts and cries from outside, and he ran out again.

Marguerite looked down at Berenger and very slowly began to weep.

'Do not die, M'sieur. Do not die.'

At the first lull in the fighting, John of Essex pulled off his bascinet and wiped his sweaty hair away from his brow. It had been a hard series of skirmishes, with men storming the walls as well as the gates, in rushes. But their assaults were badly coordinated, and the men on the walls were able to beat them off. A score or more of the enemy were horribly incinerated when boiling oil was tipped over, scalding those it struck and then igniting and enveloping still more in the engulfing flames. The screams and shrieks of agony were so intense, so frightful, that for a moment both garrison and attackers stood back, appalled. But now the French were consumed by the urge to avenge their dead, and they redoubled their assaults.

At the middle of the afternoon, both sides withdrew for a rest. The archers of John's vintaine leaned against the battlements or slumped to the floor. There were two boys in his group: one sat blubbing in the corner by the tower, while the other, a younger boy, knelt on the walkway and stared about him, his eyes wide with shock. John was relieved to see a grizzled old archer pull the lad to him and hug him, rocking him gently.

Some of the garrison were set to collecting bodies and hurling them over the walls, and then John went down to see how Fripper was.

He liked Fripper. There was something about him that encouraged loyalty from his men. John had worked with others of supposedly more experience who did not inspire that kind of confidence. Fripper did. John had tried to analyse what it was about the man, but he could not isolate it. It was something to do with the way he gave men his trust but didn't ask anything in return. He expected them to act as he wished, and his belief in them seemed to bear fruit.

'How is he?' he asked as he entered the chamber.

Fripper was still lying on the trestle where John had left him, and while Marguerite had wiped and cleaned his face, there was still a lot of blood. John could see that he was very pale. Every so often he would shiver, and a hand would twitch.

'What do you think?' she said crossly. 'He is lucky to be alive.'

'He would be dead, were it not for the stable roof.'

'He has had a blow to the head, but I do not think he will die.'

'That's a relief, anyway. Do you need anything from me to help you?'

'No.'

'Then look to him well, mistress. We need him.'

She nodded and turned back to her charge. John stood staring down at Fripper, and shook his head sadly. As he left the room, he almost barged straight into Tyler.

'Where are you going?' he demanded as Tyler stepped aside.

'Me? In there. I'm parched.'

'Get back to your post, Tyler, and don't leave it again or I'll have you flogged.'

'You aren't my vintener!'

John recalled looking up and seeing Tyler's face on the walkway after Berenger's fall. He lifted his hands and shoved Tyler hard in the breast, sending him staggering backwards.

'Hey! What are you doing?'

'You want to argue about my right to command you? You want to dispute my authority? Or do you just want to get in there and finish the job?'

'What are you talking about?'

'I saw you up on the walkway when he fell. You were there, weren't you? Be easy to make a man slip and fall, wouldn't it?'

'I would never do that!'

Grandarse suddenly appeared. Barging his way between the two, he physically separated them and glared from one to the other.

'He says I pushed Fripper off the wall, but I didn't! You were there, Grandarse, you saw what happened. He just slipped and fell,' Tyler said desperately.

'I saw him falling through the air, no more,' Grandarse said, looking at John. 'What did you see?'

'Only his face as Frip fell,' John said, and shoved at Tyler again. 'I think this prickle did it on purpose.'

'I didn't even touch him, Grandarse!'

Grandarse looked at Tyler. There was no sympathy in his eyes, but his voice was firm. 'John, we can discuss this later, but for now we have a castle to defend. Tyler, go back to your vintaine on the wall. Do not leave your place again.'

As Tyler left them, John spat at the ground. 'He did it!'

Grandarse suddenly span on him. 'Don't give me that ballocks, man.' He thrust his face forward until John could feel the spittle hit his cheeks as Grandarse hissed, 'We have a fuckin' enemy outside those walls, you understand? *They*'re the enemy. Anyone in here is a friend because we need them all! Don't you dare piss around and cost us another man on top of the ones we've already lost.'

'But he might—'

'I don't give a farthing's fuck what he may or may not have done. If it looks like he did something, we'll sort that out later, once – *once* – we've escaped this place. You understand me? You go around causing trouble inside the castle and I'll cut your throat meself!'

Chapter Forty-Three

Jean de Vervins heard them arguing from where he stood on the castle's wall. And then he heard another sound – the braying of several horns, and some shouting. With a sudden excitement he ran to the battlements, hoping against hope that this could be another English force, come to raise their siege. It would be a miracle, were they to have heard of the plight of the men here, but perhaps the English King had realised that they were in great danger, and had decided to send them help?

Then the hope was dashed from his face as he took in the flags. More men from Châlons, more from Laon, some from further afield, but all from those loyal to the French King. None were English.

He felt despair hit him in his breast like a crossbow bolt. At last he truly understood the weakness of his position here. He looked out over the men before his gates. There was not a single one in whom he could place any trust. All were devoted to King Philippe. These were the men who wanted to see him dead.

Taking his sword and thrusting it into its sheath, he walked through the little door to the winding staircase and went down to the hall.

Once there, he fetched a large pot of wine and stood staring while Marguerite ministered to Berenger. 'It would be easier if it were me lying there,' he said. 'At least then all in the castle would be safe. Once I am dead . . .'

Marguerite threw him a harassed look. 'We will all die.'

'Perhaps. And now the Abbot has arrived, the Vidame will be here, too, I will be—'

'The Vidame?'

The boy's squeak made both adults turn.

Jean de Vervins eyed Georges curiously. 'Alain de Châlons, the steward to the Abbot of Châlons, yes. And he's sworn as my enemy because he is utterly devoted to King Philippe. Since I changed my allegiance, because of Philippe de Valois's lack of faith and dishonour, I am now considered an enemy of Châlons too, and the Vidame would see me destroyed.'

'But he is at Calais,' the boy said, confused.

'His master is outside, so I doubt it,' Jean said. He sighed heavily as the clash of weapons came again from outside. 'And now we must fight again.'

Marguerite caught at her son as the men left the room.

'Let go of me!'

'What do you know of this man, the Vidame?' she demanded.

'Nothing! I do not know this man Alain.'

'But you know something of the Vidame. You were shocked to hear he had arrived with the Abbot. Why did you think he was there at Calais?'

He suddenly turned and spat, 'What is it to you? You have forgotten my father already. You only have eyes for your vintener! I hope he dies!' And the boy fled from the room.

*

After Grandarse's words, John of Essex was determined to keep away from Mark Tyler, but he need not worry. Tyler was keeping well away from him.

That night was clear and still, and the sentries saw nothing to cause alarm, but all through the dark hours the sound of construction could be heard. The rasp of saws, the thud of wooden pegs being hammered into planks, the squeak of wood forced into new positions.

The following morning, as the sun rose over the hills, when John peered out over the plain, he saw that the French were constructing a large tower, from which they would be able to send crossbow bolts or arrows directly into the English castle. It was some distance away, and throughout the day, the English could gaze out and see it rising into the sky. Already a number of great tree trunks had been cut and trimmed, ready to slide beneath the tower so that it might roll forward on them towards the castle.

'Shit!' he heard one of his men mutter. 'That's going to screw us completely.'

Sir John appeared at his side. He gazed out at the tower with a grim look in his eyes. 'They are learning, aren't they?'

'It looks bad, sir,' John of Essex said.

'We've fought worse battles, and against worse odds. At least we have a castle to protect us,' Sir John said.

He soon walked away to discuss the men's dispositions with Jean de Vervins. John of Essex watched him go with a feeling of loneliness. Having the knight beside him made him feel strong and safe.

From a short way away, he heard Clip's cheerful, 'Well, that's it. We'll all get slaughtered when that thing gets here.'

There was short squeak of pain. Then, 'Ouch! Jack, why'd you do that?'

'To shut you up, what else?'

John stood watching.

After he had been there a while, Jean de Vervins appeared at his side. 'They are keen to take my castle,' he said.

John nodded. 'You've upset the wrong people.'

'I was once the French King's favourite knight, you know. If he had only kept faith with me, I would still be his most loyal servant. But when he showed his contempt for me and transferred his affections to du Bos instead, I had no choice.'

'I see,' John said, but in fact he couldn't. The man had broken his oath. John could understand a man taking money for his loyalty, but not discarding all ties. Still, a knight had to consider his honour, of course.

'I have served your King honourably. If you return to him, tell him this.'

'I will,' John said.

'You know, they will not stop until they have my head,' Jean said.

He stared out bleakly at the tower rising before his castle walls. It was a great undertaking. He could imagine the captains about it exhorting their men to ever greater efforts. The tower itself should save many French lives, after all. They had proved to themselves that the defenders were more than competent to slay many of them. All Jean de Vervins could think of right now was what his friend Gauvain had said. What was it? Something about making sure he was not captured alive. That their enemies would seek to give them the most unpleasant death imaginable, if they were caught.

There was a thunderous roar, then drums beat and horns blared wildly once more.

Jean drew his sword. 'Here they come,' he said wearily.

Grandarse was at the far wall when the cry came, and he lumbered heavily, puffing and blowing, across the castle, up the steps, and up to the walls beside John and Jean. Jack took command of Frip's men at the right, while John held the middle, and two other vintaines waited: one at the left, the other as a reserve. There were enough French from the garrison to cover the other walls, but this was where the main attack would fall.

'Bows strung, boys!' Grandarse called, looking sternly along his line. The men were all as ready as they would ever be, he saw. That younger fellow with the pale hair and red face, he had sweat dribbling out from his upper lip so badly he kept having to wipe it away. The Warwickshire man with the badly pox-scarred face near him was trembling as if this was his first action. Well, maybe it was at that. Frip's men were all looking good, though. That damned villeiny-sayer, Clip, was looking out at the enemy and telling all who would listen that they would soon die; Dogbreath was shivering not from fear, but more in the manner of a hound that sees the hart and wants to be at it. Jack stood calmly enough, the Earl eyed the enemy with a kind of laconic bafflement, while the Pardoner glanced about fretfully, but not anxiously. And not far from him, Tyler stood staring at the men approaching with a kind of professional interest.

'Bring up oil!' Grandarse shouted. It might help. A lad fetched him a bucket of warmed oil left over from the earlier fight.

The French tower was halfway up to them now. It stood a clear three yards taller than the castle's walls, and at the front there was a drawbridge. Beneath, at the rear, men picked up the great rollers between four of them, and lumbered to the front, where they dropped them and made their way to the back again. There was a hold-up when they reached a rock that lay in their path. A section of men stood gaping at it and scratching their heads, until two peasants ran and fetched long levers and prised it from the ground. They manhandled it from the path of the tower, which began its forward movement once more, slowly travelling over the ground.

'Archers, *ready!*' Grandarse called.

It was good to give the men something to think about, but the main thing here would not be the archers' arrows, but the strength in their arms as they pitched attackers from their walls. It was going to be hard, Grandarse knew. He settled his bascinet on his head, tightening his grip on his sword with his right hand as he hitched up his hosen with his left. 'Archers!'

The tower had five men already at the top. Grandarse shuddered. Once, he had ridden in the top of a storming tower like that one as it was manoeuvred across a field. The memory of standing so high above ground while it shook and rattled over the grass was not one he would ever forget. 'Aim for the men atop! *Nock! Draw! Loose!*'

He saw all five disappear as thirty arrows were discharged into them, but then it was a case of having every arrow count.

'Hit the men with the logs!' he bellowed, and at once two of the four were felled. One collapsed in the tower's path, and as the tower rumbled forward, it pushed the logs until they rolled over his lower body as though there was no obstruction. As the man screeched in agony, the logs kept moving, and Grandarse had a brief view of a smear on the grass where his legs and groin should have been.

'Archers, *loose when you have a target*!' Sir John was roaring, and Grandarse nodded approvingly.

'Prepare to defend the walls!' he bawled in turn, and saw the tower's bridge gradually moving. When it was near enough, the bridge would fall on the castle's wall, and men would rush over it.

The bridge fell with a sudden thump, and one Englishman was crushed beneath it. Grandarse had no time to guess who it was, but instead bounded to the front as the first Frenchmen began to pelt over it. A pair of arrows took the first man down, another took the second man, but then the French were over it like beggars running for a monastery's alms. Two reached the wall, then five, then more, and all the while more were coming.

Jean de Vervins was at the forefront all the time, his sword swinging with mighty power, and men fell before him. Jack wielded a hatchet to great effect, and John swung his sword with abandon, almost taking the head off the archer beside him with one over-enthusiastic swipe. Grandarse was at the front, bringing his sword down on the head of a lunatic Frenchman who tried to push him over. He fell, more stunned than injured, but the man beside Grandarse stabbed him quickly in the face and neck as their mêlée moved back and forth over the wall.

A man had managed to grab a lance, and now he used it to push at the Frenchmen on the bridge, while archers over at the left of the wall kept up a merciless barrage of arrows.

Grandarse saw an opportunity, and hefted the bucket. With a heave, he hurled it at the bridge, and it broke on the doorway above as more men rushed through, some dying before they had crossed the pathway.

'Fire!' he roared, and as soon as a torch was kindled and brought, he flung it at the oiled patch. In a moment, the oil had caught light, and the bridge itself became a fiery vision of Hell. Men were less enthusiastic about launching themselves onto it and crossing over to the castle.

The English moved some paces away to catch their breath, and even as they did so, a second series of shouts came from the tower as the structure began to flower with flames.

A man stood in the doorway and tried to jump across, but he was killed before he had taken a pace. Then a trio of crossbowmen appeared on the tower's uppermost level again, and they loosed before the English could react. Grandarse felt the waft of the feathers pass his face, and experienced a strange elation as he realised it had missed him. And then he heard the cough and turned to see Jean de Vervins staring at the bolt's fletchings protruding from his breast.

CHAPTER FORTY-FOUR

'Help me!' Grandarse yelled to the two men nearby. 'Tyler, you come with me. John, you too,' he said, and the three picked up Jean and helped him down the steps as best they could, leaving Sir John to command the defence.

Jean was coughing and choking as they took him across the yard, but before they had reached the doorway, he waved his hands and gulped convulsively: 'Down, let me down! I suffocate!'

Grandarse looked desperately around, but there was nowhere, not even a bench, on which to sit him, so the three set him down on the ground as gently as they could.

The bolt that had hit him had penetrated his breast, and the point protruded from his back near his spine. John of Essex looked up at Grandarse and silently shook his head.

'I know.' Grandarse looked compassionately at the dying man. 'Jean, there is no priest here to give you the words as they should, but if you have anything to confess, I can say the *Pater Noster* for you.'

Jean looked up at him and shook his head. A cough sent him

into a spasm of agony, and a gush of blood ran from his mouth and nostrils; he curled up, suffocating as the blood filled his lungs. He wanted to say he was pleased to have escaped Gauvain's fate, but as he tried to speak, the blood was thick in his throat, and he could only gasp and fight for breath.

'Sweet Mother Mary, take pity on his poor soul,' Grandarse prayed – and then pulled out his misericorde. He plunged it down into the man's breast, stabbing the heart at the first attempt.

'That's that, then,' he muttered, standing again. There was a fresh clamour from the walls, and he glanced up. At the back wall, away from the tower, he saw more French fighters. 'Christ's bal-locks, but they're tricksy bastards, these,' he rasped. 'John, fetch your vintaine and be quick! Tyler, help me move this poor devil.'

Grandarse took the arms, Tyler the legs, and they half-carried, half-dragged the body through into the main hall. There they dropped it on the floor. Marguerite looked at Jean's face, then up at Grandarse.

'He's not needing any help, mistress,' he said. He was oddly affected to see how she looked at Berenger. *Frip, you old git,* he thought, *you'd best pull through, for this one's sake. The wench wants you in her bed rather than on your deathbed!*

Aloud, he grunted, 'How is he?'

'He is a lot of pain. I hope he will live.'

'Aye, so do we all,' Grandarse said.

He led the way out of the main doors, and to the yard. At the stables, he beckoned Tyler to follow him. 'See here,' he said, pointing.

Tyler stared at the mess on the floor. 'Yes?'

Grandarse had already drawn his dagger. Now he placed it at the back of Tyler's skull, at the top of his neck. 'I don't like pricks who try to kill their superiors. Normally, I'd wait until there was a court and I could accuse you myself.'

'I didn't do it, Grandarse! I was staring out at the French – I didn't even know he was there!'

They were his last words.

'Fripper's a friend of mine, you see,' Grandarse said as Tyler's body twitched and shook. 'And I won't run the risk that you'll escape punishment like you did before over the Donkey.'

Berenger opened his eyes and felt the light stabbing through them and on into his brain. The agony was exquisite and he was forced to close them again.

There was a curious movement all about him – a jolting and a jarring. When he attempted to sit up, a whole new range of pains assailed him on all sides. His back felt as if an entire army had used it for a kicking competition, while his head felt as though it was only loosely held to his neck and the slightest shock must force it free of its moorings.

A crash, and he was bumped viciously, crying out. He could have wept at the pain.

He was in a cart of some sort, that was plain. A cart that was taking him on a rough, poorly maintained road. And all about him, now he could concentrate, there was the sound of men on the march: boots tramping along, squeaks and rattles of pots and pans, of leather harnesses, the clink and jingle of chains and mail, and then he heard the voices too.

'I tell you, we'll be too late.' That was Clip's familiar drone. The vintaine was all on horseback again.

'We have plenty of time.' Berenger was glad to hear Jack's voice. 'It's unlikely that the siege will be ended any time soon.'

'What?' That was the Pardoner. 'It's been months already, and you say it's no nearer being ended?'

'Well, I don't know for sure, but it's quite likely to be carrying on even now. We've only been down here a little while, and the main thing is, the King was determined to starve the Calesians out. He's not going to go running in with his braies round his ankles. He'll make sure it's finished and on its knees and *then* he'll assault it.'

'Who,' Berenger asked carefully, for enunciating each word was making the top of his head feel as though a man had stuck an auger into it and was slowly screwing it in, 'has beaten me to a pulp? I want to know so I never insult him again. Where are we? What happened to the castle?'

Jack's face came into view. 'How are you, Frip?'

His face was pushed out of the way and Grandarse took his place. 'Oh, so you're awake, eh? About time, too. Talk about a bone-idle tart-tickler trying to escape all the hard work by pretending to be ill, eh?'

'Is he recovering?'

Berenger froze at the sound of that voice: Marguerite.

'I'm well enough, Mistress,' he said.

'Be polite to her,' Grandarse ordered. 'She saved your life, man. Don't you remember the fall?'

He could remember it now. He had come to consciousness a few times lying in the hall, but that all seemed a long time ago, and his memory was hazy, as though he was trying to catch glimpses of his history through a befogged glass. 'I remember you washing my face,' he murmured to her.

She smiled and her hand, just for a moment, clasped his, before releasing it. He was confused – alarmed too, truth be told. But she was as kind as she was handsome. He tried to smile back at her. Now he remembered more: the clatter and clash of battle, screams, the sight of a body on the floor . . . 'Jean de Vervins is dead?'

'He was hit by a bolt, poor bastard. Drowned in his own blood. So we offered to talk to the French and they agreed to a truce. They let us leave the place with our weapons, so here we are. They were happy to be rid of us without any more dead, and we were happy just to get away in one piece. I don't think we would have survived, had we stayed there longer.'

'And Jean? What happened to his body?'

Grandarse's face was grim. 'They had to make an example of him. Leave a sign to others. They hanged him from the gatehouse.'

'Poor Jean,' Berenger said.

'Could have been worse. He could have been alive,' Grandarse pointed out.

Berenger managed a thin smile. 'True.'

'No. Don't worry yourself about him. He's happy now, hopefully,' Grandarse said, and then added with a leer, glancing at Marguerite, 'And anyway, you have to concentrate on getting yourself healthy again so that you can lay siege to your woman's honour.'

'Grandarse, don't—'

'Time enough to warn me later,' Grandarse chuckled.

'What will happen to the castle? Are the local people taking it over?'

'Not now it's been the home of a traitor. The people of Laon are taking the place apart stone by stone. There'll be some fine houses built around Bosmont before long, with all that good stone becoming available. The local sheep-shaggers will have the best houses in France.'

'So where do we go now?'

'We, my fine friend, are on our way to Calais, at long last. I'm hoping that when we get there, we'll discover that it's still standing and that we're needed to help take it by storm. And then, with a little more luck, we'll be able to take a goodly share of all the plunder and put our feet up for a while!'

He gave a great guffaw and began singing a bawdy tavern song about a miller's wife and her sexual needs being fulfilled after meeting a lively pair of Northumbrians.

Berenger turned onto his side and winced with pain, but he was not thinking of his back and bruises. He was thinking about that day when he had fallen from the wall. He could distinctly recall the floor on the wall's walkway. It had been clear of all obstacles, and yet when he took that fateful step, something had tripped him. Something like a bow, out-thrust deliberately to make him over-balance – because someone wanted him out of the way. And only one man had consistently been his enemy.

'Where is Tyler?' he asked.

Grandarse didn't even look down. 'Him?' he said casually. 'Oh, he died during the last attack.'

CHAPTER FORTY-FIVE

For once the weather was warm and dry, and Berenger sat on the bench outside the tavern drinking and soaking up the sun.

His head had recovered, and the bruises and scrapes seemed to be healing well, as was the scar on his face. Only his shoulder, where the maul had struck him, was still giving him problems. It would regularly ache as the weather changed, or when there was the threat of a storm. He swung his arm, trying to release some of the tension, but nothing seemed to do it any good, apart from a large quantity of ale.

'You're looking terrible,' Archibald said. He had come around the corner of the building, and now stood staring down at Berenger with a genial sympathy creasing his crow's feet.

'I don't know what you mean,' Berenger said. 'I've never felt better.'

'Yes. Of course,' Archibald said, sitting at his side. He took hold of Berenger's jug and drank deeply. 'Hmm. Not as good as a cider, but tasty.'

'Did you leave me any?'

'Of course. A little. *Hoi!* Maid, two more quarts of this ale, if you please,' he called to the serving wench. 'With a face like hers she must be a marvellous servant, for she was not hired for her looks.'

'What, you came to discuss the merits of a woman's appearance?'

'No, I came to chat about treachery and spies.'

'What does that mean?'

'What do you think? Our young Donkey has a moderately good brain on his shoulders. He spotted a man who was regularly watching my gonnes. I didn't think much of it at first, but then I noticed that he liked to observe the English camp at different times of the day. And when Béatrice followed him, she learned that he is the clerk to Sir Peter of Bromley. Some call him Vidame, as they would call the steward of an abbey.'

'Many men wander around the town and stop to watch what is happening about our army.'

'Ah, but not many try to inveigle young fellows to watch for them, to listen for chatter, and then to report back to them.'

'This man has done so?'

'Yes. And I do not know what to do about him.'

'Perhaps you have mistaken him?'

'He tried to entice the Donkey into working for him. It is to the lad's credit that he refused. But Donkey suspects . . .'

'Tell me.'

'The other boy with you: Georges. Donkey reckons he has been running messages and giving him details of your men and what you have been doing.'

'He will have learned nothing to help the French, then,' Berenger said dryly.

'Perhaps not. But it is something to consider, when speaking in his presence.'

'Yes,' Berenger said. 'I suppose it is.'

*

It was to be a hard battle.

Three nights of rest were all Berenger would be permitted once they reached Calais once more. Three nights, and then the vintaine was called to arms once more. A mighty French convoy was on the way to relieve the town.

'Eh?' Grandarse rumbled as he pulled his bascinet on over his head. 'They must be starving indeed in that place now, with no new food since late last year. Down to eating their boots and rats, I'd think. Aye, but that's a crappy way to die, of starvation. We're doing better up here, lads, eh? If we were still at the castle at Bosmont, we'd be in a similar plight. Bugger that.'

'Somehow I don't think you're cut out to starve to death, Grandarse,' Berenger said, his tone mild.

'Aye, that's the truth. I'm the sort of man who needs a little sustenance.'

'You've had more than a little in your lifetime. Your belly is a testament to how you worship at the altar of Bacchus and—'

'Are you taking the piss?' Grandarse growled. 'I don't want to have to thump you when you haven't fully recovered from falling off that wall, man, but I will if I have to knock some sense into your thick skull!'

'We're supposed to be on board,' Berenger said. 'Archers, *follow me*!' and he led the men away from the fuming Grandarse to the quay and onto their vessel, a heavy fishing boat.

The vintener had visited Tooth Butcher again, and the barber had taken a long look at him, before drinking a large jug of ale and saying, 'You daft bastard, you. Look at you! All that bruising, it's a miracle you can still walk. Next time, take the stairs rather than trying to fly.'

Still, for all the humour taken at his expense, the fact that he appeared not to have broken any bones was a great relief. He still felt dreadfully sore, but at least there was no long-term damage, as far as the barber could tell. He volunteered to take some blood, but Berenger was so sore already that he refused to consider it.

They were out at sea for most of the morning. The French fleet had been waiting in the mouth of the Seine: ten large cogs and a barge filled with the food so desperately needed by the people of Calais. These were guarded by ten galleys and a number of armed merchantmen – some fifty-one ships all told. This was the fleet that the English were to destroy.

Berenger felt the ship come alive as he stood on the forecastle. At the quayside, she was a mere shell of pieces of wood and rope, but once she had been shoved away bodily from the land, she became something else. At first, while she was tugged out into the open, she rolled and lurched like a drunken sow who'd got to the ale slops, but as the shipmen ran about aloft, releasing sails and then reefing them in to the commands of the shipmaster, she righted herself and became like a hawk observing its prey. As she slowly moved off into the main channel, more sail was let out, and she stiffened and strained, her tension apparent to all about the vessel.

For Berenger, it was a thrill to feel the deck begin its rhythmic progress, rising and falling regularly. There was a crack and some creaking, that had more than one landsman whirl his head around, thinking a spar had snapped and the ship must sink, but it was only a wooden stanchion settling itself as the ropes gripped more tightly. Berenger smiled to himself as he saw first the Pardoner, then Aletaster run to the rails and empty their bellies. Aletaster didn't think, and his vomit was thrown back into his face by the wind, which was the cause of much hilarity amongst the rest of the vintaine, apart from two men who suddenly grew very thoughtful as the stench travelled amongst them. One was later to be seen leaning over the wale himself.

Their ships were all moving swiftly enough, and it seemed no time at all before they could see the lines of the convoy up ahead.

Berenger moved to the prow and stared ahead. With his awful eyesight it was hard to make anything out, but soon he could see a series of masts. There were so many it looked like a small forest coming ever closer. He gave the order to string their bows, and the men set to, one timing his efforts badly and tumbling as the ship rolled, sliding down the deck to the jeers of his companions.

All the archers had quivers and stacks of arrows in sheaves at their feet. They were as ready as they could be.

'Is this my bow?' Clip complained. 'It's got a knot in it.'

'Like the one that should be about your neck,' Dogbreath said.

The Aletaster glanced over. 'Yes, it's yours.'

'It doesn't look right.'

The Earl looked down at it. 'Clip, it is a *bow*!' he said. 'How much more bow-like could it look?'

'On mine the heart wood was darker than this,' Clip protested. 'Look at this: it's all light-coloured, like a good honey.'

'Does it pull? Yes. Does it loose arrows? Yes. It's adequate for its function and purpose,' the Earl said.

'It's not mine, though. Mine doesn't have this knot. How can you use a bow like this? The wood will go right where that knot is. It'll snap.'

'Clip,' Berenger said, 'shut up. You have a bow. It will do the job.'

'Ach, I don't know why I bother. We'll all be killed anyway. Whoever thought of fighting on board a ship must have been mad . . . or just hated sailors.'

'Or moaning English archers,' Berenger said. 'Now shut up.'

They were moving at a good pace now, and the distance between them and the French fleet was shrinking.

Up at the rear of the ship, Grandarse was bellowing orders. He stood like a Viking, his head encased in steel, his belly protruding beneath its covering of mail. 'Archers! We will sail into their midst and bring to action the nearest ship we can. Is that clear? When I give the order, I want all archers to loose at the same time. Now, hold to your positions!'

Berenger heard the shipmaster snap a command. A change in motion warned them that the ship was altering direction slightly, and now they were pointing straight at a barge. Her red sail was billowing, but with the weight of her cargo, she still lumbered along slowly.

'Archers, *the barge is ours!* Get ready!' Grandarse bawled, and all the ship's company stared ahead at the vessel. She was sluggish and low in the water, but her crew were doing all they could to coax a little more speed from her. They were inching closer and closer, the barge attempting to turn away slightly north, while the English cog tried to head her off.

Then Berenger was startled by a shriek from aloft: ''Ware! Galley on the larboard side!'

Turning, Berenger saw a sleek vessel plunging through the waves towards them. It had a great ram beneath the sharp prow, and he could see the rows of oars rising and dipping as it advanced. He bawled, 'ARCHERS! ARCHERS, NOCK! ARCHERS, DRAW! ARCHERS, LOOSE!'

There was a flurry of whistles, and the arrows leaped into the air, all so close together that Berenger saw some strike others in mid-air, righting themselves and plunging together with all the others.

'Archers, nock! Archers, draw! Archers, pick your targets! Loose!'

A second stream of long arrows sped on their way; by now, the English cog was turning, but too slowly ... and then the two ships struck. All could hear the impact of the ram splintering the cog's hull. And then the enemy vessel was drawing away, the rowers tugging their galley from the stricken cog before she could begin to sink and snag the ram, pulling the galley down with her. Berenger wanted to send grapnels onto her so that he and his men could clamber aboard and try to take her to replace their own ship, but the collision had knocked all the archers off their feet, and there was no time to recover themselves and hurl their ropes.

Screams and cries spoke of men trapped beneath the deck as the English cog began to fill with water, but then the ship, wallowing badly, turned her prow a last time, and Berenger saw what the shipmaster had noticed. A second English ship had tried to take the barge, which had turned back towards the archers. 'Grapnels and anything else – get that ship!' he screamed, reaching for the nearest coil of rope.

The two ships edged closer and closer. On board the barge, Berenger could see that the shipmaster was attempting to hurtle past the English cog before those on board had recovered enough to try to board his vessel. If he was fast, he might succeed. But then the two ships met with a loud squeal of protesting oak, and the English archers needed no instruction. Without a single command being given, they sprang onto the lower decks of the barge. A spirited resistance was mounted by the sailors, and Berenger saw Clip and Jack loose arrows at two strong and determined shipmen at the prow, killing them both; at the tiller, the old grizzled shipmaster laid about him so incautiously with a heavy falchion that one archer lost his hand. That was when Berenger leaped at him, his own sword striking down at the man's sword and bearing it to the ground. He then stood on the blade while he punched the older man about the face. The first blow was hardly heeded, while the second simply made the man blink – but Berenger's third punch was aimed at the side of the fellow's head, and he reeled like a rabbit hit by a slingstone, before collapsing.

The shipmaster of their cog was still at his poop. Berenger

shouted to him: 'Would you come over to this ship? Yours must surely sink!'

'This old bitch? You know how much it'd cost me to replace her? No, she won't sink – she wouldn't *dare*!' the fellow replied. 'I'll get her back to harbour.'

Slowly, the great cog turned back and began to limp her way towards the shore, while the hardy crew ran about the decks under the shipman's orders. Berenger hoped they would make it back safely.

At present, he had other things to concern him.

Jack pulled at his shoulder. 'Frip!'

Looking round, Baldwin saw that the galley had executed a neat turn and was now pointing at them once more. He saw the oars begin to rise and fall again, and then the vessel was bearing down on them.

'Bloody hell!' Jack said.

Clip was staring at the galley with a frown on his face. 'That bastard's really got it in for us! Shit for brains!' And he began to hurl insults at the men on the ship, waving his bow in the air with a rage so pure it was hard for Berenger to know whether to laugh or sympathise.

In the event, it was Dogbreath who said, 'Do you not think it would be better to try to kill the bastard, rather than waste your breath shouting at him?'

It was a call to commonsense, and the archers began to loose their arrows swiftly into the ship. At first, it appeared that their efforts were going unrewarded, but this time the galley had a greater distance to cover, and every yard of the way, a hundred arrows plummeted from the sky. Many struck the great sail, after which they travelled on and caused injuries to those beneath. Some lanced down and pinned the rowers to their benches. The drum itself suddenly gave a deep boom, then went silent, and

Berenger wondered whether they had hit the drummer or the skin of the great instrument. There came more cries, and he saw that the oars now rose and dipped irregularly; a series of oars had ceased to move, but floated in the water.

'More arrows!' he cried. 'We could take the galley! Can we catch it?' This to the shipman who had been left with them while their cog returned to shore. The man on the tiller peered ahead at the galley, but even as he stared, the galley turned and headed towards the harbour at Calais. The man looked back at Berenger and shook his head.

'Frip! Frip – look!' Jack shouted suddenly, and Berenger whirled round to see the man at the poopdeck of the galley. It was the Genoese again.

'That fucking donkey turd! Not content with stealing our first ship, now he's sunk another under us and wants to take our barge too!' Clip spat. He drew his bow and let fly at an extreme angle. Clip had always been a natural archer, with an eye for distance that was unmatched by most, and Berenger watched the arrow's flight with a mingled desire to see the cocky Genoese shipman pierced, and a reluctance to see him harmed. It was, after all, this man who had set them free from their captivity.

He was pleased to see the Genoese spring back as the arrow struck, quivering, impaling itself into the planking within a few paces of the man.

Grandarse was puffing and blowing at his side. 'Clip, man, next time, wait a minute and let a grown-up use his sodding bow rather than wasting an arrow.'

'It was the wind caught me arrow as I released – didn't you feel the gust?'

'Mayhap it was the wind from your bowels, Clip,' the Earl drawled.

'Hey, you want a taste of my fist? I'll take you on any day, you . . .'

'Yes?' the Earl enquired mildly.

'You overgrown, illegitimate son of a poxed Winchester goose!'

'Overgrown? Perhaps. Son of a whore? Perhaps that too, I confess. But illegitimate? Yes, my friend. But I was born that way, I'm not a self-made bastard like you!'

Clip went quite pale with anger, and stood rigid, at a loss for words. Berenger glanced at Jack and both surreptitiously moved nearer. However, a few seconds passed and then Clip gave a grin, conceding, 'You're not all bad, Earl.'

'I agree with you there.'

'We can be friends.'

'There you test me.'

There was a sudden roar from behind them.

'There's another vessel over there!' Grandarse bellowed at the top of his voice, pointing. 'Come on – let's see if we can catch ourselves a ship!'

Chapter Forty-Six

Archibald sat outside on his gonne's barrel and stared up at the sun. With a small barrel of ale on the earth wall behind him, and a pewter goblet in his hand, life was sweet. The ale he had won in a game of Nine Men's Morris, but the goblet, which had been liberated from a house on the way to Calais, had become his yesterday in exchange for a small charge of black powder encased in a wrap of parchment, sealed with pig's fat. Later that evening, he had heard of a near riot in a house in the town when a somewhat morose captain, who was disliked by most of his men, had been dining with a woman, and for some reason his fire had exploded when the two were growing affectionate. Archibald saw no need to investigate. His ale was tasty, all the better for being served in a noble vessel such as this, and he sighed with content. It was all good.

The smell, however, was not. The town over there, across the little dribble of water, had a right stench coming off it. He had been near towns with bad odours in the past – for instance, who could forget Exeter in the high summer, when the reek from the tanners over to the west spread all over the city, enough to make a man's eyes water . . . This was different, though. The smell had a bittersweet tang that caught in the throat like vomit. At least most of the time it was pleasant enough here. The wind tended to blow away from the little fort. And now, with the evening sun behind him lighting the town's walls with a glorious golden hue, he could almost have felt himself to be back in England instead of here, and no longer at war. The stone looked like the golden rocks used in places like Evesham. That had been a lovely town, he remembered, and sighed.

He passed a pleasant evening. Rested, he ate a good meal and went to his palliasse at the rear of the fort, secure in the knowledge that the Donkey was keeping watch. A little while after sunset, he was deeply asleep.

Béatrice experienced a wave of relief on the day the vintaine returned, but her joy was short-lived when Berenger was nowhere to be seen.

'What is it?' Ed demanded.

'He is not there!' It was only when she realised that Berenger *was* there, and sitting up in the cart that she recovered her equanimity.

'No, he's gone,' Ed was insisting.

'Who?'

'Tyler – Mark of London, of course. Why, who did you think?'

She said nothing, only blushed, but suddenly the boy's face hardened when he saw Berenger too. But then she was running to greet the vintener – and quickly forgot the expression on his face.

It came back to her now though, as she approached Marguerite's side, a look of mingled jealousy and hurt.

'I am glad to see you back safely,' she said.

'I thank you,' Marguerite replied, but there was no joy in her tone.

'I have heard that you saved Berenger from death.'

'I nursed him, but he has a hard head. It took little to save him, in truth. Only a little comforting.'

Béatrice forbore to ask how much comforting. 'You seem concerned.'

The woman shot her a glance, and then she licked her lips. 'Béatrice, you are a Frenchwoman. I am sure you are loyal to the men here, too, but you also have some feeling for our people, don't you?'

'I have no people,' Béatrice said flatly.

'But I am your friend?'

'Yes, you are my friend.'

'I am worried about my son,' Marguerite burst out. 'He is a good boy, but he is keeping something from me. He is working hard with the archers, but how can I entice him to open up to me?'

'I have no children. I cannot advise.'

'But you have Ed. He treats you as his mother.'

Béatrice shook her head. 'No.'

Marguerite said nothing, but then her mouth formed a perfect 'Oh'.

'He is desperately jealous. Perhaps your Georges has also fallen in love?'

'No, I feel sure it is something different.'

'Then you must ask him, and do not stop until he explains.'

'Béatrice, I am terrified of what his answer may be!'

'You must. It is worse to wonder,' Béatrice said. And then, with a great heave of resolution: 'Speak to Berenger. See what he thinks. You can trust his advice.'

Ed sat by the wall of the fort and stared out at the view. There was not much to look at here, only a series of braziers installed on the walls of the town. The people were petrified that the English might attempt to take the place by force, he knew. That was why they had lights all along the walls, to make sure that there were no darkened routes by which the English might cross and climb to overrun the place.

Béatrice was in love with Berenger. The truth was plain, and it hurt to know it, but at least now he could see it. She was a solid, unyielding woman, but she was comforting. He couldn't blame Berenger. Whenever Ed himself had been injured or merely alarmed, it was Béatrice who had come to give him sympathy and support. She was that sort of woman. But right at this moment, it felt as though Ed had lost her. And without her, he was bereft.

There was a brief flare of light. Nothing much, but he thought it came from down at the water's edge – not at the English shore, but on the Calesian side. He squinted in the dark, trying to see something that could have caused the flash, but decided it must merely have been the light reflecting on the sea from a brazier up on the walls. And yet, when he looked at the walls again, he realised that some of the lights were extinguished. There was a gap of some yards where no flares at all were lit. There was no movement, no indication of men. All was perfectly still, dark and calm. There was nothing for him to grow excited about.

And yet . . .

He was young, he knew, but after living with the soldiers for so many months, some vestiges of their training must have been absorbed into his soul. The thought of waking Archibald filled him with dread, for the gynour could be a terror when his sleep was disturbed, but that was less alarming than the thought that a force could have slipped over the Calesian wall and even now be hurrying to the English fortress to slaughter the inhabitants. He knew what he must do.

Slowly and full of trepidation, he crossed to the rear of the fortress and called to Archibald. 'Sir?'

'What is it?' the gynour demanded. 'There's something wrong – I can smell it.'

The Donkey was only grateful that he hadn't already been beaten. 'Sir, they have put out some lights at the fortress and now I can't see anything.'

'Show me.'

They returned to the wall and the two peered out.

'You're right,' Archibald said. 'They've shut out some of their lights. Why would they do that, I wonder?'

'I thought they could be crossing to attack us here.'

Archibald's eyes flitted over the water. There was no sign of men crossing the water, and yet ... 'There, boy! Can you see that?'

'What?' the Donkey said, but Archibald was already turning and bellowing.

'*Boats!* Boats from Calais escaping! Guards!'

Archibald scrambled to the top of the wall, thinking hard. What could the guards do? Nothing – it was too late. Yet he had his gonnes here. And what was more, he had time to use them.

Archibald grabbed the lamb'swool swab and ran to the mouth of the nearest gonne. He rammed it into the barrel, turning it to remove any dampness from the cool evening air. Then he hurried back and snatched up the powder measure. Wrenching the top from one of the powder barrels, he scooped up a good quantity. Curtly telling Donkey to put the lid back on, he went to the gonne and carefully loaded it. Then he took a bag of stones and pushed it into the barrel. Ramming it with the stave of the powder measure, he ensured that the bag was well seated before hurrying to the firing hole. There was some charcloth in his tinderbox, and he struck flint and his knife to make a spark, blowing gently on the cloth as it caught the spark and began to smoulder.

'Get back, boy!' he roared to Ed. 'Stay out there and you may lose your head!'

Over the barrel, he took a long spike and cleared the vent hole, then tipped out a little fine powder from his neck-flask. He took the match and stick, and blew on his charcloth until it was glowing nicely, and set that to the match, blowing steadily but gently until the match was red and spitting – and then he rammed it into the vent. There was a *whoomph*, a flash of blinding yellow-red light, and then a fizzing cone of smoke and flame leaped up from the vent as, with an earth-jarring roar, the gonne fired. It lighted the whole area of sea, including the two small boats which were rowing as quickly as they could away from Calais.

Through the clouds this fleeting glimpse was enough. Now the English camp was all astir, and cries and horn blasts at the waterside showed that the boats had been spotted.

'Boy,' Archibald said, his big bearded face grinning from ear to ear, 'there is nothing so satisfying as waking an entire army before dawn!'

'Yes, Gynour.'

'But don't make a habit of it, eh? I can be real grouchy without my sleep – and you can see how dangerous that is!'

CHAPTER FORTY-SEVEN

Berenger was deeply asleep when the sudden roar of the gonne woke him as well as the others in the vintaine.

'What the f . . .' he cried as he jerked awake, reaching for his sword.

Grandarse burst into their room, his eyes wild, a long dagger in his fist, hair all awry. 'Did you hear that? Fripper, the bastards have attacked us! They must have the Devil himself on their side to make that racket! Did ye hear the—'

'Grandarse, in Christ's name be silent!' Berenger halted the flow. 'What did you actually see?'

'See?' Grandarse suddenly realised the kind of figure he must cut as he looked down at his bare bony legs and shirted breast. He stuck his chin out aggressively in case anyone wanted to laugh at him, but before he could make a comment, Jack ran in.

'Frip, there are two boats trying to escape!'

Berenger raised a hand to stop him. 'Do we have any idea who's in them?'

'No.'

'That explosion: was it from the town?'

'No, it was bloody Archibald again. He was firing at the boats, I reckon.'

'Did he hit them?'

Jack gave him a withering look. 'What do you think?'

'Oh. I see.'

'So the boats are getting away, Frip.'

'Oh, God's ballocks, I suppose we'll have to try to catch them, then.' Berenger grimaced and pulled on a cloak against the cold. 'Jack, I want the whole vintaine – with grappling hooks and axes. No need for everyone to bring bows – just you, Clip, Oliver and Dogbreath. Georges, you too,' he added. He watched the boy as he pulled on a jack. There was nothing in his behaviour to show that he was in any way a betrayer of the men. Berenger found Archibald's words hard to believe. But the gynour was convinced – that much was clear.

They were soon at the waterside climbing into a large boat with a small sail and five oars each side. Berenger looked down at it with a feeling of revulsion. This was the sort of vessel that would buck and roll with every little slap of a wave against the hull, he thought, but it was the fastest craft big enough to hold his men. He climbed into it reluctantly, holding his sword against his side, and stood near the mast. The master cast off, with many muttered comments about 'Fucking archers, think they rule the bleeding harbour . . .' and were soon rowing steadily along the channel in pursuit of the two little ships.

Berenger could see the sails far away on the horizon, and felt certain that they would never catch them. Still, the master appeared convinced that with his little boat they could overhaul their quarry.

'It's a matter of the length of the craft, the size of the sail, and the width of the hull. With this little darling, I can catch about anything in half a morning,' he said. He had sparse grey hair and the kind of thin skin that looked as if it would tear like parchment, but there was a confidence and solidity to him as he stood at the tiller that spoke of years of experience. 'Look at 'em, eh? Someone in that one to port has had some experience, but the boat to starboard? He's going to be in trouble soon.'

'Why?'

'Because,' the mariner said, glancing up at his sail and nodding to himself as if pleased, 'that boat is straying too close to the shore. The sands are very shallow here – and the tide's on the turn.'

Berenger shrugged with confusion. 'Which means?'

The shipman made a comment under his breath that sounded like 'land monkeys', and then pointed. 'See the sand there? It shelves shallowly. That means the water under the boat is not deep. As the tide moves away, the water will leave him on the sands and he'll be stuck until the tide comes in again.'

Berenger nodded. 'So we can catch him. Good.'

'No.' The man closed his eyes with exasperation. 'Is this boat smaller than that? No. It's bigger. That means it goes down further in the water, which means that if *that* craft is beached, so will we be. Sooner. So we will leave that arse to his own devices and continue on this course.'

'That other boat's heading more out to sea,' Berenger said warily, not wanting to display more ignorance.

'Aye, he is. But he's too small to want to stay out. And where's he off to? London? He's an enemy of ours, so he has to come back in to the coast at some point. And that means he'll have to cut in towards us. So we'll have him.'

Berenger nodded. As he did, he looked at the boat that was in danger of being caught on the sands. Surely it was a decoy? he thought. The little craft was deliberately heading towards the sands because the sailor wanted to tempt Berenger's craft after it, and see it beached, while the other boat escaped.

But as he gazed at it, he saw that the vessel was changing direction. Now, rather than remaining over the shallow sands where it would be trapped, it was moving out towards the main channel again.

'Hold!' he said. There was something familiar about the figure in the boat. 'Jack, the man in the boat there – do you recognise him?'

'He looks like the Genoese.'

'Chrestien de Grimault,' Berenger murmured. Then, 'Master, we will go after this little boat. I had thought that the other ship was more important, but now I think our Genoese friend is the more likely to be our correct target.'

'If you say so.'

'Hold to this course, and we shall have every opportunity to catch both, will we not?' Jack said.

'Aye.'

They continued on. For once, none of the archers threw up, even though the boat was rolling and diving quite alarmingly as the tide pulled away. The ship kept as close to the shore as the master deemed safe, and all the way they kept their eyes on the vessel with Chrestien de Grimault on board.

'Frip! Look out there!' Clip said.

The other little boat was coming closer and closer now, and for a wild moment Berenger thought it would come and ram their craft, but at the last second it turned, a little more than a bowshot away.

'He's trying to tempt you out after him,' the master grunted.

'I think so,' Berenger agreed. 'Are there sandbanks out there?'

'Not that I can see. Doesn't mean anything, though. There could be, but the water is not breaking on an obvious one.'

They were approaching the Genoese's vessel now; his little boat had no escape route available. At last, Berenger saw

Chrestien de Grimault stand and hurl something into the sea. 'Mark that, Jack!' he called. 'It's something valuable, I'll wager!'

'And how do I mark it, Frip?' Jack lifted his hands with bemusement. 'You want me to go and paint the sea? Stick an arrow in it?'

'No, but remember the shore, and take a line from a building or trees. Master shipman, would you be able to mark that spot?'

'Aye, but what of it?'

'You said that the tide was on the way out, didn't you? In a couple of hours, we should be able to find what he threw in.'

They were only half a bowshot from the little boat when Berenger called to the Genoese to surrender. 'There is no point in dispute, my friend,' he said. 'You know you cannot escape, and to fight would be futile, so agree to submit and I'll hold to your oath to us. You will be safe, I swear.'

Chrestien de Grimault sat in the stern with two French shipmen who looked petrified to be confronted by the English. Only Clip had an arrow nocked, but he held his bow in the nonchalant way that told better than words that his shaft could leave his weapon and strike down a man in one second flat.

Chrestien de Grimault stood and bowed, holding Berenger's gaze. 'It would seem that you have the better of this encounter.'

'Come aboard and we shall discuss matters more easily.'

'Of course.'

It took little time to bring the two boats together, and while willing hands held the captured vessel, the three prisoners climbed aboard easily, as only men used to the sea could, while a shipman of the English crew took the painter and lashed the other boat to their own.

Chrestien de Grimault stood with an expression of sardonic enquiry. 'I suppose I shall be bound and beaten now?'

'Master, you treated us well when you had us at your mercy,'

Berenger said. 'I will not see you abused. These two, are they soldiers?'

'These?' Chrestien gave them a short glance. 'No, they are merely seamen who were told to take me away from the town.'

'Where were they taking you?' Berenger asked.

The Genoese shrugged. 'You could torture them and find out, so there is no point in my maintaining secrecy. I was to travel as swiftly as possible to Hesdin, where the King of France is gathering an army, so I understand, to break this siege. He has the greatest army ever collected together in one place.'

'And what were you to say to him?'

Chrestien gave another low bow. 'I apologise. It was all in a note, and when I saw that my honour was in danger, and that you must capture me, I committed the message to the deep. It will rest there until the end of time.'

He smiled charmingly.

Berenger smiled in return. 'That is good. So the message is lost, you think? It will never be brought again to the view of men?'

'Perhaps a whale could eat it and spit it out on the shore,' Chrestien chuckled.

'Or a whale could drink the water from the sea and expose the beach beneath the waves?' Berenger hazarded. 'Or, the tide could flow out . . .'

Chrestien's face suddenly fell.

In the end it took them three hours, while the tide withdrew and the level of the water reduced. Their boat was far too large to stay inshore, and so Berenger sent Jack and a shipman in the captured boat to go and find the item hurled in the water. One of the Frenchmen happily admitted to seeing the Genoese throwing a small hatchet into the waters, and wondered what could have prompted him to do such a strange thing. Chrestien looked daggers at this admission, but said nothing.

Berenger left the crew staring out and watching Jack as the latter searched, floundering about in the shallow water.

'Georges, come here,' Berenger said.

'Yes, Vintener?'

Berenger walked to the stern and sat so that he was at eye-level with Georges's eyes. 'I know about the clerk,' he said. 'He has been telling you to spy on us. Is that not true?'

The boy's head turned this way and that, with panic marking every line. It hurt Berenger to see his terror; it was like watching his own son being bound in a noose.

'Boy! Look at me.'

'My mother would die if you put me to the law!'

'Georges, listen. I will not hurt you or your mother,' Berenger said softly. 'Your mother has shown me kindness from the first moment I met her. I will not repay her by arresting her son.'

'You won't?'

'No. But you have to tell me all you know about this Vidame and what he seeks.'

'I know nothing. He asked me to take messages to him, that is all.'

'Messages from whom?'

'Someone in the vintaine. I don't know who.'

Berenger felt his mouth drop open. 'In my vintaine? Let me get this straight: so a man has been giving you information for the Vidame?'

'Yes.'

'What sort of information?'

'Mostly about the army, where we are going, what you are to do.'

'Is there anything else you can tell me?'

'No! I know nothing else.'

'How did you receive information to give to the Vidame?'

'It was written on a little shred of parchment and pushed into a knot hole on the cart. I pulled it out and took it with me.'

'I see. And you have no idea who put the parchment there?'

'No, sir.'

Berenger nodded. He could guess, though. 'I think your messages are over now. The man who was sending them also tried to kill me. Mark Tyler is dead, and with him dies our spy. Do not worry.'

'No, sir.'

As he spoke, Jack finally gave a cry of delight and lifted aloft a hatchet with an oilskin packet bound about it with thongs, Chrestien said nothing, but gave a slight frown and turned his back on Jack.

'You have done well to tell me this,' Berenger told Georges.

'But what if I find another note?'

'Well, if that happens, you would have to bring it to me. Understand?'

'Yes.' Then: 'Fripper, I'm so s—'

Berenger cut him off with a curt wave of his hand and walked to the prow. He had little doubt of Tyler's guilt. He could still remember the sight of the man's grin as he looked up from his fall from the castle wall. Tyler had spied, then tried to kill Berenger before getting himself slain. It was all very neat, he thought, and a huge relief to think that the spy was dead.

'Well, what is it?' he called as Jack clambered back aboard the ship.

'A letter,' Jack said with glee.

'You will not be able to read it,' Chrestien said immediately. The water will have ruined it.'

But he was wrong. The letter was all too clear.

Chapter Forty-Eight

Sir John de Sully listened as the letter was read out.

He was in the King's hall, and King Edward was pacing the chamber while reading through the note that Berenger and the men had rescued from the water. As he read, the King chuckled.

'Good gentlemen,' he announced, 'this is really excellent! Our men have managed to intercept a message being delivered to King Philippe. It is sent under the seal of the Commander, Jean de Vienne. Listen to this: "Right dear, dread Lord" – well, he's not to be feared so much, is he? "Know that, although the men are all full of courage, the town is yet in dire need". Yes, I dare say it is. He writes that they need wheat and wine and meat, ha! And that they have been eating all the dogs and cats for want of real food. There are no more horses either. He tells his King that there is nothing left but human flesh to eat!'

He broke off, then continued more pensively: 'He writes that unless they receive some help soon, they will have no option but to resort to a final attack. They will sally forth and try to fight their way through the English lines. Well, they are welcome to have a go! They do not think that they can survive such an assault, clearly, but we should regard it as a warning in any case. Tell the archers at the gates to be vigilant, and ensure that the men-at-arms know that there could be an attempt to break free. I would not want a sudden assault by half-starved wraiths to take them by surprise!'

The King set the letter down and cast his gaze over the men with him. Sir John de Sully took a moment to study them too. Here in this chamber were gathered all the most powerful men of England – barons, knights and esquires – and all were listening intently.

Sir Walter Manny sucked at his teeth. 'What will you do, now you know the condition of the men in the town?'

'What should I do?'

The Earl of Warwick gave a low snigger. 'For my part, it seems obvious: I would say that we should attack with all force. You have gathered more than twenty thousand men here. It would be a shame not to use them. We can batter their walls with your artillery – the stone-throwing machines will do good work there – and when we make a breach, storm it.'

'Sir Walter?' the King asked.

Sir Walter Manny smiled to himself, and then spoke reflectively. 'It seems to me that you hold in your hand the key to all you want, sir.'

'Is that so? Then how can we use it?' an esquire asked with a satirical tone. There was some laughter in the room, but when the King held up his hand, it ceased on an instant.

'Speak, Sir Walter.'

'Sir, you have worked towards this end: that you might draw the French to attack you in order that you might crush their army. You worked for years to achieve that at Tournai and Sluys, and you succeeded at Crécy. But now, even though you have shown the valour of your arms and have destroyed the majority of the French army, still many men will think that your achievements are caused by mere good fortune, not by design or skill. However, if you could force the French King to come and meet you again, and you could destroy a second army of his, then you would be acclaimed as the most powerful, puissant king in all Christendom. Who could deny your authority?'

'So?' Warwick asked truculently. 'How can we bring him to battle again?'

Manny indicated the letter. 'How can any King ignore a letter of that nature? The writer pleads with his sovereign for support and aid, does he not? If the King of France will not respond to the heartfelt plea of his most loyal, devoted servant, who can doubt that his entire kingdom is equally at risk? And if that is the truth, then there is no peace in his realm, and every man needs must shift for his own safety.'

The Earl nodded and smiled broadly. 'Yes! You must release that letter. Let it be broadcast all over the land so that everyone knows the French King can do nothing to protect his own realm. He'll *have* to come to defend Calais or lose his crown.'

'And how will you have all the churches announce this?' Manny enquired mildly. 'It would be difficult, for each will be looking over his shoulder to see what the French King will say or do to them. Better, sir, to merely reseal the letter. Let it go to the French King with your own appended note. Offer him the challenge. Tell him that his people are starving and dying, and that they beg for his aid. Tell him that if he doesn't come to protect his people, he is no King. Tell him you sit here, outside his town, and await his arrival. Tell him all those things, and allow that news to be spread, and you will find that he dare not evade a second battle. And with a second Crécy, his reign will be ended.'

Sir John spoke up in favour of Sir Walter. 'Your Majesty, I

firmly agree. I believe Sir Walter has struck at the heart of the matter with his advice. If the French King comes – and is destroyed – he is finished; if he does *not* come, he will be derided by all and his reputation will lie in the mud, in tatters. Yes, send the letter on with your own seal, and we shall soon see him lose his kingdom!'

The King gazed at the other men in the room with a stern expression on his face, and then he suddenly broke into a guffaw of laughter.

'Bring me my seal and wax!'

Chrestien de Grimault sipped cautiously at the wine. 'It is not so bad,' he conceded.

'Better than the water the French gave us, you think?' Berenger said.

'I think I am grateful for any small mercy, my friend,' Chrestien de Grimault said. He peered at Berenger. 'That scar,' he added, touching his own nose. 'You did not have that when I set you free from my ship. Was that fighting about the town here?'

'No, I gained this in my own country.' Berenger explained about the battle to keep the Scots at bay. 'I had thought I would die, when the fever took hold,' he said soberly. 'Yet here we both are, and still alive.'

'It is a miracle when one considers how many others have died,' the Genoese sighed. 'There are some who are not so honourable.'

'Why did you help us to escape?'

'I said at the time: I had given you my word that I would treat you as comrades. I *promised* you your lives. There was no need to execute you. I despised that decision, so I bethought myself that I would set you free.'

'We were most grateful for your help.'

Chrestien de Grimault shrugged. 'It was my pleasure. It saved my honour.'

'I am glad the arrow missed you on the deck of your galley,' Berenger said.

'It was the fortune of war. I was safe, while you have suffered greatly.' The man toyed with his mazer. 'I feel I should not drink more. I may be tempted to speak my mind, and that is not always a good idea with an enemy.'

'I don't think we are enemies,' Berenger said. He poured from the jug and refilled their cups. 'We are just on opposite sides in a war. And I think it a foolish dispute.'

'It is not mine to defend.'

'Nor mine. It is a battle between kings, and when such wars are declared, it is men like you and me who are made to suffer. Not many nobles lose their lives.'

Chrestien disagreed. 'I had heard that the French nobility lost many men on the field at Crécy.'

'Yes, but that was different. Usually it's the poor foot-sloggers who get slain. And those who seek to protect people are often punished.' For some reason, a picture of Jean de Vervins's face appeared in his mind. 'A lot of men have lost everything in this war.'

'True enough.'

Both were silent for a while, drinking companionably. Every so often, Berenger felt the Genoese's eye upon him, but he thought it was merely the appraising glance of a man who wondered what his fate would be. It was hard for someone who had been captured not to feel the concern: *what is going to happen to me?*

'You will be well looked after, I swear,' he said at last. 'You can remain here with my men, if you wish. I doubt anyone will want to keep you. You served your master, the French King, well.'

'I am only a mere mercenary, when all is said and done, my

friend,' Chrestien said. 'But I thank you for your kindness. Hopefully there is no firebrand of a bishop amongst your King's host.'

Berenger thought of the Archbishop of York and the Bishop of Durham. 'If you see one, keep well away,' he advised.

The Genoese laughed, but his laugh was stilled as the door opened and Sir John de Sully entered.

'Sir John,' Berenger said, rising.

'This is the Genoese? Good, you are to come with me. Fripper, you come too.'

'Sir John, I have given this man my word that he will not be mistreated,' Berenger said.

The knight stopped and looked at him. 'That was foolish. If the King decides a different fate, what will you do then? Fight the King to free him? Would you fight *me*, Fripper? You should not make promises you cannot fulfil.'

'He saved my life, Sir John, and the lives of all my men. At the least we were to be blinded and have our fingers cut off. This man rescued us.'

'He also attacked our fleet and almost sank the ship under you, and tried to take a secret message to the French King. He will receive his just reward.'

Berenger frowned. There was no reading the knight's expression. It was carefully blank, as though Sir John was keeping his calmness with an effort. His eyes looked bright, perhaps with anger, but Berenger had no choice; he walked with the knight and the Genoese through the streets until they reached the King's hall, where Sir John spoke with the two men at the door, and led the way inside.

'Your Royal Highness,' he said, bowing before the King.

King Edward III stood at a long table poring over papers with two clerks and the Bishop of Durham. All looked at Chrestien de Grimault with disapproval bordering on loathing.

'You are the Genoese who was taking this message to the French King?' the Bishop demanded.

'Yes.'

'Well, take it – and begone!'

Chrestien de Grimault stared at him, then at the letter. 'Me? Take it?'

The King gave a thin smile. 'Yes, man! I command you to take this letter and transport it to your King. I have ordered a horse to be readied for you. However, when you see the King, you will also give him this note from me.' He passed over a second sealed message. 'And you will say to him these words: *I challenge you to come to the aid of your town.*'

'Very well. I understand,' Chrestien managed, taking both packets and thrusting them inside his shirt.

'You had best take this too,' the Bishop said. 'A safe-conduct throughout the English lines. If you are stopped by our forces anywhere, this will protect you.'

Outside, Chrestien and Berenger stared at each other, and then burst out laughing. Within an hour, the Genoese was mounted on a fresh, fiery rounsey, and he looked down at Berenger, holding out his hand. 'Farewell, my friend. I swear, next time I see you, I will not try to sink you.'

'I will probably try to sink you, though,' Berenger joked.

Chrestien held onto his hand for a little longer. 'Do not trust your companions entirely. Not all are what they seem.'

'What do you mean?'

'Only this: there is a spy for the French King in your camp. One of your friends is determined to bring down your army.'

'So you knew about Jean de Vervins? Well, he is safe enough now – he's dead. But he spied for both sides. He was a most democratic spy!' Berenger grinned.

'No, not him, you fool. There is another, one who is close to you.'

'He, too, is dead. Mark Tyler was not a very effective spy.'

'I don't know of him. The spy I speak of is back here in the camp – right now. And he is not only spying. There is a plot to kill your King!'

And with that, he let go, dug his heels into the rounsey's flanks, and was off at a canter.

CHAPTER FORTY-NINE

After his discussion with Chrestien, Berenger was perfectly convinced that there was a spy, and he knew he must not take any risks, especially if there was truly a plot to kill the King. He would have to devise a means of learning the truth.

Before he did anything else, he sent Jack and Clip, the two men he knew and trusted best, to watch the house where Sir Peter and the Vidame were billeted. He sent the Donkey with them. 'He'll recognise the man. If that man comes out, follow him – and do not lose him, as you value your ballocks,' he growled, and then went to seek his banneret.

'Sir John, I think I have some news of importance.'

Sir John was just leaving his house, and now, striding along the road, he listened to all Berenger had to say of his suspicions and the evidence of the others. After some minutes, the knight stopped in the street. 'Say all that again, Frip.'

Berenger spoke at length, explaining about the boy's evidence, then Béatrice's, and finally spoke of Chrestien's words.

'So you think that there is a plot to kill the King?'

'That is what the Genoese said.'

'Shit! There are many who would love to stick a lance in the King's heart. But he should be safe with his friends. The lords about him would never let him be harmed.'

'What if there was a traitor amongst them? We already have the example of Jean de Vervins – apparently King Philippe's most loyal vassal, turned to treachery because of a slight, whether real or imagined. And we know that the knight Peter of Bromley is employing as clerk a man who is gathering information about the King. What if Sir Peter himself is less than reliable?'

'You capture the clerk and bring him to me. We'll have him tortured until we find your man. Meanwhile, I shall keep a close eye on Sir Peter. But keep this quiet. We don't want to cause unnecessary concern in the camp. I shall tell the King and his son, but for the rest, keep this within our circle. If there is to be treachery, we may yet work it to our advantage.'

Berenger agreed, although the thought of torture made him feel sick. After all, a man could be tortured and forced to tell everything, but unless the torturer was expert, his victim would just lie to stop the agony.

He marched quickly back to his camp. One of his men was a traitor.

But which? His sick feeling increased.

The Vidame was about to go and meet Sir Peter at the King's hall; he sent Bertucat outside to check that the road was safe for them.

'Vidame,' the big man said a moment later when he returned, a frown on his face. 'There are two men from the vintaine outside.'

'Is our man one of them?' the Vidame asked, stepping across to the glassless side-window and peering through this. Clip he recognised at once. Jack, he did not see at first. The man had an ability to conceal himself in a small crowd. 'Oh.'

'Do you want me to go and attack them?'

'No, my friend. These are not thieves and bullies from the street, but trained and competent fighters. If you attack one, you will be assailed by both. No, I think it is time for us to leave.'

It was an annoyance. Still, their information had been useful. The attitude of the men, the news of ship numbers, the position of the gonnes and weapons of war, all should aid King Philippe's efforts. And now it was time to escape.

He took a strip of paper and a reed, and quickly wrote a note. 'Take this and put it in the cart. When you have done that, come back here and wait. Our man will soon appear. When he does, you will know what to do.'

Clip had been astonished to see where the Vidame was living. *That's my yard!* he thought to himself, peering up the alleyway. He saw a man flit past the far end of the alley, and was tempted to go and check it. And then he remembered his last visit, when the mousy-haired man had attacked him, and he recalled the priest who was with him. 'Oh,' he mouthed slowly.

'Was it the man we're hunting?' Jack demanded.

'Eh? How can I tell?'

'Then go and look, but come back if it isn't,' Jack said.

While they spoke, the door opened and a tall, dark man appeared, glanced up and down the road, and then strode off up the lane.

'Didn't he come out earlier?' Jack said, but Clip was already gone.

Jack watched the man, but he was not the one he had been told to find, and a knight's house could have many servants. He sniffed, folded his arms, and leaned more comfortably against the wall. He'd wait to see the Vidame.

Clip was soon back. 'Well?'

'By the time I got there, the yard was empty.'

'Right. We'd best wait here, then.'

The spy had not expected to find a note. He'd thought that things were going to calm down once he had returned from the siege at Bosmont. He had done enough, surely, when he had shoved Berenger off the roof, risking his own life in the process?

But the note was there, with the scrawl that meant he was required urgently to see the Vidame. He wandered idly from the camp as though off to seek a cup of wine, and then picked up the pace when he was out of sight of the rest of the vintaine.

He had his own route to the Vidame's rooms. Up along the main street, then north and west until he came to a narrow alley between two sheds. He could stand here with a perfect view from the northern street to the southern, and today there was no one about. Nobody paid him any attention, so he continued on his path.

The alley took him parallel to the main east-west thoroughfares, and then he was at the courtyard behind the Vidame's house. It was the safest route to reach the place unseen.

Striding across the court, he made his way to the kitchen door and was about to knock, when a hand came around his mouth, the thumb over his nose.

Bertucat hissed in his ear, 'Sorry, but they're getting close to you. We can't let you talk.'

Panicked, the spy tried to pull away, his hands scrabbling at Bertucat's wrist to release his nostrils, but then he felt the steel enter his back ... and as he trembled in his death throes, all he could think of was the face of the Vidame, smiling so patiently as he always did. Alain de Châlons, the Vidame, the prized spymaster of the King of France.

Lying on his back in the dirt, that was the picture left in his mind: the smile of the Vidame. If he could, the spy would have cursed him, with his dying breath.

Bertucat dragged his body to a heap of garbage and scattered some planks and rocks about the corpse, but then he heard steps and shouts, and quickly ran off through the alleys, away from the scene.

He'd never liked the spy. You couldn't trust a man who would betray his comrades.

Berenger hurried to Sir Peter's house as soon as he received the message. Upon arrival, he found Jack waiting.

'Up here, Frip,' he said, unsmiling.

They walked up Clip's narrow alley to the yard behind, and there they found Clip. He was crouched beside a body.

'Who is it?' Berenger said, but he knew already. He recognised the clothes and the shock of reddish-brown hair.

Jack said, 'He came up here while we were out at the front. Clip saw him and followed, but it was too late. He must have come here through one of the alleys out at the back, and soon as he did, he was stabbed. Look: he got it three times in the back.'

'Turn him over,' Berenger said. It was hardly necessary, but he wanted to see the features of the man who had done so much to harm the army.

The dull eyes of the Pardoner were strangely sad in death. They seemed to peer over Berenger's shoulder: he felt a shiver run down his spine at the sight.

'Well, that answers one question, then,' he said roughly. 'We know who our spy was. Did you see who stabbed him?'

'A big man,' Clip said. 'Aye, with black hair like a Breton. He ran off down that way.' He pointed to another alley at the farther end of the yard.

'I see. What about the house? Has anyone checked for the Vidame in there?'

Jack shook his head. 'We've looked already. He must have slipped away when this body was found.'

Berenger nodded. 'No matter. We'll need to keep an eye open for the clerk, but at least our vintaine is safe. There is no spy now.'

It was good to have put the question of the spies to bed, for the French had worked hard to gather as many men as possible, and now news of their massive army was spreading even into Villeneuve-la-Hardie.

'We'll all get killed, you know,' Clip said cheerfully.

'If their King promises to kill you, perhaps the war will not have been in vain,' the Earl declared.

'You won't think that when you've a French lance stuck up your arse.'

Jack grunted. 'Just because they'll try to hit your brain, Clip, doesn't mean they'll think all our brains are there.'

'Oh, very witty, very clever. Just wait till you're depending on my bow in the line to protect you!'

'Dear Christ in Heaven, is this possible? Could we ever be forced to depend upon his skills?' the Earl demanded, rolling his eyes to the heavens.

'Oh, go swyve a goat!' Clip spat.

Berenger grinned to himself. The men were clearly in a good temper. The bickering was their way of showing it. They were all alive, and being English, were never happier than when they were insulting each other.

'You all right, Jack?' Berenger asked.

'Oh, I'm fine.'

So was Berenger. Since Chrestien de Grimault had ridden away, and the Pardoner had been unmasked and was no longer a threat, he had found himself feeling a great deal more relaxed. There was no sign of the Vidame. Sir Peter of Bromley was grim-faced and angry. He refused to believe that his own clerk had not been faithful to him when he had renounced his vows to King Philippe. Sir Peter considered it a reflection on his own honour. Yet although men kept their eyes open for the spies, there was no sign of them, and Berenger thought it likely that the Vidame had simply fled from the camp. The man knew his life was at risk, and had chosen to run. Killing Pardoner had been a last-minute decision to prevent any news of the Vidame from reaching the King's ears. Pardoner could have been tortured and given away details of what information had been passed on, and how. Berenger could understand the Vidame's act, but the man's ruthlessness shocked him.

Without having to worry about possible spies, he could concentrate on his men. And that was easier too, now that they had been given extra duties. The trenches had to be expanded to the south and west, and all day the men were set toiling with picks and shovels. Every few days Berenger insisted that they should practise at the butts too, and the men would groan and grumble as he led them to the sands near the seashore, where he had them set up a trio of butts and loose their arrows as quickly as they could at them. Those who missed had to buy drinks for the others that evening, complaining bitterly.

But the lighthearted mood changed in early July, when it became known that the French were approaching.

'Where from?' the Earl demanded.

'They are coming from Hesdin. That's ten leagues south of here, I'm told,' Berenger said.

'Oh, so that won't take them terribly long, then.'

'Good. I can't stand the sound of that racket much longer,' the Aletaster grunted.

Some days before, in response to the urgent pleas of the commander of the town, the French had tried to break the blockade. Eight or nine huge barges full of food of all kinds had been sent, escorted by a fleet of galleys and cogs. They had sailed to within a few miles of the town, but then the English fleet had caught them in the open sea. In a vicious sea battle the galleys were put to flight and the barges captured. Not a single pot of water or loaf of bread made it past to the harbour at Calais.

That was the last straw. The town had nothing to eat, and what there was must be conserved for the fighting men. Useless mouths were an unwanted distraction at a time of need like this. Thus the next day, the English horns had blared loud and clear as the gates opened.

'Shit! They're going to attack!' Jack had said. The vintaine was taking its turn at the far right of the line facing the gates of the town, and now he grabbed for his bow, sounding the alarm.

There was no need. Sir John ran to their side and stood with them as the men watched the unfolding tragedy.

From the gates there issued a thin stream of humanity. First came a woman, sobbing fit to burst, trailing three children. An ancient crone was immediately behind her, and then the rest poured out. All the elderly, the children, the women; those too old, too young, too infirm, too diseased or too foolish to hold a weapon, were evicted. Any who had no man to protect them and speak for them, were thrown from the gates in a knot of terror. They stood there, while armed men used lance butts or cudgels to force them through the door. One old man, struck about the head, collapsed in the path of the gates, and the men-at-arms kicked him until his body rolled out of the way and they could slam and bar the gates again.

For a long while, the English stared at the townsfolk, and the townsfolk gazed back. Their shifts and tunics hung loosely from their frames like shrouds, and their features were drawn and marked with starvation and terror. They were no longer the responsibility of the men in the town, but neither would the

English take them in. Stuck in the town's ditch, along with the ordure of the inhabitants, they were now less than humans: they were of no value whatever to either side in the struggle for power. Even as a barrier, they were useless. Whereas a rampart of stakes and barrels could hold men at bay, these frail figures could be slaughtered with more ease than so many sheep. Even sheep could run. These poor creatures, after months of deprivation and horror, could not even manage that.

Some few of the women and children implored to be allowed past. They pleaded with piteous cries, but the men had their orders. To have this little crowd pass among them could lead to the risks of disease spreading. Besides, it was better that the inhabitants should be reminded of their cruelty in turning from their own doors these people who had been their neighbours.

The vintaine stared. They had seen all the horrors of war, and most had participated, but there was something so pathetic in that crowd of people, that even the hardened killers amongst the English felt pangs.

'That's just miserable, turfing them out,' Dogbreath said.

'Can't we let them come past? They do no one any good just standing there,' the Earl asked plaintively.

'Leave them. They're not our responsibility,' Sir John said flatly.

'I wouldn't see them starve before my eyes,' Jack muttered.

'Aye, well, ye'll be dead ye'self soon enough,' Clip said, but the whining edge to his voice was stilled, as though even he felt compassion.

It was the same night that the sobbing and weeping started in earnest. Later, Berenger heard that one of the children had died, and his mother could not bear her grief but kept up her keening all night. The next day, a grandmother took over, wailing over the corpse of her daughter, and from her the baton was passed to another, and then yet another. There were no words for the suffering of the five hundred at the gates of Calais, and there were no words to describe the pity and the shame felt by the men of the vintaine. They were forced to stand and watch as the people begged for water, for food, for anything. And like torturers, they stood back and watched as the people faded, their weeping and despair growing quieter as the sparks of life were gradually extinguished.

'They'll be silent soon enough,' Berenger said grimly.

Later that day, when he saw Marguerite back at the camp, he strode to her and, without speaking, wrapped his arms about her, burying his head in her shoulder. She stiffened at first, but gradually, as he made no other move, she relaxed a little, and finally put her arms about him.

All he could see and hear were the women with their children begging and screaming for help from the moat outside the town. He knew in his heart that he would never forget that sound.

CHAPTER FIFTY

From the trenches and the main parts of the town of Villeneuve-la-Hardie, they could be seen up on the heights of Sangatte: row upon row of French horsemen, their flags and pennants fluttering gloriously in the wind. And in response, all over Calais the towns-people cheered and blew loud blasts on their horns. Fires were lit on the walls to celebrate the arrival of the French King with a force that could sweep the English invaders from his path.

'*Shit!* Archers!' Grandarse bellowed as the English horns blew to arms. 'Fripper, John, all vinteners to me: *now*!'

Berenger and the others heard the call amidst the din, and he left the vintaine under Jack's command. 'Just don't let Clip fall into another cesspool while we get things moving,' he snarled, and hared off, glancing every so often up at the cliffs.

There were at least a hundred of them. Men clad all in armour, with the mail sparkling like diamonds in the sunlight. Above them fluttered a multitude of flags and pennons, with the great flag of St Denis, the Oriflamme gleaming scarlet, distinct in the clear air.

'Christ's ballocks,' Grandarse said when Berenger joined him and the rest of the men, 'where have you been, Frip? Having a wank? Never mind that now. The French army is here, as you can see. We need to array as planned.'

'How far away is the French army now?'

'I'm told that the scouts have seen a camp three leagues from here. They are building a camp to rival ours, perhaps! There are enough of them. Frip, take your men up to the southern point of the camp. If anyone tries to force their way past, hit them hard. You've commanded a wing of archers – well, I'm giving you responsibility for half the centaine today. Take horses with you so you can ride back if it looks like you'll be overwhelmed. And don't take any risks. The lives of your archers are worth more than their knights'.'

'I'll tell them that. I'm sure they never knew you cared.'

'Don't be a thick, shit-arsed cock-quean, Fripper! An archer can kill three knights in a charge, so of course I bloody care about them! John, you and Alan and Roger will take your men and join Fripper's, and you will take your orders from him until you hear different. Now move your mother-swyving backsides and protect the south!'

Berenger and the others didn't need to be told twice. He explained where to meet him, and then raced off to find his pack. With that slung over his shoulder, he ran back to where his men were waiting.

'Clip, Earl, Aletaster, Oliver – each of you go and fetch four horses and bring them down to us. We may need to escape quickly where we're going. The rest of you, follow me. Where's our cart? Good! Georges, you can be responsible for that. We will need all the arrows we can get.'

He hurried down the clear, straight road to the south. At every intersection he glanced back at the heights, but there was no apparent movement. That was a relief. Berenger knew the French would think very carefully before attacking, after their catastrophic charges at Crécy. This meant that the English had a little more time to prepare themselves.

At the southern point, he called a halt to their mad rush and ordered the archers to attack the ground with their picks and shovels. They had brought stakes and he wanted them planted all over the land before them. Some set to digging holes, at least one foot deep and a foot square as they had at Crécy, to disrupt any charges by the French, but the sandy soil here was less capable of obliging. Still, it kept the men busy. While they were doing that, he stood on a hillock and gazed about him.

The land here was perfect for the English defence. A marsh covered the whole area from the feet of the Sangatte cliffs, and thence east. To the south of Berenger's men, there was one road that led up from Guines, and the road from the heights of Sangatte wandered from the hills up towards the beaches of the coast, and then over the one usable bridge at Nieulay. That was on a line due west of Berenger and the men, where they stood near the little church of St Peter at the crossroads leading up to Calais. But all those roads were ideal for the English: narrow, sliding into the marshes on either side. Any army attempting to move along those roads would be at the mercy of the English. Especially since the English had brought all their spare ships to lie just off the coast. These too were filled with archers. The road to the Nieulay Bridge would run along a line of archers who could hit a horse at eighty yards and more. If the French wanted to ride line abreast to charge the English, that too was impossible. The English had set up pallisades on the beaches to disrupt any assault. The bridge itself was protected by a tower, and behind this and all the other defences stood thousands of men under Henry of Lancaster, with more artillery.

Berenger and Grandarse had discussed their plan of action some days ago when news of the French advance had been reported. It was plain enough that the French could not hope to beat the English in the open, and would be very unlikely to attempt an assault on such well planned and executed defences. That would be too much to hope. But the French could be tempted to an area of apparent weakness, and here, to the south and west of the English forces, there was a road in which the French charge could consolidate. Here, where the marshes widened, they might commit themselves.

Not that it would serve any purpose, other than to injure a few score of archers, perhaps. The fact was, behind Berenger and his men were more archers, and immediately behind them lay another series of trenches that would disperse and destroy an attacking force. With archers on both flanks pouring shafts into them, the French would be annihilated. At least, that was the plan, were the French to attack here.

As the sun passed its zenith and the heat grew uncomfortable, Clip muttered, 'Are they not coming, then?'

Berenger grinned. As a weathervane to show the direction of the men's thoughts, Clip was incomparable. Now he was feeling frustrated and irritable. That was all to the good. Men in that frame of mind would fight if for no other reason than to vent their feelings.

He called to Clip, 'We're all thirsty, and as you're the best scavenger, you can go and find us some ale. There's bound to be some, somewhere.'

'Yes, Frip.'

The vintener watched his man dart off up into the tangled mass of streets and lanes, little suspecting the outcome of that foray.

Clip knew of a good place to find wine, but as he walked along the main road, he sighted a familiar figure up ahead.

It was the outlaw who had attacked the vintaine on the way to

Durham! He was not likely to forget that triangular face or gait in a hurry.

No, Clip would not forget that fellow, nor any of the others, in a hurry.

He was caught in a quandary, between the need for wine for the vintaine on the one hand, and the desire to follow this man and find out where he was going on the other.

Curiosity won the day. Taking care to remain invisible, he set off to stalk his prey.

Berenger was beginning to regret asking Clip to go and search out some wine. 'I should have sent someone who'd just go to a tavern and come straight back,' he grumbled to Jack.

'Which one of this vintaine could be trusted do that, Frip, without testing the drinks on his way?'

'That's not the point. I'll skin the bastard when he shows his face, again. He should have returned an age ago.'

'Yes,' Jack agreed, and both stared back towards the town.

'You don't think the stupid deofol's fallen into a latrine again, do you?' Berenger said at last, only half-joking.

'That would be too much to hope for,' Jack said, but there was an optimistic gleam in his eye.

Aletaster suddenly called out: 'Frip, something's happening!'

All thoughts of Clip were instantly wiped from his mind as Berenger turned his attention back to the heights of Sangatte. There, riding down a narrow track, was a small party of Frenchmen.

'*Shit!* Archers, *nock*!'

They watched the line of French men-at-arms descend the heights and assemble at the bottom.

'They're going to try to charge the bridge!' Jack cried. His eyes were keener than Berenger's.

Berenger's face grew lighter as he said, 'Good luck to 'em. They'll find that a hard nut to crack!'

The French began to ride forward, while a thick knot of men on foot ran pell-mell after them. Soon a roaring came to them on the still air – the clamour of battle. From here, it was astonishing to see how the arrows lifted and soared, then fell. It was like watching a black thundercloud on the horizon. More and more French were falling. Crazed, terrified horses, pricked with so many arrows as to look like pin-cushions, were rearing and trampling the men all about them. Flailing hooves crushed many a French skull, and yet soon, brave French fighters had arrived at the base of the tower at the bridge. With screams and shrieks, the English defenders threw themselves on the attackers, and died where they stood. More arrows flew, and Berenger saw the French fall as well, until it was hard to see which side was which, nor which men were falling. It looked like a scene from Hell: men dealing death with swords, maces, axes, anything that came to hand, accompanied all the time by the hideous whistle and slap of arrows dealing death to men and horses alike.

A group of men appeared with ladders, and these were thrown up at the tower's sides.

'They're a bit more bloody handy with a ladder than our gits,' Grandarse noted sourly. He had appeared as the first ladders hit the tower.

There was no doubting it: the tower was quickly lost. Soon there were new flags flying at the top, and the process of cleaning the building was undertaken with ease as bodies were flung from the top.

'Right, lads,' Grandarse said, hoicking up his belt and staring ahead grimly. 'Our turn now. Let's show these limp-wristed donkey-fuckers what English soldiers can do!'

CHAPTER FIFTY-ONE

In the town, Clip had followed the man slowly along the main thoroughfare until the fellow came to an alehouse; here, he pushed past other early-morning drinkers and soon was back outside again, holding a pottery horn and a jug. He set the jug on a table and drained his horn, immediately refilling it. Clip sidled into a doorway as men hurried past, and he heard horns blowing and shouts. Turning his head, he could tell that the noise was all coming from the west, not from where his own vintaine was waiting. There was the crack and boom of the gonnes going off, and he shuddered. Even after all this time he hated the sound of Archibald's horrible pots of war. Then he put the thought to one side, absentmindedly breaking off a piece of his hard cheese and chewing.

A soldier's life was mostly made up of shit jobs and bastard duties, he reckoned. The worst of it was, you never knew when it was going to go to the Devil. Well, for now, no one was aiming a bolt at him or trying to see what colour his liver was by opening him with a knife, and for that, he was more than content.

*

Berenger roared at the others to prepare. At the bridge, a company of French horsemen had gathered, and now they began to canter towards the vintener and the archers.

'They are scouting the land! We must hold our lines here!' Berenger shouted, and was almost deafened by Grandarse's exhortations to hold their positions.

'Nock your arrows!' Berenger said, and he was pleased to hear the swish of the missiles being taken from their quivers almost simultaneously. He nocked his own, and stood, the tab letting his fingers feel the string.

The men were approaching fast, and would soon be upon the archers. It was a shame that the stakes and holes had all been dug facing south, Berenger thought, before he shouted, 'Archers, *draw*!'

He could see the horses building up their speed now; the lance-points were lowering, some gleaming with that wicked, oily sheen that spoke of dead men's blood. Closer, closer . . .

'Loose!'

A shudder ran down his arm, and he saw his own arrow fly true – and miss. It slipped over the shoulder of the lead rider, but then it went on and into the face of the man behind. He disappeared, a fine spray of blood in the air where he had been, and then the archers were drawing and loosing as quickly as they could.

'Men on foot!' Grandarse bellowed, and Berenger saw the French infantry running behind the horsemen. He let slip one more arrow, sending it into the breast of a destrier that crumpled, its legs folding beneath it as it galloped, throwing its rider and rolling in a jangle of metal and legs, making the horse behind try to slow, and then attempt a leap. Two arrows struck it in mid-air, and it fell squealing, rolling onto its back and waving its legs in the air, crushing its rider, who remained in the saddle.

A lance almost spitted Berenger, but he dodged aside just in time, and heard a gurgle and choking from behind him. A moment later, the body of an archer was at his feet, a hideous rent in his breast where the lance had ripped into him. He was still mouthing words but nothing would come as he tried in vain to staunch the blood flowing from his chest. The odour of faeces came to Berenger even as the man's face sagged and his hands slipped to either side, his head lolling with his eyes half-shut.

There was no time to mourn. Only time to nock an arrow, draw, and send it into the mass of running, screaming men. He saw one hit in the head, who was knocked backwards so far he almost appeared to go horizontal before slamming to the ground. Another, who had a shaft run straight through his torso, appeared not to notice, but ran on at the English with a face filled with hatred and loathing, an axe held over his head. He brought it down with such force on the bascinet of the first Englishman he met that when he lifted it again, the bascinet of the now-dead archer was stuck to the axehead. Behind him, a man ran with eyes wide and filled with utter dread. In his shoulder, two arrows protruded; he could not use his right arm, nor dare he turn and flee, for that would be immediate death. Instead he ran on and on in among the English, ramming with his shield, hoping perhaps to make it past them and out to the lands beyond.

Two walls of men meeting men: Frenchmen running and panting, Englishmen grunting as they bore the brunt of the enemy slamming into them. A moment of tension, of terror, and then Berenger found himself borne backwards by the concussion of all the bodies. There was a feeling of dislocation, and then his feet found the ground again, and he screamed, 'Archers, *stand*!' as he gripped his sword and held it high, before bringing it down onto the head of a man who was trying to stab Aletaster.

Aletaster stood with his sword in his hands, staring at the body at his feet. Berenger clubbed him over the shoulder, saying hoarsely, '*He's* dead – *they* aren't! Protect yourself, you prick!' and then he had to duck as a polearm whirled past his head. He stabbed, thrusting hard and feeling something yield: a leather jack. He twisted the blade, jerking it downwards quickly, hearing a scream but ignoring it, lifting his blade to stop another sword sending his slithering down to the hand at the hilt, forcing it up and out of the way before headbutting the owner, feeling the satisfying crunch as his brow hit a man's nose and crushed it, then raising his knee and feeling a sudden pain as he hit a metal codpiece, and punching with his spare hand, before bringing his sword down again and feeling it slice into the man's throat ... pushing him aside as the blood sprayed, and stabbing at another man's face – but the man wasn't there any more, and suddenly there was no one left to fight, and he stood, panting with exertion, the scar on his face blazing like a bolt of red-hot iron, and his arms dangling as he watched for the next wave of men.

But for now, they were done.

Berenger was helping Aletaster to move a French body from the road when Clip arrived, leading a donkey and cart.

'You took your time!' Berenger shouted angrily. 'Last time you were this late, I said—'

'And I heard you, Frip,' Clip interrupted, 'but can I talk to you a while?'

Berenger glanced over the donkey cart. On the bed were two barrels, and from the scent that wafted towards him, he could make out the odour of apples. 'Cider'll please Grandarse, anyway,' he muttered as he followed Clip a short way off, to where they would not be overheard. 'What is it?'

'While I was in town, I happened to see a man I recognised. You remember the time I came back with a black eye? The man who did that was a big bastard. I remember him. Well, I saw him today.'

'And?'

'And he was with another man. One of the outlaws who attacked us on the way to Durham.'

'What? But . . .'

'It was the same man, Frip. Pale brown hair, sort of mousy-coloured but smelling of week-dead ferret, and a triangular face with blue eyes almost buried, they're set so deep. He was there, talking to the big bastard from Sir Peter's house.'

'There are many outlaws who've been pardoned if they've come here.'

'Aye, but this one I remember from before. I saw him here *before* we went to England.'

'Some men have travelled back,' Berenger said slowly.

'No, Frip. That outlaw was there to lead the others to attack us – I guess to get us into trouble with the commanders by slowing our journey to Scotland. That's what I think. And the fact he was with the other proves it.'

'It shows that the two know each other, nothing more than that,' Berenger said, but he knew it was too much of a coincidence for that. 'Did you hear what they were talking about?'

'I didn't dare get too close. The outlaw and I had a talk a while ago, and—'

'You saw him before and didn't think to tell me?' Berenger growled.

'Frip, he was in the yard and jumped on me, right? I really thought I was going to get killed. That was the day I had the black eye, remember? Anyway, if I'd got too close he'd have recognised me, so I kept back, but they were muttering.'

'Where did they go afterwards?'

'The big man headed to the west, the other back towards the

harbour. I went after the big man – he was easy to keep an eye on with his head standing up above the crowds. He went back to a shed out at the east of the town. And then I heard a bit of a rumpus from here, and thought you might appreciate my return.'

'Can you find the place again?' Berenger asked.

Clip gave him a sly look. An expert scavenger, he never forgot a place that could be of profit.

'Well, there's little enough we can do for now,' Berenger said. But it did mean that there were still some members of the spying team in the English camp. He noted that. 'You'll have to tell Grandarse and possibly Sir John all about your little escapades, and what you saw and heard today. It's just possible we'll have to mount a closer guard on the King in future. In the meantime, as soon as we can, we'll go to this room and see if we can catch the man.'

It was dark when Berenger, Jack and Dogbreath crept along the path behind Clip.

'That's the one,' Clip whispered, pointing. 'They'll be sure to hear us, though. If they don't run, they'll kill us for sure.'

'Shut up,' Jack hissed automatically.

Berenger studied the place in the gloom. It was a simple shed standing alone at the edge of the marshes. In happier times it might have been a fisherman's store, but now it was little more than a wreck, with the wooden shingles all broken and awry on the roof. A window was to the left of the entrance, a door that was reached by a pair of steps. The hut stood on piles to keep the floor away from the sodden sands all about.

'Careful, lads,' Berenger said. He motioned, and Jack slipped away around the side of the shed to the rear. Soon he was back.

'There's one window at the back. I don't know if anyone's inside. There's no light.'

'Go to the back and wait. If anyone hurries out, you know what to do.'

Jack nodded and was gone. After a count of sixty, which Berenger felt should give Jack enough time to get into position, he took a deep breath, pulled out his knife and stepped cautiously up the stairs to the door. He pushed at it, and it squeaked. As soon as it did, he shoved it wide, the door slamming against the wall inside. A startled grunt, and a man was sitting up on a bench. Berenger ran to him and gripped his shirt, holding his knife to his throat. 'Shut up!' he rasped as Clip and Dogbreath hurtled in behind him. There was one door to their right, and Berenger jerked his head towards it. Clip reached it as it was thrown wide, and the enormous bulk of Bertucat appeared.

'Jesus save me!' Clip yelped.

Berenger punched his prisoner to still him, and as he fell back, snuffling in pain, Berenger joined Clip and Dogbreath.

The man was not as massive as he first appeared, but he was enormously strong, and his long arms allowed him to punch or stab at men when he was still far from their reach. Clip was slapped about the cheek in a moment, and thrown to the ground. Berenger took his place, but even as he ducked and bobbed, he knew he would never get close enough to punch the man.

And then he heard a shrill squeal, and suddenly Dogbreath shoved him aside and threw himself at the man.

Briefly shocked into paralysis as the small noisome whirlwind materialised, fists flailing, Bertucat was pushed off-balance. Dogbreath sprang up and grabbed his throat, hauled hard, butted him in the face, dropped down, and kicked hard at his cods, then at his shin. Bertucat had never known such exquisite pain. He cradled his ballocks with both hands, his nose streaming, and as he did so, Dogbreath crouched low, and then exploded upwards like a rock from Archibald's gonne, and struck Bertucat with his fist right on his already broken nose.

The man's head was flung upwards by the force of the blow, and while Dogbreath gave a whistling cry, shaking his hand and dancing on one foot in pain, Bertucat tottered, took a step backwards, and then crashed to the floor.

Chapter Fifty-Two

While Clip took a malicious pleasure in tying Bertucat up very tightly, Berenger went to interrogate the other man.

After a lengthy questioning, it seemed clear to Berenger that the fellow knew nothing of Bertucat or the Vidame. He was simply an English shipmaster who had rented a bed for a night, and was happy to take one as cheap as Bertucat's. He had never seen the big man before renting the room from him, he said.

Bertucat was little more forthcoming, lying on the floor with his hands bound behind him. 'I've done nothing to you,' he said in his thick accent.

'Where is the Vidame?' Berenger asked.

'He is gone. He went days ago.'

'Then why were you talking to your friend the outlaw in town this afternoon?' Berenger said.

'What outlaw?' he sneered.

Clip answered, holding a hand three inches above his head. 'This high, with a pointy face, mouse-coloured hair and blue eyes.

Wore a faded fustian tunic and pale brown boots, had green hosen with a tear in the left knee, and—'

'Piss off!'

'Shithead!' Dogbreath shouted, and would have launched himself on Bertucat again, had Jack not restrained him.

Berenger was about to send him outside to cool his head, when he saw a flicker of fear in Bertucat's eyes, and without thinking, said, 'Jack, let him go. Clip, Jack, come outside with me. We'll leave Bertucat to talk things through with Dogbreath for a while. Dogbreath, don't kill him, but do what you need to get us answers.'

'Hey!' Bertucat called, struggling to rise. 'Don't leave me with him, he's a lunatic! Stay here with me, don't leave me!'

'No obvious wounds, Dogbreath,' Berenger said as he reached the door. He did not cast a glance at Bertucat. 'The King will want him for his own torturer.'

'Wait! I'll tell you all I know! But not this man, and no torturer.'

Berenger hesitated, one foot on the step outside. 'Not this man, perhaps. However, if you are deemed to be a traitor or spy, you'll pay for it.'

'I understand that. I'll tell you all, but no torture.'

Berenger gave a nod to Jack, who was frowning slightly at the thought of explaining this arrangement. Ah well, it was Berenger's agreement, not his.

'I was employed by the Vidame, yes,' the big man told them.

'Was it you who killed my man?'

'The Vidame ordered me to kill him. He was a traitor to you, and would have betrayed us, the Vidame said.'

'Where is the Vidame now?'

'I told you, he's gone.'

'Where?'

'He's with the army,' Bertucat said, throwing a glance up as though he could see through the walls to the hills of Sangatte.

'What does he intend to do?'

'He was just here to gain information, so that when the army arrived with King Philippe, they would best know how to break through your ranks.'

'What sort of man is he?'

'Absolutely determined. He is a loyal Frenchman, and he would do anything, regardless of the consequences, if it would help France. He often said that his duty was to destroy the English capacity to withstand the French attack.'

'How?'

'He never told me.' Bertucat shrugged. 'Look, he was only one man, and he counted the English as more than twenty thousand. What could he do?'

'What indeed?' Berenger wondered aloud.

'Frip?' Jack said. 'We need to take him to the King.'

Berenger turned to study Bertucat. In his mind's eye he saw all the men who had died in action since he landed in France last year. There were so many. From the young Frenchmen who tried to ambush him and the vintaine in the first days, to the steaming piles of corpses at Crécy, the outlaws in England, the pale face of Godefroi outside Durham, and even the man running at him down south of Calais today. Most of all, he remembered the flayed body outside Durham, and he heard again those agonised shrieks as the skin was peeled from the prisoner's body.

'I will not send him to be tortured,' he said.

Bertucat peered at him. 'I thank you,' he said. And then, licking his lips: 'I have one confession to make to you,' he added. 'When you were at the castle at Bosmont, you fell from the wall. That was not an accident. It was the man you knew as Pardoner, who tripped you. He was told to remove you.'

'Why me?'

'My master thought you were too shrewd. He felt you might realise about Pardoner and the boy, and that you would uncover the plot. He didn't want to run the risk that you would prevent it.'

'And yet you tell us now?'

'I doubt that the plot can achieve anything. What, the French break through this ring to liberate Calais? It cannot happen.'

'I see.'

'Frip, think!' pleaded Jack. 'We have to take him to the King to be questioned.'

'I will not do it, Jack. I won't send a man to be broken and cut up alive, skinned and gutted, not for anyone. It's bad enough that I've helped kill so many.'

'What, then?'

Berenger looked at Bertucat again. Then he drew his sword. 'It'll be quick,' he promised.

'You slew him?' Sir John de Sully said again with disbelief.

'He wouldn't have told us any more, except lies to stop us hurting him,' Berenger said. 'And I wouldn't have any part of that.'

'You don't make my job easy, do you, Frip?' Sir John sighed. 'Still, it was useful to learn. And at least the clerk is well away from us.'

'I don't know. I think that he has an idea.'

'Such as?'

'We had heard that an attempt could be made on the life of the King.'

'Yes, but nothing has happened.'

'Why should it? Think about it – would there be any point before the French King arrived here with his army?'

Sir John nodded and chewed at his moustache. 'Very well. I

shall speak to the King and suggest that he should have a stronger force to protect him in future.'

'What of Sir Peter of Bromley?'

'What of him?'

'His servant was the man taking messages about the army's strength. His house was where the messages were stored. Surely . . .'

'I think you should stop right there.'

'But Jean de Vervins was able to pretend loyalty to Philippe while spying and working for King Edward. What is to say that Sir Peter is not doing the same?'

Sir John nodded slowly. 'These are hard times, if even a knight must be viewed askance as a possible traitor, Frip.'

'These *are* hard times,' the vintener said.

Sir Peter was sitting alone at his table when the two men knocked and marched in.

'What is it you want?' he demanded angrily. He had enjoyed a quiet meal with four men from his household and was feeling pleasantly mellow when these impudent scoundrels entered. He stood up and was about to berate them when he saw Berenger glaring at him and hissed, 'What is that vintener fellow doing here?'

Sir John stalked to his table and stood grimly. 'When we sent men to Scotland, the Scottish were expecting us. Outlaws had been warned and tried to ambush the messenger. As it was, they succeeded in killing him. It was only the intervention and speed of this man and his vintaine that saved the exercise. Then, when the men went to Laon to try to bring the city around to our King, the messenger was again caught and the mission put in jeopardy. A spy could have warned the French about our plans.'

'And you dare to accuse me?' Sir Peter was too shocked to be angry at first. The idea that these men, who were supposed to be his allies and comrades, could suspect him of dishonour was appalling.

'No. We are here because we believe that your servant – the clerk, Alain de Châlons – is the spy. Is he here?'

'No, I have not seen him for some hours.'

'I see,' Sir John said.

'This is ludicrous! It could not be him! Why, I have known Alain for years.'

Sir John looked at him without expression, but Berenger snapped contemptuously, 'You may have come here full of the desire to serve our King, but did you not consider the feelings of your household? Did you ask the Vidame whether he wanted to follow you or not? Did you ask him for his opinion? You were prepared to show him to be faithless to his old vows, but didn't think to learn how he felt about it?'

Sir Peter was stung by the rebuke. 'Me? You dare ask me that? If you had seen your family broken up, your properties stolen, your country ravaged by the man to whom you had promised your life, your loyalty – your *all* – you too would be keen to leave, and if I was keen, then of course all those who gave their oaths to me would remain so! Alain has been my clerk for many years now. Why should I not continue to trust him?'

'Perhaps so that you could appear to be loyal to a new lord,' Sir John said flatly. And then, with no further speech, he and Berenger turned and left.

Sir Peter stood staring at the place where the men had stood, and then sat heavily.

He was finished. It was impossible to return to France and the French King, and he would forever be watched and distrusted here with the English King. He would never find rest again.

Chapter Fifty-Three

They had been there, waiting, for four long days after the two French Cardinals had negotiated a truce. Four days of sleeping in the trenches and at the barricades at the front, all the time wondering when the talking would stop and they would be sent off to fight once more. Four restless, uncomfortable days and cold, damp evenings, with poor food and worse drink.

It was the same two Cardinals who had tried, unsuccessfully, to negotiate peace all those miles before, just after they had taken Caen: Cardinal Pietro, who said he was from Piacenza, and Cardinal Roger, who looked to Berenger as though he had chewed on a diet of underripe sloes. The tracks at either side of his nose were deeply graven into his flesh like razor scars, and his posture was stiff, like a man holding in his anger with difficulty. Pietro looked more like a man who was dog tired after too much travel and too little sleep.

The two Cardinals rode to the bridge at Nieulay and waited, asking to speak with men of suitable rank. After some time, they were offered safe passage and, without glancing to either side, they went to present their messages.

Sir John was nearby and saw Berenger's eyes following the Cardinals.

'Fripper, go with them and make sure they aren't robbed again.'

The last time the Cardinals had arrived, some Welsh knifemen had stolen their horses and money. Berenger nodded to his knight and ran off after the two.

It was a curious group, more because of the way the English soldiery reacted than because of the two Cardinals themselves, who were only too aware of the contempt in which they were held. On all sides, English archers and men-at-arms watched, and while some guffawed or taunted the visitors, for the most part the men viewed the Cardinals in much the same way that they would have viewed a traitor. Berenger thought again about Bertucat. He had stabbed him quickly in the heart, and there was almost a look of gratitude in the big man's eyes as his soul passed away. It was one good deed Berenger had managed in a life of warfare: the alternative was always there in the back of his mind – the body of the young Scotsman outside Durham and the strips of flesh cut from his breast and limbs lying all about the butcher's floor where the executioners had let it fall.

The Cardinals were greeted with intense mistrust. On the other occasions when these two had appeared, it was always to argue that the English should swallow the insults doled out to them by the French and return all their winnings. It was to the credit of King Edward that he would not listen to such villainy. He believed he had come to France to correct a terrible wrong. His right to inherit France had been wrested from him by Philippe de Valois and his allies, who took the Crown, ignoring King Edward's claim through his mother by taking the outrageous step of changing the law to deny the ancient right of inheritance through the female line.

And while declaring that he had no ambitions to control England, King Philippe had drawn up plans to invade. The English had found them while searching through the records of Caen: detailed agreements with the people of Normandy for ships, men and weaponry, stipulating how the spoils would be divided. Since King Edward's publication of these discoveries at every church in the country, the English had learned to distrust French protestations of innocence. Many black looks showed the feelings of the troopers towards these Cardinals who always tried to defend the French Crown.

Berenger stood with the two men as they were presented to the Earls of Lancaster and Northamptonshire. They asked for a truce so that negotiations could begin.

This was granted. The English had great pavilions erected just inside their lines, and both sides sent earls, lords and knights to discuss terms. But while the French accepted that Calais was lost, they demanded that all the inhabitants should be released with all their goods and chattels intact and protected. They repeated the offers made before, of returning Aquitaine to the English Crown, but only as it had been held before, as a fief of the French Crown.

The talking went on throughout the four days, and at the end of the first day Berenger was already bored to madness with the whole affair. The French were haggling over a few goods and dickering about Aquitaine, but it was like a gambler offering bets *after* a race. They knew their bolt was shot: they had nothing with which to negotiate. For all the bombast and arrogance of the Dukes of Athens and Bourbon, and the others with them, it was plain that the offer of Aquitaine would never be acceptable. The English could retake it whenever they wished, and no English King, after trouncing French military might at the field of Crécy, would be ready to surrender all those victories in order to submit to a French King for lands held by right for centuries. But nor would the French delegation agree to allow the lands to pass to the

English without acknowledgement of the French claims to overlordship. That would be a humiliation too far.

Berenger heard that the French were finished on the fourth day and felt a certain relief as he took his whetstone from about his neck, picked up his sword, and began to sweep the stone along the blade. The sound was soothing.

Next morning, 31 July, a fresh delegation arrived, demanding that the English should come out of their defensive position and instead fight the French on land chosen by both sides.

'Shit, Frip – the King won't agree, will he?' Jack whispered as news filtered down to them of the proposal.

'He cannot with honour refuse,' the Earl said. His brows rose in contemplation. 'A knight must always respond to a challenge, or he will lose face. To stay hidden behind our defences when invited to an equal battle, that would be the act of a coward. Do you think our King a coward?'

'Aye, well, we'll all be killed if we go out there,' Clip said cheerily.

'Shut up, Clip,' Jack said.

'What'll we do then? Pick a place best suited for the French?' Aletaster asked.

Berenger shook his head. 'The terms offered are, that four knights from either side should agree on a field of battle, and that safe conduct will be offered to all on the march. Meanwhile, the town will remain unvictualled and effectively ours.'

'What's to stop the bastard French from sending a strong force here to push through our men and liberate the town?' Dogbreath demanded. 'They'll divide our forces in two, and then cut us down separately. Everyone knows you can't trust the French!'

The answer to that came sooner than anyone had expected.

The following evening, Berenger was called over by Grandarse.

'Fripper, what's that?'

High on the castle's topmost tower, a series of flames were showing.

'They're signalling to the French,' Berenger said.

'Shite, man! What are they saying?'

'Grandarse, do you have lard for brains? How the hell should I know?'

'You should show your centener more respect,' Grandarse grumbled, yanking his hosen upwards. He stared grimly at the castle walls. 'Well, we'll know soon enough.'

And they did. Before the second watch of the night, shouts and horns jerked Berenger from his sleep. Climbing to his feet, he rubbed his eyes bemusedly. 'What is it?'

Jack, a few yards away, said, 'I don't know, Frip, but I think we've seen 'em off.'

'What?'

All along the hills of Sangatte, an orange glow was visible, and the thick billows of smoke above could mean only one thing.

Clip began to dance and sing: 'They've fucking given up, Frip! They're burning their tents and stores behind them and fucking well fucking off! We're bleeding safe!'

Berenger wandered the streets that night filled with a vague sense of expection. English fighters were raucously, triumphantly drunk and made their feelings known to one and all. The massive French army that had appeared and given all of them such great fear was gone, and that was cause for celebration, just as much as it was a source of despair for the people inside the town.

The wretched folk who had been evicted from Calais lay slumped or curled where they had starved to death near the gates, but now those who had pushed them from the town were preparing themselves for their own deaths. Few, if any, had thought that their own King could betray them so unchivalrously. Philippe had deserted them, even after their long battle to protect his town for him, and now a constant wailing and keening could be heard from behind the walls.

Berenger hated that sound. It grated on nerves that were already raw after so many months waiting for the fall of the place. He wasn't alone, he knew. Most of the men felt the same. But it was only when he was approaching the vintaine's camp again that he realised how deeply the noise was affecting the others. He suddenly came across Marguerite, standing stock still in the roadway, her eyes full of tragedy as she listened to the cries of despair.

'They know they must die,' she whispered.

'It's likely,' he admitted. People died all the time, of course, and while it was sad when it was a friend or comrade, the death of others was less striking. He had seen so many deaths – from those of the first wave of fighters after their landing and during the long march to Crécy, to men like the young French esquire, like Tyler and Jean de Vervins. All of them were missed, he supposed, by someone.

'What if my children are in there?' Marguerite said, and her face crumpled like an old sack, making her look worn and haggard.

He had not thought about her and how she must miss her family in many weeks. Her family was broken up, and she had no idea whether her other children were alive or dead. She had maintained a dignified manner all along, but now, listening to the howls of the folk of Calais, she could keep up the pretence no longer. She was terrified that her children were slain, and her husband too.

Berenger put his arms about her, resting his cheek on her head, making shushing noises and trying to calm her as she sobbed. And he found that his heart was swelling with something like sympathy. He swallowed the lump that had risen in his throat.

'It's all right, maid. I'll look after you,' he found himself saying. 'You'll be safe with me.'

Calais surrendered.

The town had no option but to capitulate. Later, they learned that the signals on the castle's tower were to tell the French King that the town had nothing left, and that unless he came to save them, the people must surrender. Without the means to save them, the French army had packed and left, rather than witness the shameful loss of another town.

A messenger came and asked the English for terms, and Sir Walter Manny went to the town's walls. At the gates, he told them that King Edward would give them no terms: they had held out for almost a year, much to his anger, and they could not expect mercy at this stage. The English King would take what he wanted, and he would kill or ransom anyone he chose. *Those* were his terms.

Berenger heard Sir Walter as he shouted up at the walls: 'This siege has cost our King too much, in money and in lives, for him to offer you clemency.'

The answer came from Jean de Vienne: 'We have only served our King loyally as knights and squires and men-at-arms. Would you punish us for our fealty? You would do the same in our place, Sir Walter.'

It was a heartfelt plea, and one which struck a chord amongst many of the men standing listening outside the walls. Berenger could admire the man's words. They were chosen to go right to the heart of any warrior. After all, many there had the same thought: if the town were to be punished for holding true to the values of chivalry, and the men killed for obeying the orders of their King, then any man who stood to protect his own town under his King could be executed. More than one man eyed his companion and saw similar reasoning passing through his mind.

Eventually the answer was given. The English King would allow all to keep their lives, although he would arrest and ransom any whom he saw fit. However, the town must send him the six most important people, all with ropes about their necks, and bearing the keys of the town, to be at the King's mercy.

'You'll be there, Frip,' Sir John said.

Berenger nodded. He had an odd feeling that this would finally prove to be the end of their long campaign. It would be good to see the last act of this great play.

CHAPTER FIFTY-FOUR

It was, so Berenger had heard, the third of August that morning. There was nothing auspicious about the day. Just a moderate morning, with a few high clouds in a bright sky. It was not overwarm, even in the sun. The summer was waning already.

Berenger stood at the westernmost edge of the English workings with the rest of his vintaine. Before them, they could see the pavilion under which King Edward and his entourage would gather, while leftwards the road passed up through the terrible debris of war, to the gates of the town. Soon, he knew, the town would send out their sacrifices to meet the King's justice. A dais had been erected under the pavilion, and on it were two thrones.

Mass for the men was finished, and the whole of the English army had been mustered. Rank upon rank, at least two tens of thousands of archers, knights, men-at-arms, long-haired Welsh knifemen, fair Hainaulters and Flemings, and even camp-followers. Women thronged the edges, and Berenger spotted Archibald and Béatrice standing near a group of carters and tradesmen. Everyone who had been involved with the army for the last year was present.

There was a ripple of applause from his right, and he guessed that the King's entourage was arriving. He would be there with his queen, the beautiful Philippa, and his earls and knights. They would all surround him, just as they had every day while here – and more of them since the threat of assassination by the Vidame.

A sudden thought occurred to the vintener. In his mind's eye, he saw the King's household sitting up on the dais there. He pictured the men of his personal guard encircling him and the Queen, but as Berenger considered it, he knew that the King would not be ringed about. To fence him in would be impossible on this day of all days. No, the King would be in plain view, surely, staring along that road towards the gates of Calais. All his armoured knights and men-at-arms would form a thick semi-circle behind and around – *but not in front*.

Berenger had a sudden sinking feeling in his belly as the realisation hit him: if someone was determined to kill King Edward, this would be the ideal time. It would have to be a man who was prepared to face the inevitable consequences, for he would be torn limb from limb for his act. But if the man was devoted to his own King, he might risk it. And Berenger had heard tell of the ruthless determination of the Vidame . . .

The soldiers, he saw, were all grouped by vintaine and centaine, under the banners of their bannerets and captains. Any strangers in their midst would soon be noticed.

'What is it, Frip?' Jack asked, seeing his consternation.

'I just have a bad feeling . . . I think the Vidame could be here. When the King arrives, he will be unguarded here, won't he? As the people come out of the town, he will be on plain view.'

'Yes, but so what? These are all Englishmen.'

'What if one wasn't? A man up there on the horns of the army would have a perfect sight of the King.'

'A good archer could do something, but this Vidame – I don't know. Could he use a bow?'

'He only needs one good flight, Jack. A man with a crossbow could do that from the walls of the town.'

Jack glanced over to the town, then back to the King. 'What do you want me to do?'

'Take the men and go and watch the tradesmen, the carters and tranters – the people who are not in the army itself, but who support it. Our man will be in there amongst them, I'd lay my life on it.'

Jack nodded.

'And Jack? Be careful. If I'm right, this fellow is more than determined. He is a fanatic.'

The Vidame smiled at his neighbour. There were so many men and women up here on the western flank that the noise and chattering was almost deafening. Still, that was good. No one took any notice of the man who had climbed up a little above them all on the wagon's seat.

It was the perfect position. He had a clear field of view to the King some eighty yards away. Edward was just coming into sight now, his fair hair and long beard making him stand out amongst the people all around. The Vidame took a long, deep breath. The King was talking to the men about him, including that fool Sir Peter of Bromley – surely one of the most gullible idiots ever born. It was his sudden change of allegiance that had made the Vidame's task so easy. All he need do was remain one of the knight's loyal following, and suddenly he became another trusted member of King Edward's household.

But now he had a more crucial task to perform. He, Alain de Châlons – the Vidame – was to be the man who liberated France from the cruel yoke of English rapacity. Once this King was dead, that would be an end to things. The English must leave France afterwards – and with empty hands.

At his feet was the bow, ready spanned, with a bolt in place. All he need do was remove the blanket covering it, pick it up, aim and loose, and France's sufferings would be avenged. All those children and women and their men. The irreparable, intolerable damage done to so many noble families, the thieving and robbery – all avenged.

The King was seated now. Although the Vidame could see his head clearly, it was too far to trust the bolt to aim true. Until the King rose, he must wait. Otherwise there was a risk that he might hit a knight or man-at-arms in front of the King. He didn't want to have a close shot, he wanted to make sure of his enemy, of his country's enemy. He must wait and be patient. His time would come.

There was a great cry, and he turned to see the gates to Calais opening properly for the first time in almost a year. They creaked wider and wider, and at last six men became visible. From the town there came no sound. It was as if the opening gates sucked the noise from the English too, for as the six began to pace forwards, the English also fell silent.

He could see them clearly. Six gaunt, wraith-like figures, stepping forward with courage, their chins held up, while inside each must have quailed. They had no idea whether their personal sacrifices would help their people. It was possible – nay, likely – that the English soldiery would rush into their town and rape their wives and their children, killing all who stood in their path. The English had done it all before. There was no reason to think that the King would be more merciful here.

Mercy. That was a curious term to use when thinking of a King. Today, Edward had insisted that the six most important men in the town should appear like this, clad only in shirts, wearing ropes about their necks. They all knew their end would come today. They made a brave show, however, padding barefoot across the wreckage and mess of the road, all the way to the King's pavilion.

It was enough to bring tears to the Vidame's eyes. One man at least he knew: Jean de Vienne, the Constable of Calais, was a brave man, known for his courage in the face of the enemy. Rarely had the Constable confronted so implacable an enemy, however.

The King, the Vidame saw, remained seated. Men moved before him and all around him, blocking the spy's view of Edward as everyone craned their necks to see the six victims approach.

A herald stepped forward and took the keys from Jean de Vienne. He and the other five citizens prostrated themselves in the dirt of the road. The Vidame had an anxious moment, thinking that the English might show compassion and release the prisoners, but then he saw the King signal, and two men-at-arms came forward. These were the executioners.

There was an altercation on the dais: knights bowed to the King and spoke, urgently, one holding out a hand to the killers at Jean de Vienne's side, and then the Queen joined them, and bent before her husband. The Vidame swore under his breath. There was no clear view. All these men, and the Queen, were blocking his view of his target.

And then they moved away, and the King stood, his arms high, turning so that all might see him. His voice could be heard, and everyone in that great arena was silent, straining to catch his words, as the Vidame crouched, pulled away the blanket and withdrew his crossbow. He peered, and he could see the King quite clearly. Lifting his crossbow, he smiled as his finger found the large slide that fitted a slot in the nut and prevented accidental discharge.

It was time. He would make history. Today, he, Alain de Châlons, would slay a King.

He lifted the crossbow, steadied himself, and as he pulled the curved release, something hit his knees, and he went over.

Dogbreath had spotted the man up on the wagon as the men walked from the gates towards the King. He was a nondescript fellow in brown jack and broad-brimmed hat, standing well above the rest of the men. And then Dogbreath saw him bend and pull something from his feet. When he rose, Dogbreath saw the bow.

He ran. It was twenty yards, and that meant twenty paces, but it felt like a mile, it seemed to take him so long. And then he was at the back of the cart. He leaped into it, and his feet kicked out as soon as he was on it, straight into the back of the man's knees. The would-be assassin crumpled with a yelp, and Dogbreath was on him in an instant. A scream and a bellow showed that others had heard the fight, and now men came to try to separate them. Dogbreath pushed the crossbow aside and butted the man in the face, kicking up with his knee against his cods. The Vidame defended himself as best he could, punching and slapping at his enemy while Dogbreath renewed his assaults. A lucky kick caught him in the belly, and he was for a moment winded, long enough for the Vidame to grab his bow once more, but then he realised it was loosed already. The bolt had flown. He was still staring at it dumbly when Jack's sword slammed down on his head. The pommel of steel hit his skull like a mace, and Alain de Châlons fell without a word.

In the group about the dais, Sir John de Sully listened as the King ordered that all the six should have their heads cut off. There was a general acceptance, but it was not wholehearted approval, rather a sense of resignation that a King could do as he wished. Few liked the decision. These men had behaved with honour. To kill them was considered over-harsh.

Several dropped to their knees and begged for the lives of the six, but the King's face remained stern. Only when his own wife knelt and pleaded with him did he unbend.

But as the Queen stood again, Sir John heard a cry from the crowds, and a premonition of disaster made him push forward just as a bolt flew. The King was standing now, a perfect target for any man with a bow and a string, but there were others there who saw the danger too. As Sir John tried to reach his King, a group of men-at-arms surged forward – but one man shoved them all to one side.

Sir Peter de Bromley had seen his clerk standing on the wagon, and at that moment he realised the truth of the accusations against the Vidame. Into his mind flashed the confrontation with Sir John de Sully, the contempt in the face of Berenger and the others. There was but one way to prove his devotion. He leaped into the path of the bolt even as it flew straight at him. He had time to move, but he chose to hold his ground, protecting his King to the end. He was hit by it: in an instant it penetrated his eye, and he fell to the ground, already dead.

'Get him out of the way, quick!' Sir John hissed, and with the help of two others, he pulled the man's body out of sight.

Meanwhile the King remained on his feet, proclaiming that, because of the heartfelt pleas of his wife, he would allow all the citizens to go free. The army cheered and one of the six faltered and almost fell and had to be supported by his neighbours, and two of the six were weeping with relief as Sir John glanced down at Sir Peter's body.

'You poor bastard. You knew your servant was a traitor, didn't you? And this was your only way to pay for that knowledge.'

CHAPTER FIFTY-FIVE

'Are you sure, Frip?' Grandarse said again.

Berenger grunted. The two were standing outside the tavern in the market of Calais, and now that the town was theirs, and the main properties were all requisitioned by the King and given or rented to the men of his army, the memories of the last few days were fading.

They had been confronted by a hideous sight when they first entered the town and walked the streets. Berenger had been in with the first contingent of men, and he had been struck by the strange, sour smell about the place. The unhealthy, dying men and women gave off an odour that was like vinegar, both pungent and rancid. No one here had been able to bathe for months, and none had eaten properly either, in all that time. At every doorway or window, Berenger saw gaunt, grey faces, with lips that had tightened so that they could scarcely cover teeth. The people's eyes were dull, almost like the dead, and hunger had made their bellies swell.

Even more than that, the most truly dreadful thing was the lack of sound: a kind of tainted deathly hush absorbed Calais. There were no birds, no dogs, no cats, no horses. All had been consumed. Only these corpses remained: the walking dead, awaiting their entrance to Hell.

Berenger had looked about him, appalled, as the townsfolk were ordered to leave their houses. They were to be pushed from the gates and forced to leave. He wanted to give food to them all, but there was nothing he could do. He was powerless.

Later, after that first day, he had spent time with Marguerite. Not talking, just sitting with her. Georges was a short way away, playing with Ed, and Berenger watched them for a long time.

'Are you well?' she asked after a while.

He was still for a moment, then said, 'In the last year, I've been hit by a crossbow bolt, hammers, swords and fists. All I have to show for it are wounds, and the loyalty of my men. I have no woman, no home, no children to leave my money to, nor anyone to mourn me when I am dead. Marguerite, I am bone weary of death and killing. Woman, if I give up fighting, I would settle in a town like this. I'd want to fill it with happiness. I'd want to trade and make money, and fill bellies, and give alms to help the weak. Would you want to help me, if I give you a home and a home for your boy?'

'You mean you want a concubine, or a servant?' she asked lightly.

'No, Marguerite, I want a wife. Would you accept me?'

She studied his face for a long moment. Somewhere, it was possible, she had a husband and children. But with the English controlling such a broad swathe of land, finding them would be all but impossible. A woman without husband, without family, was mere prey to the men all about France. Already the stories of rapes and murders committed by English troops, whether they were English, Welsh, Irish, Flemish, Gascon or other, were circulating all around the country. Bored soldiers, some of them French, had deserted their armies and were taking over villages in their search for plunder and sex. No one, man or woman, was safe in the countryside.

At least this Berenger had shown her kindness, Marguerite thought. He had helped her when she had been lonely; he had fed her boy, had given them both the protection of his vintaine – and had made no demands on her. She had never felt threatened by him.

She looked back towards the land away from the sea. There she could clearly see the heights of Sangatte. That was where the French King had set his camp. He had done less for his people than this Berenger had done for her alone.

Berenger spoke now. 'I know you are confused. If your husband turns up, I'll understand if you want to leave me. But for now, while the land's so dangerous, I can at least give you and your son a home. I can look after you both.'

She nodded, her eyes still fixed on the distant hills. They represented freedom – and death. If there was the faintest hope that her husband was alive still, she should go and try to find him. And of course she wanted to find her children. But what was the point? They could be anywhere – if they were still alive. The chances of her finding them were remote. It was more likely that she would meet her own death on the roads.

Taking a deep breath, she wrenched her gaze away and met Berenger's steady stare. 'If I learn my family is alive, I will leave you. You have to know that. I gave my husband my word.'

'I wouldn't expect anything else, woman,' Berenger said.

'If you accept that, then before God, I declare I believe I am widowed, and as a widow, I will take you, Master Berenger Fripper. I will have you to be mine, to have and to hold from this day until death take me.'

'And I will have you, Marguerite. You will be my wife, and I will be a good husband to you, and father to your son,' Berenger vowed. And as he said it, he felt a certain lightness steal over him. It was a sign, he felt sure, of God's approval at last.

And with God's help the English would turn this little port into a great trading city in support of the English in France.

Archibald had seen her shortly afterwards, as the news was given to the vintaine.

'I have to tell you lot something,' Berenger announced, and Archibald thought how different he looked – how *relaxed*. The gynour had never seen him looking so at peace before.

'What is it, Frip?' Jack called.

'Aye, we're all to be sent on some wild-goose chase so the Frenchies can try to kill us,' Clip said darkly. 'We'll all die, you mark my words.'

'Shut up, Clip,' Dogbreath said.

'It's not that. The fact is, I am to stay here in Calais. I will marry.' Berenger looked thoroughly embarrassed now. His head hung.

'Marry, Frip?' This was the Earl. 'Do you think she will be able to make an honest man of you, then?'

'Yes: marry. I'll be settling down with Marguerite and her boy, and I intend to bring up more small Frippers while I'm about it. My name is Fripper. I may as well live up to the title and deal in your second-hand clothes. Well, obviously not *yours*, Dogbreath,' he added.

Dogbreath looked down at his stained and worn clothes and shrugged, while the other men laughed and hooted.

'So, I'll wed her.'

'Have ye not done it yet?' Grandarse called. 'She'll be changing her mind while you fuck about, you great lummox.'

'I'm to do it today. Sir John has already given us a house for my service, and the King is keen for any who will, to come and live in the new town.'

'Aye, well,' Clip said, 'as to that, I think there may be other towns.'

Archibald left them, and walked to where Béatrice stood a little way away. 'Are you well, woman?'

'Of course. Why would I not be?'

'Your face just then, I thought . . .'

'There is nothing to think.'

Ed was watching. Now he stood. 'We will be fine. Master, you will teach me all you can about gonnes, and Béatrice can teach me about powder, and in time I'll become a master gynour too, and we can ask our own price from any man who can afford us!'

'Yes, and life will be easy,' Archibald said, ruffling his hair, but even as he said it, he saw the expression in Béatrice's eyes, and felt his heart melt with pity at the sight of her despair and jealousy.

Grandarse toasted the couple in style, and then returned to his favourite tavern. There, he drank a hornful of wine to them again, before reflecting on the last year.

It had been a hard campaign. Many men had died and would still die. Disease, wounds, all had their own effect. And yet, as he sat here now, he wondered what the value had been for him. There was no more money in his purse, no riches to dangle from his saddle, not even a new, valuable horse. The campaign had been a way of filling in time between his birth and his grave.

He had made many decisions, some good, some dreadful. He had killed many men, sometimes for a good reason, but more often for bad ones. Mark Tyler, who had seemed the obvious culprit to have attempted to kill Fripper was now shown to have been innocent. Well, no matter, Grandarse had done what he had done in the best interests of the centaine and Berenger's vintaine. If he had been mistaken, so be it. Any man could make errors.

'Barman!' he bellowed, and refilled his horn.

'Bah – fuck him!' he declared, and drank again. There were many good men whom he had killed. He wouldn't worry about a one such as Tyler. Besides, it might well have been Tyler who tripped Berenger at the castle.

'What will you do, Jack?' Clip asked.

'Me? I suppose I'll go home. Work for a bit, get bored, and join a company out here again.'

'I'll get home,' Oliver said, 'and see who my wife's been screwing, then take his money at the point of my knife.'

'Me, I'll go and set up a tavern in London,' the Earl said. Meditatively chewing a straw, he smiled. 'I'll have the prettiest little geese in there, all good, buxom little wenches, the sort who'll take a man's mind off war, famine or the law for a couple of pennies. And I'll serve fine ales, and wines, and even some of this burned wine they give you out here. Aye, and all my friends from this vintaine will be welcome.'

'Oh, aye?' Clip said.

'I said *friends*, Clip.'

John of Essex was passing. 'So it's true? Fripper's going to settle?'

'Yes. What of you?'

'Me? I think I'll go on. There are opportunities in other parts of France, so they say. A great company is being formed. Once our King has peace, there'll be little enough excitement for us, after all. I'll take a new name, I think, and see what I can do.'

Clip sneered, 'New name, eh? John not good enough?'

'No, I think I need a new surname. After all, if I'm to be a great military captain, I will need a new name to strike fear into the hearts of my enemies. I think I'll call myself "Hawkwood" in future. John Hawkwood has a good ring to it.'

'Hawkwood? A name any man will forget in a week,' Clip sniggered.

'My name will be remembered for a century,' John reproached him. 'You'll see.'

'He won't,' Dogbreath said.

EPILOGUE

Six months later

Berenger sat on his bench outside his door and watched the men and women passing by.

He was content. His wife was growing large with child, and although they were not foolish young people, maddened with love, they were comfortable. Marguerite was a great asset, with her happy smile and infectious laugh, and in the months since her arrival at Calais, much of her bleak discontent has gone. She was learning to be merry again, now that she was married and safe once more.

Her son still had moments during which he would stare at Berenger as though blaming him alone for all the misfortunes that had occurred since the arrival of the English, but occasionally now he would laugh and smile, too. Like others who had survived the atrocities of the English invasion, he was discovering that life under the rule of a kindly English King could be pleasant and secure.

And Berenger himself was pleased to learn that he could rebuild his life. He was happy here, with an ale in his hand, knowing that behind him there was another barrel to be broached, and that in his shop there were clothes of all sorts ready for sale.

In the months since the capture of Calais, much had changed. All the old inhabitants, apart from a few, had been evicted and their houses taken over by colonists approved by the King. Some priority was given to those, like Berenger, who had fought hard for the town. They were deserving of reward, but also were best placed to defend the new-won lands. The campaign and siege had taken all the efforts of England, and now it was time to make the most of the territory. Men were coming from all over England to trade with the rest of France, and many French could see the advantage in coming to sell their wares. While the French King might fulminate and scheme, his people were realists and wanted peace with profit.

Today, sitting in the early spring sunshine, his cloak wrapped tightly about him, Berenger Fripper saw a tall figure striding along the road towards him. He frowned, but then his face broke into a smile.

'Sir John!'

The knight grinned in return, and stood before him. 'You are looking very pleased with yourself, Master Fripper.'

Berenger patted his belly. 'I am learning the joys of regular feeding and a bed under a roof,' he said. 'I could grow to like this life.'

'So, were I to invite you to join me . . .'

'No. There is no inducement you could offer that would be sufficient.'

'Then I am glad to have no suitable employment for you,' Sir John chuckled. At Berenger's invitation, he took a seat beside his vintener and accepted his offer of a large cup of ale. Marguerite appeared, wiping her hands on her apron and gave him a suspicious look, as though suspecting he had an ulterior motive in appearing just now. On seeing her concern, Sir John said kindly, 'No, mistress, I am not here to take your husband from you. I am simply passing by on my way home to England. It's time I saw more of Iddesleigh and Rookford – and my wife too.'

They sat talking for half the morning, as old comrades will.

'Have you heard of John of Essex?' Sir John said. 'Since he's taken up his new name, he is earning a reputation for courage and ability.'

'He always had both. Does Grandarse thrive?'

'As well as a man ever will whose diet consists of sack, cider and ale,' Sir John said sardonically.

Berenger laughed out loud. 'At least he is consistent.'

'Aye. And meanwhile, Calais continues safely.'

'Yes, Sir John.'

The knight sipped his ale. 'Mm, this is good. You have heard that Lord Neville has put up a cross to celebrate your victory outside Durham? The place will forever be known as Neville's Cross from now on. A place of great importance.'

'Perhaps,' Berenger said. All he could see, when he thought of that battle, were the faces of Godefroi and the Scotsman dying after his torture. He would spend the rest of his life trying to forget them.

'Well, my friend, be careful and God go with you,' Sir John said, rising.

'Godspeed, Sir John.'

'And if you are ever in need, you must write to me. There will always be a place in my entourage for a man such as you.'

'I am grateful for the honour, my lord, but I am happy here. I intend to avoid war and death.'

'Sometimes death comes to *us*. Have you heard the rumours? There is a pestilence affecting people in the south of France.'

'I had heard of a disease,' Berenger said, 'but that is far from here.'

'Apparently it approaches us. I hear that it is now at Caen.'

Berenger shrugged. 'We are safe enough here. We are miles from it.'

He watched, smiling, as the knight strode away.

'Why do you smile, husband?' Marguerite asked.

'Oh, just a silly story. The knight fears a mighty pestilence. As though it could affect a great town like this,' Berenger laughed, and then stopped.

An icy shiver ran down his back, as though God Himself was giving him due warning.